Shoulder Season

ALSO BY CHRISTINA CLANCY

The Second Home

Shoulder Season

Christina Clancy

St. Martin's Press
New York

First published in the United States by St. Martin's Press, an imprint of
St. Martin's Publishing Group

SHOULDER SEASON. Copyright © 2021 by Christina Clancy. All rights reserved.
Printed in the United States of America. For information, address
St. Martin's Publishing Group, 120 Broadway, New York, NY 10271.

www.stmartins.com

Library of Congress Cataloging-in-Publication Data

Names: Clancy, Christina, author.
Title: Shoulder season / Christina Clancy.
Description: First Edition. | New York: St. Martin's Press, 2021.
Identifiers: LCCN 2021006624 | ISBN 9781250239631 (hardcover) |
    ISBN 9781250271495 (ebook)
Subjects: GSAFD: Bildungsromans.
Classification: LCC PS3603.L3514 S56 2021 | DDC 813/.6—dc23
LC record available at https://lccn.loc.gov/2021006624

Our books may be purchased in bulk for promotional, educational, or business use. Please contact your local bookseller or the Macmillan Corporate and Premium Sales Department at 1-800-221-7945, extension 5442, or by email at MacmillanSpecialMarkets@macmillan.com.

First Edition: 2021

10 9 8 7 6 5 4 3 2 1

For my mom, Pat Geiger

Already I miss Troy
in the summer.
My body propped
on the raft at Booth Lake,
feet stirring the weeds.

—FRANCESCA ABBATE, *Troy, Unincorporated*

If you live,
you look back and beg
for it again, the hazardous
bliss before you know
what you would miss.

—ADA LIMÓN, "BEFORE"

Shoulder Season

Prologue

Sherri stands outside the employee entrance of the Palm Springs Art Museum and stares at the scrubby mountain behind the building. The early-bird hikers in their floppy hats have captured their sunrise photos and are making their way to the mouth of the trail that lets out just beyond the parking lot. Almost forty years earlier, she'd gone hiking there for the first time. She was drunk, and had wandered over from the Riviera in her bikini and a pair of flip-flops. She still can't believe she'd made it down without a broken ankle—or worse.

It seems everyone in town is on vacation except for her, and that's fine. She likes to keep busy, even on her days off. Her boyfriend, Bayard, keeps telling her she should retire, but she can't imagine what she'd do with herself. She takes a deep breath and prepares for her day the same way she used to brace herself at the start of her shift at the Playboy resort back when she was a Bunny.

She catches her reflection in the glass door—as a special events manager, she knows that it's important to look like she's someone who can rise to an occasion. Her hair isn't as wild as it once was, but it's still curly, and she's dyed it the color of champagne so that she won't look like George Washington. Her nails gleam, her makeup is perfect, and one extra button of her silk blouse is undone. She steps inside and shivers in the blast of air-conditioning. Her feet are tucked tight into the stiletto heels she insists on wearing despite the stern warning from her podiatrist about bunions and hammertoes. She loves the efficient clicks of her measured steps against the parquet floor and the way the sound echoes with purpose through the galleries. In the rhythm she hears the stresses in the lines of the T. S. Eliot poem her father used to recite for her each and every morning when she was a girl: "Dawn points, and another day / Prepares for heat and silence. Out at sea the dawn wind / Wrinkles and slides. I am here / Or there, or elsewhere. In my beginning."

Her first appointment of the day is with grooms Steven and Byron, and Char, their wedding planner. Char is concerned that the hallway leading out to the patio area where the couple will exchange vows features a photography exhibit of dying AIDS patients, one of whom is giving his lover a blowjob from his hospital bed. "What will their families think?" Char asks. Sherri has worked with Char before. She knows she's trying to downplay the museum because she gets kickbacks from some of the other venues around town.

"Well, I hope they'll think what *you* think," Sherri says, ignoring Char and addressing the couple directly. She can feel a special kind of energy rise up in her—she knows she has the confidence she needs to sell a space. "You guys love and value art. That's why you live here, right? And that's why you're thinking of having your wedding at the museum. This is a place that epitomizes your values. There's no denying the images are powerful, and if you ask me, they'll remind your guests that life is fragile, and the love you have for each other is absolutely precious and beautiful."

She slips their deposit check into a manila folder, winks conspiratorially at Char, and runs upstairs to the museum entrance for her next appointment, a meeting with billionaire James Wingra's much younger wife, Fiona, who is thinking of joining their board. Fiona is fresh out of USC. She's dressed for Coachella in her boho sundress and wedge espadrilles, a French bulldog at her heel. She's what people in Sherri's office call a "walker"—there are lots of walkers in town, whether they are young, gay men hanging off the arms of wealthy widows, or women like Fiona who suction themselves to much older men.

Sherri doesn't want to tell Fiona that dogs aren't allowed in the museum, so she suggests they meet outdoors instead. They sit at a table overlooking the Černý sculptures, eight-foot-tall steel babies that appear to crawl around in a giant sandpit. "Their faces look like heating vents," Fiona says with an expression of confusion and displeasure.

"Bar codes," Sherri says. "They represent dehumanization. I think they look like swarming ants from a distance, don't you? It was quite a coup for us to get them. The artist is from Prague, a real renegade. He rose to fame for painting the Soviet tank pink."

"Oh, right. Sure." Fiona gazes off into the distance. Sherri almost feels sorry for her because she's so clearly out of her element. She's lovely, with a little turned-up nose, pouty mouth, and shiny shoulders. Sherri has so much advice she wishes she could share with the younger woman, but Fiona wouldn't listen to Sherri any more than Sherri had listened to the people who'd tried to steer her down a different path back in the day. Fiona brightens. "Sculpture is my favorite!" She says this as though she's describing her favorite flavor of ice cream.

After the meeting, Sherri notices that Fiona's dog had taken a dump right outside the front door. She runs to the café and grabs a napkin to clean it up, washes her hands, and spends the next twenty minutes timing how long it takes for the elevator to travel to the third floor and back down. She needs to calculate how much time it takes to transport sixty elderly guests to the upper gallery in time for a fundraiser. Sherri doesn't mind the boring minutiae of event planning, because she knows too well that the smallest overlooked detail could turn a party into a disaster.

She chats with the security guards and the cleaning people while she works—she knows all of their names, and the names of their spouses, children, and grandchildren. They like her because she never pulls rank. She'll stay late to stack chairs and collect soiled linens. She's no stranger to hard, physical work, and she never complains. That's a lesson she carried from her Bunny days—you never let on when you're exhausted or angry. She tries not to let on that she's upset because the director of development was recently let go, and Sherri was asked to assume his duties in addition to her own. She plans to take it up with management, but she doesn't complain to her staff that her salary hasn't changed, even though his earnings were almost twice her own.

While eating lunch at her desk, she startles when she opens an email from Jerry Derzon. He almost never emails. She reads that he's suffering from stage-four pancreatic cancer, and it is time for her to return home (East Troy will always be home) to deal with the building he's been managing all these years. The news makes her heart heavy—*as heavy as a Chevy,* as Jerry would say. She doesn't have the energy or the will to pretend otherwise.

Back at the house, she sits at the edge of the pool with her submerged legs moving in slow circles, the late-afternoon sun bearing down on her, a bead of sweat rolling down her back. She's on her second gin and tonic. *So, Jerry is sick,* she tells herself, again and again, remembering the smell of the rum-soaked Crooks cigars he used to smoke. *Jerry. Is. Sick.* She thinks of the gold crown on his incisor that gleamed when he smiled, how he'd kept a yellowed linen handkerchief in his front pocket to dab away his sweat. She reverses the direction of her leg circles. *Sick, that's what Jerry is.*

Jerry's poor health will change things for her. She never would have believed that Jerry of all people would have become her unlikely savior all those years ago. It was because of Jerry that she was able to leave Wisconsin and embark on this new life. She'd read once about giant machines in Los Angeles that keep the salt water out of the fresh water aquifers under the city; if the machines were to stop working, the whole city's water supply would become tainted. Jerry had been like that for her, a force that kept her past and her suffocating guilt from contaminating her present. But now he's preparing for his own absence, and she'll finally have to go back to East Troy after almost forty years away and deal with the messes she'd made, back when she was in the midst of all her foolishness.

No. She can't possibly return. She looks around her yard and watches a hummingbird dart its beak into the chuparosa. She has a pretty, organized life with everything she's ever wanted: sunshine, a job she's good at, a lovely home in the Movie Colony district, modern furniture. The pool people come on Tuesdays, the cleaners on Fridays. She and Bayard have standing court times for tennis and golf and pinochle with friends, lots of friends. Even her underground sprinklers are on timers, watering her garden at standard intervals.

She looks at the slumbering San Jacinto Mountains in the distance. She thinks of oak trees and fields of soybean and corn, crumbling barns and dairy bars, her father's dusty poetry collections, stilettos, torn nylons, black ice, and Bach—and of that horrible day when Arthur, her dear Arthur, was suspended in the air, his back arched, his hands shot up above his head, the light on the water dazzling. The sky was a glorious backdrop of purple, blue, orange, and red. Late-summer sunsets in Wisconsin were always the most violent and dramatic, and that one was burned onto the backs of her eyelids. She saw it all the time, along with Arthur in the foreground, a floating arc suspended in Sherri's mind—an eyebrow raised in confusion, an apostrophe about to release possession.

CHAPTER ONE

East Troy, 1981

Roberta was late.

Sherri waited for her friend outside of the family store on the town square, shivering, her stomach in knots, her ears tuned for the sound of approaching cars. Under her parka she wore her favorite Junior House outfit, which she'd purchased on clearance at Waal's Department Store in Walworth, a burgundy velour skirt with a pink tie and a matching pink blouse. She'd loved it when she first bought it, but that morning she worried that her clothing made her look like a priss, and the heavy fabric felt stained from sadness because she'd worn it to her mother's funeral the week before.

In her bag she carried a pair of narrow shoes with smart heels that she wore when she played the organ, and a red string bikini that wasn't exactly stolen, but borrowed. She'd slipped it out of her friend Jeanne's sister's drawer and into the front pocket of her pants when nobody was looking, as inconspicuous as a wad of Kleenex. Claire was bustier than Sherri, and the fabric was stretched thin across the chest and rear, but where else could Sherri find a string bikini in January in the middle of Wisconsin?

She hated wearing a hood, but she pulled hers over her head

because she was freezing, and she'd spent hours trying to tame her crazy, curly hair, deciding finally to pull it back into a ponytail the size of a small hedge. She checked her makeup for the hundredth time in her reflection in the store window. If Roberta didn't arrive soon, the light mist of sleet would make her foundation and mascara run, and ruin the cerulean eyeshadow that she'd swabbed all the way to her eyebrows; she'd read in *Tiger Beat* magazine that light blue was the best color for hazel eyes like hers. Her lips were smeared with Cover Girl's Shimmering Shell, an opalescent nude shade she thought was more sophisticated than coral or pink. She hoped the sparkles would make her look iridescent, like she'd emerged from a gauzy dream instead of a small town that was notable for its rich soil. It felt strange—wrong, even—to wear so much makeup in East Troy on a cold, gray Tuesday morning.

She could have waited inside, but the apartment she'd shared with her mother had grown claustrophobic. Sherri felt so drained from taking care of Muriel while also holding herself together that she had nothing more to give. She looked beyond her reflection into the abandoned wreckage of her late father's watch repair shop below the family's apartment and felt another pang of sorrow. Losing her mother was a body blow, and the loss of her father three years earlier still managed to shock her system with grief, like a cracked tooth exposed to cold.

Sherri's father, Lane, had been a confirmed bachelor until he met Muriel. He was much older than her friends' fathers, and he was also quieter and slower. Unlike the sturdy German and Eastern European farmers in the area, he was small and balding, with bushy white eyebrows and an Adam's apple that pointed out of his neck like an elbow. He'd been better suited for intricate machines and the steady beat of time than the erratic natures of people. Sherri used to love working by his side while the chorus of clocks hanging on pegboard walls dinged and chimed behind them. He didn't talk much, but he did love to read poems out loud to Sherri, especially the ones that made him sad, as if sadness were a form of pleasure for him. Rilke was his favorite:

"Everything is far and long gone by," he would say at the end of the day, and "harry the last few drops of sweetness through the wine." By the time Sherri was twelve, she could dismantle, clean, and reassemble the whole movement on a watch and recite the first section of *The Sonnets to Orpheus* from memory.

The shop had been silent since his death. Between the slits in the shades, she could see the empty cash register yawning open, and boxes of yellowed paperwork and his remaining inventory of crowns, gaskets, rotors, hands, and wristbands gathering dust. The Chamber of Commerce was always after her mother to wash the porous cream city bricks and rent out the neglected storefront space, fearing it made the town of East Troy appear less prosperous—what a joke. They finally hung a FOR LEASE sign in the window and hadn't had a single bite in over a year.

Sherri's mother had suggested she open a "this and that" store in the space, selling stationery, pinecone wreaths, painted pots, and other useless stuff she referred to brightly as "bric-a-brac." "People will come from all over," she'd said, but Sherri had no desire to hawk useless junk, because she had other plans—plans that hinged on Roberta's arrival.

She turned to face the square. There had been several fierce blizzards that winter, and the snow was piled so high around the perimeter that she could only see the American flag hanging like a frozen sheet on the pole beyond the squat, red brick bandstand. Part of her wished she were a kid again so that she could climb the snow bluffs and sled down the small berms on her mother's vinyl placemats. She'd loved playing in the square until she'd overheard Roberta's mom say that hooligans with nothing better to do hung out there. Sherri hadn't wanted to be thought of as a bad kid, and she wasn't, not with her mom to take care of. Unlike Roberta, she'd never had the luxury to misbehave. It was *Roberta* who ended up smoking cigarettes and drinking cheap wine at the picnic tables, Roberta who lost her virginity in the bandstand, Roberta whom their classmates thought of (respectfully) as a "bad kid."

The businesses around the square were slowly limping to life. Giles was serving breakfast, and the air smelled of sausage and their famous cinnamon rolls. The desk lamp in the window of Haskell's Insurance glowed green, and on the other side of the square, probably in front of the tavern, she could hear someone shoveling snow and ice from the sidewalk.

Marshall's department store on the corner wouldn't open until nine o'clock, the same time her interview was supposed to start, which was in, what . . . twenty-five minutes? Sherri checked the time again on her art deco antique watch. Like the bathing suit, it wasn't exactly stolen. An old lady from Whitewater had brought it in for repair and never picked it up. After a year or so, her father had told Sherri she could keep it. Sherri didn't generally like old things, but she loved that watch. It had a delicate gold chain for a band and an elongated, angular bezel that suddenly reminded her of the shape of her mother's coffin. It was 8:38, and it took twenty minutes to get to Lake Geneva. Sherri began to hope that Roberta had overslept so that she could avoid this fool's errand, but just then Roberta veered off Highway 15 at breakneck speed and pulled up in her rusted-out Chevy Chevelle. She came to a loud stop and reached across to unlock the passenger door.

"Think we'll get there in time?" Sherri asked before getting in.

"We're fine." Roberta threw her cigarette out the window. "Let's go. It's just down the road a piece. Traffic in Milwaukee was the shits. Should have only taken half an hour to get here."

With her red blush, thick eyeliner, and blue mascara, Roberta looked like she was ready for a night on the town. They'd been best friends their whole lives, a friendship that felt predestined and sisterly because their mothers had delivered the girls on the same day. When they were younger, Roberta had buck teeth so severe that she needed to wear headgear to school, while Sherri had massive curls like Slinkies for hair, and a loud laugh.

The girls had been lost in their own private world. They'd wear their clothes inside out and their shoes on the wrong feet, and they'd walk backward down the hallways, their ponytails on their foreheads. When the kids looked at them funny, which they always did, Sherri and Roberta would say, "Didn't you hear? It's backwards day!" and squeal with laughter. They were boy crazy. In winter, they'd spend long afternoons in Roberta's bedroom composing love notes that they'd never send to their latest romantic interests. In summer, they'd have picnics in the square, eating peanut butter and jelly sandwiches and drinking milk out of Roberta's dad's empty whiskey bottle because they thought it made them look cool. They'd lie on their backs and stare at the sky, planning their weddings at Linden Terrace and picking names for their children. One summer, Sherri and Roberta both had a crush on Trent Eagan, the lifeguard, and they'd go to the deep end of the public swimming area at Booth Lake and practice the dead man's float, holding their breath almost as long as the Japanese pearl divers they'd read about in Social Studies, trying to trick him into thinking they needed to be saved.

In middle school, Roberta's brown hair was always greasy, parted down the center in permanent wilt, and her face bloomed with acne. "You have a great face for radio," Jan Stone once told her, leaving Roberta in tears. But then, in high school, Roberta's skin cleared up. She cut her hair and feathered it like Pat Benatar's. And when her braces were removed, she emerged a regular butterfly with a perfect, toothy smile. She got a job in the kitchen at Camp Edwards and started dating Ian, a British guy who worked there. Everyone in East Troy listened to rock and roll because Alpine Valley, the outdoor music amphitheater, had opened when Sherri and Roberta were sophomores, and it transformed the town from a sleepy farming community into a place that was actually cool. Alpine was just down the road, drawing all the big acts to the area in the summer, from James Taylor to the Doobie Brothers. When the Grateful Dead played, the fans took over the whole town. They'd hang out in the square with their tie-dyed shirts and long braids, and use people's hoses to shower in their yards. Most kids sold tickets to shows or worked as ushers, and come fall they'd return to school bragging about the famous musicians they'd met, showing off their autographed tickets and albums. Roberta had been the biggest rock-and-roll freak Sherri knew, especially for the Allman Brothers, but all that changed when Ian introduced her to British music that people in East Troy had never heard of, like Siouxsie and the Banshees and the Sex Pistols. She'd gone from being a first-class dork to one of the smokers that all the other girls were afraid to even walk past. She took up menthol cigarettes, sported a black leather bomber jacket that must have weighed as much as she did, and wrapped a Union Jack bandana around her wrist.

Roberta's ascent to tough-girl popularity was hard for Sherri, who felt left behind. Sherri had always been pretty enough, but she was too socially awkward to get much attention for her looks, and her free time for the last three years had been spent taking care of her mother. Even though they both understood that Roberta couldn't be seen with her anymore, Roberta watched out for her old friend, making sure nobody teased her or made her life too miserable. The kids stopped asking Sherri if she'd stuck her finger in a light socket to make her hair so wild and giving her a hard time for checking books out of the school library from the "Coping With" section with titles like *Coping with Cliques* and *How to Be Your Own Best Friend.*

After they graduated from high school, Roberta moved to Milwaukee to work at the Wooden Nickel store selling jeans in Southridge Mall, while Sherri spent the next year taking care of her mom. She was touched that her friend had returned home to pay respects at Sherri's mother's funeral. Roberta genuinely cared for Mrs. Taylor, who had taught her how to play the piano. Sherri's mom had known that Roberta's father got rough with them sometimes, and even though Muriel could be bossy and adamant with Sherri, she was always available to offer Roberta quiet support without interfering.

After the service, Sherri stepped out of the receiving line, shattered.

Roberta, her eyes red from crying, gave her a big hug. "Sorry, Sher. This must be hard."

"It was a long time coming," Sherri said, exhausted from trying to say the right thing to the funeral attendees, as if she were comforting them instead of the other way around. She didn't want people to feel sorry for her, or to worry. She did her best to appear poised and appropriate. Sherri thought she'd done well; she had a gift for remembering her parents' friends' names and the connections between the family's few and distant relatives. Her father had been an only child from neighboring Burlington. She'd met a few of his aunts, uncles, and cousins over the years, but Sherri didn't know them very well. They were farmers, and her father, the black sheep, preferred to stick his head in a book. He had no interest in animal husbandry or big tractors. He didn't like to get his hands dirty—he couldn't even stand to get Jismaa oil on his fingers when he repaired a watch. Her mother had been a loner for different reasons. At thirty, she'd left her parents behind in Albany, New York, when she'd heard about the church organist job in East Troy. When Muriel was in her teens, her parents converted from Catholicism to Christian Scientist, and had refused medical treatment for her beloved brother when he came down with TB. She'd never forgiven them for rejecting her entreaties to seek medical attention as he grew sicker. *Just call the doctor!* Muriel often noted the irony that in the last years of her life she'd seen one doctor after another, and they'd all been useless.

Sherri held each attendee's hands and looked them in the eyes when they spoke to her, her smile caring and authentic. "Honestly, we were just waiting for her to pass so she'd be relieved of her pain." She used "we" to make herself feel less alone, although it only made her more aware of her new status as an orphan. She repeated what she'd said a hundred times that day to Roberta, this time with sarcasm.

"Still." Roberta could see through Sherri's act. She knew there was more to it.

"Yeah. Still." Sherri tried not to cry. "It's just. I had to do every-thing for her. Literally *everything*." Her mother had battled against a mysterious neurological disease that made her dizzy. The doctor called it cerebral atrophy—her cerebellum had turned into scrambled eggs. She had a sound mind, but her body slowly became a cage for it. As an only child, Sherri was the only person to care for her. The last year had been especially brutal. Her mother couldn't even go to the bathroom without help. Though Sherri got along with her just fine, Muriel had been stubborn and strident even before she got sick. She had strong ideas about how things *should* be: music should be played at tempo, daughters should be obedient, and Muriel should be able to do all the things she used to be able to do.

"I had to watch her like a hawk," Sherri said, thinking about the accident that led to her mother's final decline, when she fell down the stairs. Sherri looked around the church. "She's just *nowhere*. I know it sounds crazy, Roberta, but now that she doesn't need me anymore, I'm all alone, and I'm—I'm useless."

Sherri needed to vent, and aside from her friend Jeanne, there were very few people in her life she could confide in. Roberta, she felt, could absorb some of her emotions. "I can't believe she's really gone, even though I have a death certificate to prove it. The coroner typed out the technical term for the disease. I couldn't even tell you what it is, but I counted. It was twenty-three horrible letters long."

Roberta fixed Sherri's collar and kept her hand on her shoulder. "Have you thought about what you'll do next?" Roberta asked. "You can do anything now."

Roberta was right: Sherri could walk right off a cliff if she wanted to. This new freedom she'd guiltily anticipated during her mother's decline was at once frightening and exhilarating. Everything was changing. The people she'd gone to high school with had moved on to jobs or to college. She had the building on the square, she supposed, but she felt too young to be saddled with real estate. She couldn't even afford to pay the taxes without someone to lease the space downstairs.

It seemed everyone else had a plan, but what was Sherri supposed to do? She'd been so busy taking care of her mother these past few years that she'd never had the luxury of thinking much about her future. She was smart, but she had no money for college, and she didn't know what she'd even major in. She knew one thing for certain: she didn't want to become a nurse.

"This might sound crazy," Roberta said, "but my friend Ellen from the store told me that they're interviewing for Bunnies at the Playboy resort. I already mailed in my application, and they called me for an interview."

"You did?" Sherri had a hard time imagining Roberta without her leather jacket on.

"Sure, why not? They pay serious money, more than I make at the mall, that's for sure, and it sounds fun, doesn't it? Think of all those men."

"I wouldn't know what to do with them. I've never even had a boyfriend."

"What about Tommy?"

Sherri rolled her eyes. She'd dated Tommy briefly when they were sophomores. He played the clarinet and made patterns in the spit that fell on the band room floor. He took her to a dance at the youth center, and then on a date to see *Exorcist II*. He put his arm around her, but he might as well have placed a dead cat across her shoulders. When he leaned forward to kiss her good night, she saw his greasy forehead and thought of all the drool that came out of his mouth. She closed her eyes and winced as his lips, like two earthworms, landed on her own. She hadn't enjoyed it at all. That was the only time she'd ever been kissed, and it was nothing like the passionate kisses she'd seen on her mother's soap operas.

Roberta said, "You don't want to date anyone from around here. Besides, you already know everyone. The men at the resort have good jobs. They open doors for you and chew with their mouths closed. You could find someone decent to marry."

Sherri felt like her life was just getting started. "I don't want to get married."

"Not yet, but someday you will, so you might as well find someone handsome and rich."

"At the Playboy resort? Aren't the guys there a bunch of perverts?"

"No, are you kidding? The guys there, they have an *outlook*." It had always struck Sherri as strange that someone as tough and seemingly independent as Roberta would worry so much about having a boyfriend and a husband. She'd already designed her own wedding dress. Sherri figured it was because her family was more "normal" than her own. Mr. Fletcher worked in management at Trent Tube, and she had siblings. They always ate dinner together as a family, drew lines on a special wall in the basement where they marked each kid's growth on their birthdays, and they went on beach vacations to Florida every other year. If it weren't for Mr. Fletcher's short temper, Sherri would have given her eyeteeth to be part of their family.

"Berta, are you crazy?" Nobody called Roberta "Berta" anymore except Sherri. "You really want to work at the Playboy resort?" Sherri said these words softly, because they weren't meant to be spoken in a church. The resort opened more than a decade ago and there were still some people in town, mostly older ladies, who couldn't even talk about the place out loud, while the men would brag openly about owning membership keys to get into the club. They'd take out-of-town visitors there for dinner and drinks, and make it sound like they were friends with Hugh Hefner himself. Between Alpine Valley and the Playboy resort, there were people in town who felt that they lived on the edge of the center of the universe. "You seriously want to work at that place?"

"You know how much money you can make? Thousands—not a month, but in a *week*. You can save up for your car. Didn't you always want to move to California?" When they were in middle school, they'd sneak into the Community Hall and play "California Dreamin'" on the jukebox over and over, dancing until they could hardly stand. That was Sherri's favorite song, because she couldn't believe there was a place where the weather was nice every day, all year long.

Roberta said, "My interview is next Tuesday at nine. They said to bring heels and a bathing suit. I can call and see if you can come with me."

"No, that's OK. That's not for me." What Sherri meant was that becoming a Bunny would permanently change her reputation in a small town where your reputation was all you had. Everyone knew you, and they knew your aunts, uncles, grandparents, siblings, and second cousins. Even her relatives in Burlington would get wind of it.

"Oh, come on. What have you got to lose? You can always say no if they want to give you a job. And they have a dorm."

"You mean we can live there?" Now, *that* appealed to Sherri. She couldn't imagine spending another day alone in the apartment she'd shared with her mom. She'd already talked to Jerry Derzon, the town Realtor, about finding someone to buy or lease the building.

"Don't you want to see what it's like? What else are you going to do? Let me just ask."

A few days later, when Roberta called to tell her that she'd arranged for Sherri to join her for the interview, she couldn't say no—then again, she could never say no to her old friend. The idea of the resort, while "pie in the sky" as her mother would say, offered a nice psychic refuge from the sad work of cleaning Tupperware dishes from the noodle casseroles the church ladies had dropped off and writing thank-you notes for flowers and memorials.

Sherri tried to imagine how she'd answer the interview questions they'd ask her. Could she really be a Bunny? *Sherri Taylor?* No way. But maybe they'd hire her to work in the laundry room folding towels and ironing sheets, or cutting vegetables in the kitchen. She remembered in seventh grade when Greg Thielan told their teacher with a perfectly straight face that he wanted to be a photographer for *Playboy* magazine. Greg's aspirations seemed about as realistic back then as Sherri's did now, only *she* was actually going to try.

Just before Sherri got into Roberta's car, she heard a little girl's voice. "Hey, Sher!" Sherri looked up and there, in the apartment above the flower store, she saw Raylee's face hanging out the window. She was the pesky neighbor kid, with thick glasses, a smattering of freckles, and massive gerbil cheeks. She was just as lonely as Sherri was. Her dad was a long-haul truck driver and her mom, Donna, worked the second shift in a nursing home, where there were lots of emergencies. Donna was always asking Sherri if she could do her a "little favor" and watch Raylee. The kid was always desperate to talk to someone—she'd even talk to Muriel as though she were able to hold up her end of the conversation. "Did you know glass is made from melted sand? Mozart could play the piano upside down and backwards. Could you do that before you got sick? Could you? Could you do a backflip? I heard about a man who could eat forty hot dogs in a minute. Do you think the sky is blue on other planets?" Sherri heard her voice and felt the girl's eyeballs on her everywhere she went. "Where are you going?" Raylee asked.

"It doesn't matter. Shut the window, it's freezing! Your dad doesn't drive for two days straight to pay to heat the outside." That was exactly the kind of thing Muriel would have said, and this made Sherri impossibly sad. But Raylee did everything Sherri told her to do, so she slammed the window shut with a startling *bam*.

Roberta's car smelled like exhaust, cigarette butts, and the Little Tree air freshener hanging from the rearview mirror. She turned onto Highway G. The ride from East Troy to Lake Geneva was pretty, even in the heart of winter. Off in the distance, Sherri could see the lifts on the ski hill at Alpine Valley, worn tracks from ski runs, and the domes of giant floodlights. Bare old oak trees lined the roads. Dilapidated barns, silos, and weather vanes were tucked into the rolling hills. The black cows looked like semicolons against the snow.

It had always been a big deal to go to Lake Geneva. There were only about three thousand residents in the winter, a number that swelled in summer, but people in East Troy considered it a real town second only to Milwaukee. It was only an hour away from Chicago, and the area had a certain mystique, because it had been a playground for mobsters like Al Capone and John Dillinger in the 1920s. There were nice restaurants, bars, and a little shop she liked called Barden's on the main drag, but the real attraction was the giant, deep lake. When Sherri was ten years old, her father had splurged and taken her and her mom on a tour on a converted steam yacht called the *Louise*. Everything seemed huge to Sherri back then: Lake Geneva, yes, but especially the Gilded Age mansions that the Chicago industrialists had built around it, like Stone Manor with its rooftop swimming pool, and the Alta Vista, Edgewood, Wrigley and Black Point estates. Decades later, Hugh Hefner had built his Playboy resort nearby so he could have a country playground escape from his Chicago mansion, which gave Chicagoans yet another reason to visit.

They passed near Bower's farm and the old schoolhouse, and suddenly Sherri felt herself come loose. She didn't know what was wrong with her. She'd kept it together all week since her mother's funeral, so why fall apart now? Maybe it was leaving East Troy for the first time in months, the exhaust making her feel light-headed, or seeing Berta, her old friend. Maybe she felt bad about yelling at Raylee, who was just lonely and lost—all she'd wanted was Sherri's attention. Why had she barked at her to shut the window instead of just saying hello and asking nicely?

When Roberta gunned the engine at the bottom of the hill, Sherri's stomach dropped, and suddenly she was in tears. She leaned forward and began to cry, really cry, for the first time since her mother had died. She sobbed without feeling embarrassed, jerking with grief.

Roberta reached her arm across the seat and rubbed Sherri's back. "It's OK, Sher. It's OK. Here." She grabbed an A&W napkin out of the glove compartment. Sherri appreciated that Roberta knew her well enough to just be there; she didn't offer the stupid platitudes Sherri had been bombarded with since her mother had gotten sick, and especially since she'd passed. The worst was *God doesn't give you what you can't handle.* Sherri especially hated that one.

She wiped her face, dabbing under her eyes, knowing her makeup would be ruined, and her pale china doll skin would be splotchy with tears. She blushed easily, which made it hard for her to conceal how she felt. She knew this was why it was so easy for the girls to make fun of her; unlike Roberta, who'd learned how to let their teasing roll off her back, Sherri's hurt blared like a neon sign. Everything got to her.

Soon her sobs, like thunder after a storm, grew less frequent, and Sherri slowly sank back into the cold, hard bucket seat, exhausted but also feeling better, cleansed even. She pressed her face against the window in hopes that the coolness would restore her complexion. When she pulled away, she saw she'd left an ugly smear of tan foundation on the glass.

"Hey Sher," Roberta said, "remember? Two all-beef patties, special sauce, lettuce, cheese, pickles—"

Sherri mustered a smile. "—onions on a sesame seed bun!" They said this last part together. The girls used to sing the McDonald's jingle over and over again, and in rounds. By the time Roberta turned off Highway 50 Sherri felt better, but the knot in her stomach tightened again when she saw a little booth with an attendant and the massive wooden sign advertising the Playboy resort with the familiar, giant white profile of the bunny head with the blank eye carved into it, and she remembered why she was there. Roberta stopped to tell the guy their names, and he waved them in. Sherri flipped down the mirror on the visor. "I'm never going to get this job." Long black streaks of mascara ran down her face. "Look at me. I look like I just finished a shift in a coal mine!"

"You'll be fine, you just need to get cleaned up. You're so pretty, Sher. Just wash your face when we get there. If anyone can get away with a natural look, it's you."

Sherri didn't believe Roberta meant what she'd said. Roberta was always the pretty one; she liked having Sherri as her sidekick, not her competition.

The road up to the resort was almost a mile long, and it wound up and down gentle hills. Sherri had always imagined that the main building would be closer to the lake, but when she turned and looked through the rear window, she could hardly see the icy expanse glinting in the distance.

"This place is posh *posh*," Roberta said. "They have their own airplane landing strip."

"You've been here? You never told me that."

"Just once. My dad has a key. They give them to all the managers at Trent. He brought me to see Gabe Kaplan perform in the Cabaret. All I remember is his stupid joke about teaching a monkey how to shave."

"You saw Gabe Kaplan?" Sherri was impressed. She loved *Welcome Back, Kotter*. She loved all the shows; whatever happened to be on TV was her mother's only form of entertainment, so Sherri left it on in the background for hours at a time. But her mother's true pleasure had been to listen to Sherri practice the organ, nodding along to the music she knew by heart, a look of concern crossing her face when Sherri missed a note.

As they crested the hill, Sherri saw the building. It was modern and earthy, with massive overhangs and stucco walls, sprawling and as flat as a sheet cake. It was easy to look at; it didn't compete with the landscape but managed to appear as if it had grown out of it. Most of her life she'd imagined the Playboy resort as a dirty place, forbidden. But up close it was almost disappointingly normal, not tacky at all. Tasteful, even. What had she expected, some brothel like the ones in the movies about the Wild West?

Roberta had to drive around to find a parking spot. The resort was pretty busy for a blustery Tuesday morning. "Hurry," she said. "The interview starts in two minutes."

"You go ahead," Sherri said. "I don't want to make you late."

"But the woman I contacted, she's expecting you."

"I don't even care if I work here."

Roberta was visibly annoyed. "Then why'd you come?"

"Because you asked!" Sherri started to cry again, and a fresh round of tears began to flow. "I wanted to do something with you. We never do things together anymore. You were my best friend."

"Oh, Sher." It was clear that Roberta was moved. "I'll always be your best friend. Just do this for me, OK? I really want this job or I'll have to sell jeans at the fucking mall forever. Please don't make me look bad by skipping out now. Just interview. It won't take long."

Sleet began to gather and thicken on the windshield. What could Sherri do? "Fine. Go on ahead, you go first. I'll be there in a few minutes." It didn't matter; they'd never hire her, not with Roberta for competition, and not the way she looked that morning after crying her guts out.

When she finally approached the building, the doorman opened the thick glass doors. "Welcome to Playboy, dear!" He said it as if Playboy was more than just the resort; like it was a way of life. Maybe for some people, but certainly not Sherri.

She half expected a bolt of lightning to strike her dead the minute she crossed the threshold. The entrance was grand, and the sound was muted because the walls had millions of small pebbles pressed into them. The ceiling was covered with wood beams that were stained almost black. A woman in a brown vest sat at a switchboard with a headset on. A happy Bunny with blond hair and a bright yellow outfit worked a table covered with Playboy merchandise—mugs, pens, stacks of magazines. "Here for the interview?"

"I guess," Sherri said. She didn't want this woman, so perfect and poised, to see her blotchy face, so she looked down at the navy carpet. Even the carpet was decorated with the bunny logo—bunnies everywhere.

"You're going to need to show more enthusiasm than that," the Bunny said, although her voice was kind, concerned.

"Where's the bathroom?" Sherri asked. She looked up, and the Bunny frowned when she saw streaks of mascara on Sherri's cheeks.

"Tell you what, I'll walk you there. Follow me." She led Sherri by the arm down the hall. "I'm Bunny Tina."

Sherri felt so dowdy in her parka and velveteen, her face stained and mottled, while Tina could have walked right off the cover of one of the

Playboy magazines. Embarrassed, she stared at the black leather furniture and the floor of the main area, which, unlike the lobby, wasn't carpeted but covered in fieldstone. Between the stones was a sheet of plexiglass, and beneath it ran a river that streamed from a waterfall. It made Sherri think of her father reading Coleridge's "Kubla Khan" to her:

In Xanadu did Kubla Khan
A stately pleasure-dome decree:
Where Alph, the sacred river, ran
Through caverns measureless to man
Down to a sunless sea.

"What's your name, hon?"

"Sherri," she said, still thinking of the next lines she knew by heart. She looked up and noticed the sunken indoor pool behind a glass wall, right there in the middle of the resort. Little bistro tables surrounded it, and there was a bar in the distance with a wall glittering with bottles of liquor under the lights. The air smelled faintly of chlorine.

"We just lost a Sherri."

"She died?"

"No, silly, she quit! But that means that when you get the job, you'll be able to keep your own name—you'll be the only Bunny Sherri for miles around."

"I'm not going to get this job."

"Don't say that! Come on now."

"Are you really Tina?"

"No, my real name is Mary, but forget I ever told you that. Here I'm Bunny Tina. We say 'Bunny' in front of our names the way you say 'Doctor,' even with each other. Did you know that Sonny and Cher bought Hugh Hefner's jet? And when they did, they had a party out there on the landing strip." Tina pointed beyond the big floor-to-ceiling windows. "Frankie Valli and the Four Seasons played. Just for us Bunnies! There's always something fun here—well, in the summer at least. Back home everyone just watches the corn grow." They entered the bathroom, and Tina handed Sherri a towel. "Start washing up. Don't go anywhere. I'll be right back."

Sherri did as she was told, grateful for Bunny Tina's calming chatter, her kindness. She soaped off her makeup. The mascara, like ink from a busted pen, swirled down the drain. She ran the water until it was cold and pressed it on her eyes with the hand towel to get rid of the puffiness.

Bunny Tina returned with a purple Chivas Regal bag made of soft velvet. She pulled out foundation, fake eyelashes, lipstick, and blush. "I can do this in record time. Trust me, I've had lots of practice."

"But those are *your* eyelashes."

"My drawer is crawling with these little caterpillars! I've got plenty to spare, and you're going to need to learn how to do this."

She stepped closer to Sherri and told her to look up. Bunny Tina smelled good, like cotton candy. It was hard not to stare at her ample breasts sitting on the shelf of her uniform, so Sherri fixed her gaze on the black bow tie at the base of her neck instead.

"You have to be pretty to be a Bunny, and you are, but there's more to it. The Bunny Mother wants each of us to have our own look. You've got that, did you know? A look. Real distinct. Plus, you seem sweet, and Gloria wants girls who are wholesome. She wants happy girls, friendly girls. So when you interview, trust me, smile until your mouth breaks. No drama, no tears. Here, let me put some blush on those cheeks." She bit her lip as she dabbed puffs of pink with a giant makeup brush and lined Sherri's lips before filling them in and asking Sherri to blot them on a paper towel. "I'm so jealous of your heart-shaped mouth."

"I have a heart-shaped mouth?"

"Sure you do. And a heart-shaped face, with your wide cheekbones and cute pointy chin. That's part of your look, see? What do you think?"

Tina placed her hands on Sherri's shoulders and adjusted her stance so that she could see herself in the mirror. The eyelashes made her eyes look huge, and her cheekbones appeared more angular and distinct. She looked better than she ever had, she really did.

"Now let's free up that gorgeous hair and unbutton your shirt. You look like you've come to interview at the library!" Tina set Sherri's hair loose and puffed it with her fingers. "You're a regular Bernadette Peters with those ringlets, has anyone told you that?"

"Oh, I hate my hair," Sherri said.

"We always want what other people have, but trust me, it's amazing. Look at you, Sherri. You're beautiful! What on earth made you so sad? Did you and your friend get into an argument?"

"No. My mother died."

Sherri could tell that Bunny Tina wasn't prepared for something *that* bad to have upset her. "Oh, you poor thing." Instead of brushing her hair, she started to pet it. "I'm sorry to hear that, I really am, but listen, don't mention it. Gloria won't even hire a girl if she hears her parents are divorced. Remember, no drama. This is a family resort. You need to ooze sweetness and smiles. Just tell her what she wants to hear, even if you have to lie. Trust me, it doesn't matter to her if you're telling the truth—all she cares about is how you look and how you *seem*." Bunny Tina led Sherri out of the bathroom and down the stairs and pointed to the door for the locker room. She gave her a big hug. "When you get the job, I'll look out for you. Remember, Sherri. If you've got an edge, don't let Gloria see it, and don't let her scare you. She scares the crap out of all of us, but you won't make it here if you show it. Good luck!"

When Sherri entered the locker room, she was overwhelmed by all the activity. The walls were covered in full-length mirrors except for one wall that had a door and a big window with the shades closed, and there were a few women in hot rollers applying makeup and shimmying into their costumes. The air was thick with perfume and hair spray. The women paid no attention to Sherri. Where had Roberta gone?

She stood with her bag hanging off her shoulder, unsure what to do. She took off her coat and folded it over her arm, and yanked off

her ugly winter boots and hid them in a corner. After a few minutes the door opened, and Roberta walked out wearing her bikini,
a frightened expression on her face. Sherri had never seen Roberta
look so small or so vulnerable with her pale skin and rib bones. She
was followed by a woman who must have been the Bunny Mother,
based on the silence that fell over the room when she entered it. She
was older than the other women by a decade or so but still beautiful.
Her cinnamon-colored hair was styled in a fashionable bob, with her
bangs cut bluntly across her forehead, and her lipstick was bright red.
She wore a loose, ivory silk kimono with orchids embroidered on the
neck, and her eyeglasses were propped at the bottom of her thin nose.
"What's your name?"

"Sherri," she said. She could feel everyone's eyes on her. "Sherri
Taylor. I'm Roberta's friend."

"Well, Sherri Taylor, which part of nine o'clock did you not understand? I usually have the interview before I see you in your suit, but I
don't have time for that today. Get changed, pronto. I've been waiting.
Come to my office when you're ready."

Sherri remembered what Bunny Tina told her: smile, be wholesome
and sweet. So Sherri forced herself to smile even though she felt like
dying. "Absolutely!" She was so rattled she didn't know what to say. Was
she really supposed to change in front of all these women? Then she saw
a topless Bunny standing with her breasts hanging out for all the world
to see, Sherri stripped, fumbling with her snaps, zippers, and ties because her hands were shaking and cold. Finally, she was in the borrowed
bathing suit, which seemed grubby and worn. There was still sand in
the crotch from last summer at the lake.

She stuffed her feet into her narrow organ shoes with modest heels
and Mary Jane straps and tapped the door to Gloria's office. "Stand
there, against that wall, so your knees and ankles touch," Gloria said
without looking up. Gloria got up and shut the door so that it was just
the two of them in the room. She bent down and inspected Sherri's legs;
Sherri realized that she was counting to see if she could see three tri-

angles of light shining through between her feet and ankles, between her ankles and knees, and between her thighs. Fortunately, Sherri had lost her appetite with her grief, and she was skinnier than she'd ever been. When Gloria saw her shoes, shaped more like dress shoes for men, she frowned with displeasure. "What are these?"

Sherri didn't want to tell Gloria that she played the organ. "It's my only pair."

"Well." Gloria stood up. "Take a seat."

Sherri lowered herself onto the chair next to Gloria's desk. She crossed her legs and set her hands on her lap, feeling more naked than she'd ever felt before, covered in a rash of goose pimples. She could tell that Gloria was inspecting everything about her as if she were a hog at the state fair: her skin, her hair, her bust, her waist, her teeth. "Why were you late?"

"Oh, I got here as quickly as I could. I was waiting for my ride, and—" She just blamed Roberta for making her late. She wished she could push the words back into her mouth. She decided to change the subject. Sherri smiled and fixed her eyes on the bracelet watch on Gloria's wrist. "I can put a new battery in that for you if you like. That's why your second hand is skipping."

Gloria seemed taken aback. "I thought it was broken."

Sherri repeated something her father had taught her: "Swiss watches don't break."

Gloria scribbled some notes. "You have work experience?"

"I brought a résumé. It's nothing much, but I've waitressed—"

"You don't need a résumé. And we don't call this '*waitressing*.'" She said it like the word was dirty. "Where'd you work?"

"Inn the Olden Days. In Mukwonago." Sherri had picked up a few shifts a week while a church deacon stayed with her mom. She worked hard and was lucky to leave with twenty bucks in her pocket after a four-hour shift. There, she'd waited on old ladies who farted and played bridge, and farm-equipment salespeople passing through town who called her "doll." She never wanted to smell chipped beef on rye again.

"And what do you like to do? Hobbies? Interests?"

At this point, Sherri figured she had nothing to lose by following Tina's advice—*even if you have to lie.* She channeled Tina's people-pleasing personality. "Well," Sherri said, smiling the way Tina did, and pulling her hair back behind her ear. "I guess you could say I'm your typical small-town girl." She giggled. "I love to play volleyball and golf and tennis, and I volunteer at the Salvation Army camp as an aide—I just adore kids. And I'm in 4-H, like everyone in my town. Lop-eared rabbits are my specialty." This was partly true. Sherri *had* been in 4-H, but her rabbit, an American Dutch named Radio, had bit the judge on the knuckles and was disqualified.

"I know it might sound funny," Sherri said, "but I just love spending time with my family. My mom is in charge of the annual cookbook for the East Troy Lioness Club, and she knows everyone in town." Ha! Sherri's mother would never have joined the Lioness Club, not in a million years. She thought the local women were busybodies with nothing better to do than gossip and exchange recipes. In turn, they considered Muriel a foreigner because she was from New York. "Between my dad's Rotary friends and my mom's potlucks, and all my brothers, our house is practically as busy as this resort!"

After everything she'd been through, it felt so good to be someone else for a change, good to imagine herself surrounded by siblings in a close-knit, unmarred family. Sherri tried to think of more lies to tell Gloria, but before she could say anything else, Gloria asked, "You're not planning to go to college, are you? You don't strike me as a college girl."

"No." Even though she had been trying to be someone else, Gloria's comment made her feel exposed; it was directed right at her, the *real* Sherri, and it hurt. Sherri was bored easily, but she'd been a good student, and she had a keen memory and proficiency with numbers. She could balance her father's books when she was just eleven years old. At the restaurant, she could tally her tickets and tax without an adding machine. She received perfect scores in her business simulation accounting classes, but the teachers only praised the boys for their good work. She liked how numbers made sense, and she loved that feeling of correctness when they clicked, but everyone assumed Sherri was a dip because of her loud laugh and awkwardness—and so did Gloria, apparently, right at first glance.

"We aren't so busy now, but by summer it'll be a madhouse. I need someone who can live here and work year-round, someone reliable to pick up shifts and work doubles, even triples sometimes."

"Oh, I can do all that. I'm a hard worker, I am. And I want to work here. The resort is so beautiful and classy." Just saying it made Sherri realize this was true—she really did want to work there. Suddenly it seemed as if the job was the answer to everything. She smiled and said, "I have the heart of a Bunny."

Later, on the drive back to East Troy, Roberta would die laughing when Sherri told her she'd said this, but Gloria seemed moved by the sentiment. She'd slipped off her watch and handed it to Sherri. "You'll get a letter from me in a few days. When you come back, bring this with you, and don't you dare lose it."

Sherri couldn't help herself. She reached out to Gloria and tried to give her a hug, which would be the first and only time she would ever try to touch the Bunny Mother. Gloria recoiled. "I didn't say you got the job," she said, her voice cold and firm. Sherri felt more stupid than ever—even more stupid than the time she tried to take the steno machine down from the top shelf at school and dropped it on her head in front of everyone.

Gloria opened her office door and ushered Sherri back into the dressing room. She frowned when her eyes fell on a Bunny in a pink costume who wore a cowboy hat with a turquoise stone and feather. "Bunny Carmen," Gloria said to a messy-looking Bunny with a shaggy Dorothy Hamill bob haircut, "let's talk about what happened last night." The pink-costumed Bunny's face fell. She ran into the office and the door slammed shut.

A few days later, Sherri got a letter offering employment. Training would start the following week. It seemed impossible. For someone who didn't plan to take the interview seriously, she suddenly felt like she'd won the gold wrapper on the Willy Wonka chocolate bar.

She called Roberta and blurted out her news. "We're going to work together, Berta!"

"You got it?" Roberta asked, dismay creeping into her voice.

"Didn't you?"

"No," Roberta said.

"Sure you did. Check your mail."

"I *did* check my mail, Sher. I got a letter of rejection yesterday. They don't want me."

Sherri was shocked. Was it because she'd mentioned that Roberta made her late? Or because Sherri didn't have a chance to share Bunny Tina's advice and tell her friend that she should act wholesome and never show her edge?

"I'm so sorry. I didn't even think I'd ever, you know, it wasn't even something I'd wanted, and you're so gorgeous."

"I didn't want to work at that trashy resort, anyway." Sherri knew Roberta well enough to know she was lying. She didn't think the resort was trashy. A ripple of guilt braided with pleasure ran through Sherri when she realized how good it felt to step in front of Roberta for a change. It was the first sensation of a new life. She clutched the Bunny Mother's repaired Provita watch like a talisman.

CHAPTER TWO

Sherri didn't tell a soul about her job for a few days, even though she wished she could shout the news from the top of the bandstand on the square. But then she'd look around at the practical farmer's wives and staid church parishioners and hold her tongue. A bigger part of her wished she could live a secret life that nobody would know about, but that was impossible in East Troy. Word would get around soon enough, and she'd no longer be thought of the same way ever again. She could already imagine the tongues wagging. *Did you hear about Sherri Taylor?*

Raylee was at the apartment as usual, working on homework at the kitchen table, yammering on and on about how many pull-ups she could do and how she'd burned her leg climbing the rope in gym class. Sherri only half listened, because she was sorting through piles of paperwork and worrying about bills. The invoice from the funeral parlor had just arrived. It seemed to Sherri that hearses and caskets ought to be free. At the funeral, she'd overheard Jim Kubiak from the feed store knock the thin aluminum casket Sherri had chosen with his knuckle and, after hearing the tinny sound, say to his wife, "Sherri must have got a good deal."

Jeanne, Sherri's fallback friend after Roberta became cool, stomped up the stairs and entered the apartment without knocking. She'd started checking in on Sherri when she finished her shift at Marshall's. She was quiet and reliable. She had short, frizzy hair and wore a constant uniform of thermal shirts and Earth shoes, and dreamed of becoming a park ranger.

"Guess what?" Sherri said to Jeanne, figuring she'd need to tell people sooner or later. "I found a job in Lake Geneva."

"That's great! At one of the stores?"

"No. I'm going to be a Bunny at the Playboy resort."

Jeanne fluffed her hair and stuck out her chest. "Ha! Me too."

"No, I mean it."

Her friend's face went pale. "You're joking, right?"

Sherri thrust the Bunny Mother's letter in Jeanne's face. "I'm completely serious."

"No. A *Bunny*! Think about that, would you?"

"You're going to be a *Bunny*?" Raylee said, genuinely confused. "How?"

"Oh no she's not!"

"Am too!" Sherri put her hands in front of her and scrunched up her nose for Raylee's benefit and began hopping around the apartment, causing her mother's china to clink in the cabinet. Her mother had thought of herself as a Yankee blue blood. She believed that owning good china was important and felt her Wedgwood collection set her apart from locals who ate off of unbreakable Corelle dishes and drank juice out of old jam jars.

Raylee laughed, but then she saw the alarm on Jeanne's face.

"You'll set us back, you know," Jeanne said.

"Us?"

"Women."

Jeanne made it sound like women were about to be liberated from jail and Sherri alone had the power to save them all, and here she'd gone and swallowed the key. "I hardly see how I'm helping women if I keep waitressing at the Inn."

Jeanne said, "What about college? You're so smart. You could go to UW-Whitewater, it's close."

"I don't even know what I'd want to study, and besides, I'm broke." She held up the accounting ledger she'd carefully filled out in red and blue ink. "Jerry Derzon just listed the building, but interest rates are through the roof. If he can't sell it, I'll need to find someone to lease it, and we've been trying to get someone into the store forever."

"You used Monopoly Jerry?" He was the biggest Realtor in town, hence the nickname. He owned a bunch of houses that he rented out, and had been badgering Sherri to sell her family's building ever since her mom got sick. She had a feeling he wanted to snap it up himself for a low price and make it part of his empire.

Jeanne had a new strategy. "There's an opening at the insurance agency. Why don't you work there?"

"You think I'll liberate women as a secretary to that disgusting Mr. Haskell? He's chased every skirt in town. Oh hey, honey, go get me a cup of coffee why don't you?" Sherri pretended to pinch Jeanne's ass, trying to make her laugh and lighten up, but Jeanne swatted Sherri away, frustrated.

"You're not in the best position to make decisions right now. I don't want you to take that job. I'm serious."

"I'm serious, too. Why on earth would I want to make three bucks an hour as a secretary?"

"That's what I make and it's fine by me for now. If you want more money, why don't you work at the factory?"

"Don't even suggest it." Trent Tube made stainless-steel tubing, and they were the town's biggest employer—and polluter. Sherri couldn't imagine a more boring (or loud) job than stamping metal all day long. Besides, now that she knew she was pretty enough to be a Bunny, she couldn't *unknow* it. It was confirmation that despite the teasing she'd endured throughout high school, she possessed all the physical qualities people found appealing. To someone who hadn't known her since she was a kid, she might even be considered beautiful. "I want to do something different. I want to go somewhere else."

Raylee looked at Sherri with alarm. "You mean you're really leaving?"

"I won't be far."

"No, stay here, Sher. We'll do stuff."

Sherri hated the thought of leaving the girl on her own, but Raylee wasn't her kid. It wasn't Sherri's fault that her parents didn't have time for her. "I'll visit all the time, I promise, and you can come see me at the resort."

"Are you crazy?" Jeanne said. "She's just a kid. She can't go there."

"It's a family resort," Sherri said.

Jeanne snorted and rolled her eyes. "Right. You know those men, they aren't going to pay attention to you because you're interesting."

"But I'm *not* interesting."

"You can balance a spoon on your nose," Raylee interrupted.

"Sher, don't you want to be valued for more than what's on the outside? This is not you. This isn't who you are."

"You don't even know who I am. And you know what? Neither do I. How am I going to figure that out if I stick around here? I don't want to be *Sherri the sad orphan*. I want to have a good time for a change." Tears pricked her eyes, and she turned to the empty living room to hide them. She saw her mother's empty wheelchair with the worn armrests sitting in the corner and thought of every spoonful of food she'd tried to get her mother to swallow, all the soiled sheets and clothes she'd washed, the bedpans she'd changed. It took every bit of reserved strength for Sherri to say clearly, firmly, "I'm taking this job. I start training on Monday. It's my turn to have a life."

"But it's not the life you want."

Sherri gestured at the lonely apartment. "This isn't either. So for now, I'm just going to make some money and have some fun." She was angry, so angry and upset she wanted to cry. She could never experience just one emotion at a time. "Why can't you just be happy for me?"

"Because I'm afraid you're going to forget who you are."

"Geez, I didn't say I was going to be a spy for the KGB. It's a job, just like you have a job."

"No, it's not just like that at all."

Deep down, Sherri knew that Jeanne was right. Sherri's job *would* be different. She wasn't just going to work somewhere; she was going to live her work, and become something she hadn't been before. Even the possibility of change made her feel different about herself already.

Despite Jeanne's reservations, she agreed to drive Sherri to the resort the following Monday. That morning, Sherri walked Raylee to school one last time. She was sullen, and pleaded with Sherri not to go, her lip quivering. "You were going to teach me how to play the organ."

"We can set you up with lessons from Mrs. Vogel. That's who taught me."

"I don't want Mrs. Vogel. I want *you*." Raylee's palm was soft and sweaty, and she gripped Sherri's hand as hard as she could.

When she returned home, Sherri stood with her duffel bag on her shoulder holding everything she thought she'd need and looked around the grim apartment above the store, taking inventory of the incredibly high ceilings, the transom window above the front door, and the view of the square. The spider plant sat atop the oak plant stand. It would need to be watered—who would do that? There was the Steinway that needed to be tuned and the threadbare arms on the scratchy, matching rose-colored wing chairs with doilies on the headrests. Her parents' framed black-and-white wedding portrait hung above the davenport like a portal to a different time. How could they both be gone? It was hard to remember that her mother had once been buxom and full of spirit; that her father, slight and inward even as a younger man, would have been both terrified and relieved at the prospect of an end to his solitude by getting married.

Sherri wished someone, anyone, were there to say goodbye to her, but then again, nobody in their family made proper exits. Her father's stroke was sudden, and her mother slipped away when Sherri least expected it. She'd left her in her bedroom so she could cook dinner, and Muriel died in the time it took to fry an egg.

CHAPTER THREE

There were six other girls in Sherri's training group, and each possessed her own "look," as Tina had called it, although Sherri wouldn't have ever guessed they were Bunnies if she had to pick them out of a crowd. Gathered together in the lobby before the start of the tour in their heavy wool sweaters and jeans, they all seemed to have come from good homes, whatever that meant, good enough that they felt the need to explain to each other why they were there—to save money for college or a car, or to help their families get by. But when it was Sherri's turn to say why she'd applied at the resort, without a trace of apology she said, "Because it sounds fun."

Maryellen was short, muscular, and cheerleader cute with her French braids secured by ribbons, while Lucy was rugged and self-assured. She taught horseback riding at her parents' stables and had ruddy cheeks, a flat butt, and looked like she could kick a horse in the ribs without hesitation. Rhonda was sweet and tiny, with a pixie haircut and elfin ears. Sherri's mother would have said she was so small she fell off a charm bracelet. She seemed as terrified about becoming a Bunny as a young virgin sold into an arranged marriage. She'd brought along a stuffed-rabbit toy and her own sewing machine.

On the other end of the spectrum from Rhonda was Ginger. At almost six feet tall, she possessed the statuesque glamour of a 1940s movie star, although her teeth were slightly crooked and her nose was large. It seemed her features needed to be big to accommodate her outsized personality. She told Sherri in her husky voice that she'd recently quit her job at nearby Lakelawn Resort, where she'd dressed like an Indian princess and wore a heavy suede beaded and fringed costume. "All the people from Chicago think this is the North Woods. If I have to dress up to work, I may as well dress like a Bunny so I won't sweat so much."

Like Sherri, the women mostly came from small towns and unincorporated townships like Honey Lake and Barneveld. Maryellen said she was from "The five O's" and clarified that this meant Oconomowoc. Gwen was from Milwaukee. She was one of the only black people Sherri had ever met, and from what Sherri could tell, she was the only black Bunny working at the resort. Aside from a few Hispanic families, there had been no minorities in East Troy; the only black children Sherri had seen attended one of the Girl Scout, Salvation Army, or YMCA camps on the area lakes. It was like a one-way exchange program, where city kids were expected to visit East Troy to learn how to swim, ride horses, and build a campfire, but country kids were never encouraged to learn how to do anything useful downtown. The city loomed in their imaginations as shadowy and dangerous, especially after the televised riots that sprang up after the 1977 New York City electrical blackout, when Sherri had heard a few local people complain about the "n" word, a word Sherri had said aloud only once, when she was four years old after she'd heard someone say it outside the tavern. She didn't know what it meant, but her mother did, and she promptly washed Sherri's mouth out with Lava soap and admonished her to never, ever say it again.

Sherri thought racism was limited mostly to extremists like Bob Dwyer, a regular at Giles, who'd joined posse comitatus and believed the postal service was involved in a conspiracy with the IRS. He'd tried to get Sherri's mother fired from the church after claiming she was Jewish because of her curly hair. Sherri was ashamed she even knew people like Bob. She wanted to convince Gwen that she wasn't racist without coming across the way Rhonda did when Gwen said she was saving for college. "Oh, good for you!" she'd said in an overly congratulatory tone, and Gwen shot her a look that made Rhonda seem even smaller than she already was.

And then there was Val. She was from Beloit, a factory town on the Illinois border. Most of the girls had fathers who ran dairy farms, drove trucks, or worked as boilermakers, although Val bragged that her father worked at the Parker Pen factory, which didn't seem like much to get excited over. Val said she'd taken the job to help her boyfriend Curtis buy his own carpet store. "It'll be *our* store once we're married. I'm investing in our future." Val was gorgeous and cool, with feathered brown hair and cobalt blue eyes. She described herself as "Black Irish," a term Sherri had never heard before. But she was rougher than sandpaper, and because her interest in the job was purely financial (or at least that's what she said), she wasn't nearly as impressed by the resort as the rest of the girls. To them, everything was *So pretty! So exciting! So wonderful! So interesting!*

"Open your mouths any wider and you'll catch flies," Val said. She scraped her nails with an emery board, a sound that made Sherri's skin crawl. How on earth had Val convinced Gloria that she was wholesome? She made Roberta look like the Virgin Mary. She probably got the job because she knew their mentor, Bunny Starr, who was also from Beloit.

Sherri looked up to Starr. She was so poised and glamorous that she was in a category all her own. She called Hugh Hefner "Hef" as if he were an old friend, and said she hung out with Hef's girlfriend, Barbi Benton. She impressed the trainees with stories of her stints at the Playboy Clubs in Chicago and Los Angeles, and at the resorts in London, Jamaica, and New Jersey. "You wouldn't even believe those

Bunnies. Most of them are centerfolds. I mean, I was a centerfold a few years ago, but these ladies are runway gorgeous. Anywhere else you go they'll tell you you're just cute *for Wisconsin,* so don't get a big head just because you work here."

Starr made everything she had to teach them—especially the rules—seem as important as collecting secrets for the CIA. "Pay attention," she said. "Some of you won't make it through training. They weed you out if you can't keep up. It's survival of the fittest around here. And even when you get the job, it's hard. It really is. Look around. I'll bet good money that in six months, only a few of you will still be here. Just yesterday we lost someone who'd only been here a month because she had a kidney infection."

"How'd she get that?" Ginger asked.

"The stays in the uniform. They hit some girls in a bad spot. It just happens."

She led them around the Sidewalk Café on the first floor and showed them the darkened Playboy Club, the Cabaret, and finally the VIP lounge, where the Bunnies wore silver velvet or blue velvet costumes. The air was still heavy with the residue of smoke from the night before. "You have to work your way up to the premier areas. And unless you can speak two languages, you'll never get to work in here."

Sherri nudged Ginger. "I eak-spay ig-pay atin-lay."

Ginger roared. "I'm also fluent in pig latin!"

Val shushed them angrily. "What are you, seven years old?"

They passed posters advertising upcoming events, from a boxing match and ski lessons to performances by comedian George Gobel and jazz musician Joe Williams. Long hallways with hotel rooms shot away from the lobby and seemed to extend into eternity. "If you get caught setting so much as a toe in the hotel part of the resort, you'll be dismissed *immediately.* I've seen it happen more times than you'd like to know."

After the tour, they stopped at the basement cafeteria for lunch. There were sandwiches, pasta, and a giant salad bar. "You can eat anything you want. Just show your employee key. It's free, but it'll cost you, if you know what I mean." Bunny Starr tapped her belly.

The girls were making conversation while they ate at one of the long tables when Val shot Sherri a look. "Stop dragging the fork across your teeth, would you?"

Sherri thought she'd left girls like Val behind in high school. She felt that familiar dread at the prospect of having to deal with her. Becoming a Bunny had given Sherri the idea that she had the power to change who she was. She desperately wanted to be different. So when she took her next bite of cottage cheese, she bit her fork and pulled it slowly out of her mouth, her teeth scraping against the tines, looking Val right in the eyes the whole time. She wasn't used to being defiant, and this gesture ran against her nature, like rubbing fish scales in the wrong direction. She could feel her chest and cheeks becoming red and hot. She wanted to laugh and cry at the same time.

Gwen smiled approvingly and gave Sherri a discreet wink that further emboldened her. Lucy pretended to stare at something of interest off in the distance, while Rhonda's eyes grew big.

Val popped a cherry tomato into her mouth. "I'm surprised you still have all your teeth coming from East Troy. That's why you're showing them off, huh?"

Ginger leaned back in her chair, slapped her thigh, and laughed out loud, a throaty sound that echoed in the cavernous room. "Oh boy, let the games begin."

Sherri wished she could think of something biting to say about Beloit, but all she could think of was the world's largest can of Hormel chili that sat by the freeway. Instead, she lost her nerve, reverted back to the old, awkward Sherri, and let out a loud, nervous laugh, attracting the attention of Tina, who stood in line at the salad buffet. "Is that Sherri? *Bunny* Sherri?"

Before she knew it, Bunny Tina, again in her yellow costume, had set down her tray and sprinted toward her in her heels, wrapping Sherri up in a huge embrace that made her feel important, especially in Val's eyes. "I just knew you'd get the job. I told you, didn't I? Training is the worst. Like boot camp, but maybe that's good for you now. It'll keep you busy so you won't have time to be sad about your poor mom."

Sherri still felt tender and raw. She didn't want to think about her mother, not in front of the girls she'd just met, and not at the resort, a place Sherri had thought of as set aside from the pain of her real life, set aside from *everyone's* real life. Wasn't that the point of a resort? It was a whole separate world. Besides, she worried about what would happen if Gloria learned that she'd lied about her family.

"Training isn't bad so far, but we just started."

"Oh, just wait. But you can do it, you can. I've got to run, but let me know if you need anything. Anything at all." Tina meant it—she looked Sherri in the eyes and made her feel protected and chosen.

After Tina disappeared, Val looked at Sherri with a glimmer of compassion in her eye that took Sherri off guard. "What's wrong with your mom?"

"Oh, nothing," Sherri said. "She just hurt her hip."

Val was suspicious. "My mom was in the loony bin," she said. "They told her to bite down on a mouthguard and then they shot her up with electricity. Now she sits on the front porch all day watching the birds."

"Seriously?"

"No." Val sneered. "God, you'll believe anything I tell you, won't you?"

After lunch they were shown to their dorm rooms in a cement block building everyone referred to as the Bunny Hutch. It looked like a prison, because it was surrounded by a twelve-foot-high barbed-wire fence; whether that was to keep the men out or the girls in, nobody said.

"The security guards will bring you here after your shifts," Bunny Starr said. "You should never, ever walk back alone, especially when it's dark. You never know if some stalker might follow you. Play it safe. They're happy to shuttle you over in their carts. And if you want to go into town to do laundry or meet with friends, they'll drive you there, too, if they aren't busy. No need for a car, but if you have one, you park it over there, in the employee lot."

The rooms were simple and nondescript, with twin beds on opposite sides of the room, matching desks in the middle, and institutional chairs one might find in a dentist's waiting room. Not everyone would live there; Gwen commuted to work from Milwaukee, and Lucy and Maryellen rented an apartment in town. Sherri's heart was set on rooming with Ginger, who'd played competitive volleyball in high school and seemed like she was used to being around other women. Already she made Sherri feel like they were on the same team. She also would have been OK with mousy Rhonda—anyone but Val, so of course that's exactly who she was paired with. She couldn't believe it. Rhonda, sorry for Sherri but clearly relieved at her own good fortune, told her how sorry she was. "Val," she whispered. "Ugh."

And in no time at all, Sherri discovered that Val *was* ugh. She snuffed out her cigarettes in the cans of Tab she'd left on every countertop, and Sherri almost broke her wrist when she fell after tripping on the shoes Val had kicked off and left in the middle of the room late their first night there, when she'd breezed in after partying and threw on the lights. She didn't care if she woke Sherri up. One morning, she left her wet towel plopped right on Sherri's bed. The only good thing she could say about Val was that her boyfriend Curtis supplied them with a huge purple, orange, and red shag remnant, which made their corner room with two sets of windows the largest, brightest, and most inviting of all the dorm rooms. If only Val's personality weren't so acerbic. The other women quickly learned to keep their distance.

A few days later, Sherri could see what Tina meant about training being hard, and she understood why Gloria didn't want to use the word "waitress" to describe the work the Bunnies had to do. What waitress trained for an entire week, or stayed up late trying to memorize the contents of two huge binders that were bigger than the Old Testament? Memorization was easier for Sherri than for most of the other girls. She was able to take a mental picture of just about anything she saw and store it in her brain, but still she was overwhelmed by all the rules Bunny Starr ticked through. "Don't let guests see you wear jewelry, chew gum, eat, or sit. You'll get demerits for having dirt under your nails, if your ears are bent incorrectly, if you don't keep your locker organized, or if you don't keep the changing room cleaned. You need to look at the bulletin board every day for updates and attend Bunny Council meetings. And don't ever forget to check the ashtrays."

Bunny Council sounded important. They had their own employee newsletter, called *The Hare's Head*. Wouldn't Jeanne be impressed to learn that there was more to Sherri's job than strutting around in a Bunny suit? Sherri had underlined a line she'd found in the Bunny Manual twice, once for herself, and once for Jeanne: "The Bunny has become what the Ziegfeld girl was to another generation, synonymous with the most glamorous young women in the world." She was part of a tradition. She was finally part of *something*.

Sherri even got benefits. She felt like a real adult filling out her forms for accident, life, and health insurance. She had a week's paid vacation and a free subscription to *Playboy* magazine that she could read two weeks before the subscribers. Guests could practically eat for free with Sherri's family discount, but this perk only made Sherri sad that she didn't know anyone who would visit her. Sherri was told she would be welcome at the Playboy Clubs in Chicago and Los Angeles and all over the world. When she heard this, she smiled at Rhonda. "We should go to Chicago."

"That's OK," Rhonda said. "I went there on a school field trip to see the King Tut exhibit. I couldn't stand all the shadows."

"The shadows?"

"From the skyscrapers. The middle of the day in the city feels like the middle of the night. And the El is so loud. I'd be fine if I never went back there again. The loudest thing I hear in Barneveld is a screech owl. That's enough for me."

The most important rule, and the one that bothered Sherri the most, was that Bunnies were forbidden from dating not just coworkers, but also keyholders and guests. The women broke out in a collective groan when they heard this.

"We're disappointingly moral here," Bunny Starr said in a voice that could break up a party. Disappointing was right: Sherri had had a million crushes on the boys at school, and she'd daydreamed about encounters with celebrities like Leif Garrett and Shaun Cassidy. Her notebook was filled with her signature combined with the last name of whichever boy she liked at the time: Sherri Parker, Sherri Hackbarth, Sherri McBride, all with a heart as the dot for the *i* in "Sherri." But, aside from Tommy, she'd had little experience. She didn't know how to flirt, much less act sexy. She'd hoped to change all that—wasn't the resort supposed to be the sexiest place on earth? But with all the rules, she felt like the mystique around Playboy was a total lie. Rhonda seemed relieved, while Sherri felt she'd been betrayed. "We may as well have joined a nunnery," she whispered to Ginger.

"Don't worry." Ginger winked. "I heard there are ways to have fun."

"Don't ever let a guest touch you," Bunny Starr said, "and if they so much as give you a sideways glance or ask to squeeze your tail—and trust me, they will—tell security. This is a family resort first and foremost. See?" She pointed at some teenage boys who were taking a break from skiing. They played cards at a table in the lobby area and blushed when they saw the group of women looking at them.

Liquor was the hardest part for Sherri to keep straight. Sherri was no stranger to alcohol—nobody was in East Troy, or all of Wisconsin for that matter, because the Tavern League reigned supreme. The drinking age was eighteen, but even when she was underage, she could get served alcohol at a restaurant or bar if her parents were with her. And if they weren't, she could always find someone's older brother or sister who would buy. But Sherri's parents hadn't been drinkers, and she'd never been exposed to the highbrow stuff they served at the resort. She and Roberta used to drink super-sweet wine, like strawberry kiwi Mad Dog 20/20, or Boone's Farm varieties called Tickle Pink and Country Kwencher. Sherri's only exposure to hard alcohol included sneaking sips of her mother's crème de menthe that she used to make grasshopper ice cream drinks on special occasions, or the scotch she'd chugged out of Roberta's flask when she ran into her in the bathroom one day at school, upset because she hadn't had enough time to finish an English quiz. "Go ahead, it'll relax you," Roberta had said. Later that day Sherri was so "relaxed" that she fell asleep in typing class. When she woke up, her mouth was dry and she had a black mark on her forehead from the typewriter ribbon, which was why Lynn Jenkins called Sherri "Ash Wednesday" straight up to graduation.

By senior year the kids in her class, many of whom had turned eighteen, would spend their lunch hours drinking Schlitz on tap at Denny's Bar, an old saloon on the square just a few blocks from school. The place was rumored to be haunted by the ghost of Eugene Chafin, the universally despised East Troy native who'd run for president as a representative of the Prohibition Party. They'd return for their afternoon classes smelling like the bleacher section of a baseball stadium on a hot day, belching and running to the restroom all afternoon. In summer they drank in the "ETBT," or the East Troy Beer Tent, to benefit the Lions Club, and they'd go to a farm out on County Trunk D, where they rolled kegs out to the edge of the cornfield so the cops wouldn't see them and partied all night.

But that wasn't the kind of rarefied drinking the guests did at the resort, where Sherri felt like a real redneck as Bunny Starr taught them about the most important part of their jobs. "The drinks need to be ordered and served in a sequence. Whiskey, bourbon, gin, vodka, tequila. Got it? Whiskey, bourbon, gin, vodka, tequila. Say it after me. Hard liquor comes in a shot glass with a separate twelve-ounce highball filled with ice." She held up the glass and clicked it with her painted nail. "Unless the drinks are already blended, you mix them for the guests at the table. Remember, it's all part of the show. Slow down and exaggerate your guest's experience of being waited on by a Bunny. And smile the whole damn time."

A week ago, Sherri didn't even know what went into an old-fashioned; now she knew every variety. Mike, the head bartender, who bore a striking resemblance to Burt Reynolds, led a session on drinks. He said they could be made with bourbon, brandy, or rye, with soda water or 7UP to make it sour, sweet, or press, and served with two maraschino cherries. The Bunnies, not the bartenders, garnished the drinks with the bunny-head plastic stir sticks the guests liked to collect. He said that Cuba Libre was served with lime, and a whiskey sour was served with a citrus cherry flag. Daiquiris were made with Malibu rum, Harvey Wallbangers with Galliano that smelled like butterscotch, and Rusty Nails with Drambuie. There were seemingly infinite combinations and preferences: neat, up, on the rocks, shaken, dirty ice on the side, salted rim, blended, stirred. Sherri focused intensely on everything he said, imagining that he was reciting a poem for her to memorize. She broke his advice down into lines and stanzas, repeating his words back to herself again and again.

"Always be nice to the bartenders," Bunny Starr said, winking at Mike. He had giant biceps and a vampire-like widow's peak on his forehead. "They're the most powerful people you'll work with."

"She's right," Mike said while drying out a glass with a bar rag, the bottles of liquor arranged on the wall behind him like books in a library bookshelf. "We can make your life a living hell, or paradise on earth."

Who knew there was so much to think about, starting with how Bunny Starr taught the trainees to approach a table? "Make eye contact with each guest. Remember, they're here to have a good time. Smile and introduce yourself, and stand with your hips squared. Check the ashtrays and place napkins down with the bunny emblem facing the guests. Ladies first—always ladies first. Remember to seek the approval of the wives. It's more important to talk to the women than the men, and avoid flirting with the husbands at all costs. The women need to know that you aren't there to be a home-wrecker. I'll tell you, the more insecure the woman is in her relationship, the more she'll hate your guts. You want them to realize you aren't the trash they think you are. You're just working." Bunny Starr smiled.

The drinks were arranged in a very specific order on her tray, and the women were taught how to serve them with the famous "Bunny Dip." "You don't want to be seen bending at the waist or appearing to sit. You are absolutely forbidden from reaching across a table." Bunny Starr was so serious she might have been leading a lesson on gun safety.

Dipping was much harder than it looked. Sherri put her knees together, leaned into her right leg, and attempted to serve sideways and backwards from her tray. The empty glasses slid off and clattered to the floor. The move reminded her of the weather girl on television pointing at the map. "No, not like that," Starr said, reaching for her arm, spotting her like a gymnastics coach. "Like this." She thrust Sherri's arm behind her so that her shoulder ached. "Try again. And again. It'll be even harder once you're in heels." They practiced for an entire afternoon, over and over, until Sherri's hips and back ached. "You need to get this right."

And if she didn't? Well, there were room captains, Bunny Starr explained, and they watched every single move the Bunnies made. They would be written up daily for their dips, along with their attitude and appearance. The Bunny Mother would hear about every little thing that could possibly go wrong: the slightest grimace or pea-sized stain on their uniform would get them a demerit. "Enough demerits and you'll be out in the parking lot on your ass," Bunny Starr said.

The costumes came last. The girls were ushered into the dressing room and were told to strip to their underwear. The room was in the basement, and outside the temperatures had dropped below zero. It was drafty and cool inside, and Sherri, shivering to her bones, found it awkward to mingle bare-breasted with these women she'd just met. She could feel the girls taking inventory of each other's bodies in front of the full-length mirrors and making comparisons, while Bunny Starr went from girl to girl, telling them what they needed to work on. When it was Sherri's turn, Bunny Starr stuck her finger in her hair and yanked out the ponytail holder, setting Sherri's hair loose.

"I know, it's a frizzy puffball," Sherri said. She was used to apologizing for her hair.

"Whatever gave you that idea? Your hair is your distinctive feature, so make it even bigger. A lion's mane." Bunny Starr sprayed her with Aqua Net and stood so close to Sherri that she could smell her Binaca-scented breath. "You've got good skin. Great skin, actually. But your eyes need help. You need eyeliner. Try gold eyeshadow instead of blue. That blue is so wrong for you, so seventies. You put on makeup like a teenager. You need to be camera ready at all times." Before Bunny Starr moved on to the next girl in line, she said, "And darken up the lipstick. It's supposed to be vivid. You'll get a demerit if the color is too light. Go for big lips, big hair."

Bunny Starr walked away, and in the mirror, Sherri's eyes caught Bunny Gwen's. She'd been standing next to her the whole time, watching. "Big lips, big hair, huh? I'll tell you something: I walked in here with a 'fro and Gloria said I had to relax it or cut it short. I'm surprised they haven't asked me to cut my lips off."

"I'm so sorry." Sherri wished she knew what to say.

Bunny Gwen shook her head. "I didn't ask you to be sorry."

Biata and Ola, the Polish wardrobe "mistresses," entered the room. Bunny Starr hung two uniforms next to Sherri, one in brown and orange paisley, and the other a bright Kelly green. "I picked these colors to go with your chestnut hair."

Sherri had chestnut hair?

"Here are your stockings. Two pair, you put one right over the other."

"Two?"

"The good news is you won't need to shave your legs anymore. None of us do. At least when it isn't summer, nobody will see them."

Sherri put the stockings on and remembered the compression hose her mother had worn to keep the blood circulating in her legs. She stood and faced the mirror again, feeling especially naked with her legs black as night and her bare torso seemingly the only part of her that existed. She fought the urge to cross her arms over her breasts but she didn't, because none of the other girls did. They were adults! Biata came over and asked her to slip her feet into the leg holes of her green uniform. Her strong old hands tugged and pulled the costume up over her hips as if she weren't really there, yanking and pinching the fabric. She set Sherri's breasts on the shelf inside the bustier part and squeezed as dispassionately as if she were testing peaches for ripeness at the grocery store. Ola came over, and the women measured and pulled, murmuring to each other in Polish, their fingers hard and cold, marking the satin with the safety pins they held between their pinched lips. Sherri thought there was something wrong. The uniform was so tight that she could hardly breathe, reminding her of something her mother used to tell her when Sherri complained as she roughly ran a brush through her mess of hair: "Beauty hurts."

But once her costume—no, her uniform—was on, she gave herself permission to really look at her reflection, something she was never allowed to do at home because her mother believed mirrors made people vain. Muriel said that five seconds was long enough to see what you needed to see. The only mirror in their home was on the bathroom medicine cabinet, and it was old and pitted with age. Her father used to recite a line from Auden every time he caught his own reflection: "O look, look in the mirror, / O look in your distress; / Life remains a blessing / Although you cannot bless."

That afternoon, in her uniform for the first time, Sherri lingered in front of this clean, smooth reflection and liked what she saw: Her shoulders and chest were milky white. Her arms, just arms before, seemed as long and delicate as tulip stems, and her legs seemed wispy and elegant, especially when she stepped into the pointy satin shoes she was told she'd need to take into town to get dyed to match her uniform.

Bunny Starr showed the girls how to put on their bow ties, and demonstrated how the bunny-head cuff links on the white wrist cuffs had to face each other. "Everyone is going to want to squeeze your tail. Don't let them. And don't ever let them take it. Or your ears. They'll ask, and trust me, they'll offer you money and favors, but you can never, ever let them out of your sight. These are only yours to borrow, and you'll get charged if you lose them. They were custom made."

Last but not least, just before her first inspection, Bunny Starr put the bunny-ear headband on her head with all the pageantry of a royal coronation. Next, she affixed the tail to the clip in the back. Sherri hardly recognized herself in the mirror. She could almost feel her former life become severed from this new one, and she wasn't sure if she was changing into someone else, or connecting with her most true self. She didn't yet know that this was a critically important distinction.

Under the recessed lights in the dressing room she saw it all come together: her eyes now outlined like Cleopatra's, and her hair an auburn mane, with little tendrils of baby bangs on her forehead. She never knew she could be this person—this truly beautiful woman. *Sherri*, she thought, *meet Bunny Sherri!*

Rhonda stood next to her, as awed as Sherri was. "Look at us," she said. Rhonda had gone from mousy to adorable, her eyes big and round, her high cheekbones rosy, her chin pointy and cute. "We're all Bunnies now."

Gloria, in her trademark kimono, walked up to Sherri. She was holding her ever-present clipboard, and appraised every inch of her flesh. Sherri smiled, but Gloria frowned. What was it about her that made Sherri feel like a dog at the pound? She was suddenly gripped by panic. She remembered what Bunny Starr had said: "Some of you won't make it through training." What if Sherri was that girl?

"You have lipstick on your tooth," Gloria said, handing Sherri a Kleenex. "Wipe it off." Sherri exhaled with relief.

But then Gloria walked over to where Lucy stood, still topless and in her black tights, waiting for Ola and Biata to fit her. Gloria looked her up and down. The entire room went quiet. "You're not going to make it, honey. Ola? This one is headed home."

Lucy was stunned. "What did I do?"

Gloria turned to walk back into her office. "It's nothing you did."

Rhonda and Sherri caught each other's gaze in the mirrors—*oh my God!* It was bad enough to get fired, but to get fired while you were half naked in a room full of girls, and for no given reason? Poor Lucy.

But Sherri made it. How odd it felt to walk out on the floor in her costume and heels for the first time, her hair loose and wild, the air cool on her bare shoulders. It was like one of those dreams Sherri often had that she'd shown up at school dressed in just her underwear. But nobody was shocked. None of the guests in their heavy sweaters and sport coats who sat in the Sidewalk Café where she worked pointed and made fun of her, or insisted she should cover herself up; instead, she was as expected and as welcome as the cocktails she set on the table in front of them. When she did, the men gazed at her with raw approval.

It only took a few shifts for Sherri to begin to enjoy all those eyes on her. She knew that she was there to be seen, and for the first time in her life she learned that she liked being looked at, she did, as much as she liked to be told that she was beautiful, something she now heard every single day.

Kids were always at the resort, whether to have brunch with their grandparents or warming up with hot cocoa after a day of skiing, and they'd hide behind the giant pillars and muster the energy to ask Sherri for her autograph. At first, she felt like saying, "Who, me?" But soon she learned to smile and sign her name with flair.

And then there were the men who stared at her as if she were the answer to every problem they ever had. She could move them with the smallest gesture, from an extra napkin to calling them "hon," and offering up a sincere smile. *You're a good-looking girl, aren't you?* they said. *Well, hello, gorgeous! Have I died and gone to heaven?* Men asked to have their photos taken with her. They complimented her skin, her button nose, her hair, her long, elegant neck.

If it weren't for Roberta suggesting she interview here, she might never have experienced this revolutionary rush of power; never learned that she had control.

That thought made her smile. When she did, she could see why Gloria chose only happy, wholesome-looking Bunnies. Her smile worked. It reminded her of the shift in sound on the organ, when she would change the registration from a 16' Bombarde reed stop to the light, charming sound of a 4' flute. After so much heavy sadness, she finally felt light and free.

CHAPTER FOUR

The brutal January weather extended into the first couple of weeks of February. The resort's slopes were covered in ice. Not even the die-hard skiers were up for a visit or a swim in the heated outdoor pool by the ski chalet. During the week the resort was lucky to fill twenty rooms. The Bunnies' shifts were cut back, and they were happy for any work that came their way, even if it meant spending hours rolling silverware into napkins. It was so cold that it felt even time had frozen still. Sherri rotated through endless shifts in the game room, playing cards with one or two little kids, the boys trying to sneak peeks at her cleavage. "Want to play a game called taxi?" she said to one particularly naughty boy, remembering when Lynn Jenkins had done the same thing to her in seventh grade. When the boy said yes, she held the deck of cards in her hands and said, "OK, you're the taxi driver." She flipped the cards onto the floor. "Those are your customers, now pick them up."

Working at the Playboy table as a greeter the way Tina had wasn't much better, not when her skin broke out into goose bumps whenever someone opened the wide front door. One Saturday, Gloria invited her and a few of the other Bunnies to work their first off-site event at a car show in Janesville, where she stood in front of a Buick Skyhawk like a game show hostess with her feet in a T, her arm outstretched, a smile frozen on her face, and her back killing her. She thought she'd die from boredom, but at least she wasn't stuck in the dorm.

Val was gone a lot, hanging out in Beloit with Curtis (Ginger called him the "the Pile Prince" and "the King of Shag"), but that all changed when he picked up a second job at the Frito-Lay plant in Beloit to make more money for the carpet store, which meant that he dominated less of Val's free time. Nights he didn't work, he'd drive the half hour from Beloit to Lake Geneva to hang out at the end of the bar in the club, where all the Bunny boyfriends gathered. He didn't have a roving eye; he cared about Val and only Val, and he watched her while she worked, smelling of corn chips, his camo John Deere cap perched low on his forehead.

One night, Sherri was feeling sorry for herself because she had nothing to do after Carmen, the girl who'd gotten into trouble with Gloria when Sherri had interviewed, canceled plans. Carmen was gregarious and fun—and a total mess. Nobody wanted to be her roommate, so she'd somehow managed to have her dorm room to herself. It was cluttered with mounds of clothes, half-empty cans of soda, and dirty ashtrays. She was the girl who always seemed to have a piece of toilet paper stuck to the bottom of her shoe, or a glob of ketchup on her shirt. She'd been at the resort for over a year and kept getting demoted, which meant she hung around with the new recruits while most of the other Bunnies stuck with the girls from their training groups. "I can't help but get into trouble," Carmen told Sherri. "I'm an All World Division One talker."

Carmen explained that she'd started working a second job at the Sugar Shack one night a week. The club was on a rural road on the outskirts of Lake Geneva, and became briefly famous for adding male strippers to the lineup even before Chippendales dancers were a thing.

"You're going to be a stripper?" Sherri asked, awed not just that Carmen could do that job, but that she knew a real-life stripper. She couldn't stand to be seen naked in the shared shower in gym class, much less in front of leering men who threw singles on the stage. Carmen wasn't the prettiest Bunny by a stretch. If anything, she was "normal." Sherri was just beginning to see that the line that separated "those girls" from "us girls" was thin and permeable.

"It's for my brother," Carmen said. "The stupid little fucker goofed around with some friends and put gasoline into the carburetor of his Mustang, and it exploded. His face looks like a pan of lasagna. Now he needs skin grafts, and my mom, she works at a diner. She can't even afford the ointment he needs. It's three hundred dollars a jar because it's made with real silver."

"What about your dad? Can he help?"

"He died in Korea. I'll happily jiggle my tits in a stranger's face if that's what it takes to make Mark beautiful again. He's my brother bear."

Val was also suddenly left without plans, because Curtis had to fill a shift for someone. Val seemed relieved, yet desperate for something, anything to keep her occupied—she was one of those people who had to stay busy every single second. She sat at her desk (Sherri thought it was funny that the dorm rooms had them), throwing dime after dime at her box of Vantage cigarettes, trying to topple it over. Both of their desks were cluttered with makeup, fake eyelashes, roll-on deodorant, and bottles of Love's Baby Soft, what Val called her "signature scent," and crumpled pink messages scattered all over the desk like dirty Kleenexes. Ola and Biata were like secretaries, because they had access to the only phone the girls could be reached at. In their hasty block handwriting they'd write *CURTIS CALL FOR YOU. CURTIS SAY CALL NOW.* Sherri had received only one message the whole time she'd been there. It had been from Jerry Derzon, whom Sherri called frequently to see if there'd been any movement on the sale of the building. *JERRY D. NO NEWS.*

Sherri sat on her bed looking at the photos in the latest issue of *Playboy*. There was an article about sex in Chicago. At least people were having sex somewhere, she thought, wishing she weren't a virgin. Rhonda was in the next room practicing shorthand so that she could become a legal secretary, and Maryellen was probably writing letters to a prison inmate in Arizona she'd been communicating with for years. Whenever he sent her a letter, she'd run into Sherri's room, sit down on her bed, and read the whole boring thing aloud. "Did you know there's a cactus that takes ten years to grow just one inch? That's what Hank says. He says he once saw a jackalope, too, but my dad says there's no such thing as a rabbit with horns." She'd clutch the letter to her chest, his handwriting like child's scribble. "I'm going to marry Hank when he gets out. He's already proposed to me and we've never even met. Hank knows my heart."

This was not the Playboy lifestyle the magazine promised. Men wrote letters to the advice columnist asking about the best ways to please "my lady," and used words Sherri couldn't say out loud, words she'd only heard whispered about at slumber parties by girls like Roberta. They still made her cringe. All her life she'd had ideas about sex being dirty and forbidden, but every page in the magazine expressed that it was OK to look and that sex *wasn't* a sin, and it wasn't dirty. The revolution had happened. The more sex you had, the better, but Val was the only girl she knew who was getting any action.

Val saw the model in the open centerfold of Sherri's magazine and did the strangest thing: she struck up a conversation with Sherri, who was so surprised that she looked around the room to make sure someone else wasn't there. "So last night some guys were sitting at a table," Val said, "and they put a quarter, a nickel, and a dime in front of them. 'Which are you?' they asked."

"I don't get it."

Val rolled her eyes and tossed one of the crumpled notes at her. "You really don't know? Sister Sherri, they were asking about my nipple size, you idiot."

"Gross! Did you call security?"

"Hell no! I pulled out a Susan B. Anthony coin and slapped it on the table. And they left me a twenty-dollar tip!"

"Wow," Sherri said.

"*Wow.* Can't come up with anything better than that?"

Sherri closed her magazine and thought for a second. "OK, I would have slammed a dinner plate on the table and said *that's* how big!"

Val started laughing, a sound that was truly magical. She was even more beautiful when she was happy. "Nice one."

The window in their room was black—it got dark so early in February. The radiator hissed. "What would you do in East Troy on a night like this?" Val asked. "Counted cross-stitch?"

Just like that, Val was back to being Val. Sherri tried to ignore her.

"Go on a hot date with your first cousin?"

Sherri wished she could come up with another good reply. Val's digs about East Troy made Sherri want to defend the place. She was often surprised by how much she missed it. She was known there, and everything was comfortable and familiar as a warm bath. "You know why they call it Beloit?" Sherri asked, remembering a joke Roberta had told her. "Because that's the sound a quarter makes when you drop it in the toilet."

"You really think I haven't heard that before? That's not even funny." Val stood up and ran a brush through her hair. She passed a cigarette to Sherri, who'd never smoked. She took it, fearing she'd seem uncool, not sure how to even hold it. She sucked hard—too hard. Her lungs felt like they were filled with broken glass. It was all she could do not to cough.

"Get dressed," Val said.

"Get dressed for what?"

"I'm going to take you to Danny's."

Sherri felt like she'd just been invited to the prom. Danny was at the center of resort life. He'd worked there for years, managing the golf shop and the pools. He knew everyone—the fellow employees and the guests, and even the celebrities who visited. He'd briefly dated a centerfold who'd visited the resort for a photo shoot. "Oh man, did I ever love her," he told Sherri. "But then again, I've loved them all.

I tell you, I've been in love many, many times." He told stories about catching the members of Fleetwood Mac skinny-dipping when the pool was supposed to be closed, playing poker with Ricky Nelson and golfing with Jim Brown and President Ford. He walked through the halls as if he were Hef himself. He drove the resort van that took the women to off-site events, and he was so powerful that he had a master key that unlocked every door. Hefner hadn't been to the property in years, and his room had become a sort of museum, reserved for special guests. Danny had once taken Sherri and Carmen upstairs to show them his suite. "Go ahead, jump on the waterbed," he said.

"He even carpeted the walls!" Carmen was impressed.

Danny led them out to the patio that looked out onto the outdoor bar and dance floor. "He just stands here and watches the action from a distance."

Sherri had heard all about Danny's parties from the more seasoned Bunnies, although she hadn't been invited to one yet, which made her feel like she was still in high school, where the popular kids had all the fun and everyone else was left to wonder what they were missing out on. Anyone could go to the bars, but a house party was special. And now Sherri had an invitation. She could feel the social sands shifting beneath her feet.

Val pulled a bottle of Galliano out of her drawer and poured two shots. "Bottoms up, Sister Sherri," Val said, flicking her lighter and setting the surface of the liquor on fire. "Let's show you how to have a good time."

Val drove a rusty green Gremlin that was so light it skidded around on the icy roads like a Frisbee. The floor of the car was covered in pennies. When Sherri reached for one, Val stopped her abruptly. "Those are for luck. Don't touch."

It was cold outside and the snow was pretty, but so heavy that she could practically hear the snowflakes fall, and so thick that she couldn't make out the farm fields on the ten-minute drive out to Delavan. The rare streetlights appeared as refracted blobs in the ice crystals on the passenger window. Finally, Val pulled into the long driveway of the only house with lights on for miles around. The home was giant and squat, with stone walls and big wooden pillars in front of the door; it was part cottage, part estate. "Nice, huh?" Val said, her pace picking up as she approached the entrance and rang the doorbell.

Danny opened the door. He was broad-shouldered and so blond his hair was almost white. He wore a Milwaukee Brewers T-shirt and shorts, impervious to the cold. "Your house is so nice!" Sherri exclaimed.

"It's my nana's," he said. "She's a snowbird."

"What's that?"

"She winters at her house in Sarasota."

Sherri loved hearing the word "winter" as a verb. She couldn't imagine owning two houses, especially when one of them was this nice.

"I thought Sherri could use a good time," Val said.

"You came to the right place. Come in, come in." Danny's smile was broad and easy; he liked Sherri, but then again, he liked everyone, and everyone liked him, because he was so happy and seemingly uncomplicated. Val lit a cigarette and passed one to Sherri. She wanted to look cool with a cigarette, although she'd catch herself pinching it between her fingers in a death grip and staring intently at the smoke when she exhaled. Cool smokers, she noticed, acted like they'd almost forgotten they had a cigarette in their hand.

Danny handed Sherri a plastic Solo cup. "Go get yourself some wap," he said.

"Some what?"

Danny laughed and pointed at a metal garbage can in the kitchen. Bunny Ginger was pouring a bottle of peppermint schnapps into it. She wore her long, ashy-blond hair pulled into a ponytail on top of her head, like a palm frond, and it made her seem even taller than she was. "Sherri's here! Have some wapatui!" She grabbed the end of a hockey stick and stirred the mixture. "Pour a bottle, mix it up, all night long you throw it back up."

She dipped Sherri's cup into the brown sludge and handed it to her. "Here you go, honey. Just don't smell it first. You'll get used to it." Sherri inhaled anyway, and felt the astringent burn cut through her sinuses. Across the room she saw Bunny Tina, now a regular earthling in jeans and a blouse, but still golden and radiant like the first-class Bunnies Bunny Starr told them about in training. She was talking to Bunny Sheila with the red hair and freckles, and waved at Sherri the way a beauty contestant might and returned to the conversation. Sherri approached but was too awkward to nudge her way into the circle of more established Bunnies. She overheard Sheila say that her father was ashamed to have a daughter work as a Bunny, but that he also asked her to have the Bunnies sign each latest issue of *Playboy* so he could take it to his machine shop to show to his friends.

Sherri stood by herself, not sure what to do next. Bunnies she recognized from the resort but had never spoken to were smoking cigarettes and dancing with other workers whose names Sherri also didn't yet know. She looked around and realized she'd never been in such a nice house in all her life. It was hardly a cottage, with its massive picture windows and screened-in porches with ticking-stripe rugs and wicker furniture. The living room was paneled in wainscoting, and the ceiling had thick wood beams. A deer head with glassy black eyes stuck out of the wall above a giant stone fireplace. In front of it was a seating area with a deep, fat couch upholstered in red and black plaid fabric and overstuffed leather chairs that seemed to beg for someone to sit down and smoke a cigar.

Andy Gibb's "Shadow Dancing" was playing, and everyone swayed to the music. Sherri, already a little drunk, took a long gulp of the wap and closed her eyes, hoping to get drunker still so she could enjoy herself. She was a good dancer with a strong sense of rhythm, although she'd never danced in front of other people outside of a high school

gym or with Roberta in the Community Hall. She could do the Bus
Stop and the Hustle without missing a step. The music changed to
Van Halen's "Runnin' with the Devil." The lyrics and the alcohol emboldened Sherri to let go. *I got no love, no love you'd call real / Ain't
got nobody, waitin' at home.* Soon other guests joined her, and before
she knew it, she was in the center of a group of dancers, sweaty and
breathless, feeling suddenly drunk enough to forget about everything
that made her sad. When she finally sat down on the couch, exhausted,
a few of the Bunnies gave her high fives. Val stood in the distance,
leaning against the bookcase, and nodded with approval.

One of the busboys plopped down next to her and put his arm
around her back. "I'm Frank," he said. He was about her age, with
wire-rimmed glasses that were big for his face and long, wavy hair that
hung almost to his shoulders.

"Sherri," she said.

"I know. We know all the Bunnies' names, but they never know
ours."

"Oh, I'm sorry," she said. She was always apologizing. "I just started
a few weeks ago. I don't know anyone or anything. This is my first
time at Danny's."

"I practically live here. Nice place, huh?"

"It is," she said. "Super-duper nice."

"Oh, just wait until summer. Pretty soon the rich Chicagoans will
host after-bar parties at mansions on the lake that'll make this house
seem like a dump." He pointed at the blackness beyond the giant picture windows. "That's where they buried the elephants."

"The what?"

"Back when Barnum and Bailey trained for the circus in Delavan.
When the elephants got sick, they'd walk them out on the icy lake,
and they'd sink through and die right in front of this house, where the
water is deepest."

"That's horrible." It really was awful to consider, especially on a
bitterly cold night.

Frank continued, "Did you know that in Elkhorn there's a graveyard for the clowns? They have special markers in front of the head-
stones."

Sherri laughed out loud, so loud that people turned to look, but not
the way they had in high school. It was more like she was contributing
to the kind of laugh track they play on a sitcom. How liberating to
discover that she could be her loud, silly self at a party when everyone was drunk, and it was OK—better than OK. "A clown graveyard!" She started to laugh again, so hard she couldn't stop, and Frank
started to laugh, too, pleased that he'd provoked such an enthusiastic
reaction. Sherri took another sip of wap and ran to the bathroom. On
the way, Danny tapped her on the shoulder. "Frank's not a bad guy,"
he said, "but he likes to think he's part of the 'initiation process' if you
know what I mean. Just know what you're getting into."

Sherri smiled. "Thanks," she said, but it came out *zanks*, and she
had to put her hand against the wall to keep from falling down. Once
she made it to the bathroom, the black and white checkered tiles on
the floor seemed to move around, making her dizzy, a state she vis-
cerally feared after watching her mom lose her balance. On her way
back she passed a group of Bunnies leaning over an antique pub
table in the den. What were they all looking at? She looked closer and
saw Tina snorting white powder into her nose. Tina? Cocaine? She'd
heard about it at school, read about it in the newspaper, but had never
seen actual drugs up close. She shouldn't have been surprised. She'd
heard people talk about coke. Yet even in her drunken state she felt
disappointed. She wanted to believe that Tina was as virtuous as she
thought she was, and that the resort was as clean as the reputation
they touted at training.

"Want a bump?" Bunny Barb asked. Those were the only words
Barb had ever said to Sherri. She was the head Bunny in the VIP
lounge. She made more tips than anyone. "It makes your eyes warm."

"No thank you," Sherri said politely, as if she were declining sugar
in her coffee.

When she returned, she sank back down into the couch, even closer to Frank. She let his fingers travel up and down her arms and thighs. Her plan was to become more experienced. She felt the gravitas of the word "initiation"; it meant more to her than Danny knew. All her life she'd wanted to be initiated into something. Instead of pushing him off, she gave in to the pleasure of being touched and paid attention to. Soon his tongue was in her ear and his hand was pawing her breast, and she felt herself lean into him, hungry, even if they were both awkward, and Frank's kisses were wet and sloppy and she wasn't sure what she was supposed to do with her hands. The room began to clear out as some people went home or paired up and disappeared into the many guest rooms. Frank stood and reached for Sherri's hand the way a gentleman might, a small gesture of kindness. They laughed and stumbled down to the basement, where Val and Danny played beer pong on the Ping-Pong table. Val winked and said, "Sister Sher!" Soon the sound of the ball bouncing against the table stopped; everything was quiet and everyone was gone except Frank.

She was drunker than she'd ever been, and it was dark. Frank led her to a plush floral couch. Her head was spinning, and she didn't have the energy or the desire to stop Frank when he slid her pants down. She wanted to lose her virginity under better circumstances, with someone she was madly in love with. But her virginity had gone from a romantic concern to a practical one. She was convinced that she was the only virgin at the resort, and she was nervous but ready to change her status. She figured Frank, still in his sweater, grunting with his eyes closed, was doing her a favor—a favor that suddenly blossomed into more hurt than she'd expected, but just when she thought she couldn't take it anymore, the whole thing was over. Frank sank on top of her, heavy as a pile of bricks. Soon he was sound asleep and snoring. Sherri wished he'd at least said something nice to her. He could have told her she was pretty.

The next morning, she woke up alone, cold and still dizzy. She didn't know where Frank had gone off to. She saw a red Solo cup sitting on the coffee table and thought of all that brown liquid that ran through her veins. She rushed into the bathroom to vomit, just missing the toilet, making a mess on the floor and all over her jeans. She was a mess, a mess! Had she really lost her virginity? She wiped herself up with a hand towel and sank down onto the cold floor. She wanted to go home—not home to the Bunny Hutch, but *home* home, to East Troy. She wanted her mother so badly she couldn't stand it. Muriel had once told Sherri that she had the grace to get through hard times, although Sherri wasn't sure anymore. She'd been trying so hard to grow up and be an adult, but at that moment she wished she could be a little girl again, sitting next to her mother on the piano bench as she introduced the lines of the treble clef. "EGBDF. Here's how you remember: Every Good Boy Deserves Fun."

After a good cry (she didn't think she'd cry after losing her virginity!) she dug around in the medicine cabinet for aspirin and came across something she hadn't expected to find in a grandmother's house: a Massengill douche. Carmen said that douching prevented pregnancy, and the very last thing Sherri needed at the moment was a baby to take care of. She could practically hear all the doors of possibility for her future slam shut.

Sherri pulled the rubbery thing out of the box and used it, she hoped correctly. She thought that sex would be beautiful and easy. It wasn't. She was disgusted by the dirtiness and smells, the cycles of her body, the fear of pregnancy. Sex had seemed so easy in books and on TV; she imagined it would be as clean and as odorless as it was in the magazine.

She looked at her watch: nine o'clock. Her shift would start in an hour. She dashed upstairs. The house was completely quiet and still. The living room was strewn with empties and smelled of stale cigarette smoke. Beyond the windows she could see the icy lake, half expecting to spy elephant tusks jutting out from the surface like the ribs of a shipwreck. She went door to door, swinging them open. All the bedrooms were empty until she got to the last one. That's where she discovered Val curled up next to Danny in a giant four-poster bed with a rose-colored canopy. She was sleeping with *Danny*?

Val sat up straight and pulled the comforter up her chest. "Knock first, would you? Jesus!"

"I have to get to work. Please. I don't know what to do."

Val wiped her eyes and yawned. Her hair was a mess but she looked lovely, her skin rosy. The room smelled pungent, musky. "You should have told me you had an early shift."

"I didn't think we'd stay here."

"Hey, Sher." Danny set one hand on Val's bare shoulder and pulled her close. Sherri saw something go soft in him. This was nothing like Sherri's experience with Frank; Danny said he'd loved many women, and now it was clear that he was crazy about Val.

"Please." Sherri's eyes filled with tears. "If I'm late, Gloria will fire me. I don't know what I'll do if I don't have this job." Her stomach flipped. She raced out of the room, found the guest bathroom, and threw up again. She rinsed her mouth out and returned to Val's room, but the door was locked. Sherri banged on it. "Please, Val. I don't even know where I am."

She could hear Danny saying, "I'll drive her, I don't mind."

Bam, bam, bam.

"Oh, fine," Val said, annoyed, but why should she be? It was her idea to go to the party, her idea to drive there. "I'll be out in a few minutes."

Sherri waited in the fancy hallway and looked at all the framed photos on the wall, including lots of pictures of Danny as a little kid with his brothers and sisters and cousins, all of them healthy, robust, and blond and seemingly always looking into the sun, because they squinted at the camera. There was Danny as a little boy in a life vest sitting on the end of the dock, Danny fishing with his grandfather on a rowboat, Danny's senior portrait, Danny in a suit, standing between what must have been his grandmother and mother. Sherri didn't even have a family anymore; she was jealous of his cottage life, jealous of all of his lake memories.

On the ride back to the resort, Sherri was so nauseous she could hardly speak. Her head spun. Val had to pull over so Sherri could barf on the side of the road into a pile of snow.

"Look," Val said. A bit of fear crept into her voice. "Don't you dare say anything to anyone about me and Danny. Not a word."

"I won't, I promise."

"I mean it. If Curtis finds out, God knows what he'd do. He walks around with an X-Acto knife in his pocket."

"Why don't you just break up with him?"

Val lit a cigarette and took a deep drag. "Because, Sherri, Curtis is forever. Danny is just for now."

At work, Gloria eyed Sherri so critically she was surprised she let her walk out onto the floor. She could hardly even talk to her customers, grinning through her hangover as she set Cuba Libres in front of them, swearing to herself that she'd never, ever drink or have sex again. The resort was busy because Olympic skier Billy Kidd was there to give demos, and everyone gawked at him in his cowboy hat and ski vest.

When Sherri saw Frank they exchanged knowing glances, but that was all, which was a relief, even if it made Sherri feel cheap. She imagined him keeping a spreadsheet with all the new Bunnies' names and little check marks after them. Bunny Sherri: *check!*

At the end of her shift, she leaned against Carmen in the locker room. "I'm so damn tired."

"Sorry baby duck, but I've got you beat. I had to take my brother to the doctor yesterday, work an afternoon shift here, and then I got called to the Shack because one of the girls didn't show. My hips hurt from all those lap dances."

"What's it like to, you know, to do that?" Sherri didn't want to sound like she was passing judgment, but in truth, she was. She cared too much about what people thought of her to work at a strip club.

Carmen had a faraway look in her eyes. "It's like I'm there and I'm not there at the same time, like Cinderella doing a miserable chore but there are birds chirping in her ear? That's me. I smile and do my thing, but in my mind, I imagine I'm a doll walking through my old dollhouse, and I go room to room. I try to remember everything, from the wallpaper to the little tiny teacups. And when my time is up, I take the money and move on. It's like it never happened."

Carmen wasn't one to wallow. She smiled, reached into her purse, and pulled out a piece of metal jewelry and plunked it on Sherri's tray. "Here's a present for you."

"Is this an earring?" Sherri asked, flipping it around in her palm.

Carmen couldn't stop laughing.

"What's so funny?"

"Honey, that's a nipple clamp."

Sherri threw it across the room as if it were a cockroach, and Carmen roared with laughter. The "gift" made her feel even dirtier than she'd already felt after losing her virginity to a relative stranger. She was convinced that people saw her differently now; that the men she waited on could see the tackiness of forgettable sex all over her. She didn't want to believe that all men were like the guys who wanted Carmen to dance on their laps.

After her shift, Sherri returned to the dorm room, trying to sort through the dissonance of moving between nipple clamps and doll-houses. She was dying to slip between her sheets so she could fall asleep and wake up on the other side of this overwhelming new phase of her life. She found Val in the room, dressed in her fringed, brown suede coat, checking her hair in the mirror. Val kissed her lipstick on a tissue. "Curtis has to work again, and Danny's having another party. He invited some of the guys from Cheap Trick."

"For real?"

"It's not such a big deal. Those guys are around the resort all the time. There's a world-class recording studio downstairs at the club. You know that, right? Shade Tree. You coming?"

Sherri looked like hell, felt like hell. But if she went to the party, she wouldn't be alone, thinking about how badly her first sexual experience had gone. "Sure!"

She reached into her pocket and felt the pink slip of memo paper Ola had handed to her at the end of her shift. It was from Roberta, who shared her birthday and never, ever forgot.

ROBERTA SAY HAPPY BIRTHDAY TWIN HELLO HOPE YOU ARE FUN.

CHAPTER FIVE

Sherri felt like she'd been holding her breath until she got her period, a tremendous relief after her night with Frank. She'd been so happy to find blood in her underwear that she ran up and down the hallway in her dorm happily screaming, "I'm not pregnant, I'm not pregnant! No baby for *meeeee*!" This was the perfect excuse to let everyone know that she wasn't a virgin.

Carmen and Ginger ran out of their rooms to share in her excitement, and agreed to celebrate Sherri's empty womb at Thumbs Up—or "Thumbs," as they called it. There was a line in front of the dive bar—there was always a line—but every bouncer in town knew the Bunnies, partly because they were there so often, and partly because Sherri's third week on the job, all the Bunnies had bought fifty-dollar fur coats from some guy Bunny Carmen had met at Sugar Shack. He'd parked a VW van in the farthest corner of the back lot. He said he'd inherited the coats from a rich aunt and had no use for them.

"Your aunt sure had a lot of coats," Sherri said.

Val nudged her. "They're hot."

"I know!" Sherri said, modeling the rabbit-fur-and-leather hooded coat she'd picked out. She'd never owned anything so fabulous in her life. "I'm boiling."

Val rolled her eyes. "'Hot' means *stolen*, you dip."

"These are from Vegas," Carmen said. "But you never heard that from me."

Sherri and her friends, dressed in sable, mink, and rabbit fur, sailed ahead of other patrons waiting in line to get into the bar when the bouncer signaled for them to go in. Sherri vaguely recognized a few of the front-desk workers from the resort. They glared at the Bunnies who were spared from the chilly weather—the dampness was bone-chilling. Once they were inside, it was only a matter of time before the guys sitting at the bar sent drinks over. The Bunnies gave careful little waves of thanks that didn't offer too much encouragement.

Carmen, Val, Rhonda, and Ginger were like the sisters Sherri always dreamed of having. They offered advice about contraception, making her promise to get a prescription for birth control the very next day. "You're lucky," Ginger said without the slightest judgment. "What you did was like driving through an intersection with your eyes closed."

"Like eating raw hamburger!" said Carmen. She wore so much lip gloss that Sherri could almost see her reflection in it. Ginger ordered a round of Everclear shots, her voice low and authoritative like a man's.

"You should have been more careful," Val said, but who was Val to talk? She'd gotten Sherri drunk, left her alone most of the night, and hadn't even wanted to drive her back.

Rhonda said nothing. But being around the other women, who spoke openly about sex, a forbidden topic back home, was an exhilarating new experience for Sherri, and it felt like an admission ticket to the world of female solidarity. It was one thing to go to parties at Danny's. Talking with her friends that night about the downsides of the diaphragm and IUD, she felt very grown-up—she was finally, *finally* one of the girls.

When the shots arrived, Ginger initiated a toast. "For poor little Frank, Jr., who is not to be."

Rhonda clinked her shot glass so hard against the others that it almost shattered.

"So," Carmen said. "I'll let you in on a little secret. Frank just started dancing at the club."

"He's a *stripper?*" Sherri couldn't believe that was who she'd lost her virginity to. "But he seems so . . . so ordinary."

"Like me?" Carmen winked and spoke in a fake Southern drawl. "Honey, as you know better than any of us now, that boy is hung like a can of soup." It had hurt enough for Sherri to know that this was true.

"He has this act where he struts on stage dressed like Paul Stanley. He wears a black wig and the white face makeup and a star over one eye. He has these black leather suspenders and a choke collar and chaps. The women go wild for that shit. I think he wants to be a Chippendale someday."

Kiss? Sherri could feel herself flush with embarrassment. When she and Roberta were freshmen, Mr. Fletcher found Roberta's secret stash of records and burned them in the firepit in their backyard. He said Kiss was a band full of devil worshippers and threatened to kick Roberta out if he caught her listening to them again.

Rhonda pushed her stool away from the table and hopped down like a little kid. She seemed troubled. "I'm going to head back." She threw a few bucks down to cover her drinks. "See you later."

"You OK?" Ginger asked.

She looked like she was about to cry. "I just want to go to sleep, OK?"

Ginger stood up and grabbed her keys. She was the unofficial dorm mother, always tending to the emotional needs of her friends. "Let me drive you. Come on." She was almost twice as tall as Rhonda. When they walked away, her arm was behind Rhonda's back, protective as a boyfriend's.

After they left, the women looked at each other. "What was her problem?"

Val rolled her eyes. "That's what happens when you're in the middle of sewing a quilt."

Something about Rhonda's abrupt departure seemed off to Sherri. It felt directed at her, and she couldn't imagine why.

At work the next day, because of her period and the Everclear, Sherri felt particularly awful. She grew more uncomfortable as the hours of dipping and drinks stretched on. The sharp edge of the corset cut into the skin under her arms, the stays of her uniform dug into her back, and the now-lopsided headband pinched behind her ears. She was terrified her period would bleed through, but if she unzipped her uniform to change her tampon, she'd never get it zipped up again. And if she leaked, she'd have to change into her other uniform, and everyone would notice that she'd gone from paisley to green.

Every time she blinked, her eyes got stuck from glue from her hurriedly applied false eyelashes. Her head throbbed. After two months she could finally walk in the requisite satin three-inch pumps without feeling like Minnie Mouse. For the most part, she'd grown used to the pain, but that day, because she was so bloated, it got to her. Her arches screamed, and her heels stung from blisters. She knew that when she finally slipped the shoes off, her toes would be molded into the V shape of the points, numb and white from lack of blood. She couldn't wait until the end of her shift, when she could massage her feet with golf balls or roll them on ice. Some of the Bunnies would even sit on the tank of a toilet, put their feet in the bowl, and flush over and over again—and then they went dancing.

If only she could rest for a few minutes. She was forbidden from sitting in front of customers unless she was teaching backgammon to kids in the lounge on Sundays. Bunnies were only allowed to perch for temporary relief. "The Perch" was an actual position she was taught in training, like the Bunny Dip.

At least she could walk, she scolded herself, thinking of her mother's debilitating illness. Sherri stuffed a three-dollar tip into her waitress wallet as she cleared a table and thought that the pain was worth it. A single table's tip was the same amount she would have earned after an hour at the insurance agency. Free food, free housing. She was making so much money she didn't even need to keep track of it, and she certainly didn't have time to spend her earnings. She loved the feeling of sitting on a pile of cash. The more she accumulated, the more possibilities she saw for her future.

She walked into the kitchen so she could lean against a wall for a moment without getting written up. That was where Bunny Tina saw her. "Blisters?"

Suddenly Sherri wanted to cry—what was it about Tina that made her feel so vulnerable? "Everything."

"Play your cards right and Gloria will give you some shifts at the ski chalet. You can wear a white turtleneck and Bogner ski pants with the tail on the back. I worked there yesterday and a Catholic school group came in. Would you believe the nuns skied in their habits? You should have seen them. And in summer you can work the golf hut. Last year that's where I was during a pro-am tournament. It was heaven! I was allowed to wear ballet slippers and a golf sweater, and I could take off my tail and sit at the table with the millionaires from Chicago. They play high-stakes poker games in the back rooms—you'd think it was Monopoly money. I made over eight hundred dollars in tips in a single day. That's how I made my down payment on my car. If you put in the work now, there's a good chance you'll get a few sit-down shifts there this summer."

A sit-down shift appealed immensely to Sherri. She was beginning to feel the first stirrings of ambition and planned to buy herself a car, too, as soon as she'd saved enough—assuming she could lease or sell the building on the square. She wanted a maroon Monte Carlo with a power sunroof, and had torn the ad for it out of the pages of her

Playboy magazine and taped it on the wall next to her bed. But before she could make big money, she needed to be promoted, and promotions were based on seniority. She couldn't wait to advance out of the Sidewalk Café. The real fun was in the Cabaret and the Club. Next to the Bunnies with those jobs, she felt like she was sitting at the kids' table.

Carmen saw Sherri and Tina talking and sauntered over to join them; she could never resist a conversation.

"Gotta go!" Tina said.

Everyone liked Carmen, but she was always getting into trouble and dragging other Bunnies along with her, like the kid in school who'd talk to you when she thought the teacher wasn't paying attention. Tina disappeared, her tail sitting high on her ass, and Carmen and Sherri looked out onto the floor of the Sidewalk Café. The resort was busy with middle-aged teachers from all over Wisconsin who were attending a special-education conference.

"I should get back to work, too," Sherri said.

"Did you hear that Maryellen gave her two weeks' notice?"

Sherri stalled. She had to hear more.

"She said it was just too hard." Carmen pretended to wipe her eyes with her fist like a crying baby. "She was as homesick as a seven-year-old at summer camp."

"I had my money on Rhonda being the first to go," said Sherri.

"Rhonda? That girl is tough. And strong for someone so tiny. Have you seen her carry her tray? She looks like she could twirl a school bus on her little finger."

Sherri noticed that a guest had taken a seat in her section against the glass that separated the café from the sunken pool in the lobby—and when he turned, she saw that he was not just any guest, but Jerry Derzon. "Oh no," Sherri said to Carmen when she saw him sitting in her section. "That guy with the creepy eyebrows? He's from my hometown." She didn't say that he was her Realtor.

"Oh, that's the Barnacle."

"What?"

"That's what we call him because he's here all the time, but he's usually in the Club. Looks like he found a cute friend." Across from him sat a skinny guy with shaggy brown hair that hung heavy over his eyes.

In high school, she'd walked past Jerry's football trophies in the display case in the lobby every single day. It was hard to believe he'd ever been the star of the East Troy Trojans—or that he'd once been capable of running down a field. He was only a decade or so older than Sherri, but already he looked like he'd struggle to walk up a flight of stairs. His years of heavy drinking showed in his potbelly and ruddy cheeks.

"Want me to cover for you?" Carmen asked. "I actually kind of like him. He's harmless."

"That's OK. I've got it." Maybe he had news for her; maybe the guy sitting with him had bought her building. That's what she thought as she approached his table feeling like her entire body was under assault. Had someone put sandpaper inside her shoes? Were there tiny knives twirling around inside her abdomen? Was there an ax in her forehead?

She took a deep breath. She just needed to keep smiling, and *endure.* That was the word her mother used on the hard days, back when Sherri could still understand her speech. Endurance—now, that was a trait Sherri had inherited, and it was how she'd made it this far at the resort when girls like Maryellen gave up after their first blister.

Jerry wore a checkered polyester shirt with a wide collar spread like wings over the lapels of his brown suit jacket. A gold chain twinkled between the folds of skin in his neck, and a rum-soaked Crooks cigar was wedged between his fat fingers.

It was one thing to be dressed like a Bunny in front of strangers, another to be dressed like that in front of people she knew. As she approached Derzon's table, she took a deep breath to prepare herself. She was suddenly intensely aware of her costume *as* a costume.

"Good afternoon, I'm your Bunny Sherri." She said it the way she'd said it hundreds of times, only this time she didn't need to introduce herself. Sherri did what she always did. She set down some bunny-logo cocktail napkins from her tray. She stood with one foot behind the other, her hips unnaturally squared toward him just the way she was taught.

"Well well, Bunny Sherri, huh? Arthur, this here's Sherri Taylor, a back-home girl." It was jarring to hear her real, proper name spoken aloud here. Jerry took a juicy drag off his cigar. "No movement on the building, I'm afraid. Interest rates—" He whistled. "—sky high. It's a tough market. Nothing's moving. Not a thing."

"I've left you some messages."

"Wish I had news. But don't worry, we'll get it sold. You can always sell it to me. I told you my price. I know it's low, but these are hard times."

"I'll think about it," she said, and she had been, although her mother made Sherri swear not to sell too low. She'd said they'd worked too hard on the building to let it go for a song.

"Tell me," Jerry said. "You still play organ?"

"Not at this exact moment."

"Arthur, Sherri here plays like an angel," Jerry said. Sherri could hardly remember seeing Jerry in church on the few occasions she'd filled in for Mrs. Vogel. She gazed at the indoor pool through the thick sheet of glass. People swam and lounged poolside, while Danny, Joe, and Flip, the attendants, tried to connect with the guests, hoping someone would offer them a job or an investment opportunity, anything to give them a chance to become captains of industry. In the summer, Danny said, they'd work the outdoor pool and offer to apply Native Tan to the guests for a dollar, and they made a fortune. Danny had all kinds of schemes to skim money from the pockets of visiting businessmen. He saw Sherri and waved, but she was holding her tray, so she couldn't wave back.

On the other side of the plate glass, it seemed everyone was having fun. For the first time since she'd started working as a Bunny, she wondered what it would be like to be a guest, to be served, to be a watcher instead of the watched.

Jerry, trying to be impressive, a regular Mr. Realtor, pulled his gold Playboy key out of his pocket and began to wave it in front of her face with pride. Smoke dribbled out of his nose. "I'm a member." The card slipped out of his hand and landed on the plush orange carpeting without a sound.

Sherri tried to pick it up, awkwardly bending backwards instead of forward, her chest cantilevered while trying to hold the tray so it wouldn't tip. She had a lot of stuff to balance: ashtrays, mugs, lighters, matches, bar checks. She wondered if he'd dropped the damn card on purpose.

Derzon gave his friend a nudge. "They're not allowed to bend forward, you know."

They? He could have been talking about an animal at the zoo. "But you are," she spoke under her breath, risking a demerit.

"I'll get it," Arthur said. He scooched back his chair to help her, but she already had the card in her hand. Their heads bumped, and when they both stood up at the same time, their faces bumped, too, almost like a kiss. He smiled, a sweet, funny smile. He had firm lips, a sharp nose, and a nice, square jaw, although his features didn't all go together; he had the kind of face she needed to look at a few times. She adjusted her ears and set the key on the table in front of Jerry. "You know you don't need to show your key here. Just in the club." She wanted to embarrass the jerk. She didn't think of him as a *real* guest, he was just a guy from town, but then again, wasn't that what most of the guests were? The only difference was that Jerry was the guy she knew.

He tapped the ashes of his cigar into the ashtray as casually as if he were sitting in his own den. "You know, I didn't have you pegged as a Bunny. Not that you can't pull it off, I don't mean it like that, but . . ."

"But what?"

"Well, you being from home and all. Remember how you and that friend of yours used to pretend the bandstand was a fort and you'd throw pinecones at anyone who walked by and shout '*Intruders!*'?"

"We were dumb little kids." Sherri could feel herself blush. Arthur could tell she was embarrassed and looked into his lap.

"Sherri grew up right on the square," Jerry said. "Great building with a storefront and, above it, a nice two-bedroom apartment."

"You should buy it," Sherri said. "It's for sale."

Arthur seemed impressed. "You're from downtown?"

Jerry roared with laughter. "Downtown! I never heard nobody call it that in my whole damn life. Downtown, heh." It felt as if everyone in the café turned to see what the noise was about.

The only person who didn't laugh—or even smile—was Arthur. "I love the square," he said, his tone serious. "I really do. It creates order, a feeling like there's a center. It's so European. Every town should have a square, and to have grown up on it? And in East Troy? There are some places that just make you feel good. I can't explain it, I feel like myself there. I feel right."

Sherri had never heard anyone speak so effusively about the town, not even the mayor. It was hard for her to imagine experiencing it as an outsider. As Sherri's mother used to say, East Troy was the kind of place where they rolled up the sidewalks at night.

"First time I pulled into East Troy," Arthur continued, "I knew I wanted to stay. I wish I'd been there my whole life. You're lucky."

"I guess." Sherri was confused by this sentiment. All her life she'd thought everyone else had been lucky, from Roberta with her Sunday dinners to the kids from the big farm families who got into mischief in the barns.

Jerry said, "He's not kidding. First day I took him to look at houses, he told me to write an offer."

She couldn't believe anybody would actually choose to live there. East Troy was where you ended up by accident, like her father, because his settler-ancestors had lost steam on their trip west and plunked down in Wisconsin, or, like her mother, because she would have gone anywhere to escape her parents. Muriel used to say that the only thing missing from East Troy was a city.

Judging from Arthur's smile he was clearly still pleased with his purchase. "I knew I wanted to live there as soon as Jerry turned off Highway J."

"You bought a house on Lake Beulah?" Now the story was starting to make sense. Lake Beulah she could understand. It was a beautiful, big, spring-fed lake.

"Not just on Beulah. On Jesuit Island," Jerry said. "The house is all the way at the end of Island Drive."

Sherri was impressed. Jesuit Island wasn't really an island but a peninsula that stuck out into the lake like a skinny finger, separated from the rest of the land by a small, man-made channel that connected the lake to other, smaller lakes. It was named for a group of Jesuits who had owned a huge old retreat house there. When Sherri was in high school the Jesuits decided to sell, and they divided the land into half-acre lots and stipulated that the minimum price for a house was five hundred thousand dollars. Everyone in town talked about it. Half a million bucks! Now the "island" was home to some of the biggest, newest houses in East Troy, with views of Lake Beulah on one side, and Mill Pond, as the locals called it, on the other.

Arthur was young—older than she was, but not by a lot. Where'd he get money like that? "You bought one of those big new houses?"

"No, I got a little one."

"But there aren't any little houses left," she said.

"Get this," Jerry said. "There was a lone piece of property with an old cottage on the point between Mill Pond and the main lake. So overgrown you can hardly see it. That's where the retreat director stayed. It wasn't part of the initial sale because the lot was nonconforming. They just left the place for the raccoons. So when Arthur comes to me and says he wants to buy himself a lake house, an old one, 'cause for whatever dumb reason this guy likes places that make you tired just thinking about 'em, you know what I do? I call the superior general—the Black Pope himself! Turned out they'd forgotten all about it. So now Arthur here owns a tumbledown cottage that's been abandoned to time. But you stand there and look out at the lakes and I swear to God, you feel like you're standing on the prow of a ship."

"That's great." Sherri suddenly missed East Troy, especially the lakes. She didn't understand why she'd occasionally feel these pangs of homesickness for a place that all her life she'd wanted to leave. She was thinking about the lake when she looked up and saw that the room captain was watching her. She had to move it along. "Excuse me for a moment," she said, and stepped away to deliver the bill to the customers at the next table.

"What can I get you boys to drink?" she asked when she returned. She'd learned that men Jerry's age loved being called boys. She wiped down the table, set a clean ashtray on top of the dirty one and picked them both up in one hand, set the dirty one on her tray and put the clean one down on the glass table with an efficient tap.

Jerry said, "How about two Harvey Wallbangers?"

Sherri thought it was rude of Jerry to order for his friend the way he'd order for his wife.

"Harvey Wallbangers." Sherri was taught to always repeat their order. "That's OK by you?" She smiled at Arthur, who smiled back, and when he did, she felt something strange shift inside her, a sort of rightness, like the feeling she got when she'd add up her tickets at the end of her shift and come to the correct number. She finally looked at him, really looked, and he looked right back. He was wiry and intense. His brown eyes, almost obscured by his long bangs, were fixed on her. He wasn't appraising her the way the other men did; he was studying her, *learning* her, the way she did when she looked at sheet music for the first time.

She needed to wait on her other tables, but she felt suspended in his gaze. "What brought you to town, anyway?" she asked.

Arthur said, "I'm part of the group that's hoping to resuscitate Rainbow Springs."

Sherri gasped. "*Rainbow Springs?* You're working on that place? It gives me the creeps!" She saw another of her other tables fill up. She couldn't talk for long, but she'd always been haunted by the massive resort that never opened. The property was tucked into the woods in neighboring Mukwonago. It had a huge conference center, hundreds of hotel rooms, and a main street complete with empty shops. The rooms were all set for visitors, complete with boxes of tissue, towels hanging from the racks, and beds turned down for guests. The pool just waiting to be filled with water. But the complex was financially stillborn the day it was set to open a decade earlier. The owner, who lacked the sexiness and savvy of Hugh Hefner, was once worth millions, but he'd squandered his fortune on the property and didn't trust banks to help with the necessary financing, so he went bankrupt. For years it sat empty. All the kids from her school ignored the NO TRESPASSING signs. They'd throw rocks in the windows, get high, have sex, hold séances, and seek out messages on their Ouija boards. "They should burn that place down," Sherri said.

"That, or maybe we can save it somehow."

Jerry jumped in. "I thought Arthur should see how the Playboy resort works, how it's designed, get some ideas."

"Seems like everyone wants to build a paradise out here," Sherri said. "Resorts, camps."

"This corner of the state is practically Eden," Arthur said. "Fresh springs, the lakes, the hills. Why not share it with other people?"

"People who can afford it," Sherri said. "You know, sometimes I think how different this place would be if a woman designed it. We wouldn't have men walk around dressed the way I am, I can tell you that. Honestly, I don't think we'd have men at all."

"I wouldn't have expected you to turn into some women's libber once you zipped yourself into that Bunny suit," Jerry said.

"I'll bet Doris would agree with me. She's probably giving your kids a bath while you're ordering Harvey Wallbangers. Where's a good place for her to go have fun?"

Jerry crossed his arms over his chest. "I bring her here for steaks sometimes. What's gotten into you? This place has made you sassy."

"I'll go get your drinks," she said. The room captain was scratching notes into his book. She'd stayed too long.

"Sherri," Arthur said, with something like admiration in his eyes, "make mine a Manhattan."

Arthur's order, and his assertion of independence, pleased her, just as she was pleased that he took her seriously. She went back to being a Bunny. "Would you care to have your cocktail in a specialty mug so that you'll have something to take home?" She stuck out her chest and held the black bunny-logo mug, forcing herself to smile, knowing she'd get twenty percent of the bill. Anything with the bunny logo seemed to sell; men had a primitive response to it.

Arthur cleared his throat. "I'll take one if it'll help you out." His voice had a rare quality she loved in the male singers in the church choir. Low, but with a cry in it, like Springsteen.

"And you?" she asked Derzon. "Would you like a mug?"

"I can't bring any more of those home with me. The trunk of my car is full of them." He winked at Arthur.

"Got it." She began to write their order down, distracted by the way Arthur looked at her, as if he really saw her, not as Bunny Sherri but as Sherri Taylor. Who was she anymore? "Did you say an old-fashioned?" How could she forget? She never forgot. She felt a warm rush of blood between her legs. No, no! She couldn't bleed through. She looked around at the other Bunnies servicing their tables and thought about how the costumes made it look so easy to be a woman, but it wasn't. It was horrible.

Arthur asked, "Are you OK?"

His sincerity took her off guard. She paused and looked skyward at the lofted ceiling to hold back tears. His concern moved her in a way she didn't want to be moved. His question, so human, so nice, pierced her somehow and made her freshly aware of how raw she still felt about the loss of her mother and the shock of this dramatic turn in her life. She loved working at the resort, she did, but the familiarity of Jerry and the talk of Lake Beulah made her feel as homesick as Maryellen had felt—only Sherri couldn't indulge these pangs of emotion, because she didn't have anyone to return home to. She couldn't sort it all out, so she did what she was trained to do: she smiled. "Oh, I'm just fine," she said. Gloria had told her that she needed to speak in a higher voice so the guests could hear her over the din, that she needed to *e-nun-ce-ate*. "I'll be right back with those drinks."

She walked away as quickly as she could, her legs pressed tightly together, her springy hair bobbing up and down. She made a beeline for Carmen and asked if she could cover for her so she could change into a fresh costume. She was fighting back tears, her ankles wobbling just a bit.

What was wrong with her? Sherri didn't know then that the entire architecture of her life existed in that moment, and that Arthur and Jerry Derzon would become the post and beams of her future.

CHAPTER SIX

Sherri's mother once told her that when you're young you have good days and bad days, but when you get older you have good years and bad years. Sherri had occasional bad days, like the one she'd had when she broke down in the locker room after meeting Arthur, or days she missed home or was blindsided by grief. But those days were folded into the mostly good ones. And on those good days, Sherri could feel herself grow larger and more expansive. She was learning how to unapologetically take up space in a room. She began making grand entrances at the start of each shift, puffing her hair and walking with her chest proud as a lion's.

She was thrilled to hear the words "Sherri's here!" when she entered a bar or a party, her hair loose and wild, her arms jingling with brace-lets. She'd once been so ashamed of her cleavage that she'd strapped her chest down with Ace bandages, especially after Pete Becker told her that he bet her breasts were saggy like the ones on the naked women he'd seen in *National Geographic*. Now she smiled to herself when she took a few pairs of the old nylons Ola and Biata washed and left in a basket for the girls to stuff inside their bras for more lift—she had never imagined wanting to look even bigger than she already was.

After baring so much of her torso in her costume, she no longer felt the need to be modest in her street clothes, wearing low-cut blouses and tube tops that revealed mountains of carefully padded flesh.

She was looked at now, but she'd never felt less *seen*, which was just fine by her. After all, that was the point of a costume. Charismatic and confident "Bunny Sherri" took over for the real Sherri. She went out every single night and managed to get by without ever revealing much about herself. Nobody wanted to hear about the organ or poetry or her sad, dead parents. Sherri accepted every invitation to go out—it didn't matter how tired she was after her shift. Now she had a reputation to manage, a persona to craft that would be different from the one she was saddled with in high school. She wanted to be not just fun but *reliably* fun. She was the first to shoot back a shot of Rumple Minze or Jim Beam, and the last person to step down from dancing on the bar until closing time.

She felt like she was in a tribe. She had girlfriends. In the morning, they'd come into her room and sit on her bed to complain about their hangovers and rehash the previous evening. They shared clothing and makeup and offered fashion advice. Even their menstrual cycles were in sync. She was part of something. She belonged.

But the work itself was often boring. The guests were fun at night, but during the day it was slow, and the air was soggy with worry. The place crawled with workers from the massive GM plant in Janesville who spoke in hushed tones about hiring freezes and other plant closings. A group of Gary Works employees visiting from Indiana complained about job cuts due to cheaper Japanese and Korean steel imports, along with reduced demand for their galvanized steel from lower new car sales. And businesspeople complained to each other about high interest rates, "stagflation," and lingering problems with the energy crisis. Farmers were the saddest and most anxious guests of all. Just like back home at Giles, they complained about debt and cursed Jimmy Carter for halting grain shipments to the Soviet Union.

They said his name like it was an obscenity. No wonder Gloria wanted the Bunnies to smile. That's what these worried men needed to see.

It was during those slow shifts that she could chat with the other Bunnies and learn about their hobbies, boyfriends, and aspirations. She loved hearing juicy bits of gossip about who had the clap, or who'd slept with a visiting entertainer. The Bunnies never tired of speculating about Gloria's private life. Rhonda had heard that she'd been married three times already. Gwen said Gloria was connected to the local Mafia. Carmen had caught her crying once when she'd walked into her office and slammed the door. "It was like watching a stone bleed."

Despite her troublemaking, Carmen was Sherri's favorite. She was also the best person to share shifts with when the work was slow. She always had great stories from the strip club, and she couldn't keep anything a secret. Because she'd been there a while, she had inside dirt on the other Bunnies. "Bunny Sue was paid a thousand dollars to fly to Las Vegas to take off her shoes and step on a guy's face," she said. "And they didn't even have sex!" She could tell stories about the regulars, from the executives with big-time jobs who tried to hire away Bunnies as personal assistants, thinking they could "save" them, to the lonely farmers who blew their life savings at the resort. "Men don't know how to talk to each other," she said. "They just don't. That's why they come here, because they need someone to listen. Someone to smile at. When it gets right down to it, this place is lonelier than a church."

Were men really that lonely and misunderstood? Or did they just want to get laid? This was the puzzle, and Sherri made it her mission to figure it out. She'd had no brothers or male friends, and her father, with his girl's name, had been a sweet and sensitive soul. Men—real men—were as mysterious as the aliens that had scared her to death when she watched *Close Encounters of the Third Kind* with Roberta.

She'd waited on her share of lonely men, that was for sure, but then there were the awful guys she'd encountered at bars like Papouli's. One night, a group of men called Sherri and Ginger over to where they sat. "Hop on over, little bunnies." One set five crisp twenty-dollar bills on the edge of table. "How about I make it rain?"

Sherri didn't know what he meant until he blew the bills onto the floor—this was like the grown-up version of the card game taxi she'd played with that little boy in the game room. "It's all yours if you'll pick it up on your hands and knees."

Ginger shrugged. "Easy money."

"No, I'm not doing that. The floor's dirty."

"Tell you what," Ginger said. "I'll let you have three and I'll have two. Then we'll take ourselves out for a nice dinner."

Ginger was always in charge. Plus, Sherri was drunk, and the money was enticing, although Sherri felt cheap and humiliated as soon as her hands touched the sticky barroom floor. She felt everyone's eyes on her backside. The men whistled and pushed the bills farther away with their boots. She hoped nobody who knew the old Sherri would see her like that. Finally, she and Ginger stood up and pocketed the twenties. "Let's go," Ginger said, blowing her hair out of her face.

"I don't even get a thank-you?" The man ran his fat hand over Sherri's ass. Ginger slapped it and told him to fuck off. He didn't argue; she was taller and stronger-looking than he was, and the expression on her face could stop the earth from rotating on its axis. Sherri was grateful for Ginger. As long as she was surrounded by her friends, she felt she would always be protected.

"Listen, if they're stupid enough to part with their money that quick," Ginger said, "take it."

Sherri didn't want anything to do with guys like that. Instead, she wanted a confident *real* man, the kind of man Hefner imagined as the ideal reader of the magazine—someone like Prince Charles, only better looking. He and Lady Diana had recently announced their engagement, and it was all anyone talked about. Everyone was jealous of Diana, even the Bunnies. Her life, like Cinderella's, had changed entirely because she'd been noticed by the right sort of man, the kind who opened doors for her, called her "darling," and told her she was lovely. Sherri wanted that to happen to her. She imagined someone debonair, sophisticated, and well read. He'd have an aristocratic countenance and melt her with his eyes, make her tingle with electricity. He could fill up her emptiness, make her complete. Sherri thought the resort was designed for exactly that sort of man, the perfect, rich guest who would emerge as if from the pages of a Harlequin romance: suave and remote, worldly, smart, strong and chiseled, yet tortured by some sort of secret or feeling of being misunderstood. But where was he, this mythical, masculine man who was just sensitive enough? The only men she saw had comb-overs and beer bellies and stress acne on the backs of their necks. She wanted to meet someone who could show her some excitement, someone who would notice she was especially suited for him, like the butterflies she'd read about whose wing design matched the flowers they drew nectar from.

The management was serious about transgressions with patrons, although, from what Sherri could tell, it happened all the time. Dating a keyholder was a real badge of honor, as long as you weren't caught. Retired Bunnies often returned to visit the resort, and when they did, they hung off the arms of men they'd once waited on, their diamond wedding rings sparkling under the recessed lights. Sherri didn't want to get married, not yet. What she wanted was a boyfriend who could open her up to a world of new experiences and opportunities. The resort was the lever.

That was her state of mind when Sherri met Sam, who stayed at the resort during a Cattle Raisers convention in nearby Waukesha. He'd cut his thin, wind-hardened lip on the rim of a broken glass, and the manager tripped over himself to make it up to him, telling Sherri to bring him bandages and club soda for the bloodstain, and a towel to wipe it up. After all of her mother's falls, Sherri was a pro at cleaning injuries. For years, her mother had denied that her dizziness was a serious problem and she'd fallen all the time, cracking her head and breaking her ankle and wrist until her doctor had insisted first on a walker, then a wheelchair. A cut lip? As far as Sherri was concerned, that was nothing.

Sam called her "sweetheart" in his lazy cowboy accent. With the towel covering his mouth, he said, "You're cute as a speckled pup under a red wagon, you know that?"

Sherri smiled. She *did* know that.

"I understand you're not supposed to cavort with the clientele," Sam said, lingering over the word "cavort," "but I sure would love to see you outside of this place if you'll do me the honor."

She was grateful that he was discreet. The male patrons learned through word of mouth that the security team at the resort was as protective as an army of older brothers. She could tell that he was angling to ask her out, and even though he wasn't exactly Warren Beatty handsome—not by a long shot—she decided she'd say yes if he asked.

Bunny Carmen had told her about a place on the other side of Lake Geneva where Bunnies went to meet guests. Carmen knew the ins and outs of everything.

Sam winked at her. "What do you say?"

Without looking around to see if a room captain was watching, because she knew that would make him suspicious, Sherri surprised herself with her boldness. "There's a restaurant called the Crow's Nest," she said. She knew she had to be careful. "I'll be there tomorrow at seven. Maybe I'll see you." She smiled coyly even though she felt nervous, and dipped the soiled towel into a glass of water. Sam's blood swirled in the clear liquid.

The next night, Sam showed up in a bolo tie, a Stetson hat, and alligator-skin cowboy boots. Guys from the area like Frank, Danny, and Curtis wore cowboy hats and boots, too, but Sam looked like a *cartoon* cowboy. Maybe it was just fine to dress like that where Sam was from, but in Wisconsin it seemed like he was in a costume, drawing attention to himself the way *her* costume was designed to draw attention, only his getup made him seem old, and he *was* old, maybe forty?

Sherri wanted her first real date with a guest to go well. She'd hoped to find Sam interesting and appealing, but he'd talked about how it felt to hold a cow's eyeball in his hand, and told her cows don't have any upper teeth, stuff she could learn from any old farm boy in Wisconsin, and there were plenty of those. But he wasn't a farm boy from Wisconsin—at least he had that going for him, and he had to have been rich with all his talk of his ranch, so big it could have taken up the whole state of Texas.

The other Bunnies met men who would send them on trips, which was exactly what Sam did when he surprised Sherri by handing her an envelope with a plane ticket to Houston. Now, *that* interested her. She'd never been farther away from East Troy than a 4-H bus trip to the state fair in Des Moines, and she'd never set foot on an airplane. She felt she was due for a real, grown-up vacation after a lifetime of constant servitude. She agreed without hesitation and begged the other Bunnies to cover her shifts for her, knowing she'd have to return their favors, and there would be lots of doubles in her future.

She couldn't wait to tell Val. When she did, Val seemed worried instead of impressed. "Let me tell you some things you didn't learn about at the nunnery, Sister Sher: Don't ever let a man know he's given you an orgasm or he'll think he owns you. You've had an orgasm, right?"

"Sure," Sherri lied. "Lots of times."

Val clearly didn't believe her. "Right. Let's practice your sex face."

"My sex face?"

"Like this. Get on your knees." Val sank down on the shag carpeting and patted the space next to her. "Now do this." Val arched her back, parted her lips, and gazed at the sky. Sherri did the same thing.

"How's this?"

"It's great if you want to look like a large-mouth bass." Val began to laugh so hard she couldn't breathe, and soon Sherri was snorting. She never would have dreamed she'd become that comfortable with Val. "Call me if you have an emergency. Tell Ola and Biata to find me wherever I am."

"I'll be fine."

"No. You're like Anne of Green Gables walking into a lion's den."

"I can do this. Haven't you heard of feminism?"

"God, you're clueless. Here." She opened her drawer and pulled out a box of condoms. "You just started on the pill, so make sure he wears a raincoat."

Bunny Gwen offered to drive her to the Milwaukee airport on her way home from her shift. Sherri liked Gwen, even if she kept to herself. She seemed like she saw everything and had something to say but she always held her tongue. She also seemed to know that Sherri wasn't headed to Houston to visit an uncle, as Sherri had claimed. "Don't do anything stupid. Pay attention to your surroundings. You have keys?"

Sherri reached into her bag and jingled her key chain.

"Hold them in your hand wherever you go. Anyone messes with you, gouge their eyes out and run. Got it? I don't want you ending up like the girl in *Looking for Mr. Goodbar*."

Ginger told Sherri that travelers were supposed to dress for an airplane ride the way you might dress for church, so Sherri wore her favorite fitted daisy-print polyester dress with puffy shoulders and a pair of slingback heels. She loved everything about the flight at first, from the hum of the engines to the stewardesses in their slim navy suits, smart caps, and wispy neck scarves. They were poised and friendly in the same service-oriented way that she'd been trained, and reminded her of all the Bunnies at the resort. Maybe, Sherri thought, she should go to flight attendant school in order to become a stewardess. She could try to work on *Big Bunny*, Hugh Hefner's plane, the one he'd painted black and outfitted with special lights on the wings so that everyone could see it from the ground. She'd heard his plane had a big, round waterbed with a possum-fur cover.

Her dreams of traveling the world on *Big Bunny* ended as soon as the plane hit turbulence, and she gripped her armrests so hard her fingers turned white. She looked out of the window and saw how far she was from earth and home and everything she knew.

The flight attendant could tell that Sherri wasn't doing well, and showed her the long, narrow waxed bag in her seat pocket that looked like one of the doggie bags from the Sidewalk Café. "It's for airsickness, hon. You can throw up in it."

When the plane landed in Houston her stomach was still uneasy, and she was suddenly terrified of what she'd agreed to, and everything she'd risked. She understood that Sam hadn't invited her on this trip for mere companionship; the Trojans in her purse were proof. Accepting his offer had made her feel sophisticated and worldly; now she just felt dirty. She figured people in East Troy had whispered and spread rumors about her once word had gotten out that she'd taken a job as a Playboy Bunny. Wouldn't this prove them right? Then again, they'd never need to know. Those people back home sitting with their legs crossed tight couldn't even find Houston on a map.

Sam would be there in the airport lobby, waiting. She pictured those awful boots, and remembered when he'd kissed her in his car after dinner, ramming his big, wet tongue into her mouth, the feeling of his scar against her lip, his large hand cupping her breast. She hadn't even told anyone where she'd gone off to. What if something happened to her in Texas? What if Sam flew girls like her out here so he could murder them? He was a rancher; he was used to putting animals down. She'd read about a girl her age who'd been missing for months, and they could only identify her by a big pink curler that was still stuck in her hair after they'd dug her skeleton out of the dirt.

No, no, Sam was nothing like that. She told herself that this was just a date—a long, exotic date. She was nineteen years old now, a real grown-up, and she wasn't even a virgin. So why couldn't she unbuckle her seat belt? She thought of something her mother told her near the end of her life: "It might be hard to be responsible for other people, but it's even harder to be responsible for yourself. You'll see."

She stared at the baggage handlers and air controllers out on the hot tarmac as the passengers walked past her. Maybe Sam would figure she'd decided against coming. If she delayed long enough he'd leave, and she'd be free to explore this strange, humid city all by her lonesome.

A stewardess asked her if she needed help. "I just feel woozy," she said. "Woozy" was a word her mother had used when she first got sick. The attendant offered to walk her off the plane. When they entered the lobby, Sam was standing there in a suede jacket and tight jeans, waving. He was both shorter and fatter than Sherri had remembered. "See?" the attendant said. "Your dad's here."

Sam had a pleased grin on his face and a bouquet of red roses in his hand. Roses, Sherri thought, were for old ladies.

The air in Houston was so humid she could feel her curls grow tighter. Sam led her to his lemon-yellow Cutlass Supreme and drove her to a stately old building called the Rice Hotel. Not until she walked into the ornate lobby did she realize how accustomed she'd grown to the Playboy resort, which felt sexy and muted in a way that the Rice Hotel did not. With its wingback damask chairs and stiff couches, it was stuffy and formal.

"This is where John F. Kennedy spent the day before heading to Dallas," Sam said. "We all know how that story ends."

Sherri smiled weakly. Was she supposed to be horrified or impressed?

Their room was on a high floor and he'd pulled the curtains against the afternoon sunlight. He set her luggage down and ran his hand lightly up and down her back. "Welcome to Houston, Bunny Sherri," he said, kissing her neck with his hard lips. His hand searched down, further down, until he'd lifted the hem of her dress and slipped his fingers inside her underwear, making her jump. She fought the urge to slap him. He must think she did this all the time! He led her to the bedroom and gently pushed her to the mattress.

Couldn't he have at least taken her out to eat first? Offered her a drink? "I'm exhausted from the flight," Sherri said. "How about I take a nap?"

Sam threw his hat onto the floor and unbelted his giant metal belt buckle with a horse's head on it, dropping his pants. "Oh, you can't go to sleep on me now. Look how excited I am to see you." She'd never actually looked at a naked man before. He was proud of himself for luring Sherri there, that was for sure, the way he might have beamed over a winning bid for a prize calf.

"I brought these," she said. Her hands shook so hard that she could barely open her purse. She pulled out a condom and tried to remember if she'd taken her pill that morning.

"We don't need 'em," he said. "I'm fixed. You've got nothing to worry about."

Sherri closed her eyes, gripped the sheets in her hands, and tried not to show she was nervous; it had been easier last time, when she was with a boy her own age, and after a shot of Galliano and a few cups of wapatui. She had thought that losing her virginity would make her first encounter with Sam easier and more comfortable. She was wrong.

Without much ado, Sam pushed himself into her, exclaiming, "Oh Lord, girl. You're tighter than wallpaper!" She bit her lip and closed her eyes and tried to decide if Sam was telling the truth about getting "fixed" and how not being fixed implied he once was broken. She should have insisted he wear a condom, but he hardly gave her a chance to assert herself, not that she even knew how. She couldn't even say the word "condom" out loud.

She remembered what Carmen had told her about escaping into a dollhouse. She closed her eyes and tried to distract herself by imagining she was working, adding up orders, calculating tax.

It was almost worse to spend time with Sam outside the hotel than in bed—that was when she felt the dirtiest for what she was doing. She tuned him out when he spoke to her, because he talked about cattle futures, highways, dry spells, and Elvis's death. On the few occasions when they left the hotel, he took her to the Barbecue Inn and Brenner's Steakhouse, always looking around to make sure he wouldn't see anyone who knew him. He didn't live in Houston but in a town called Crockett, partway between Houston and Dallas—close enough that he must have known people there, given how alert he was, like a kitten under a sky full of hawks. "If anyone asks, I'm going to say you're my cousin and you're going to college at Rice," he said. "Got it?"

In the years to come, she would try hard to forget everything about Sam: that he smelled like a tannery, and that once, twice, three times he'd accidentally called her Loretta. She would also try to forget that morning when she took a long, hot shower, wishing she could go back in time to make herself pure and new again.

He was asleep when she returned to the bedroom. She quietly packed her things and checked her wallet for cash. Knowing she'd need more to get her through the next three days before her return flight, she slipped several twenty-dollar bills from Sam's wallet into her own. In the process, she spied a photo of his three young sons in matching cowboy hats, sitting on top of a high fence. The boys looked just like Sam, and she guessed that in his "real life" people liked and looked up to him, thought he was a great cowboy, husband, and dad. How could he be both that person and the guy in the hotel room? The photo made her flush with guilt and shame and something even worse—the feeling that she'd lost herself the way Jeanne had told her she might. His kids were probably the most important people in his life, and he hadn't even felt her worthy of mentioning them to her. She wasn't special to Sam, she was a commodity. She understood that she was a warm body, that was all she was to him, and this understanding made her feel hollow and sad.

She grabbed her things and took the elevator to the lobby, eager to escape before Sam noticed she was gone. "How do I get to Galveston?" she asked the doorman, who directed her to the nearby Amtrak station. Galveston was a place she'd overheard a lady in the bar talking about; she'd called it "the New York of Texas," which sounded perfect to Sherri, although she discovered the sleepy sandbar was nothing like a big city.

Sherri felt very adult handing eighty-nine dollars to the hotel attendant when she booked two nights in the stately Hotel Galvez. After she'd tired of the touristy shops and looking at the brightly painted Victorian houses on the strand, she sat by the pool in her new polka-dot string bikini reading fashion magazines. She was grateful to be away from Sam, content to listen to the waves gently roll into the sandy beach off in the distance. When she looked up, she saw a tall man standing at the end of the diving board, arms stretched out. He had long, wavy blond hair. He was broad-shouldered, his waist tapered, the golden skin on his back free of the moles and wiry hair she'd seen all over Sam. He might have been a statue of a swimmer until he jackknifed his leg and sprang high into the air, landing in the water without a splash. Sherri ran to the edge of the pool and waited for him to emerge. When he did, she clapped for him. "Hey, that was perfect! Just perfect! Will you do it again?"

He did. Afterward, they got to talking about the cold winters in Wisconsin and places to go in the area. He was the most handsome man Sherri had ever spoken to. He had a husky, low voice and aloof manner. She was charmed by his blue eyes, and the cleft in his chin she wished she could reach out and touch. He was about to return for another dive when Sherri said, "Guess what I am."

"What do you mean?" He didn't strike her as the kind of person who liked to play guessing games.

"I'm a Bunny. A *Playboy* Bunny."

His demeanor changed. "They have Bunnies in *Wisconsin?*" She saw a flash of disbelief—was it because of the unlikely place for the resort, or because he thought she didn't look like a Bunny? His skepticism mellowed into satisfaction. He seemed oddly pleased with himself, as if he'd accomplished a difficult task. When the waitress walked past in her white blouse and navy-blue skirt, he stopped her and ordered two Long Island iced teas. He told Sherri that his name was Mitch Spaulding, and he was from a place called Calabasas. When Sherri asked him where that was, he said it was near Malibu, a place she only knew about because of her Barbie.

"Los Angeles?" She'd never thought of LA as a city where people actually grew up and settled—imagine being *from* there, instead of a small town with a VFW Lodge and an old-timey bandstand in the square! His long legs hung off the edge of the lounge chair next to hers.

"And what do *you* do for a job?" she asked.

"I'm a stuntman." He showed her a small scar on his collarbone she hadn't noticed before. "This is from when I worked as a double for Evel Knievel. My motorcycle flipped once, twice. I thought I'd nailed the jump, but the stagehand, a new guy, he moved the ramp. Just a quarter of an inch and bam, lights out. I was in the hospital for over a week."

She couldn't imagine Mitch taking a greater risk than jumping off the hotel diving board. He was as calm as the current in Honey Creek.

"There's nothing I won't do," he said.

Sherri took a drink. "But why does Evel Knievel need a double? I mean, doesn't he do all the tricks himself? Isn't that the point of being a stuntman?"

"Bobby likes me to try the tricks first."

"Bobby?"

"Robert's his real name. Know what he said to me? He said, 'If I couldn't be me, Mitch, I'd be you.'"

"That's funny!" She imagined Val rolling her eyes at Sherri's weak response.

Mitch said Pete Townsend had signed his guitar and he went to high school with Jerry Lewis's kid. His father was some kind of movie producer. He had five brothers, and he was in Galveston because one of them had married a girl from there. Her father was in the oil business, and he was so rich that he'd rented out the entire Opera House for the wedding. The rest of his family had returned home to California, but Mitch had decided to stay for a few extra days to buy a new car, a red Ferrari Berlinetta Boxer. Before she knew it, she was sitting in the passenger seat, and they were cruising Sewall Boulevard. Strollers lazily ambled along the sidewalk. The waves crashed against the abandoned Pleasure Pier, which had been decimated by a hurricane; it was just a hunk of piles with rusting steel beams. Gulls nosedived for fish. Mitch reached for Sherri's hand and slipped it under his jeans as he drove.

"This is the life," she said. "We were meant to meet each other, don't you think?"

"Sure, babe," Mitch said. She'd never been called "babe" before.

She found his tan skin, clean, angular surfer's good looks, and carefree manner incredibly appealing after Sam's squat bluntness. How was it that men could be so different from each other? Mitch seemed wonderfully untouched by tragedy in a way that Sherri couldn't fathom. Her short life had already been steeped in loss: first her father, then her mother. Mitch hadn't even lost a dollar.

When it came time to have sex, Sherri didn't ask Mitch to use a condom. It was so embarrassing, she thought, remembering how put off Sam had been. She'd be fine; what were the odds? With Frank and Sam, Sherri had felt like a rabbit who'd wandered into a trap. Mitch was different because she'd gone after him. She thought the sex would be better, more exciting, and it was, but not by a lot. After, she'd lie in bed and listen to Mitch snore, wondering if she'd done everything right.

In the mornings, rumpled and messy, they'd drink coffee on the porch overlooking the pool. Mitch wore his cool gold-rimmed aviator sunglasses. When Sherri looked at him, she saw only her own reflection in the metallic orange surface, which made her think that she was the only person in his world. He was her closest encounter with the kind of real man she was dying to meet. Mitch was handsome, traveled, successful, interesting, and remote.

"Are you as happy as I am?" she asked him one morning, playfully nibbling his earlobe—even his earlobes seemed perfect and clean. "Tell me how happy you are."

"So happy," he said. He stood up abruptly and went into the bathroom and stayed behind the closed door for almost an hour. If he was that happy, she thought, wouldn't he want to spend every last second with her, because he knew their time together was fleeting? She wanted to say something about this and thought about the actual words she might use to express herself, but the more she thought about it, the more she realized she wasn't really in a position to talk with him as though they were close, even if they'd been naked together. She wished she could leapfrog from just getting to know him to being his actual girlfriend.

After wasting her money on two nights on a hotel room she'd never used, it was time for Sherri to fly back home. That third morning, Mitch dropped her off at the Amtrak station to begin her return to the airport.

"I thought you'd give me a ride to Houston in your new car."

"Wish I could. I've got to catch up on some work."

"Work? What does a stuntman do when he's not, you know, running into a burning building?" She ran her finger along his nose. "Will you come see me?"

"Sure." He kissed her, a kiss that felt like a goodbye. "I'll add Wisconsin to my list of places to visit."

On the ride back to the airport, Sherri felt funny about Mitch's aloof manner, and she was nervous that she'd run into Sam. And she did. He was waiting for her at the gate with more roses, yellow this time. Her stomach lurched. "Where'd you go, honey?" He seemed sad. Pathetic, even. Angry.

"I just needed some time to myself," she said, wishing Sam didn't exist, but then again, if he didn't exist, she wouldn't have met Mitch. She still believed in fate back then.

"I didn't spend all that money to fly you out here so you could have time to yourself. I could have bought a steer for what I paid. And my wallet's a little lighter."

"I'm sorry." She wasn't one bit sorry, but she didn't know what else she was supposed to say.

"Well, I'm sorry, too, sweetheart." He handed her a small jewelry box. "I was going to give this to you if you'd stuck around."

Sherri didn't want a gift from Sam, but what was she supposed to do? She opened the box. Inside was a gold chain with a pendant on it shaped like Texas, with a small diamond star in the middle. She wished it were Mitch standing there, Mitch who'd given her the gift. "This is sweet, Sam. Real sweet. Thank you. But I can't keep it."

The attendant announced they were boarding.

"I've got to go," Sherri said. "This trip was a whole lot of fun. Here." She tried to return the necklace, but Sam leaned closer to her and put his face next to her ear.

"You're just a dumb little fuck, you know that?" He threw the roses on the ground, leaving her holding the necklace, before turning and stomping down the terminal, creating quite a stir at the gate. She felt like everyone on the airplane knew more about her than she wanted them to.

She returned to Lake Geneva on a grim, rainy spring afternoon, ricocheting between feeling dumbstruck by Sam's comment and lovesick for Mitch. The two men seemed to represent the two possible ends of the romantic spectrum. She chose not to think of Sam, and let her mind linger over all the moments she'd shared with Mitch, from taking a bubble bath together to the way his golden hair gleamed on his legs in the afternoon sun. *You look like a real prince,* she'd told him. She'd stuffed his soft, white undershirt in her bag and smelled it occasionally when nobody was looking in hopes that his piney scent would obfuscate Sam's musky odor and harsh words. She'd given Mitch the phone number for the resort so that he could call her. She couldn't wait for Ola and Biata to come find her with a pink "while you were out" memo when he did. She was already mythologizing Mitch, forgetting that when they made love, she felt they were doing so alongside each other instead of together. Why had Mitch kept his eyes shut? Why did she fumble with him, unsure how to give him pleasure? They seemed to have different rhythms. His desire seemed almost athletic, like he really had to try hard and focus. She certainly hadn't reached the height of passion—she only pretended she did. She was certain that once they got to know each other better, that would happen. Sex had seemed more straightforward with Sam, more animalistic and instinctual. How horrible, she thought, that her more primal attraction was to that awful man. The mere thought of Sam made her shudder with the feelings of shame, guilt, and embarrassment she knew she deserved. She'd given herself away like she was trash. Sam had taken her dignity from her, but she'd let him. She wanted to believe that Mitch could give it back.

One day, she decided, she would live somewhere like Calabasas. She felt she belonged in a place where the weather was warm year-round, and where there were palm trees. She wanted a prettier life, one where everyone was having as much fun as they did in the magazine. She'd wake up next to a handsome, trouble-free man whose tan skin glowed against fresh, white sheets.

CHAPTER SEVEN

She spent her first morning back at the resort dressed in a light pink Bunny costume working the Easter egg hunt on the resort's back lawn. Parents stood around chatting while their greedy little kids dressed in their Sunday best ran each other down to snatch up candy-filled plastic eggs. It was cool out for April, and it was hard to walk, because her heels sank into the damp, recently aerated soil. Rain sputtered from the sky. Her ears wilted, her hair flattened, and she shivered uncontrollably.

It was her first holiday away from home, and she felt nostalgic for the scratchy sound of Rimsky-Korsakov's *Russian Easter Festival* overture that used to flow through the speakers on their RCA stereo cabinet—her mother listened to "pagan music" to cut loose after playing the more serious liturgical pieces for Easter Mass. She told Sherri that Rimsky-Korsakov hadn't heard a full orchestra until he was twelve years old, and the sound of all the instruments had overwhelmed him with joy, a feeling she could hear in all of his compositions, especially the overture. "Some feelings stay with you your whole life," Muriel had said. She was usually so practical and stern, and only waxed poetic when she spoke of music. Sherri had loved the unique time signatures of the piece, and the movement in tone from solemnity to hedonism.

Sherri would have given anything to spend five minutes back in the warm comfort of her past, enjoying a lazy Easter afternoon day-dreaming on the davenport. She always remembered her parents in separate rooms—her father tinkering with an antique radio in his shop while her mother cooked scalloped potatoes and sugary baked ham. She could picture the kitchen table with a vase of daffodils, and the wicker bowl bulging with the decorated Easter eggs that smelled of vinegar.

But she was farther from home than ever. She felt her fake eye-lashes coming loose from the moisture and did her best to smile. The little girls in Florence Eiseman dresses looked at her with adoration, while the boys, even the little ones, tried to peek down her top when she bent over. She tried to forget what Sam had said to her. Instead, she lost herself in that familiar music in her head.

Everyone had off that night, so the Bunnies gathered at a tall table at Papouli's. Sherri told Carmen, Ginger, Val, and Rhonda about her trip, modifying the details to only mention Mitch, not Sam—how Mitch smiled when he said her name, and how he looked like a cross between Robert Redford and Clint Eastwood. Val lit up a cigarette and exhaled with her lower lip sticking out, pushing the smoke right into her blue mascara and feathered bangs.

"I'm not buying it. If that guy was so perfect, you never would have come back. You would have stuck on him like a tick."

It had never occurred to Sherri that she could have chosen not to return. The resort was her home now; it was her community.

"I think he sounds amazing," said Ginger, who was always single. She had no patience for men who bothered her with unwelcome advances. "And he's over six feet? How come short girls like you and Rhonda always get the tall guys? All I ever see are bald spots."

"Don't get too excited," said Carmen, who'd just gotten a perm and whose hair was painfully curly, not like Sherri's loose locks but tight

and springy as steel wool. She'd come into Sherri's room and cried
and cried when she'd first returned from the salon. Her hair made her
seem even more unhinged. "I hate to tell you, but most men are just
looking to leave a scratch on your bedpost."

"Not Mitch," said Sherri. "He's into me."

"That's what they all say. Anyway, I don't need a man," Ginger said,
picking up a swizzle stick and raising it in the air. "I've got an electric
toothbrush."

They sank back shots of Jägermeister that a bunch of guys in hunt-
ing camo and blaze-orange hats had sent over. "You think he's married?"
Val asked.

"No way." The thought hadn't even occurred to Sherri, but of course
that was something Val wondered, since she was a two-timer herself.

"Say he was," Carmen said. "Would it matter?"

"Sure, it would matter," Sherri said. "I couldn't possibly share a
man with someone else." Already she was imagining Mitch out in the
world meeting other women, who might be prettier, smarter, richer,
and more accomplished than she was. The thought made her crazy.

"See, I prefer to share a man," said Carmen. "Let their wives do
all the dirty work. They bleach the stains out of their husband's underwear, make their meals, raise their kids, and we get to have all the
fun without having to listen to them brag about their golf swing or
complain about how much they hate their jobs. What do you want
to be tied down for, Sher? Let someone else sit at home and worry if
Mitch's parachute will open when he jumps off a cliff."

All the women back home acted as if the goal was to find a
husband—a good one—before they were all taken. Sherri's mother
raised her to believe that mating was a game of musical chairs, and Sherri
didn't want to be the last person standing, because that was how Muriel
had ended up with Sherri's dad. She'd described herself as having been
an old maid when she landed in East Troy in her late twenties. Lane
was the only bachelor in town. Sherri hated to think of her father as
a last resort, but he was older than her mom by a good stretch, and

he was bookish and solitary, more of a partner than a spouse. It was hard for her to imagine that any passion had ever existed between her parents. Sherri had overheard her mother describe her father to her friends, her tone drenched with defeat. "Oh, you know Lane. He wears well." That was the most romantic sentiment Sherri had heard from her. There were worse marriages, like Roberta's parents'. At least Sherri's parents didn't scream or fight. But Sherri often watched them eat dinner together without exchanging a word and she vowed that she would never, ever be stuck in a marriage like that. She wanted the kind of romance that tore people apart, made them insane with jealousy and desire.

Carmen said, "Mitch is the one who should worry about you, Sher. The season starts just after Memorial Day, and the men are going to come out of the woodwork, just watch. And when they do, you'll need to be organized. Arrange to see them in shifts. Afternoon, dinner, night. Just do your best to keep their names straight. Organization is key."

"Yeah," said Rhonda, her tone acerbic and directed at Sherri for no reason Sherri could understand. Rhonda made Sherri feel seen for who she was becoming, and it hurt. "You'll need to start keeping track of all the guys you sleep with."

Sherri was already drunk but ordered a round of Baileys (Sherri thought cream drinks were a sophisticated choice) without giving a thought to the calories. Rod Stewart's "Da Ya Think I'm Sexy" began to play. Carmen said she'd met Stewart last summer when he'd performed at Alpine Valley, and she'd even danced with him in that very bar. Another summer was coming, and with it, the promise of celebrities, musicians, endless parties, and multiple boyfriends. The impending peak resort season was like a wave seen from a distance, slowly approaching shore. Sherri couldn't wait.

She was still wasted at three in the morning when she was woken by Val and Danny, who stumbled, giggling and drunk, into the dorm room. The security light from the outside of the building shone through the slats of the blind. She could see Danny standing behind Val with his hands wrapped around her. When Val was with Curtis, she seemed sullen and aloof. She'd return to the dorm with a split lip or a bruise on her arm that she'd have to cover with the same concealer she used on her face. Danny brought out something soft in her prickly friend. "Danny?"

He put his finger over his lips. "Shhhh."

"You're not supposed to be in the dorms," Sherri said.

"What are you going to do, call the cops?" Val asked.

Val was right. There were rules, but from what Sherri could tell, they were relaxed. Carmen had rescued a kitten and kept it in her room, and nobody seemed to care about the "no pets" policy. Besides, Val had never asked Sherri for anything before, and she didn't want to be on her roommate's bad side—something that could happen with the slightest gesture. Even though their relationship had warmed, it was only on Val's terms, and Val still scared her. Sometimes she'd be nice, offering to do her makeup for her, and the next minute she'd say something biting but in a passing manner. She'd called Sherri big-boned, and told her that her incisors were like fangs. As much as Sherri wished she could dismiss these barbs, they stayed with her every time she looked in the mirror, and they reinforced Val's position of dominance in their relationship. Sherri looked up to Val the way she'd looked up to Roberta. She put up with everything she did.

"Come on, Sherribelle." Danny tussled her hair. "My grandmother is at the cottage with a bunch of women from her Bible study. We have no place else to go. Help a horny guy out."

"Fine, but this can't happen again."

"Don't tell anyone!" Val said.

A few minutes later she heard groaning and a rhythmic thump, thump, thump coming from Val's side of the room. "I love you like crazy," Danny whispered to Val, just loudly enough for Sherri to overhear before she wrapped her pillow around her ears. Sherri wished

Mitch would someday love her that much, but he hadn't even called once since her return.

A few weeks later, at weigh-in, Gloria adjusted Sherri's ears to center them on her head, even though Sherri was certain she'd already centered them perfectly. But she smiled through her teeth, anxious to get through the now-familiar ordeal at the beginning of each shift, a painfully thorough inspection of her hair, makeup, outfit, cuffs, bow tie, nylons, shoes, and smile. Sherri was convinced Gloria even inspected her soul.

"Stand up straight. Shoulders back." Gloria hadn't softened a bit. She was still the coldest and most powerful person Sherri had ever met, and she seemed determined to find something wrong with her. She reminded Sherri of a younger, more exotic version of Mrs. Vogel, the Bavarian organ teacher who'd kept a folded wooden ruler on the music rack and slapped Sherri's knuckles with it whenever she pressed a wrong key. Like Mrs. Vogel, Gloria was unsmiling and grim. She seemed to have it in for her. "Silly Sherri," she called her, and Sherri supposed she *was* silly, and what was wrong with that? She was finally having fun, she really was. Somewhere along the way her grief had begun to ebb. She'd catch herself experiencing enjoyment without having to think about it.

But then she stepped on the scale and sucked her gut in, suddenly worried by the pounds that had been inching up at each weigh-in, and the expression of disapproval on Gloria's face. She'd half-heartedly tried the grapefruit diet, but that hadn't stopped her from drinking, and it hardly made a dent in the Texas-sized food she'd eaten a few weeks back on her vacation. Fried chicken, giant slabs of steak, baked potatoes with mounds of sour cream, pineapple upside-down cake, rum and Cokes. How could she have let herself go like that, in every possible way? She wanted a promotion from the Sidewalk Café and couldn't blow it.

"You're up seven pounds," Gloria said.

"There must be a mistake."

"There's nothing wrong with the scale. And there's nothing wrong with my eyes, either." Gloria put a pencil between Sherri's knees and nudged it up her legs. When she let go, it stuck in place between her thighs. Gloria shook her head. "Vacate the premises, and don't come back until you drop some pounds. You can weigh in again next Monday, Memorial Day. We'll be slammed. You gain ten, you're back to being a civilian."

Sherri was so mad at Gloria's stubborn smugness that she wanted to hit her on the head with the sharp heel of her shoe. *Vacate the premises?* It didn't matter a hill of beans to the Bunny Mother that Sherri was one of the best Bunnies they had. She was always on time, took extra shifts, and covered the ones she had to miss. Her daily write-ups were almost perfect, and, unlike the other girls, she never, ever made mistakes on her tickets. That ought to count for something, shouldn't it? But it didn't.

She returned to the locker room, embarrassed and angry, her arms crossed in front of her to hold in that familiar surplus of emotion that made her want to scream, punch the air, cry, have a fit. She changed back into her T-shirt and red terry cloth short-shorts, her curls stiff as steel springs from the shellac of Aqua Net. The hair spray alone could have weighed a pound! She had to get out of there. She couldn't face the other girls, who were probably already talking about her disciplinary. Bunny Council met later that day, and word would spread. The Bunnies were her friends, sure, but deep down each of them believed that she was the only Bunny who mattered.

She went to her dorm room and quietly threw her clothes and makeup into her duffel. Fortunately, Val was still asleep—and alone.

"Where are you going?" Val asked, her voice groggy.

Sherri couldn't lie to Val. Nothing got past her. "Gloria is sending me home."

Val shot up in bed. "Are you kidding? She fired you?"

"No." Sherri began to cry. "She's sending me home for a week because I tipped the scale."

Carmen poked her face in the door. She could always be counted on to show up whenever there was drama—she lurked in the hallway, popping into everyone's room at the slightest sound of trouble. "Oh my God," Carmen said. "I overheard. *Fuck* Gloria."

Val threw a box of tissues at Carmen's head. "Get out of here, you nosy bitch."

Carmen, who was never fazed by Val, winked at Sherri, blew a kiss to Val, and disappeared.

"She's like a Mrs. Potato Head with that big nose," Val said.

"And her big mouth. Now everyone'll know," Sherri said.

"So what. They'd find out anyway. It's just because you went on the pill. Everyone gains weight at first." Sherri hated the pill. Ever since she started on it, her face broke out in pimples, her breasts ached, and she gained weight.

"I wish I could tie my tubes or rip my ovaries out. I don't even want a baby, not ever." It was so unfair. Women had to deal with everything.

"Look, just enjoy the break," Val said. "Do something crazy while you're back home. Crash a Knights of Columbus meeting or something. It'll be nice to have the room all to myself for a week."

Carmen was at the door again, listening to everything. "You'll be miserable without Sherri to kick around."

"I said *get out*, stripper."

Carmen shook her ass and threw back her hair. Sherri couldn't help laughing, although her spirits sank when she left the dorm with her duffel bag and was shuttled to the main building, wondering how she'd even get home without a car. How she wished she had her own set of wheels! She was going to ask the security guy if he'd take her to East Troy but decided against it when he complained about how busy the resort was that day.

Sherri walked into the lobby and spied Jerry Derzon sitting on the couch with his legs splayed apart, his gold-wire sunglasses resting on top of his balding head. A woman with large plastic hoop earrings and a low-cut pink top sat next to him, her hand casually pressed against his thigh. When Jerry saw Sherri heading in his direction, he sat up straighter and drew his legs together. He whispered something in the woman's ear and she quickly got up and walked away, her skirt pulled tight across her rear. Jerry, who liked to throw his weight around back home, was visibly nervous.

"Well, well," he said. "No ears?"

Sherri had no patience for Jerry, trying to deflect attention from his indiscretions. "That's not Doris."

"No, she's my—"

"Look, I don't care. It's none of my concern." She stood with her hands balled up at her sides. "Don't worry, I won't say anything." She wished she could. Doris was always so high-minded, sending her boys to church with plaid bow ties and wax in their hair, and organizing etiquette classes for the girls in town as part of the Lioness Club. Sherri bet that, after her training to become a Bunny, she now knew more about table settings and manners than Doris ever did.

"I need to go home. Are you headed that direction?"

Jerry checked his Seiko watch, the same watch her father had once fixed for him after he'd dropped it a fish pond, probably because he was drunk. "As a matter of fact, I am. I'm meeting my friend on the square. Arthur, you remember him."

"Sure, I do. I got written up for talking to you guys for too long."

"Well, we're having a late breakfast at Giles. Join us. Or join him. I've got a busted pipe at one of my rentals that needs fixing, so I can't stay. I'm sure Arthur would enjoy getting to know you better. Anyone could see he has eyes for you."

Sherri didn't want to eat at Giles. She wanted to work. The resort was getting busier. She'd miss the chance to make lots of tips and brush up against celebrities, and she'd planned to go to the bars that night with her friends. What if Mitch called while she was gone? How would she ever get the message? She was certain she'd miss everything, and everyone would forget about her. She'd become inconsequential, Cinderella after the ball. Worse, returning to East Troy meant she would return to her old self.

"I'll walk ahead and meet you by the entrance," she said. She couldn't be seen leaving the building with Jerry.

The transition from the muffled and cave-like atmosphere inside the resort back outside to the bright light was always jarring. It was finally nice out, and the golf course was a lush sea of green, although the beauty of that late-spring day was wasted on her because of the mood she was in. She twirled her bag in the air and thought of Gloria wearing her dumb kimono to cover up her jelly rolls. She's the one who should be sent home.

The management company had built condos on the edge of the property and started selling time-shares, offering free or discounted stays with a tour and the kind of heavy sales pitch that was geared for people who had a hard time saying no. Sherri didn't like the time-shares, because they took away from the feeling of the main resort building being the center of activity. The salespeople were always on the make. One had told a couple that if they bought a time-share, they were welcome to take one of the paddleboats in the tiny lake by the golf course. When they went to pick it up, security stopped them and told them they weren't the salesperson's boats to give away.

Service trucks buzzed past her, delivering food and boxes of liquor. The roads leading into and out of the resort were like veins and arteries serving a beating heart. It was hot for May, and the outdoor pool was finally open. She could have gone sunbathing with the other Bunnies, but no, she was headed home.

By the time Jerry pulled up in his black Chevy Nova, Sherri had calmed herself a bit, but she was still edgy and rattled when she slid into the passenger seat. A hula-girl doll was glued to the dashboard. Her hips swung when he took tight turns along the winding roads, which he did with his ample thighs gripping the wheel instead of his hands.

"You've got a few days off?" he asked.

"Not exactly."

"Why are you going back home?"

"Because I'm a fat cow." Sherri could hear her voice break. She didn't want to start crying. She looked down at her thighs spreading across the vinyl seat like underbaked loaves of bread.

"Are you kidding me? You look great."

"Tell that to the Bunny Mother, the Wicked Witch of the Midwest."

Jerry's laugh was gravelly and surprisingly warm. On Highway D they passed a little white church with a small graveyard next to it. The weather was so confusing; cold and rainy one day, warm and humid the next. Now that the soil was damp and warm, farmers were busy plowing their fields, driving tractors they'd bought in Milwaukee and driven all the way from the factory back to their farms. Through the vents she could smell the familiar and strangely appealing scent of manure. Jerry sank a Mark Lindsay eight-track cassette into the player—old-guy music. She cringed when he began to sing along. "'She must belong to San Francisco / She must have lost her way / Posted up poster of Pancho and Cisco . . .'" He strummed the wheel. Sherri remembered the blunt end of her father's index finger. It had been cut off when he'd chopped wood as a boy, and, without a nail, made the fine watch repairs more difficult. He called it his tapping finger, and he'd tap it against the cover of a hard book to the beat of "Green Tambourine" by the Lemon Pipers. When Sherri played the organ, she sometimes imagined the metronome was beating out time to that reassuring, firm tapping sound. Jerry had no such sense of rhythm.

He said, "East Troy's not a bad place, you know. A week home will do you good."

"It's boring."

"No, it's not," Jerry said, sounding like a chaperone. "Show some Trojan pride. It's beautiful. Everything you're looking at was carved out of ice thousands of years ago. Booth Lake? Lake Beulah? They're just buried glacial ice. Richest soil in the country is right here in Walworth County. I've lived here all my life and it still takes my breath away. Arthur acts like he's some Christopher Columbus discovering new land, but we've been here all along.

"Is Arthur from Chicago?"

"Isn't everyone?"

"Is he rich?"

"That's a rude question. If he is, he's a cheapskate. There are plenty of nicer homes on the lake with indoor plumbing and heat. Do me a favor. Introduce Arthur to some people, show him around. He shouldn't be out there on his own getting tired of his own company. A young, single guy like that could turn into a hermit."

Sherri was worried she was the one who would turn into a hermit—that was what she'd been all through high school while taking care of her mom. In that time, she'd missed out on a proper adolescence. She inspected her nails. She'd painted them in her signature color, Cutex peach. All the girls had favorite colors. The dorm always reeked of nail polish and remover.

"Did you hear what I said? Young. Single. Guy. He's different, sure, but he's got prospects, and the last time I counted, he had ten fingers and ten toes."

"I already have a boyfriend. Besides, I don't want to date someone from home. And I sure don't want to get married."

"Who's going to take care of you?"

Sherri had been on her own for so long that she almost couldn't imagine what it would be like to be taken care of. "You mean the way you take care of Doris? Who was that woman you were with?"

Jerry lit a Viceroy, took a deep drag, and offered it to Sherri, who took it. The car filled up with smoke. He looked at her sideways, serious, no longer the cartoon Jerry the Barnacle she liked to reduce him to, but an actual man. "Doris wants nothing to do with me. Hasn't for years. I'll give you some free advice, Sher. Never presume to know what it's like inside someone else's marriage."

At Giles, Arthur waited for Jerry at a table by the window and lit up when he saw Sherri walk through the door. She felt sheepish about being seen and sat as quickly as she could, without looking around to see who noticed her. "Jerry said your new house is old and dark and filled with raccoons," she said.

"Nothing a pellet gun, a bulldozer, and a chainsaw can't fix," Jerry said.

"It's perfect," Arthur said.

Jerry stood behind Arthur and slapped him on the shoulders. "It's your house now, pal. Do what you want, like what you want, build a hippie-dippie commie commune at Rainbow Springs. I've got to skip out and take care of some business. Your future wife here can show you what's what in this town." Sherri blushed, because Arthur smiled at her in a way that made her feel like they shared a secret.

"Well, thanks for the ride back," Sherri said.

Arthur seemed suspicious. "You were at the resort awfully early, Jer."

"Well, Sherri here called and asked me to drive her back home. How could I say no? I've never been one to turn down a damsel in distress. If I'm nice enough, maybe she'll sell me her building." He gave them his best Kojak wink, set his sunglasses back on his nose, and headed out onto the square.

Sherri was glad that Jerry was gone. She liked having Arthur all to herself, and she was grateful to delay her return to her old apartment. She wasn't sure she was ready for all the emotions that would slap her when she walked through the door. Sherri looked with longing at all the food spread out in front of Arthur, the cheese melting on top of the eggs, buttery slices of bread, and the giant, golden pancakes hanging off the edge of his second dish. From that day forward she would always associate Arthur with feelings of insatiable hunger. "Want me to order you something?" he asked. "My treat."

She shook her head. "I'm good."

"But I feel funny eating in front of you on our first date."

"This isn't a date."

"Whatever you say." He smiled. At the resort, Arthur had looked like a scruffy imposter who cared more about how the corners of the ceiling came together than the backsides of the Bunnies who walked by. In East Troy, he seemed smarter than every other person in the room, more interesting and alive, an entire force field twitching with energy. He even ate differently, holding his fork with his left hand, the tines facing down, gently pushing his eggs with his knife.

It was easy to strike up a conversation at the resort, but she struggled now that she was sitting across from Arthur, eye to eye instead of standing in front of him, no longer emboldened by her costume or distracted by Jerry's bravado. "Where's your family?"

"Nearby," he said.

"Nearby where?"

"The Chicago suburbs. Lake Forest."

She knew that Lake Forest was a wealthy community from the movie *Ordinary People,* which had come out a year earlier. She pictured Arthur's family living in a classy Tudor with a circular driveway and winding staircase.

"You don't seem like a flatlander."

"Is that what you call people from Illinois?"

"I was just being nice. We usually call you FIBs. Fucking Illinois bastards. This town swarms with them in the summer, just watch. But you seem different."

"Different how?"

"You aren't a big show-off, that's how. How old are you, anyway?"

"Twenty-eight."

"Why would a young guy like you want to live out there in the cottage all by yourself?"

"I'd love some company. Come join me." He winked at her and she giggled. Men flirted with her all the time now. It seemed harmless when she was wearing her Bunny costume—how odd that an outfit so revealing could also feel like armor. But in that moment, she was plain old Sherri, and she wasn't sure how to respond.

"You'll love the cottage," he said. "I wanted to tear it down at first, build something new, but then I walked inside and that old-cabin smell reminded me of my grandpa, of this cabin he took me to when I was a kid. It activated all my senses, and I started to cry."

Did he just tell her he cried? Sherri had never before met a man who seemed so comfortable sharing his feelings. Mitch would *never* cry in front of her. "Jerry says it's a dump."

"Nah, it's perfect, just neglected. It's dark because of all the trees, but it's the best kind of darkness, like a peaceful din."

A peaceful din? "I could help you decorate. What about shag carpeting, the kind that's super plush, so you have to clean it with a rake? That's what we have in my dorm room. My roommate's boyfriend could sell it to you. And how about one of those freestanding cone fireplaces?"

"It already has a fireplace."

"You should make it super cozy."

She hadn't even noticed that they were leaning closer to each other, their heads forming the tip of a triangle. He cleared his throat. "You ever hear of a Krugerrand?"

Arthur set his utensils down and fingered a Giles matchbook, bending down every other match to make a pattern. He was the kind of person who needed to keep his hands busy at all times. She thought of the collectible matchbooks she was instructed to set on the tables when she prepared them for her guests, advertising Playboy clubs in Jamaica, Seattle, Denver, and London. They were so much more exotic than the Giles matchbooks that said HOMEMADE BREAD AND PIES. FAMOUS FOR NOTHING BUT WE'RE TRYING.

"A Kruger*what*? Is that some kind of pastry?"

"No," Arthur said, laughing. "They're coins. I like to buy and sell coins."

"My dad did that, too. He had one of those big binders with thick sheets of plastic with coins he'd collected since he was a kid. I don't know what to do with them. I never thought they were worth any-thing."

"I can take a look if you want. But these coins, the kind I buy, they're from South Africa, and they're made of solid gold. You like gold, Sherri?"

"Sure I do."

"So do I," Arthur said, and she could tell from his smile that he really did. "It's rare, like you. Brilliant, like you. Timeless. I like the weight of it. The past few years I've been buying as much as I can get my hands on, although I think it's time to sell my gold and invest in stocks." He lowered his voice to a whisper. "Ever heard of Digital Switch?"

"No."

His eyes lit up. "I plan to buy some of their shares next week. I have some inside information. Want me to buy some shares for you?"

"Sure," Sherri said—never mind that she hardly knew Arthur. There was something about him she trusted, and buying stock seemed almost as grown-up as paying for her own hotel room. "I have so much cash. May as well do something with it, because I don't have time to spend it." She reached into her purse and pulled out a wad of bills.

Arthur covered her hands, and her money, with his own. In a hushed voice he said, "You can't carry cash around like that. You'll get mugged, Sherri. Someone could follow you out of here."

"But I didn't want to leave it in my dorm room, and I didn't have time to go to the bank. Besides, this is East Troy."

"It doesn't matter if you're in Timbuktu, you can't wave money around in public. Sherri, look around."

Sherri liked the way he said her name out loud. She looked up. Sure enough, the people at the tables next to them were staring—her father's former customers, church members, neighbors, the parents of former classmates, all of whom, Sherri imagined, had formed some kind of opinion about her job at the resort. She became even more aware of the warmth of his fingers and looked from the people in the restaurant to the knot their hands made. Anyone who'd seen the exchange might have thought they were lovers. "Here." She pressed the money into his palms and folded his fingers around it.

"What if I run off and spend it?"

"I can tell you're not the kind of person who would do that."

Arthur seemed flattered, but wary. "I'm not. But you can't just—I mean, you shouldn't be so trusting, even though I'm basically asking you to trust me." He tapped her hand. "I don't want you to get taken advantage of."

"I'm not a little kid."

"Just—promise to be more careful. I feel protective of you for some reason, not that you can't take care of yourself. And you know, the market is for the long haul. It'll go up and down. If you want security, you should put this in a CD."

"I've already got some of my money in a CD because I'm saving for a car, and I calculated the interest. It won't amount to a pile of beans. This is extra." Her father had read her a poem—how did it go? She remembered the line: "Money is external."

"What did you just say?"

"It's from a poem. 'I am everywhere, / I suffer and move, my mind and my heart move / With all that move me, under the water . . .'"

"Oh yeah, John Berryman. I learned it in school."

"He killed himself jumping off a bridge into a river in the middle of winter. Jesus, that just gives me the chills. How can something so sad be so beautiful?"

Sherri couldn't believe it. There were other men who knew poetry and liked it? The boys at school would groan and make fun of anyone who took it seriously the way Arthur did. He seemed shaken, and surprised to be so impressed. His eyes were light brown, the color of cinnamon. "Sherri Taylor, I think I just fell in love with you."

Sherri felt for a moment that they were the only two people in the restaurant—actually, they'd ascended to another realm, a feeling that lasted about as long as a spell of déjà vu. She heard chairs scraping across the linoleum floor and coffee cups clinking against tables and laughed, embarrassed. She realized their hands were still touching. She pulled hers away, leaving the money with him.

He cleared his throat, gathered the bills, and counted them discreetly. "One hundred and sixty-five dollars."

Sherri reached for the money. "No, there should be two hundred and twelve." She counted as efficiently as a bank teller. "I swore I had more." She bit her lip and looked in her purse to see if the money had fallen out of her wallet. This wasn't the first time her money had gone missing. Sherri kept track of everything; was it possible that Val was skimming her cash? She felt guilty for even having the thought. "Well, anyway, just take it."

"You sure?" He stuffed the money into his shirt pocket. "I just want you to know that the markets are crazy. You invest, and then you forget about it. You can trust me with this, but it's a risk."

"I'm OK with risk," she said. The truth of what she said next made her sad: "And I've got nothing to lose." Arthur seemed smart and capable. His steadiness blunted any fears she might have had.

"Oddly enough, it's actually *you* I need to trust."

"Why?"

"Because, like I said, I shouldn't even tell you this, but I have inside information. My dad sits on the Chicago Board of Trade, and I overheard him talking with a friend. I wasn't trying to eavesdrop or anything, but I heard what I heard. I'm a 'Jr.,' so I can't buy the stock under my name, so if I open an account for you, we'll use your name, and I'll put some of my gold money in it."

"So we're doing each other a favor."

"That's exactly right. I'll even pay you some of my gains to make it worth your while."

Sherri was so wrapped up in Arthur's spell that she hardly noticed the waitress with the syrup-and-butter-stained apron tied at her waist stopping at the table with a pot of coffee. "Refill?"

Sherri looked up, startled. "Berta?"

"Yeah, it's me." Roberta seemed embarrassed to be working at Giles. She pointed the coffee pot in Arthur's direction. "Who's this?"

"I'm Arthur," he said, clearing his throat, standing and extending his hand for her to shake it like a real gentleman. "I'm new to East Troy."

"I can tell."

"How so?"

"By the way you left your fork and knife on the side of your plate to let me know you've finished eating," she said. "I hope you plan to stir things up around here."

Arthur smiled and stood to go, patting the bulge in his shirt pocket as he did. "I'll see you later, Sherri," he said.

Roberta raised an eyebrow at Sherri as if to say, *Who is this guy?* "Hey. I'm off in five minutes. Want to go to Booth Lake?"

CHAPTER EIGHT

The public beach was empty. It wouldn't open for another week, not until Memorial Day. So far, only the high dive had been put in, and it looked strange out there alone in the deep end without swarms of people scrambling to take turns jumping off. The restrooms were still locked up, and the candy store on the first floor of the simple city-style house built into the dandelion-covered hill next to the beach was shuttered. All summer long, kids would stand in line after swim lessons, wet and shivering, with quarters clutched tightly in their little fists. They'd buy Laffy Taffy, Bazooka gum, candy cigarettes, or ice cream Push-Ups to eat on the bus that would drop them back off at the square. One summer, Roberta figured out how to insert tweezers into her mother's piggy bank, and she loaded up with loose change that she willingly shared with Sherri. It was fun until Roberta's father found out and whopped her backside with a hairbrush.

After talking about Lake Beulah with Arthur, Sherri found it hard not to compare the lakes. Beulah was farther from town, and much bigger and more prestigious than Booth. It was really three lakes merged together with channels that were dug through the land that separated them. But that lake, much as Sherri loved it, had a quality of otherness, because it felt like it belonged to the Chicagoans. "Poor Man's Lake Geneva" was what people called it, but it was still too rich for the townies. A state representative lived there, and so did families with names like Gillette, and the people who'd built railroads and bridges all over the world. It was the home of sailors and spoiled kids who filled up the churches in summer, when Sherri would look around and not recognize a soul. Booth Lake was much smaller and simpler, and sweeter, even, if a lake could be sweet. It had the Girl Scout camp on one side and simple cottages dotting the shoreline, and a small island with a cabin on it sat smack-dab in the middle. She felt this lake belonged to her. Actually, with Roberta standing next to her, she felt like it was *theirs;* the very best part of their childhoods had happened here.

On one end of the beach sat the raft. Only the teenagers went on it, and couples would sneak underneath it to make out in the air space between the wood and the empty barrels while the adults, oblivious, sat on blankets or in tattered folding chairs chatting with neighbors about farm subsidies and corn futures, whose kid did what to whom, and the annuals they'd planted in their gardens.

Roberta walked over to the big and little slides, set sideways in the sand on the opposite side of the beach from the raft, staged to be put into the lake next. "Do you think Walter's finger is still out there?"

Sherri pretended to make herself vomit. "That was so disgusting."

When they were kids, Walter Dougan, goofing around as always, had tried sliding sideways and gripped the rusty undersides of the handrail, catching his index finger on an errant bit of metal as he slid down. When he'd surfaced, he'd looked at his hand and screamed bloody murder. He'd bled so much everyone thought he would die. For years after that, the kids would plug their noses and swim upside down, saying they were looking for Walter's finger, or they'd make up ghost stories to tell around campfires about the finger gripping the ankles of swimmers and pulling them into the depths of the spring-fed lake.

"I wish we'd brought our suits," Roberta said. She wore a baseball-cut T-shirt and cutoffs, and still had a glob of syrup stuck in her hair.

"I know. I'll bet the water is freezing." In summer, Sherri and Roberta were always the first in the water and the last to emerge, the skin on their hands and the bottoms of their feet shriveled like raisins. They used to escape the roped area and swim to the island, or furtively sneak around Camp Alice Chester, pretending to be Girl Scouts, even getting free lunch in the cafeteria a few times. One summer, the camp had installed a new fiberglass pier, and the girls decided to sunbathe on it, ignoring the KEEP OFF signs. They had ended up with tiny shards of glass all over their skin that itched and burned like crazy.

The stillness of the lake made Sherri ache to be in it and swim the way they did when they were kids, not the way adults swam at the resort, afraid to get their hair wet, doing a stupid half breaststroke.

The sand was cool and damp beneath them, and the lake was turquoise blue the way it always was that time of year, and crystal clear. The pool at the resort was nice, but Sherri much preferred to swim in the lake in the height of summer, when it thickened with life and turned a luxurious dark green. She thought it was wonderfully illicit to swim in the deep, away from lifeguards and the milfoil that tickled her legs near the shore. She preferred to float high above all that green-gray nothingness below. Unlike the salty, buoyant ocean she'd swum in when she'd been in Galveston, she found lake water sensual and lush, like a languid embrace.

"Who's that Arthur guy you had breakfast with?" Roberta asked.

"Beats me," Sherri said. "I practically just met him." This felt like a lie, but why? She *had* just met him, yet something had passed between them that morning, and already she felt as if she were attached to him by an invisible thread. Her fingers still buzzed from the feeling of his hands on hers.

"From the way you were talking, you guys could have been married. He's cute."

"Think so?" Roberta's opinion mattered to Sherri. He *was* cute, Sherri thought, although "cute" wasn't the right word for him. He wasn't pretty or classically handsome, perhaps because he didn't seem to care what he looked like. The shirt he wore could have been a hand-me-down from an older cousin or brother, his jeans were high-rise, and his Converse high-tops were stained, the laces torn. Sherri could picture him perfectly, from the way his hair curled behind his ears to the pointy tip of his nose. It was the crinkle in the corners of his eyes that really got her. But she didn't want Roberta to know this; she didn't want to know it herself, because she'd already established a different ideal man to strive for. "Arthur isn't really my type," she said.

"Oh, so you have a type now?"

Sherri couldn't help feeling that she needed to introduce Roberta to this newer version of herself. She wanted her friend to recognize that she'd changed. "I do. You should see my boyfriend Mitch." The word "boyfriend" didn't sound right, especially after her encounter with Arthur. "He's tall and blond. And he's from *California*." Sherri emphasized the last word the same way Roberta had said "*England*" when she'd dated Ian.

"Yeah?"

It was still strange to detect jealousy in her friend's tone. It was such a new and heady experience for Sherri that, instead of being sensitive to Roberta's feelings, she went further. "He drives a red Ferrari. He's a stuntman, actually."

"A stuntman for real?"

Sherri nodded her head. "He's friends with Evel Knievel and everything."

"You met him at the resort?"

"No," Sherri said, looking off in the distance. "I met him in Texas." She said this as if she'd been all over the world. She did not mention Sam. She knew that for the rest of her life, she would never mention him to anyone. He would settle in her memories like the stone Roberta had just thrown into the lake. "We stayed in this hotel in Galveston called the Galvez. It was so fancy that they even turned down the covers for us at night, and left chocolates on our pillows."

"That sounds top shelf." Roberta was straight-up jealous, and Sherri was being a first-class jerk. "He flew you out there?"

"Yeah," Sherri lied. "We just knew we were meant for each other." She thought not of Mitch, but of Arthur saying *Sherri Taylor, I think I just fell in love with you.* She added, "Like how you thought you and Ian were meant for each other."

Roberta rolled her eyes. "Ian had two other girlfriends who worked at the camp, and another one back in England. When I found out, I cried into my pillow for a whole week."

Roberta's confession made Sherri feel guilty for baiting her friend, but there was more to it: she also recognized that something had changed in Roberta. She'd grown more mature, mature enough to admit things weren't perfect in her life, while Sherri could see that she was acting like a dumb teenager.

Roberta's tone was wistful when she said, "I'll bet you meet all kinds of men at the resort." It was a relief that they could finally talk about her job.

"I do," Sherri said, "but to be honest, some are real creeps. This one guy told me he'd give me a hundred dollars if I'd wear his socks for a week. He took off his shoes, slipped them off, and handed them to me. They were all damp and practically steaming."

"No! That's gross. So what'd you do?"

"A hundred dollars, Berta. Are you kidding? I sprayed deodorant on them, stuffed them in a paper bag, and a week later I gave them back. I don't even want to think about what he did with them after that."

The expression of displeasure on Roberta's face made Sherri laugh. Soon they were engaged in one of their contagious laughing fits that caused them to lose their breath. Tears sprang out of their eyes. As soon as they began to calm down, they looked at each other and burst into another fit of laughter, almost forgetting what it was that had caused them to begin laughing in the first place. As much as Sherri adored her new friends at the resort, she couldn't laugh like this with Carmen, Tina, Val, Ginger, or Rhonda.

Roberta said, "I would have fucking slapped him." This, Sherri realized, and not in a way that made her proud, was the reason Gloria probably gave Sherri the job instead of Roberta—because Roberta would stand up for herself, and they wanted girls who wouldn't do that, girls like Sherri.

"Do you think—" Sherri began to ask, not sure what it was she really wanted to know. "Do you think all men are like that? Even the good ones? Deep down, do they even care about us, or are we just—warm bodies?"

"I don't know," Roberta said. "My brothers, sometimes they seem like that, but sometimes they don't seem so different from me. I mean, we want sex too, right?"

"Yeah. Sure. But I guess I want more than that."

"Like more what?"

That was a good question. Sherri didn't have words for what she wanted. She'd hoped that the right man could fill her loneliness and dispel her insecurity. That's how it seemed on TV and in the movies, like a woman was otherwise incomplete. She couldn't say this out loud, because she also knew that women were supposed to be independent and liberated, but her independence terrified her. "They're like aliens."

"I guess." Roberta pulled a pack of Virginia Slims out of her purse and handed one to Sherri, who lit hers off the tip of Roberta's, almost like a kiss. "So, you like it there?"

Sherri paused, wondering if she should confide in her old friend, and also wondering if she should admit the downsides of her job to herself. "I do, but the uniforms are killer. They make them two sizes too small, so you're really stuffed in. And Gloria is a bitch. She really is. I feel like everyone is watching every single thing I do, like I'm under a microscope. I have to be perfect all the time. Every minute. For the room captains, for Gloria, for the guests, for the other

Bunnies, for everyone." Until she'd said that out loud, she hadn't realized how much it had bothered her.

"You're making me feel better about Giles. My manager only cares that I show up. I think he's afraid of me, if you want to know the truth."

"I was so surprised to see you there. I didn't even know you were back."

Roberta sat up and threw another rock into the lake. The town had probably just stocked it with fish. Sherri could smell the dead ones—there was always a die-off of perch and bluegill early in the season. "Well, my roommate moved out and I lost my job at the mall, and I was like, why the fuck *not* move back to East Troy? Plus—" She hesitated.

"What?"

"This isn't public yet, but my mom and dad are finally getting a divorce." The word "divorce" in East Troy sounded harsh to Sherri's ears, scandalous. It was a word people whispered.

"I'm sorry. Did your dad meet someone else?"

"No, it's my mom. She finally had enough. She's leaving him, and I'm so proud of her. She said she's tired of pretending everything's fine."

Sherri grabbed Roberta's hand and squeezed it. She thought of the empty bottles of whiskey on their countertops, of Mrs. Fletcher's black eyes and bruises, and all the times Roberta had slept at her house because her dad had flown off the handle. She could hear her mother saying Mr. Fletcher's name under her breath, and remembered the coldness in Muriel's greeting when she saw him at church. "Look at Karl, trying to atone for his sins," she'd say.

"I was always afraid they'd get divorced, but I feel relieved."

"Everything's changing," Sherri said.

"It is. I'm back in East Troy, sure, but I don't know, this place doesn't feel like home anymore. It's not the same here when you're an adult. I don't know what I'm supposed to do. I mean, look at you. You've got this fun job and you get to meet celebrities and go to Texas and I'm just . . . here. Sometimes it feels like this is the only place I belong, and other times I wonder what else is out there."

Sherri felt just as scared and uncertain as she did. She paused, wondering if she could confide in her old friend. "It's good you're home. You're here because your mom needs you. I don't regret helping my mom. Not for a second."

Some geese flew overhead in V formation, and a gentle wind picked up, roughing up the surface of the lake.

"Berta, are you mad I got the job?"

"Nah," she said. "Honestly, I don't think I even could do it."

"So we're still friends?"

Roberta nudged her with her shoulder. "You're a fucking idiot, Sher. We'll always be friends."

CHAPTER NINE

Sherri couldn't stand the thought of entering her old home again. She paused, looked at the sign that now read FOR SALE OR LEASE in the front window of the store, and reached for her keys. She heard Raylee's voice coming from down the street.

"Sher! You're back!" The little girl seemed like she'd been waiting all her life for her to show up. It felt good to be missed, good not to be alone.

"I'm not here for long, just a few days."

Raylee didn't want to hear that Sherri's return was only temporary, so she changed the subject. "Do you know what camblet is?"

"Camblet? No. But I have a feeling you're about to tell me."

"It's a kind of fabric made out of goat hair. It's also called 'camelot.' I'm memorizing the whole encyclopedia. I just started on *C*."

"Want to come in?"

Sherri didn't need to ask. Raylee ran up the stairs in front of her. She was wearing stiff carpenter pants and the kind of striped T-shirt Peter Brady wore. The minute she opened the door to the apartment, Sherri felt the particular, sharp quality of loss that existed in the space. Since her mother's death, she saw their home as if in photo reverse, defined not by her parents' presence, but by their absence. Everywhere she looked she saw what was missing instead of what was there: her father was not sitting in the empty wingback chair, her mother's slippered feet weren't propped on the needlepoint ottoman. Whenever something had seemed off, her mother would say, "This is potato soup without the potatoes." That's how the house felt to Sherri now: it was missing the main ingredient.

When her mother was sick, the apartment had seemed sick, too—dark and listless, the thick wooden shades turned down. But Sherri had left the shades open when she'd left. The apartment was filled with light, and the air, once so stale and heavy, no longer smelled like skin. Sherri wondered why this didn't make her happier.

Raylee took her usual place in front of the television and flipped on *Days of Our Lives,* the soap opera Sherri 's mother watched religiously. Sherri hadn't had time for television at the resort and hadn't kept up. Apparently, lots had happened in Salem. Julie wanted to kill herself and someone Sherri didn't recognize was playing Hope.

After the episode was over and *The Price Is Right* had begun, Sherri thought she might lose her mind if she spent another minute in the apartment. How would she survive a whole week at home without her mom to keep her busy? She flipped off the television and grabbed Raylee's hand. "Let's get out of here. It's depressing."

Raylee slipped on her shoes and gazed wide-eyed at Sherri.

"Do you have a bike?"

Raylee shook her head. "I wish I did. Mama says I'll get hurt."

"You probably will, but that's OK." Sherri pulled back her bangs and bent down to reveal a scar along her hairline. "I got this when I wasn't paying attention and rode my bike up the back of a tractor that was parked on Swoboda Road."

Raylee seemed fascinated by the scar. She ran her finger slowly across it with clinical detachment. "Did it hurt?"

"Hey ding-dong, what do you think? And don't call your mom 'Mama.'"

"Why not?"

"You're old enough for plain old 'Mom.'"

"I'm just talking how I want to talk."

"Trust me. People will make fun of you, and you don't want that." Sherri saw her own self in this lonely little girl on the square. "The girls around here, you know how they are, especially the farm girls. They've got lots of brothers. You say one thing they don't like and they'll sit on your face. C'mon, let's find some wheels for you before you turn into a mushroom."

Deep in the back corner of the garage, Sherri discovered her old orange Huffy bike with a banana seat and streamers hanging from the wide handlebars. The Sundance. Her father had given it to her for her eighth birthday, when she was just about Raylee's age. That was when life had really started for Sherri. She and Roberta could finally explore the country roads, go to the little convenience store in Miramar for candy, ride to the playground at Stone School, and swim at Booth Lake. She loved discovering the world beyond the town square, and loved her first real taste of freedom. She pedaled furiously, her hair flying behind her and her mouth clamped shut because once she'd accidentally swallowed a big, hairy moth and felt the furious beating of wings in her throat. Looking at that old bike, covered in spiderwebs and dust, she felt a surprising tug of nostalgia for the childhood she'd never thought she'd cared much about. Up until that afternoon, sitting at the lake with Berta, she'd never even thought of her childhood as a separate part of her life, or as a thing to leave behind.

She pulled the bike out onto the driveway. The wheels were flat, the rusty chain sagged, and the vinyl seat was yellow and sticky.

"I can't ride that," said Raylee. She stood with her hands on her hips.

"Sure you can. Once we get it fixed up it'll be good as new." Sherri wished Raylee could be *normal*. Life was easier for girls who could smile and giggle and get excited about something as simple as a bike. Raylee was more complicated. Sherri appreciated that the kid wanted to stuff the entire world in her brain by reading the encyclopedia, but where would that get her? "You need a bike. You'll never have friends around here if you can't get to where they are."

"I don't want friends. I just want to be with you, but you're never here."

"I have a job. I need to work, just like your mom and dad need to work. C'mon, we'll take it to the Mobil. They've got oil and air. And if you act stupid enough, those guys'll do anything for you. Just watch."

Sure enough, Pete Becker was working at his father's station. Pete was big and blond, and he'd played football. His dad owned a pontoon boat on Potter Lake—or "Potter's pee-hole," as everyone called it, because the lake was man-made and not as clear and fresh as Booth. All the popular kids took the boat out on nice summer days. Sherri used to have a crush on Pete until one afternoon, when they were juniors and were alone in the hallway, he told her she needed "a tickle" and started pawing her breasts right under her bra. She had to kick him to make him stop. She never said a word to Pete about it after the fact. She felt shame, but she figured that was the way guys behaved. Not until she'd started working at the resort, where a man could get thrown out for so much as tapping a Bunny on the shoulder, did she see how wrong he was to do what he'd done.

As soon as Pete saw Sherri approach, her hair still stiff and shiny and her face made up for her aborted shift at work, she saw him look at her with actual interest. She was no longer that awkward girl with the loud laugh who played the church organ. Now she was a *Bunny*. The women in town snickered at her behind her back, she knew—she'd assumed they were gossiping about her at Giles—but she could see by Pete's expression that her status with men was newly elevated.

"Smile sweet as you can," Sherri whispered to Raylee, who managed to look like she was frowning even when she tried to grin.

"Sherri Taylor, that you? What're you doing home?"

"I have a few days off. And the kid here wants to ride my old bike, but just look at it."

Raylee, wanting to please Sherri, smiled coyly.

Sherri bit her lip. "Do you happen to know where I could take this thing to get fixed?"

Pete peered over his shoulder to make sure his father was occupied. His dad, who looked just like an older, thicker version of Pete, had his arms buried deep in the guts of a pickup.

"Oh, I think I can help you with that. Let's give 'er a look."

Sherri winked at Raylee, who winked back.

Before long, he'd cleaned, greased, and reset the chain, patched and pumped the tires, and rubbed the chrome handlebars with a rag to make them shine. It was almost good as new. "What do I owe you?" Sherri asked.

"My treat. How about you let me take you to a movie?"

How much had changed! There was a time when this would have given her a thrill. Now Sherri wasn't interested in the likes of Pete, not after what he'd done, and not after spending a weekend with Mitch Spaulding, who wore a silky red Christian Dior smoking robe instead of an oil-stained work shirt with his name embroidered over the front pocket. Pete would work in this garage his whole life and die with grease under his nails. She looked around the shop disparagingly and frowned. "Sorry, my boyfriend in *Los Angeles* wouldn't like for me to go on a date with a *hick* mechanic." She felt like someone else was saying those words for her.

She pushed the bike out of the garage. "C'mon, Raylee." Sherri was giddy with her new strength. It wasn't just her job as a Bunny that had emboldened her; Arthur's flirtation made her feel beautiful, and Raylee stood by her side, admiring her and paying attention to her every move. Sherri liked to have an audience, someone to impress. "Let's get out of here."

As she was leaving, she heard Pete mutter under his breath, "Bimbo." The word snagged her confidence.

"Why don't you like Pete?" Raylee asked.

Sherri put her index finger in her mouth and pretended to gag.

"He felt me up. That's when a boy—never mind. I suppose you're too young."

Raylee tugged Sherri's arm. "Tell me!"

"I'll tell you when you're ready, don't you worry. There are all kinds of things I can tell you." There were little buds poking through the fabric of Raylee's shirt. Poor girl, Sherri thought. She didn't know what she was in for.

Raylee stopped and stared at the bike as if she were suspicious of it.

"Hey, it's nice now, right? And it's all yours. We can decorate it for the Memorial Day parade on Monday, stick playing cards in the wheels, wrap streamers around the handlebars, whatever you want." Memorial Day was a big deal in East Troy, marking the start of summer. There were parades, school bands marched and played patriotic songs, cheerleaders cheered, guest speakers orated from the stage, and Badger Boys and Girls, the top students from the district, had a chance to speak and show off while everyone ate hot dogs and bratwurst sold by vendors on the square. The day was capped with a grave count at area graveyards, where people somberly tallied the number of graves of fallen veterans.

"Your bike is mine for real?"

Sherri had a feeling that nobody had ever given the kid a gift. "What am I going to do with it? It's all yours." She reached into her pocket and gave Raylee a dollar. "Now go to Javell's and buy yourself some candy."

"Seriously?"

"Get lost," Sherri said. She liked being with Raylee, but another place was calling her: St. Peter's.

The church doors were unlocked, and Sherri was glad to find that all the pews were empty. Good. This was *her* space, and she was surprised how much she missed it. She was gripped by the familiar smell of old Bibles and candle wax. More than the apartment above the store, this place was where she truly felt at home.

St. Peter's was old, built by settlers in the mid-1800s. It wasn't the biggest or grandest church—her mother had often complained about its narrowness and lack of pillars. It had no frescoes, no dome. The pews were not original. It was neither traditional nor modern. But to Sherri it always seemed big and grand—sacred even. She wasn't a particularly religious person, because her mother had turned away from the church but not the music, and her father was agnostic at best. Playing the organ here was a deeply personal and even transcendent experience for her, a way of escaping herself and her life. That afternoon, escape was exactly what Sherri needed.

Her sandals slapped up each creaky wooden step of the curved staircase that led to the narrow balcony, a *clap, clap, clap* that echoed as loud as holy thunder. The console sat waiting for her like an old friend. It was common for an organ to face the pipes in the back of the congregation; still, it struck her as odd, as though the organist were somehow being punished, sitting with their back to the priest. She could only see the altar in a mirror that hung at a slant in front of the instrument.

She slid the wooden roll top up, which made another loud clatter. Mr. Richardson had taken over when—three, four years ago? He hadn't bothered to clean up, and the space was just as her mother had left it. Muriel loved candy, and her tin of Hoffman's cherry drops was still on the bookcase, along with a glass jar filled with circus peanuts. The top of the console was cluttered like a bedside table, with a pile of St. Gregory Hymnals and a yellowed German prayer card that had been handed out at Otto Heinrich's funeral a decade ago. It featured a kneeling St. Thomas praying to an angel. Sherri's mother and Otto used to play duets together, her mother on the piano, Otto on the violin. They exchanged books, they met for coffee, and, before her legs gave out, they went on long walks. Sherri's parents' marriage felt more like a business arrangement, as if they'd agreed to keep each other just a little less lonely. Her mother and Otto seemed more married than her parents ever had. Her mother had been despondent after Otto died. "He had the most wonderful vibrato," she'd said. "Such expression. He could live inside the music."

Sherri slipped off her sandals and sat down on the bench. She hadn't played in almost half a year, and for a moment she worried she might have forgotten how. She had an excellent ear, and she could memorize and play just about anything she heard, but no matter how hard she tried she wasn't any good at reading music, and she couldn't improvise like a jazz musician. Her playing was too passionate, and she lacked the patience to develop technique. She always knew that she'd never, ever play organ in the fine cathedrals in Europe that her mother had told her about—she'd probably never even *go* to Europe.

She began with some finger and foot scales, working her way to "Gentle Shepherd" and a few bars of Pachelbel's Canon, a song that moved her mother to tears, partly because of the music itself, and partly because that was the song that had been played at John F. Kennedy's funeral, and her mother had loved Kennedy so much that she hung commemorative plates with his image on her bedroom wall, although now Sherri would always think of Sam and that hotel in Houston when she thought of the late, beloved president.

Sherri played the canon because it was a way of connecting with her mother, although she found the song slow and laborious. She preferred romantic music that was big, fast, and exciting. Her mother and Mrs. Vogel were always saying, *Slow down, Sherri, slow down.*

She hadn't realized how battered her body had become until she started playing. Her feet, hips, arms, and fingers were sore, and her wrists ached from carrying heavy trays. Soon she forgot about work and allowed herself to get lost in what she thought of as the space between the notes and feel the music move through her. It was hot and stuffy in the balcony, and there was only one small window louvered out from the middle of the stained glass, propped open with a tattered hymnal. She was sweating.

Her mother had loved Baroque music. What made it special, she'd said, was that all voices were supposed to be equal. That was why, that day, Sherri chose to play Buxtehude, her mother's favorite. Bach was rumored to have walked twenty-five miles to Lübeck to hear him play the organ. Sherri had memorized the Prelude in G Minor, a piece she found exciting and energetic, with two fugues that gathered together the three melody lines and lots of funny little parts, so that's what she decided to play.

Soon the sanctuary was filled with sound. The organ made her feel powerful in a way that no other instrument could match. Her mother said that when she was a girl, she'd loved the organ because it was the only truly big thing a woman was allowed to be in charge of.

Sherri understood how incredible it felt to have an entire orchestra at her command. The organ could capture the full range of her always intense emotions, from abject grief to sheer bliss. She never understood people who said they didn't like organ music. Her favorite sound was the diapason, the only stop that wasn't supposed to sound like anything else; not the clarinet, not the cello—this was the true organ, as simple as pressurized air moving through pipes. But that afternoon, it wasn't enough. She wanted to hear the roar of trumpet, the booming bassoonlike fagotto, the wanky sound of the oboe. Sherri set up her preferred registration for the prelude—full organ plus mixtures on the great, full pedal plus Bombarde on the pedal. The prelude began with a fast improvisation passage on the great, then the pedal entered with a slow ostinato. Her mother would have taught her to register the fugues and little connecting pieces differently, lighter, but she wanted as much sound as possible. It was awful, she knew, all that noise—completely inappropriate for the piece—but it was also somehow lush and expressive. She could almost hear her mother say *Sound doesn't disintegrate!* Sherri didn't want it to, not ever. She had power in this space, and in this moment, even if it was only the power to create a cloud of noise. She played so loudly that she imagined her mother and father could hear it in heaven. Soon she'd somehow drifted from the wild ending of the Buxtehude to the chorus for the Rolling Stones' "Shine a Light."

As she approached the final notes, she pulled out the stop of the Zimbelstern, the little star with bells that rotated and chimed. In fancier churches, you could see the star twinkling as if it sat on the top of a Christmas tree; here it was hidden behind the wall that covered most of the pipes, and it made Sherri sad that it wasn't visible. She wished the organ at St. Peter's were as grand as the one at Holy Trinity Church in Milwaukee, where her mother had taken her for a few lessons. The pipes there were meant to look like the steeples, and were engraved with etchings. Once, at Mass there, she was transfixed when the organist turned on the Zimbelstern and it sounded to Sherri as if every clock in her father's store had chimed all at once; the entire congregation turned to look for it. The sound was more beautiful than life.

When she was finished, she felt a rush of joy, took a deep breath, and set her hands on her lap to compose herself. She sat like that for a long time in the warmth, the notes she played floating like dust motes in the air, sweat dripping down her back.

She canceled the stops, turned off the organ, pulled the cover back over it, and slipped back into her shoes. She was spent; physically, emotionally. She descended the curved staircase slowly, her mind clear for the first time in a while. And there he was, Arthur, sitting in the last pew.

"Oh! I didn't think anyone was here." Sherri was embarrassed. She'd unwittingly revealed a part of herself to him, and felt he knew her now in a deeply intimate way.

His smile, so awkward and genuine, twisted something inside of her that the music had made space for. She felt a powerful rush of feeling for him.

"You drowned out all my prayers," he said.

Although the church was lofty and grand, she felt the walls sealing them into the space as if it were large enough to accommodate only the two of them; it was almost suffocating. She led the way to the heavy wood door, pushed it open, and entered into the richness of a warm, humid early evening. Everything was coming to life. The air smelled of lilacs and freshly turned soil.

"What are you doing here?" she asked.

"I followed you." He seemed suddenly bashful, his face flushed, his hands stuffed deep into his pockets. Mayflies circled around in the lights of the church sign behind him that advertised the spaghetti dinner. Somewhere in the distance a trolley car clanged along the rails. "I wanted to see if you'd go on a date with me."

A "date"? The term sounded so old-fashioned to Sherri's ears, so sweet for someone as intense and brooding as Arthur.

"I was calling after you earlier but you didn't hear me. So I followed you into the church and had my own personal concert."

"I wish I'd known you were here," Sherri said. She'd played her most, but definitely not her best. He'd seen—or heard—her passion and her flaws.

"I'm glad you didn't know. It was nice. Brought me back. I went to grad school in England, and sometimes when I needed to think I'd sit in the pews in the cathedral and listen to the pipe organ."

"This organ is nothing like the organs in *England,* give me a break."

"It's not the organ that concerns me, but the player." He stood close to her, close enough that she could smell him. He didn't reek of cologne like the guys who came to the resort; he smelled fresh and woodsy, like pine needles. "There's something about you, Sherri. I felt it the minute I first saw you. I don't mean to be too forward, but you feel it too, right? Like there's a little snap of something between us?"

"I guess," Sherri said, blushing. He both confused her and made everything seem so simple.

She watched him read her response, consider it, and back off. He cleared his throat. "Will you show me around? It's such a nice night. I wish I'd spent my life here like you."

"This is just East Troy."

"There's nothing *just* about it."

Sherri was baffled. "What is it about this place that you like so much? It's so ordinary."

"Ordinary in the best way. I have this theory that we all have our own ecosystems. Some people are most comfortable in the desert, others the mountains, the ocean. But I've been all over the world, and I don't know why, I'm most comfortable here."

Sherri understood that East Troy was comfortable, but that was the problem—it was as comfortable as a warm bath. "I already can't wait to leave."

"There's really no such thing as leaving," Arthur said.

"What do you mean?"

"Wherever you go, there you are."

"Easy for you to say."

The streets shot off in all directions from the square. Sherri led him down Division. "See that pharmacy? My dad told me that back in the day, there was this crazy pharmacist who was obsessed with pyrotechnics. He hired a teenage girl to make firecrackers in the back room, and one day she blew up. A few days later, they found her hand stuck between the open sign and the store window. When my dad told the story, he'd say the accident left the pharmacist shorthanded."

"Ha!"

There were flags hanging on tilted poles in front of the Victorian houses in preparation for Memorial Day. "Actually, the girl's mom went to work for him after that. She was there for years. Mrs. Tiller."

"I guess the heart is truly a resilient muscle."

"This is the house that was built by a man with one arm," she said, pointing at a Victorian with a crooked porch. "My dad always said it *looked* like a house that was built by a man with one arm. And that's where Mrs. Cable lived." Mrs. Cable's house used to be charming, but during the energy crisis she replaced the big windows with little ones, and she'd covered up the gingerbread siding with thick strips of white aluminum. "She didn't like to do dishes, so she set them on her back stairs. They'd pile up until she finally cleaned them." They turned onto Main Street. "And this bungalow here? An old lady named Festa lived there with another woman and everyone knew they were, well, you know."

"Wow, even in East Troy."

"That could be our town motto. All the houses on this street used to be connected on the same party line, and whenever there was an emergency call, all the neighbors would try to get to the fire or accident before the ambulance and fire trucks. That's probably the most fun you could have here."

She showed him the jungle gym at her old school, and they swung in the swings where she and Roberta had done underdogs until one summer when they were eleven years old, and Sherri fell and dislocated her shoulder. Then they walked over to the baseball field and sat in the old bleachers, their shoulders and knees lightly touching. The scent of freshly turned fields, cut grass, and the distant lake hung in the humid air. Soon there would be June bugs and fireflies, bonfires, brats and corn sold under the tents.

"My dad loved it here," Sherri said.

"Tell me more about him."

"He kept Marathon candy bars for me in the back of his cash register. He'd give them to me as payment for replacing crowns and pushers on watches. The store was never very busy, and he liked being alone. It gave him an excuse to read to me all the time. He loved this Herman Hesse book called *The Glass Bead Game*. It's about a man with no purpose who spends all of his time playing with glass beads. I didn't really understand it. He said it was about the importance of math, music, and art. He told me those were subjects I was good at, but I was still reading Trixie Belden. He was so much smarter than everyone else I knew. I always felt like he had to explain everything to me, and even then, he was just skimming the surface."

"That doesn't mean you weren't smart. You were too young to understand Hesse." She noticed that he pronounced the author's name differently than she'd said it, a gentle way of correcting her. "I read *Steppenwolf* in college and hardly got it. You were, what, eight?"

"Nine, maybe ten."

"He might as well have read Nietzsche to you."

"He did, actually. I'm still trying to understand eternal recurrence."

Arthur reached for her hand. "I understand it perfectly. It means we get to spend this time together over and over, into eternity."

They walked down Graydon Avenue still clasping hands. "When he had his stroke I visited him in the hospital. He'd been there for a few hours already but nobody would be straight with me about his condition. I sat by his bedside and said don't go, don't go. I begged. He was so weak, but he squeezed my hand. I thought he was saying he wouldn't die, but later I realized he was saying goodbye. I never felt so alone."

She hadn't spoken about her father to anyone for years and couldn't believe she was confiding so much in someone she'd just met. Her mother had been of the opinion that bad things happened, that was just life, and you took it on the chin and moved on. She wasn't one to indulge Sherri's grief even though she must have been in pain herself. They'd comforted each other more through silence than words, and that had been OK, but that was also part of the reason Sherri had a hard time articulating her memories of him.

"I'm sorry you lost your dad." Arthur really did seem sorry. "As Ovid said, 'be patient and tough; someday this pain will be useful to you.'"

"I can't imagine pain ever being useful. Pain is just pain."

"I don't know. I think it changes with time. You were lucky. It sounds like your dad was really kind. That's not a word I'd use for my father. He only cares about money. He's one of those guys who raised himself up by his bootstraps. Part of the reason I went to school so far away was to escape him, first to Swarthmore in Pennsylvania for my undergrad, and I studied economics in Nottingham."

"*Swarthmore,*" Sherri giggled. "*Nottingham.* And here you are a stone's throw from *Mukwonago.*"

"What I really wanted to study was architecture. My dad said I didn't have a sense of design, and I don't know why I listened to him. Maybe he was right, but really, I think he wanted to steer me towards the only thing he understands: money. He gave me everything," Arthur continued. "He even gave me his name, Arthur St. John, *Jr.* And he gave me stuff I never asked for or wanted, but then he resents me for what I have. He wants me to be just like him, and you know what? I can't, it's not how I'm wired. He was on my back all the time, so I bought this house, and I decided to have a simple life."

"What about your mom?"

"She's really old-school, really fifties. She's constantly polishing the silverware. She just cares what people think of us."

"We were just the Taylors."

"Well, for what it's worth, Jerry told me that everyone in town admired you for taking such good care of your mother when she was sick."

"That's news to me." She didn't want to think about what people were saying about her now that she was a Bunny, and she didn't want to talk about her parents anymore. "So now you know everything you need to know about East Troy."

"This is the perfect place to grow up," Arthur said. "I want to raise my kids here so they can have the same childhood you had."

"You mean you want them to be ordinary?"

"You're anything but." He ran his fingertip along the slick peach surface of her nails and pressed the tip of her index finger into the flesh of his palm until it made a half-moon dent. Everything felt exactly right. He reached for her hair and gently twirled it around his finger. His eyes were warm and gentle. He leaned forward and pressed his lips against hers. They were nice lips, not pillowy and damp like Frank's, or rough like Sam's. His kiss was perfect. Mitch hadn't smelled like anything, but Arthur's breath smelled sweet. This felt like her first real kiss. But when the kiss deepened, she pulled away.

"What's wrong?"

"Nothing," she said. She didn't want to tell him that the inside of her mouth had exploded with painful canker sores from all the grapefruit she'd eaten on her diet. This yanked her back to the reason she was in East Troy in the first place; she was exiled. "Can't you see, Arthur?" she said. "You seem like a nice guy and all, but you're coming and I'm going. You know that, right?"

"Shhh." Arthur put his finger over her mouth. "Come to the lake with me," he said. "I want to show you my house."

Arthur drove a red Camaro, a car that reminded her of a giant tongue. He kept the interior sparkling clean. The shiny dials on the dashboard reminded Sherri of the watches in her father's shop; all the arrows spun wildly when he turned his key in the ignition. He drove fast, nailing the curves, accelerating at the exact right moment. Even though he was new in town, he knew that the best route to Jesuit Island was via Stringers Bridge Road. He drove like a townie.

Arthur's edges were too sharp for him to be traditionally handsome. She thought he looked best in profile, with his aristocratic nose, and the little knob at the anvil of his square jaw. His arms were thin and muscular and laced with prominent veins, not unlike the legs of the horses in the stables at the resort. She felt the electric thrill of his hand occasionally brushing her thigh when he reached for the stick shift and wondered, now that she had some men to compare him to, why it was that Arthur's touch could spark something in her while Mitch's was just . . . nice. But Mitch had that California-golden-boy look. And Mitch was so . . . *Mitch*. She tried to conjure him, but he seemed fuzzy with Arthur right there next to her.

The taste of their kiss still lingered. She ached for more and felt kittenish, holding back the desire to lean closer and nestle her head in the crook of his neck as if he were her real, old-fashioned boyfriend. He glanced sideways at her with an admiring look, never letting her forget that he was aware of her presence.

He turned off Highway J onto Island Drive, a road that ran like a spine across the wisp of land Sherri had never set foot on. They crossed over a little bridge and came to a gatehouse, where an attendant waved him through without even looking up from his book. "Who do you suppose they're worried about?" Sherri asked. "Nobody comes back here."

"It just makes people feel rich, that's all. Rich people love to be reminded of their wealth."

The land still seemed scarified and raw in the areas surrounding the new homes. Fortunately, there were still giant old oak trees and lots of brush on either side of the road to create a leafy archway to drive through, and the foliage grew thicker the farther he drove along the peninsula. The energy seemed to change and become more solemn in a way she couldn't explain, the way the energy in the church changed the minute she lifted the cover over the organ keyboard. It was dark, but the moon was bright and the water in the inlets he drove past appeared milky and radiant. She half expected to glimpse the ghosts of the Jesuit brothers walking through the woods in their medieval brown robes and leather sandals, meditating about poverty, obedience, and chastity.

Arthur approached a fork in the road. "Close your eyes," he said. She felt gravel under the wheels, and the car stopped. He came around and opened her door. "Are they still closed?"

"Yes, but I'll peek. I'm a peeker!"

He kissed her nose—nobody had ever done that before, kissed her like she was adorable. "Don't peek tonight. Just this one time. For me."

He stood behind her with his arms around her waist, propelling her forward. She giggled. The ground was unsteady under her sandals. "I'll fall."

"No, you won't. I won't let you."

She didn't really care about seeing the house. What she wanted was to lean back and press herself against him as if she'd done so a million times. She felt so pent up. She wanted to pull him to the ground, wrestle and laugh, run through the woods, go skinny-dipping, make love—she would have done anything with him that magic night.

They came to a stop. He shifted her shoulders to the right and kept his hands in place. His head was next to hers. She could smell his breath. "OK, open."

She did, and then she could see where they were, on a sloping bluff right at the end of the peninsula. Water was all around them. The Mill Pond portion of Lake Beulah was to her left and the main lake to the right, and the channel in front. She was acutely aware of the between-ness of seasons. The ice and the fishing shacks were gone, but the summer people weren't there yet. She felt as though she and Arthur were the only two people in the world.

He turned her around. There it was, the sleepy little cabin. It had been there for so long that it looked organic to the place, covered in ivy and shrouded by trees. The roof was pitched, with small windows poking out from under the eaves on the second floor. Hostas lined the stone path that curved toward the entrance. The home wasn't a bit like Danny's grandmother's house; it was small and quaint, with a sunporch made from rusty screens. It was as reassuring as an old blanket. Just beyond it, she saw a rowboat tied to one side of Arthur's pier, and a pontoon on the other side, a double-decker. "How do you like my martini boat?"

"Your what?"

"That's what we call them, you know, because they ride so smooth that your martini won't spill." The word *we* reminded Sherri that she and Arthur came from different worlds. "It was just delivered a few days ago. It reminded me of the double-decker buses in London. I figured I'd splurge because I'll own it for another twenty or thirty years. Someday my kids will jump off of it."

Sherri saw things differently. "That would be a great boat for a party!"

Arthur didn't seem as excited. "Maybe."

"What's the point of having a lake house if you don't invite people over?"

"The point is to retreat. I'm a regular Thoreau. 'I went to the woods because I wished to live deliberately' and all that."

"Well, I went to the Playboy resort for the same reason."

Arthur seemed pleased. "Here, let me show you inside. It's rough, but I'm making progress."

A fat yellow Lab with sensitive brown eyes sat on a circular rag rug in the living room, hardly acknowledging them when they entered. "That's Goldie."

"Why isn't she happy to see you?" Sherri asked. She could tell that something was wrong with the dog the same way she could tell that, despite Arthur's worldliness and accomplishment, there was something a little off about him, too. She only knew this because she recognized the same quality in herself. They both seemed alone in the world.

"Goldie has a slipping phobia. She doesn't want to step on the hardwood floors. She looks like she's drunk when she walks."

The dog's fat tail rose and slapped the ground. Arthur walked to where the poor dog sat on the area rug, rubbed her ears, and lifted her up to carry her outside. Sherri followed him. They leaned against his car, still warm from the engine, while Goldie sniffed around the bushes and the evening cooled around them.

"I've never heard of a dog with a phobia," she said.

"We've all got our problems," Arthur said.

"What's yours?"

He stood next to her, so close she could feel the heat radiating off his body. He kissed her again, gently, and put his hand on the curve of her hip. "I have a feeling that you are." His voice cracked. "You're my problem."

She laughed, flattered and awkward, but he was serious, and this made her uncomfortable. She'd always wanted passion and intensity, but now that it was actually available to her, she was scared to make herself vulnerable. Arthur had snuck up on her. He wasn't the guy she'd pictured herself falling for. It was easier with men like Frank, Sam, and Mitch, who didn't expect more from her than a good time. "Why am I your problem?"

"Because you don't see how rare this is."

He was right. She didn't. Sherri wanted to believe that the world was full of Arthurs, and that every sort of man was available to her for the choosing.

"I felt something the minute I saw you. A tug." He kicked his shoe in the dirt and waited for her to respond.

She felt the same way, but she was afraid to say so. He was older than she was, old enough to know when a relationship was special, old enough to buy a house on Lake Beulah, old enough to have traveled to the far corners of the globe. Sherri came from a world of church potlucks, hayrides, and bratwurst festivals, while his father sat on the Chicago Board of Trade—Sherri didn't even know what that meant exactly, but it sounded important. She was learning that there were different kinds of confidence. She'd mastered the kind it took to walk into a room wearing a skimpy costume, but this moment required her to have the confidence she didn't have—to make herself emotionally vulnerable, and to meet Arthur where he was. "How about you make us some drinks?"

Arthur seemed caught off guard by the change in subject. He paused. "Ever had a Snowball?"

"No, and I thought I'd heard of everything."

"It's a drink made with Warninks and lemonade. Snowballs got me through a few rough London winters."

She imagined him walking down a sidewalk in England and all the other places he'd inhabited. She didn't understand in that moment that his gait, his words, the sound of his voice, the way he looked at her when he clinked his glass against hers and said "to us"—everything that made Arthur unique was becoming indelibly etched in her mind.

She woke alone, startled by the mellow surroundings. Instead of staring up at cold ceiling tile and listening to the chatter of Bunnies waiting to take showers in the hallway, she heard birds and crickets. Old, yellowed curtains with pom-poms along the edges fluttered in the breeze. Knotted-pine beadboard covered the sloped ceiling. She looked around the room. A small, military-style sink was in the corner and Arthur's clothes, mostly plaid shirts, hung off a simple metal bar that ran along one side of the room and his shoes, scuffed and worn, sat in a neat row on the floor below. The room smelled musky, of sleep and pine and a hint of coffee. Where was Arthur? His side of the bed was neatly made, and she was still dressed in the clothes she'd worn the day before. Goldie had been slumbering against her legs but wiggled when she detected that Sherri had woken. She stood, her tail wagging like mad, and leaned down to wipe Sherri's face with her tongue.

Arthur entered the room carrying a cup of coffee, a glass of water, and a bottle of aspirin. "How do you feel?"

"Like I'm buried under an avalanche."

His hair was messy, and his unshaven face was dark and shadowed. His features appeared sharp and angular, and his eyes were intense. "I didn't mean to make your drink so strong. One minute you were telling me about watching full-length films about International Harvester at the cinema, and the next you were sound asleep."

"I don't even remember." She shouldn't have had so much to drink on an empty stomach. "I feel like I haven't slept in months."

He wore a soft old T-shirt, the kind men wear under dress shirts, and a pair of boxers. His legs were hairy and skinny but strong. "You know what time it is?" He pointed at the Westclox travel alarm on his bedside table, a clock her father could have sold to him. Maybe it had even come from his store.

"It's almost noon?" Her mother would have disapproved. *Idle hands do the devil's work,* she always said. "Where did you sleep?"

He pointed at the door beyond her. "I was on the sleeping porch."

She reached out and fingered the hem of his boxers. She could see his erection, straight and true. "Why didn't you join me?"

"Because our first time should be special. I want you to remember it forever." Arthur bent over to kiss her. "God, just look at you." He set the drinks down. Her shirt was scrunched up, and he set his hand on her bare torso. "Is this OK?"

"Yes," she said. She grinned, thinking she'd die if he didn't touch her.

"God, I can taste your smile," he said. He inched the shirt up further, gently lifting her bra over her breasts. He pressed his cheek against her stomach and groaned. His fingers gently circled her nipple. "Oh, Sherri." He traced a line up the center of her abdomen with the tip of his nose. "I wish you could see yourself. I stood here watching you for the longest time. I have this feeling that I longed for you before we even met. It's spooky. Do you feel that, too?"

She wasn't ready to admit to him that she did. She was still trying to sort out who he was and what he possibly saw in her. She felt she was so simple and inexperienced.

"You being here makes this place complete. It's like this house was waiting for you as much as I was."

She'd never felt more beautiful than she did in that moment, even though her thighs touched when she walked. Carmen had told Sherri that men don't notice the things women worry incessantly about; that women are really trying to impress other women. Judging by the expression on Arthur's face, this had to be true. She had a feeling he could see a kind of beauty in her that Gloria missed.

The other men she'd been with had worked quickly; sex was fast and efficient. Arthur was in no hurry, luxuriating over every inch of her flesh. He took off his shirt. His back was bare and knotted with small muscles. His hand worked its way under the elastic of her underpants. She was embarrassed. That part of her had always been private, but she felt an urgent need for him to get closer, closer, so close that she could become inhabited by him, so close she thought she could die from pleasure.

She was curious about his past and wondered how he'd learned his tricks, but whatever he was doing with his fingers made her stop thinking, stop wondering. She closed her eyes and gave in to this new form of communication. This was a language that existed only between them, a call and response. When at last they came together she reached for his hand and bit down gently on his finger. His back was slick with sweat. He moaned with pleasure and said her name in a way she'd never heard it. She allowed herself to make the smallest sound, a tiny gasp. Their lovemaking felt generous, like an exchange of thoughtful gifts. It was different and more meaningful than anything she'd read about in the magazine. After so many months of shielding herself from grief, their closeness led her to feel a dangerous pang of tenderness for him in the place where she protected her feelings—dangerous because she knew too well that love led to loss, and she'd already lost so much.

Arthur provided Sherri with a wonderful excuse to stay away from her empty apartment on the square. Whenever she talked about going home, he'd nuzzle her. "Don't," he'd say. "Stay." And she did.

"Don't you have to work?" she asked. His lifestyle confused her, and made him harder to put into any kind of social context. He was away from his family, away from any sort of office. That's how he seemed to her, away.

"You're my job this week," he said. "Can't beat the benefits."

The closest they got to real work was filling out paperwork for Arthur's broker so that he could purchase her stocks. Otherwise, they played house. The work that needed doing after so many years of neglect required elbow grease instead of special skills—Sherri had never minded hard physical labor. She preferred to be busy. The toilet bowl was filled with rust from the high mineral content in the water. Spiderwebs clung to every crevice and corner, and the walls above the beadboard needed to be painted. The house had been sold furnished, but the upholstered furniture was musty and dank. Sherri lifted the cushion on one of the camp chairs to take outside to dry out in the sun. It seemed heavy and suddenly it broke open. Sherri and Arthur laughed until they cried when dog food the mice had squirreled away spilled onto the floor. They hauled the chairs and old pillows and stained twin mattresses with springs sticking out of them to the dump. Fortunately, the caretaker had left some antique furniture worth keeping. Sherri polished the charming bookcases with their leaded glass windows and the matching prairie-style rocking chairs with black leather seats that sat sentinel by the fieldstone fireplace. The stained oak dining table with claw feet gleamed like new with a few coats of Pledge. She carried the rugs out to the laundry line and slapped them with a broom while Arthur pruned the bushes and pried off the thick slatted shades that hung over the windows. The dim house filled with the gentle, dappled light that streamed through the surrounding trees, which had only recently burst into bloom. "You don't even need shades here," she said. "Who's going to see?"

Arthur reached for Sherri and pulled her down to the floor in front of the fireplace. "It's just us, and it's perfect."

"Just us" was OK for Arthur, but Sherri had other ideas. "We made your place so cute, and the lake is so nice. Please can you have a party?"

"Oh Sher," he said. "I don't even know anyone here aside from you and Jerry. A party is a lot of work."

"I'll do everything. And I know people. I can order the keg, and string up little lights. Please?" The cottage was so cute, so woodsy. She loved the idea of having her friends there. She imagined them sitting in the chairs, drinking beer on the sunporch, standing just beyond the windows on the bluff overlooking the lake. She could hear the hum of conversation and the distant splashing of swimmers jumping off the pier. "Please?" She could almost feel how he softened to her entreaty. "Think of it as a housewarming."

"The house is already warm."

She straddled him, took off her shirt, and smiled. She could see what it did to him. She enjoyed this newfound power. "Please?"

They couldn't keep their hands off each other, and they couldn't stop talking. They chatted while they worked, and on long walks through Beulah Bog, and in the middle of the night when they'd take the row-boat out to the middle of the lake with some beers, a candle, and a sleeping bag and look up at the stars. Sherri lay with her head against Arthur's chest, listening to the reassuring thump of his heartbeat.

"The old chapel used to be somewhere over there," she said, pointing at a fancy new Mediterranean-style home on the island. "People around the lake would take their boats for Sunday services there in the summer, but we never did, because my mom was busy at St. Peter's."

"You remember it?"

"Mostly I remember when they burned down the monastery. Something you'll learn soon enough is that watching controlled burns is the height of entertainment here. That's how they train the volunteer firefighters. When they torched the old hotel and the building where the brothers lived it was ten times better than fireworks." She felt sad that the retreat center was gone. In its way, it must have been like a more holy and meditative version of the Playboy resort, and it must have meant a lot to the people who'd been there.

"My mom told me that the monastery had a flat-bottomed steamship," Sherri continued, "and the brothers would sing church songs so loud that their voices would echo off the water in order to make friends with the farmers, who were Protestant and didn't approve of Jesuits. I feel like I can still hear them, do you?"

"I do," he said. The sound of water rippled against the metal hull of the rowboat. "Lakes are so mysterious."

"It's like they can remember," Sherri said.

He kissed her on the top of her head. "Exactly."

"Arthur, why aren't you married?"

"I was engaged once, to a woman named Victoria, but she fell in love with her professor. It was horrible. I was so heartbroken that I bummed around Europe for a year and tried to find myself. I worked in an olive orchard in Spain, hiked the Basque country, slept in a tent on the beach. I read a lot of poetry, too. That's what you do when your heart breaks. I'll bet your dad had it bad for someone and never really got past it."

"Did you? Did you get past it?"

"Yes. Entirely." Arthur pushed Sherri's hair away from her face and gave her a kiss that felt like the period at the end of a sentence.

Arthur's hair was messy from sleep, and she could still see a crease from his pillow on his face. It was nice of him to wake up so early to drive her to Lake Geneva. He stood by the front door holding a plaid thermos filled with coffee. "Do you really have to go back?"

"It's my job," she said.

"Stay. I want to be your job."

"It's not like you'll never see me again."

The resort had a very small gym downstairs with a few treadmills, a vibrating belt to put around your waist, a tanning lamp, and a sauna. Mondays the gym was closed, but Danny had a key and had told Sherri that he'd sneak down and open it for her at seven so that she could sit in the sauna and sweat off any extra ounces before the morning weigh-in. Sherri wanted to become as dehydrated as a piece of old fruit. She would miss Arthur, but she couldn't wait to get back to work, and back to her own life.

The closer they got to the resort, the more the lightness she'd experienced at Arthur's disappeared, like a chord change from major to minor. Her empty stomach felt like it was twisting into knots. Her eye began to twitch, and she jiggled her leg.

"Nervous about weigh-in?" Arthur asked, sensing her tension. Normally she loved that he was closely tuned in to her, but that morning her anxiety sealed her into herself. She didn't want to have to explain it. As usual, everything was so new to her that she couldn't articulate how she felt, even if she wanted to.

"I keep thinking about that evil scale."

"They shouldn't weigh you. You look great. You'd look great even if you gained ten pounds. A hundred! More for me to—" He smiled and blushed. The word "love" hung in the air unsaid, exciting and potent—too exciting, too potent. At any other time in her life her stomach would have flipped. Now it churned.

He set his hand on her leg. She admired his fingers, how they were thick and strong, his wrists bony. But suddenly the warmth and pressure of his hand made her feel as though he were holding her down, keeping her in place. She felt carsick and had to look out the passenger window. Ordinarily, she'd appreciate the simple beauty of the fields of soybean and corn and the bur oaks that looked as lonely as scarecrows. The light was golden and new. But the beauty wasn't simple anymore. Nothing was. If she'd never left East Troy and had continued living her old life, she would be able to show off Arthur like a prize she'd won at the fair. They could cheer on Raylee at the parade and attend the grave count like a real couple. She could imagine herself in Arthur's life the way he was imagining it, but she had a harder time imagining how Arthur could fit into hers.

"I used to have this soccer coach named Jeremy," Arthur said. "He would have loved the resort. He was from South Africa and fancied himself a real ladies' man. He wore an ascot and white driving loafers. When I broke my ankle, he came to my house and gave me a collection of Somerset Maugham stories to keep me occupied while I recovered. He made a point of telling me to read the one about the tennis player who had an affair. He thought it was a good coming-of-age story." He laughed to himself. "I was only fourteen years old."

She'd spent a week with Arthur and talked with him about things she didn't talk about with her closest friends at the resort, and still she hardly knew him. He came from a different world—a world of Somerset Maugham, tennis, and soccer coaches from South Africa. He'd eaten blood sausage at a country café in Spain, and he'd drunk Turkish coffee out of tiny cups in Greece. She grew up with 4-H, frozen custard, and the Top Forty countdown. Dinner was often corned beef hash out of a can.

Their differences seemed more apparent with every inch of pavement on Highway G that led her closer to the resort. He had the resources to travel and explore the world, and the confidence to do so alone. He'd traveled so much that he'd grown weary of it, while she'd moved just twenty minutes from home—even spending time on Lake Beulah, that much farther from the nucleus of the square and everything she'd always known, gave her a different perspective on her town. She felt like she could talk to him about almost anything, yet she didn't know how to give voice to these feelings. She was hesitant to point out inadequacies he hadn't yet observed.

He turned up the long drive to the resort and shifted into a lower gear. "I feel like I'm dropping you off at college," he said. "Like I should tell you to study hard and be good."

The word "college" hit an already raw nerve. "You wish you were, don't you?"

"I wish I were what?"

"Dropping me off at college."

"I don't think that would be a bad choice for you. Hey, what's wrong?"

"Oh, gosh, I don't know." She wished she could light a cigarette. She hadn't had one all week. Smoking in front of Arthur felt like smoking in front of a grandpa. "I'm sorry. I'm fine."

"You're perfect." He pulled into the resort property and began to crest the hill. "Jeremy. God, I haven't thought about that guy in years. He also gave me a tube of Toblerone chocolates. Have you ever had them?"

"Arthur," she said, frustrated. "I can't ever eat chocolate again."

"You could quit. I'll buy you all the chocolates you want."

"Don't you get it?" Suddenly the air in the car felt tense. "I don't want to quit. I like my job. I love it, actually. I had to train for it. I have friends here. You make it sound like quitting is easy. But say I quit, then what? College is expensive. And everyone I know who went to college started almost two years ago."

"That doesn't mean your ship has sailed. College is still there. You can still go. I could help you apply." The resort came into view and she saw it through Arthur's eyes as silly, a diversion. She felt like picking a fight, rebelling. She'd never before had the luxury of rebelling against anything or anyone. What had gotten into her? "You have a problem with it, don't you?"

"With what?"

"With my job. With me being a Bunny. You've had everything handed to you. You said so yourself. I don't think you get to say what I should or shouldn't do."

Instead of answering right away he was quiet, thoughtful. "When I told you about stock options, you know, puts and calls, you picked it up right away. You calculated in your head my net return after taxes when I sold my gold. Not many people can do that."

"So?"

"I'm not telling you what you should do. I'm just pointing out that you have other gifts that have nothing to do with how much you weigh. You could study finance or accounting. I've heard you play the organ. You hum all the time, you don't even know that, do you? There's always a tune in your head. You could study music, write compositions. It's not just me who thinks so. Remember the glass beads you told me about? Your dad, he thought so, too."

How manipulative, she thought, for him to invoke her father. "You don't get it. I love my job."

"That's great. Not many people can say that. But I've never seen a thirty-year-old Playboy Bunny is all. Sherri, don't you see? I'm not judging you."

His words rang hollow. Everyone judged her: Arthur, the people back home, the other Bunnies, Gloria, all the guests. She wanted her relationship with Arthur to be as simple as it seemed at his cottage.

"You shouldn't be offended if I recognize your potential. All I'm saying is that you might want to consider using this time in your life to become something rather than *be* something."

"You don't get it." She felt like crying. "Just being something, being anything, it's hard for me."

He parked the car and ran the knuckle of his index finger down her cheek. "I know."

The doormen in their caps and black suits stood like palace guards in front of the entrance. "I've got to go."

"Sherri, you can't be mad at me for telling you that you're smart and special." He leaned across his seat for a kiss, and she responded by kissing him back like a brother. "Come on, we had a great time this past week. Remember?"

She nodded. Just returning to work and Gloria was anxiety-producing enough, and now she was wrestling with all the ways that Arthur made her question her decisions and her future.

He pulled her into his arms. "I'm going to go insane with desire for you. Like a horse rearing up with blinders on."

Sherri blushed, embarrassed. She wasn't used to talking about sex out loud.

He gently turned her head so that she had to look at him. "It's not just me with these feelings, right? It's so good between us, so easy. Like how it's supposed to be. You feel it too, right?"

"Sure," she said. "I do." This was true. What she didn't say was that those feelings were problems in and of themselves. She reached for her bag.

"When's your next night off? I'll pick you up after work. I'll rub your feet . . . and everything else."

"I don't know if I'll even have a job."

He sank back into his chair and sighed. "You want to have a party? Would that make you happy?"

Sherri brightened. The word "party" chased away the word "college." "I'd love that, Arthur. I really would."

"So, let's have a party."

"How about Sunday night? That's when we're slow. People will have off."

"Sure," he said. "Invite a few friends over." He reached his arm across the back of her seat and fingered the baby hairs at the nape of her neck. "Don't forget about me, Sher. Don't forget about *us*."

She kissed him—his kisses were so nice. Too nice. If she weren't so anxious, she could have kissed him for hours. She said goodbye, stepped out of the car, and watched him drive away.

Later, and for the rest of her life, she'd wonder what would have happened if she hadn't gained those extra pounds that caused her to return home and meet Arthur. It would amaze her that something as trivial as her weight was the first domino to fall in a long line of dominoes that stretched all the way to Lake Beulah and deep, deep into her future.

CHAPTER TEN

Sherri leaned against the wall clutching her towel to her chest, afraid she might faint after sitting in the hot sauna for almost half an hour. She watched Danny spin his muscular legs on the exercise bike. The huge front wheel was like a room fan, blowing the announcements on the bulletin board loose. The breeze felt good.

"Did you hear about Bunny Rhonda?" he asked.

"No," Sherri said. "What about her?"

"Preggers."

"What?"

"She got herself knocked up."

"Little Rhonda?" She wanted to clean out her ears. "She's pregnant? I didn't think she even had a boyfriend."

Danny smiled. He loved being surrounded by women, and he took delight in gossip. "Frank."

"*Busboy* Frank?"

He nodded.

She was still in disbelief. "Frank the *stripper*?"

"I told you he liked to break you girls in."

"But Rhonda?" Now Sherri really did think she could faint. Frank could have gotten *her* pregnant. How easy it would be to be in Rhonda's shoes, just a shuffle of the deck of fortune. Now she understood why Rhonda seemed to have turned on Sherri after she'd been so public about sleeping with Frank.

"She's working the coat check now. Her parents won't let her come home."

"What's she going to do?"

"She made Frank propose to her. You should see him, he's sadder than a pound dog."

"Maybe they'll be happy," Sherri said.

"Frank and Rhonda? They go together like a giraffe and a hedgehog. I wish them the best and all that, but I don't see it."

"I guess I don't either," Sherri said. Poor Rhonda. She'd been training to be a legal secretary, but what she'd really wanted was to go to law school—there were plenty of Bunnies who settled for the next best thing, but even the next best was something. Now she was stuck having a kid with a guy who slept with Bunnies as a rite of passage, and strutted around a strip club in a wig, makeup, and studded dog collar. If she'd been terrified of becoming a Bunny, imagine what she was thinking about becoming a mother.

"Speaking of couples," Danny said, "Val keeps saying she's going to break up with Curtis. Think she ever will?"

"She should. That guy is such a creep. He's not even nice to her."

"I know, and look at me. I'd lick the bottom of her feet. You know, I'm starting to wonder if that's the problem. Maybe I'm too nice." Danny's sentiment touched a raw nerve in Sherri. Arthur was so sexy and so accessible, so why was it that Mitch still hovered on the edge of her thoughts, a delicious and enticing mystery?

"Val cares about you, Danny. She does."

"I don't want her to just 'care' about me. I've already got sisters, you know?"

"How about you and Val come to my party Sunday." She'd never thrown a party before; it felt good to say those words. "I know of a place on Beulah." A place: how detached that sounded, when she could have said that it was her boyfriend's cottage. Was Arthur her boyfriend?

"Yeah, sure. I'm actually off at four that day."

"Can you help me spread the word?" She wanted all the same people who went to his parties to come to hers. If anyone could get people there, it was Danny.

"Yeah, sure," Danny said. "As long as Val comes. I want her all to myself."

"Deal. I'll ask her." Her stomach tightened. "I'd better go weigh in. I hope I can keep my job."

"Don't worry. You're light as a feather," he said.

She didn't feel light, and what did Danny know, anyway? He'd never had to step on a scale in order to work. "And if I'm still fat, then what?"

Danny hopped off the bike, reached deep into his pocket for a bottle and shook some little white pills into her hand. "These'll help."

"Diet pills?" All the girls were on Dexatrim; it was basically speed. She'd seen other girls take it but she swore she'd never try the stuff herself, not after watching her mother's bad reactions to all the medications she'd taken—pills that made her vomit, made her sleep for days, tore up her gut. She remembered the medicine cabinet filled with all those amber-colored bottles she detested, and the mornings she'd spent pinching them into piles. To Sherri, pills meant disease and problems that weren't easy to fix. But these pills were small and harmless-looking. And Danny was a good guy—he wouldn't let her have them if he thought they'd hurt her. There had been an unspoken closeness between Sherri and Danny since she'd found out about his relationship with Val. Sherri was the keeper of their secret. He trusted her, and so she trusted him.

Any other day and she would have politely declined. It was too early to pop pills, not even eight o'clock in the morning! But the day had already been a doozy. Reckless and desperate to pass muster and keep her job, she washed the pills down with just a small sip of water, wishing she could drink the whole glass without fear of the ounces the liquid would add to her weight.

"Whoa, just one of those black caddies'll do ya," he said.

"I'll be fine."

The changing room was a hive of activity, the air thick with hair spray. There were lots of new Bunnies Sherri had never seen before, college girls who'd been hired for summer. College, college. She could hear Gloria say, *You don't strike me as a college girl.*

The week away had stripped her of the confidence she'd once felt. She was jealous and threatened. Why did she put herself through this? She could leave, she could. One phone call and Arthur would collect her in a heartbeat, but then what? She'd be stuck in East Troy forever, her future as closed and certain as Rhonda's.

She could feel eyes on her. Everyone knew she'd been sent home on demerit, even the newbies. She looked at the floor to avoid their gazes and solemnly changed into her uniform, wondering as she yanked her tights over her hips and applied her fake eyelashes if this would be the last time she'd ever shimmy into her costume or stuff her bra with someone else's old nylons, the last time she'd stand on a scale or finish a day's work with blisters on her feet and wads of cash in her hands.

It seemed she'd missed so much during her week away. She overheard someone talk about an INS raid the previous week, when the Mexicans who worked in the kitchen had to hide in the tunnel that led to the employee parking lot. One of the new girls, a gorgeous wispy redhead with freckles, asked another new girl if she'd seen Steve Martin sitting by the pool the day before. "He talked to me! He's so nice. And cuter than he is on television and the movies. But pale as a dead fish." Sherri had missed Steve Martin?

"Welcome back," Val said. "I wore all your clothes while you were gone." She winked.

"Who's that?" Sherri whispered.

"Oh, she goes to DePaul. They call her Boo because all through training she didn't say boo."

Sherri stood in front of the mirror and tried to zip herself up. "Let me help," Bunny Tina said. Sherri had been so distracted that she didn't notice that her first Bunny friend was standing next to her, as golden and glorious as ever. Sherri turned and lifted her hair up so that Tina could nudge up the zipper, which wasn't as hard to do this time. She was certain she'd lost weight, but the outfits never felt like they fit well. Tina said, "I don't know what you did while you were away, but you look great. You got some color in your cheeks. I have a feeling you're going to have a good day."

"I hope you're right."

Tina whispered, "No matter what happens with that bitch, you'll be fine."

Sherri sucked in her gut. "Here goes nothing." She bit her lip and walked to the corner of the room where Gloria stood. "Hello, Bunny Mother," she said, her voice dripping with sweetness. She stepped on the scale, holding her breath as she waited for the swinging lever to come to a stop. Gloria pulled her pencil out from behind her ear and banged it against the metal bar, impatient. She frowned, disappointed. "Four pounds."

Sherri's heart raced and her eyes filled with hot tears. She couldn't even remember when she'd last eaten. How was that possible? The girls were starting to whisper, which made Sherri mad. "I gained four pounds?"

"No." Gloria spoke as if Sherri were an idiot. "You're down four."

What a relief! Sherri exhaled hard. She usually tried to stay calm around Gloria, but she couldn't help it: the pills Danny gave her were starting to kick in, and she suddenly felt as though even the blood coursing through her veins sparkled, fizzed, and popped.

"Hallelujah!" she said, and all the girls in the fitting room, even the new ones she didn't know, began to clap. *Go Sherri!* they said. She turned and waved at them as if she'd won the Alice in Dairyland beauty pageant. But Gloria's expression was still grim. Why couldn't she be pleased for her? Instead, she looked like she'd just heard that a close relative had passed away.

"I lost weight, just like you asked," Sherri said, angry. "What's wrong?"

Gloria propped her little glasses back up her skinny nose. "Let me ask you something," she said, her voice low enough that the other girls wouldn't hear her. "Do you have a plan?"

"A plan? What do you mean?"

"For yourself. Your future."

Maybe if, at that very moment, her brain hadn't started to light up like the neon A&W sign at sundown, the Bunny Mother's words might have sunk in. Instead, they bounced around the room like a rubber ball. "I just want to work. That's my plan."

"You can't do this forever, you know. You might want to start thinking about what's next."

"I thought you wanted someone who could work here for a long time." Sherri felt her face and chest flush red. She wanted to explode. "Gloria," she said, "are you firing me?"

Gloria paused. "No." She held her clipboard close to her chest. "Although I'm not doing you any favors by keeping you on. There's more to life than this place. Most of the girls already know this. You, I'm afraid, do not."

Sherri stepped off the scale and gave Gloria a fake smile. Gloria knew it was fake—Gloria knew everything! "Thanks for the pep talk."

Gloria began to inspect Sherri's nails. "I've got all these new girls here," she said, "so I'm sure you'll be pleased to learn that I've moved you to the Cabaret."

The *Cabaret*? In what other job could she be forced to take a week off and return to news of a fabulous promotion? The Cabaret was where famous comedians and musicians performed. She was leap-frogging some of the other girls, who'd worked the Sidewalk Café

longer than she had, and this would ruffle some feathers. But who
cared? She let out a squeal and smiled for Gloria, knowing better than
to try for a hug again. "Oh, thank you! That's, I mean, that's just ter-
rific!"

Gloria didn't smile back. "You'll shadow Bunny Tina. Listen to
every word that comes out of her mouth."

Three hours into her first shift, Sherri felt like she could serve every
single guest that ever walked through the front door of the resort, run
to Chicago in her heels, climb a mountain, fly an airplane, jump out
of it, and make a perfect landing on earth. She felt great, and clear!
She dutifully weaved behind Tina as she explained how they set up the
tables in the club. She couldn't wait for her second shift, when the place
would fill up with guests, the lights would go down, and the performers
would take the stage. Unlike the Sidewalk Café, the tables here were
huge, seating ten people, and were covered in beautiful white linen
cloths. The porcelain plates with the bunny logos gleamed as white as
Tina's teeth, and the napkins weren't rolled but folded into the shape
of swans. There were two forks instead of one, a spoon above the plate,
and beautiful goblets for water. The menu featured French dishes
Sherri had never heard of. "I love it here," Sherri said. "It's so classy."

Tina smiled. "I can tell you're on something. Be careful with that
stuff. When you come down, you really come down. And when you're
up, like you are now, you have to watch yourself. Be mindful of your
voice, you've practically been screaming. And focus, OK? Are you
with me? Here, you're going to need to say these words with a French
accent." Tina pointed at the menu, divided into Les Entrées, Les
Grillades, Les Desserts, and Les Cafés. The meals cost around eight
dollars, more than twice the price of the meals in the Sidewalk Café.
"The chef is from Paris. Read this."

"*Lays Grill-aids,*" Sherri said.

"No, *Ley Grillahds.* And this—" She pointed at the smaller print.

"*Pra-vyance* sauce."

Tina laughed. "You sound like you're pinching your nose. *Prah-vance.*"

"Nobody around here even knows how to speak French."

"Some of them do. And the ones who don't, well, don't try to correct them when they butcher the language the way you just did. Just smile and write their order down."

Arthur spoke French. He was the only person she knew who'd actually been there. He told her about country houses made of stone, fields of lavender, and grapevines that were hundreds of years old and worth thousands of dollars—just the vines! He'd called Sherri "*ma chérie*" instead of "Sherri" and told her it meant "my darling." He whispered to her in French when they were intimate. It was sexy to hear him speak that strange, liquid-sounding language.

"Tina, why did Gloria move me up here to the Cabaret?" Sherri asked.

Tina's expression grew dark, serious. She looked intently at the napkin she was folding while she spoke. "Because she needs someone to replace me."

"*Replace* you? What are you talking about?"

Tina nodded, her chin quivering. "I gave my notice."

"No!"

"People quit jobs all the time. It's not a big deal."

"But you can't leave. You're the reason I'm a Bunny. You love it here."

"I do!" Tina gave up folding the napkin and instead expertly tucked it under her bottom eyelashes to catch her tear. "I really do. You and the other Bunnies, you're like my family. I'm having the very best time."

"So why are you leaving?"

"It's my grandfather."

"He's sick?"

"Sick in the head is what he is! He's horrible, one of those holy rollers. My brother told him that I'm working here, and now the old man thinks I'm a prostitute. He doesn't listen to a word I say about all the security guards and the rules. I told him that this is a *family* resort, and it is, you know that. We play tiddlywinks with kids in the game room for crying out loud. I've even seen nuns have lunch here! He doesn't listen. He says I'll burn in hell."

"Let him think what he wants. So what?"

"So what? He says he'll cut me out of his will unless I quit. He means it, he really does."

"So let him cut you out!" The speed made everything seem simple. Sherri didn't have patience for problems. Much as she loved Tina, she was having a hard time sitting still and listening to what she had to say.

"You don't understand. He's loaded, Sherri. Ever heard of Schnitz Sausage?"

"The bratwurst? Who hasn't?" Everyone in the state ate Schnitz. They'd partnered with Schlitz beer and made a commercial about soaking the brats in lager. The ad campaign included a tongue twister that got harder to say the more people drank: *A Schnitz soaked in Schlitz is a scrumptious Schlitz Schnitz.* Nobody could eat a Schnitz without trying to say that ten times fast.

Tina's hands were shaking. "My brother would be happy to have it all: the house in Racine, a cottage on Green Lake, the condo in Sarasota." Tina gazed out beyond the massive glass windows that overlooked golf course. The golf balls were flying, and Nick, one of the caddies, stood with a pair of golf bags over his shoulders chatting amicably with an old guy in a yellow shirt and Bermuda shorts. "I figure I'll have to leave sooner or later. I'm already twenty-three. That's like fifty in Bunny years." Tina grabbed a handful of forks and efficiently set them down next to the plates. "Look for water spots. Always wipe the silverware down. When I gave my two weeks, I insisted that you were the best Bunny to take over. I've always liked you. You work hard, and you've got such an amazing memory, everyone talks about how you could work as a spy. You'll need a good memory to work here. You don't have much time to get all the drinks before the show begins. You need to order them with the bartenders in just the right order, *bam bam bam*. It's really hard, Sher. The money is good, and the shows are great, but you have to hustle."

"But what'll you do once you leave?" Sherri asked.

Tina shrugged. "I've always figured I should either break up with my boyfriend back home or get married, so I guess we'll get married."

Sherri couldn't stand to see someone as gorgeous and bright as Tina settling on her future, especially after hearing about Rhonda. Weren't they all too young to become mothers and wives? Sherri was getting her first terrifying inkling that her youth might not last forever.

She could have encouraged Tina to reject her grandfather's threat and take her chances on living her own life, but what did Sherri know about being an heiress to a sausage fortune? This only confirmed to Sherri that Tina was from another world. Besides, she couldn't stand to dwell on problems and just *talk*. She didn't want Tina to leave, but she was thrilled to take over her job. "I'm having a lake party Sunday night," Sherri said. If she were still in high school, this would be the equivalent of inviting the prom queen to a party. "Can you come?"

"You're sweet, Sher. Sure, I'll try to make it. It'll be my swan song."

Her first few nights at the Cabaret, the work proved to be ten times harder than at the Sidewalk Café, but she was making twice as much in tips, and she was meeting interesting people—a radio DJ, Jack Nicklaus's caddy, Cher's personal stylist. The pills helped her get through.

She was so swept up in her triumphant return to work that she'd forgotten she'd made plans with Arthur to return to his cottage for a night when she finished her early shift. She could feel the energy in the Cabaret change when she looked up and saw him leaning against the doorway. He smiled and waved. Something caught in her chest at the sight of him, a feeling of snapping into place. She dropped her tray—never before had she done that. When she leaned down to pick up the broken glass, an older lady said, "Is that your boyfriend?" She nudged her husband. "Honey, remember when we were like that?"

"We still are, aren't we?"

"Ha! There's nothing like that feeling of young love. Just look at the way he looks at her."

Sherri felt exposed. Bunnies threaded their way between the tables. Frank Sinatra piped through the speakers. Then she looked in Arthur's direction again. Everything else fell away. She'd only known him for a week, but it had been an intense seven days, and now she couldn't shake the feeling that he'd been standing there her whole life, off to the side, waiting for her.

Shit, she thought, a piece of broken glass in her hand, thinking about what the older couple had said. *I'm in love with that guy.*

CHAPTER ELEVEN

Sherri didn't recognize how much she'd missed Arthur until they were together in the enclosed space of his car, and she was still a little high. Judging by the bulge in his jeans, he missed her, too. Before, they'd been feeling each other out, getting to know each other. She'd been more guarded. Now, because of their brief time apart, she practically climbed into his seat while he drove. What could be sexier than watching him shift gears?

She tried to kiss him while he kept his eyes on the road, one hand rubbing her shoulder under the collar. As soon as he pulled into his driveway and parked, they were out of the car, grabbing on to each other, animalistic. They couldn't even make it to the house. Arthur leaned Sherri against the potting shed and tore her shorts down. His tongue darted more aggressively in her mouth. She slipped her hands under his shirt and felt the soft warmth of his back, pulling him closer, closer—she couldn't get close enough.

There, under the canopy of trees, she allowed herself to stop worrying whether she looked OK to him, or whether she was doing what she was supposed to do. She closed her eyes and abandoned her thoughts, not escaping the moment but living inside of it the way she did sometimes when she'd get lost playing music she knew by heart. In that moment, she and Arthur were the only two people in the world, and nothing was more urgent than the desire she felt.

And then something happened. Her back arched, and her toes curled. She felt a blossoming, an explosion, a crescendo, a physical quake of warmth and pleasure unlike anything she'd experienced— what a revelation that her body could feel that way. She didn't have to make the sex face, she became it. She'd had sex before, yes, and she'd enjoyed it, but now she understood in a new way what drove people to the resort, and what made them read the magazine. Everyone was chasing the experience she'd just had, that feeling that seemed too big for her body. She began to cry—not because she was sad, but because it was too much.

"Hey, what's wrong? Are you OK?"

"Yes," Sherri said. She'd never felt anything better, and yet . . . She pulled away from him. "No!"

"Did I hurt you? Tell me I didn't hurt you." He stroked her hair. "What happened?"

She didn't say anything.

"Let's sit down." He threw his shirt on the ground for Sherri to sit on and wrapped her in his arms. "Talk to me."

She was still sweating and stunned. "Why'd you do that?" she asked.

"Do what? What did I do?"

She shook her head, frustrated. She knew the word for what had happened to her, but it had been off-limits for so long that she was too embarrassed to say it out loud—even in this most intimate of moments, and even to Arthur. "You made me feel something. In my body. Something *big*."

He stroked her cheek, genuinely touched. "Sherri, that was your first orgasm, wasn't it?"

She nodded, speechless and spent.

"What you felt, it's natural. It's beautiful. It's what happens."

But it didn't happen with Frank. It didn't happen with Sam. It didn't even happen with Mitch. "It scared me." She was afraid to look at him, because she knew instinctively that meeting his gaze in that tender moment would forge an even greater connection between them. "*You* scare me."

"Oh Sherri, did it ever occur to you that you scare me, too?" He lifted her chin and forced her to look into his soft brown eyes, and that's when she felt that some part of her she could never get back was his now. It would remain captured forever in his gaze.

Val was right. He owned her.

The weather was warm and humid the day of the party, a perfect early-summer afternoon. Sherri hadn't seen Arthur since that revelatory night they'd spent together earlier that week. This time, when he picked her up from the resort, she was tense and quiet, too nervous for affection. She was worried that her new friends would be able to see her—really see who she was—in her hometown. A party was a test, one that would reveal who really liked her. What if nobody showed up? Or what if they did, and they were bored?

Arthur told her not to worry. He put out plastic tablecloths and bowls of chips while he tapped the keg. What would her friends think of him? He wasn't like anyone she knew from the resort. He wasn't gregarious or wild. He was more like her father, preferring deep, involved conversations over small talk. She watched him work and saw him for the first time through her friends' eyes.

That was also how she saw Roberta, their first guest. Sherri had invited her because she really wanted her there, but also because she was afraid nobody else would come, and if they did, she wanted to show off her new life. Roberta walked through the door wearing a green sundress that showed off her freckles and ivory skin—Sherri hadn't seen her dressed like that since they were little girls. She looked pretty instead of tough. It occurred to Sherri that her friend had taken more time with her appearance since she was going to hang out with Bunnies. Arthur struck up a conversation with her as if they'd just met. He didn't recognize her from Giles. Before she could remind him, Sherri heard wheels on gravel and ran outside. The resort van that usually took Bunnies to off-site events pulled into the carport. Danny was driving—of course Danny had somehow figured out how to access the van. The door slid open and the Bunnies spilled out full of giggles, squeals, and hugs. Even Tina came to the party.

"I thought we said just a few friends," Arthur said.

Sherri clapped her hands in delight and kissed him. "I guess word got out."

Sherri felt as if someone had flipped a switch from off to on. Soon more cars pulled up and boyfriends in Levi's jeans and cowboy hats carried bottles of Jim Beam and six-packs of beer into the house. Jerry Derzon pulled into the lot in his Nova. He seemed thrilled to have an invitation and handed Arthur a bottle of Rumple Minze. "Just look at you two lovebirds playing house and hosting parties," he said, winking at Sherri. He wore a Cuban-cigar shirt and giant wing tip loafers, an outfit that made him seem like an old man, even though he was only in his thirties.

"You invited Jerry?" Sherri whispered, disappointed.

"I like him," Arthur said. "He's an acquired taste."

Curtis, another unwelcome guest, arrived with Val. He chewed on a toothpick and wore a gold chain necklace with a Virgin Mary pendant resting on his hairy chest. He had muscular arms from laying carpet, and he kept Val in a strong grip. When Arthur offered to give him a tour, he stood in the living room and said, "You should put some carpet down here." He eyed the space as if he were calculating square footage.

"I like the look of the wood," Arthur said.

"Suit yourself, but your floors are Doug fir." He reached down and sank his fingernail into the grain of a floorboard, leaving a mark. "Scratches like glass."

Carmen came up from behind Sherri and planted a kiss on her cheek. "This place is so classic, Sher. I feel like I'm at summer camp!"

"Like a grandmother's house in a fairy tale," said Bunny Boo. She'd told Sherri that her real name was Cynthia.

Sherri overheard Curtis whisper to Val, "I'm surprised this place even has electricity. I've never understood why rich people want to go on vacation and live like they're poor."

Chip, one of the bartenders in the Cabaret, collected twigs and loose brush from around the property and started a campfire. Sherri ran into the house and found musty old camp blankets for people to sit on. Arthur gave more tours of the cottage. "Here's the first indoor toilet ever invented," Sherri heard him say. He sounded like someone's father, making dumb jokes and asking people where they were from, how long they'd been at the resort and what did they like about it? Sherri wondered if they enjoyed talking to Arthur or if they were just being polite.

Sherri introduced Roberta to Bunny Tina, who shook her hand. "Oh right, I remember you from your interview." Roberta's face fell.

In high school, Roberta had never invited Sherri to parties, but Sherri had extended an invitation to Roberta because she wanted to show off her new friends and perhaps even bridge her two worlds. Now she was sorry. She felt responsible when she saw Berta standing alone, and she felt obligated to draw her into conversations that died on the vine. Sherri usually appreciated Roberta's cynicism and wariness, but not here, not with the Bunnies. Sherri knew Roberta well enough to read her mind, and she could tell that she thought her new friends were shallow. She didn't know that they had their own aspirations and complicated lives.

"Sher," Danny said, "think you can arrange for us to take a ride on the pontoon boat?"

Arthur had come outside with a pile of newspapers for the fire— Sherri had thought it was impossibly sexy to watch him read *The New York Times* from front to back each morning when they were in bed.

He interacted with the news, circling articles about the shooting of Pope John Paul II and a story about a Russian cosmonaut who swore he saw a UFO that looked like a transparent barbell. Arthur underlined "transparent barbell" and in the margins he wrote, "What does that look like?" She'd paged through an old *New Yorker* on his bedside table and saw that he'd underlined some lines from a poem called "Like Wings" by Philip Schultz and wondered with a bit of a thrill if he'd been reminded of her: "I think of the light that opened over you our first morning, / how the glass in my lungs turned to sound, / and I saw you woman and child, and couldn't breathe, for love."

"Artie?" she asked, trying out the nickname that fit him like a bad suit. "Can we take the martini boat out?"

"No, sorry. I need to stay here and watch the fire. It's too close to the house. This place will go down like a bag of sticks."

"I can drive, I'm a lake guy," Danny said, patting Arthur on the back. "Your boat is in good hands."

Arthur still seemed worried. "But she doesn't even have a name yet. Isn't that bad luck?"

"Nah," Danny said. "A boat has to earn her name."

"Please?" Sherri asked. She ran her hand along the back of Arthur's neck, knowing it was easy to get him to say yes. "What's the point of owning a boat if you never use it?"

"I'll go get the key."

"I can stay here with you," Roberta said to Arthur. "I didn't know I was supposed to bring my suit." Her tone was accusatory.

"It's a party, Berta. Nobody's *supposed* to do anything," Sherri said.

"Do me a favor," Roberta said. "Stop introducing me to these people as your 'old friend.'"

"But you *are* my old friend."

"Sher, listen to yourself. You don't have to impress these people."

Nobody at the party knew Sherri better than Roberta did. Sherri knew this, and it terrified her, because she didn't want to be that Sherri anymore. "Maybe you don't know me that well."

Roberta's laugh was indignant. "You know what? I know you better than you know yourself."

"Then you must not like me much, because you pretty much ignored me our whole senior year."

"I was going through stuff. I was changing, Sherri."

This sounded like an invitation for Sherri to ask Roberta what she'd been going through, but there was too much happening. "Well I can change, too. I *have* changed. And I don't need you to tell me—"

Ginger, team captain that she was, interrupted their conversation by rushing Sherri, grabbing her by the arm and leading her to the water before Sherri could say more. It was hard to go from Roberta's scowl to the group of smiling friends waiting obediently at the shore station, like switching channels on the television from *Masterpiece Theater* to *Three's Company*. Danny was already straining at the wheel to lower it to the water. Sherri looked back at Roberta and saw her standing with her arms crossed hard over her chest. Even though Sherri was upset with her, she wished she could return to their conversation, make things right, tell her she loved her.

Jerry hauled over a cooler filled with beer and set it down on the boat.

"The circle is complete," Ginger said to Sherri under her breath. "Now the boat has a barnacle."

All of her resort friends packed into the pontoon. Danny was perfectly at ease as the driver, pushing a button on the lever to put the gearshift in neutral before pumping the engine. He backed it away from the pier without incident, leaving the rowboat on the other slip with the oars crossed like arms across a sleeping chest. Arthur waved from the shore. "Is that guy your boyfriend?" Danny asked. There was no way Arthur could hear him over the sound of the motor.

That guy? Suddenly she looked at Arthur differently, trying to see through Danny's eyes. "What do you think of him?"

"He's nice. Different. Deep." His pause made Sherri uncomfortable.

"Deep how so?"

"When he was showing me his house, I told him my place was always a mess, and he started talking about this philosopher named Carl Jung, and said that's a good thing not to worry about my physical environment because it means I have a 'life of the mind.' I wanted to tell him that all I think about is sex, but yeah, OK, sure."

Danny brought the boat to a stop in the middle of Mill Pond. The sun was low in the pink sky, and the water was so smooth that it reflected the cottages and boathouses along the shore. Danny dropped anchor, but didn't hit bottom. "Shit, it's deep here," he said. "This is thirty feet of line."

Curtis stood next to Danny. Sherri had always believed that everyone should be drawn to a certain type. It amazed her that Val could take an interest in two men who were so unalike. Curtis was as dark, deep, and unfathomable as the lake, while Danny was as light as the sky. "You don't need an anchor," Curtis said. "There's no wind." Curtis's tone was intended to make other people feel small—he wasn't even speaking to Sherri and even she felt diminished. Danny bristled, pretending not to hear him. He set the anchor down heavily on the floor of the boat, just missing Curtis's foot.

Sherri looked over at Val, expecting her to be worried, but instead she seemed amused at the prospect of having the men fighting over her. Jerry, trying his best to be one of the guys, cracked open a beer, leaned on the railing, and regaled the men with history. "Used to be a gristmill on this lake. It must go down sixty, seventy feet. In the thirties, this is where gangsters dumped their slot machines during police raids."

"There are a million lakes in this whole damn state, and everyone thinks their lake had a gangster on it," Curtis said, skeptical.

"Ours really did," Jerry said. "They pulled up a suitcase with a skeleton tied to it by a chain a few years ago. Saw it with my own eyes."

Sherri needed to shake loose. She climbed the ladder to the top of the boat and hesitated for a moment before diving in. The first swim of the season was always special. It felt like getting reacquainted with a friend she hadn't seen in a while. The water was bracing, icy cold and crystal clear. When she emerged, she felt like she was awake for the first time in her life. Somewhere in the distance she could hear a bull-frog, and a small plane flew overhead. The cabins around the lake were mostly dark, the windows like closed eyes that would soon open wide when the season kicked into gear. She'd never been anyplace better.

Val jumped out and joined her. "I didn't want Curtis to come. He showed up just as I was leaving and overheard us talking about the party. What could I do?"

"Poor Da—"

"Shhh," Val said, concerned, even though they couldn't be heard over the sound of the guys competing to make the biggest cannonball splashes after jumping off the top deck. What was it about men that made everything a competition?

"Careful!" Jerry said from the comfort of the boat. "Beulah's a hungry lake!"

Time passed more quickly on water than on land. Before she knew it, the sky was dark and the lake was even darker, a pool of onyx. More importantly, the beer cooler was empty, which meant it was time to head back.

Arthur met Danny at the pier and tied his boat against the shore station while everyone hopped off and walked past him toward the campfire, as if he were a carnival worker at the end of the ride. Not even Sherri thanked him; instead, she flitted from person to person, begging Tina to stay at the resort, complaining about Gloria with Carmen, and gossiping about regulars and comparing schedules and shifts. Arthur and Roberta stood by, outsiders to her world, unable to find a way to enter the conversation.

Sherri began to see the boundaries that separated her two worlds. There were Arthur, Jerry, and Roberta, people who knew her one way, and her friends from work, who knew her as someone else.

Danny had brought a big boom box and played ELO. A group of

people started to dance in the light of the fire. Curtis didn't. He whit-
tled a stick with the knife he kept in his pocket for cutting carpet. He
looked up and saw Val and Danny talking to each other, and his eyes
narrowed with suspicion. Jerry, wasted, snored in the hammock strung
between two white pines, a bottle of Jim Beam at his side.

Sherri was drunk and oblivious. She swayed to the music. Roberta
and Arthur sat in plastic folding chairs, watching her. Goldie rested
at Arthur's feet—even the dog looked bored. Sherri grabbed Roberta's
arms and tried to get her to stand. "Come on," she said. "Dance with
me. You guys look like chaperones."

"When did you learn how to dance like that?" Roberta asked.

Sherri stuck out her tongue. "You're no fun anymore."

"And you're nothing *but* fun. That's it."

"That's because I've never had any fun until now." Sherri gave up
on Roberta and moved on to Arthur. "You'll dance with me, won't
you?"

He stood, but he seemed stiff and uncertain.

"What's wrong?" She pressed herself against him.

"How long do you think people will stay?"

"I hope forever!" Sherri twirled away from Arthur's sullen heaviness
and fell into a circle with Ginger, Carmen, and Boo. She didn't notice
when Roberta left, or when Arthur went upstairs and didn't come back
down.

The sun was starting to rise when the van finally pulled away. Jerry
snored contentedly. The house was scattered with empties, and cigarette butts were all over the yard. Sherri, buzzed and pleased, plopped
into bed next to Arthur, a huge smile on her face. She kissed him and
his eyes fluttered open. "Oh Arthur, thank you so much. I had the best
time!"

Arthur pulled her close to him and smelled her hair, which, like
her clothes, must have smelled like lake water and campfire smoke.
"I'm glad," he said, although he didn't sound glad. He sounded frustrated and resigned.

"Can we have another party?"

"No." His voice was serious. "Sherri, I've been meaning to tell you something."

"What?"

He looked concerned. "I know this is awful timing."

"Tell me!"

"I have to leave, Sher. I'm going to France for the summer."

"The whole entire summer?" Although at first Sherri had been confused by Arthur's apparent lack of responsibilities, she'd quickly grown used to it. Now it was hard for Sherri to imagine Arthur anywhere but at the house with nothing to do, always at her beck and call. She was shocked he had other places to go, other things to do. "But you just bought this place."

"I know. I know. The timing couldn't be worse. My parents are celebrating their thirtieth anniversary and have a big tour lined up for us. I tried to get out of it, but it's very difficult to say no to my father."

"What about Rainbow Springs?"

"Oh, that fell through for the same reason that Jerry can't sell your building. We're going to sit on it for a while, see if interest rates go down."

"What about us?" She kissed him. "We just met."

"I know, although it doesn't feel like that, does it?" He reached for her hand and wrapped it around him. "You entered my life like a grenade. I'd like to think we have control over our emotions, but mine are running amok." His voice cracked. "I know we haven't known each other long, but I feel you in the very fiber of my being. You have no idea how much I'm going to miss you. No idea at all."

"I'm going to miss you, too." She was heartbroken. She was. So why was she also relieved? She'd miss him terribly, and she'd miss the cottage, but with Arthur out of the picture she could have her fun without feeling tied down. She figured that by the time he returned she'd be ready for him. "Arthur? Are you my boyfriend?"

"Even better: I'm your *lover*."

It was the perfect thing to say, thrilling. To Sherri's ears it sounded romantic, and ushered her into the realm of the kind of adulthood she'd dreamed of. He ran the tip of his nose down her sternum and kept going down, down. He hesitated, looking up at her the way Goldie sometimes would look up in the middle of eating from her bowl.

"Don't stop. For the love of God."

"First you have to promise you won't forget me while I'm gone."

She gripped fistfuls of his thick, dark hair and tried to push him down.

"I mean it. Promise me."

"Oh Arthur," she said, loving the sound of his name in her mouth, loving that he knew what he was doing to her. "I promise. I promise! How could I possibly ever forget about you?"

CHAPTER TWELVE

Despite her promise, as she entered the full swing of summer at the resort, Arthur, so far away in a place she couldn't even imagine, sank deeper into the recesses of her mind with every shift she worked, and every late night.

She hardly recognized the season—it bore little resemblance to the quiet breeziness of the summer days she'd known from her childhood. Back then she could spend hours with Roberta swimming, playing hopscotch, drinking malts at the Dairy Bar, and sunbathing on blankets in Roberta's backyard on Hodunk Road, talking about boys like Trent Eagan while searching for four-leaf clovers or racing grasshoppers. The quiet of East Troy and the peacefulness Sherri had experienced at Arthur's cottage didn't exist at the resort. Soon the smell of the old pine beadboard and gas off the motors of the trolling fishing boats just beyond Arthur's pier was replaced by the mingling odors of cigarette smoke, carpet cleaner, chlorine, and men's cologne.

Everything was in movement: golf carts scooted around the grounds, guests rode horses at the stables, musicians arrived to record records at the studio in the basement or to perform at Alpine, and the lobby was so packed with guests that it was, as Rhonda described it, like a shopping mall before Christmas. She no longer ran into Rhonda in the dorm, because she'd moved in with Frank, but Sherri saw her multiple times a day as she passed her in the lobby, where Rhonda was now stationed, and also in the bathroom, where she threw up almost nonstop. Sherri felt awkward and nervous around her friend, as though she'd been diagnosed with a contagious disease.

One evening, Sherri took her break outside on the chunk of cement overlooking the golf course. What started out as an occasional cigarette when she was drunk had turned into a constant craving. She loved everything about smoking, right down to the crinkling sound of the thin plastic wrapper around the package. Smoking gave her jittery hands something to do, and at parties the ashtray was something to gather around, like a campfire.

Sherri took in the warmth of the evening. People always complained about the humidity in the Midwest, but she loved the thick, sensual quality of the summer air, the way it held everything in suspension. "Hey," someone said. She jumped and saw Gwen sitting in profile at the employee picnic table, her legs crossed. She had a long neck and slender wrists and ankles, and looked glamorous when she smoked, like a movie star.

"I haven't seen you in a while," Sherri said, sitting across from her.

"You're probably the only person around here who noticed I was gone. I took some time off."

"Are you OK?"

"Yeah, I'm fine. I needed to study for the bar exam."

"You're a lawyer?"

"I hope so. Why so surprised?"

"I just didn't know." Sherri knew that backpedaling would make the situation worse.

"I should find out how I did on the test in a few weeks."

"That's amazing," Sherri said. "I'll keep my fingers crossed for you."

She was supposed to be happy for Gwen, and she supposed she was, but this meant that she would leave. Sherri hardly knew her, but she wanted everyone to stay in place forever. Summer was just kicking into full swing and already she was beginning to feel like the stagehands were taking down the set at the end of a production. Why couldn't the resort mean as much to everyone else as it did to her? Why did it have to be temporary? As Arthur had said, people were *becoming* rather than *being*.

Gwen stood and wiped down the front of her outfit. "First thing I'm going to do when I get my law license—well, after I quit this place—is sue the property owners on your boyfriend's 'island.'"

"Jesuit Island?"

"Uh-huh. I went to that party of yours. Or I tried. The guy in the gatehouse at the entrance wouldn't let me drive my black ass past him."

Sherri's stomach turned. "God, Gwen. I'm so sorry. I wish I'd known."

"And if you had, Sherri, tell me: what would you do, huh? What does anyone out here do?" Gwen stubbed her cigarette out on the picnic table. "I've got to get back to work. I can't believe people pay good money to see Engelbert Humperdinck. An old guy at my table is watching the show through his goddamn bird binoculars."

Gwen breezed past her, her heels clicking against the pavement. Soon they'd click down the hallway of a fancy law office.

Sherri returned to her shift, smiling to cover the bad feelings about what Gwen had told her as she poured shot glasses of rum into Coke for the steelworkers' union members who'd planned their annual meeting at the resort. Their mood wasn't any more upbeat than her own. They spoke of inflation, deregulation, and interest rates—the same stuff Arthur read about in his newspapers. Sherri liked to think those were problems that existed elsewhere and didn't concern her.

"Good thing you girls aren't unionized," one of them said to her, "or you'd come to work wearing turtlenecks and overalls."

At the Bunny Council meetings, there was occasionally talk about forming a union, but it sounded so serious, and nobody lasted long enough to make it happen. Besides, what other job would pay anything close to what she was making? She was picking up as many shifts as she could. She worked doubles and triples and pocketed more money than she knew what to do with. She stashed it away in a new hiding spot in the back of her underwear drawer in hopes of buying a car. She never said anything to Val about the missing money. She tried to convince herself that she'd miscounted, although Sherri didn't miscount.

Gloria never praised Sherri, but Sherri knew that she was pleased with her, because she invited her to work many of the coveted off-site events, from a Brian Piccolo golf tournament with O. J. Simpson to car shows to charity fundraisers. Her dorm room filled up with the perks the sponsors gave the Bunnies, including Estée Lauder makeup sets and giant bottles of Ralph Lauren perfume.

On the rare occasions when she wasn't working, or when she was between shifts, Danny often invited her and his other favorite Bunnies to sit by the pool in their pink Catalina Playboy bikinis. He could only pick twenty girls a day, and an invitation was a real honor. Without one, the Bunnies had to sunbathe outside the dorm, just inside the barbed wire fence, while the golfers beyond the partition gawked at them.

She had her own clique now, and each woman had her role: Ginger was the organizer; Carmen was the life of the party, always inappropriate and gossipy; Boo was like the audience member of a live television show, providing the laugh track, happy to be included. If her friends were the kerosene, Sherri was the match. She was always up for another shot, always the first person to climb up onto the bar to dance, always the last to leave at closing time.

In the mornings, Carmen, Ginger, and Boo would come into Sherri's room—the door was always open and Val was often gone—and lie in Sherri's bed with her to rehash the evening. Carmen always had good stories from Sugar Shack. She still only worked one shift a week, in the afternoon, and wasn't making much in tips. "They call it the C-section shift," she said. "I work with the moms." They kept track of each other's diets, traded clothes, painted each other's nails and did each other's makeup, and gossiped about the case of crabs that was spreading like brushfire. The critters hopped from uniform to uniform, and soon the Bunnies were all grimacing while carrying their trays because they wanted to scratch their crotches so badly. Ola and Biata had to take all the uniforms to be dry-cleaned, something the girls were supposed to do themselves but obviously hadn't, and the older women were none too happy about it.

Sherri felt as though she had sisters. Nothing was private. Sherri regaled them with detailed accounts of her exploits with Mitch and Arthur, and they listened, wide-eyed and jealous, not nearly as experienced as Sherri had assumed her friends were—even Carmen.

"Which one would you pick if you had to choose?"

"Oh gosh, I don't know," Sherri said. Never mind Mitch hadn't made a single attempt to reach Sherri. As much as she adored Arthur, Mitch still had some appeal because he was elusive.

"You should see your face when you talk about Arthur," Boo said. "You're going to marry him, aren't you?"

"It could happen, I suppose, but not anytime soon." Sherri was enjoying the feeling of having Arthur in her back pocket. She fantasized sometimes about becoming Sherri St. John, the mistress of his cabin, the mother of his children. If he was game for an entire summer in Europe, surely she'd be able to convince Arthur to live somewhere besides East Troy. But that fantasy competed with all the fantasies she'd indulged before she'd even met Arthur—of Mitch and celebrity crushes, and some of the men she waited on or met at the bars and parties. All the lives she could possibly lead dangled in her future, still deliciously unknown to her. What made her youthfulness so deliriously exciting was the cornucopia of possibilities that awaited her, although she was blissfully unaware that most would necessarily go unrealized.

Besides, she was too busy in the present to be haunted by her past or to worry about her future. Even when she wasn't working, the orders swirled around in her head: roast rack of lamb, make the Sidecar with cognac instead of cheap brandy, up, not on the rocks, cream with the Jamaican coffee, no ice in the water, lemon on the side, separate checks please, more butter, bring us another round, honey, only make mine a double. She smiled and tried to playfully avoid the men who'd try to grab her tail. She dipped and dipped until her knees felt like they'd get stuck in a bent position.

The pills worked better than any diet. Food? She didn't want it. Not a bite. Food was another country, suddenly strange and foreign, gross even. So warm, so brown. She'd look at her guests' plates and see dressing that was thick and oily, and gravy that was a curtain of goop. Cheese was chunky, potatoes were the color of dead flesh. The meat, all marbled and red, bled and bled. She could see every single calorie.

One afternoon Carmen organized a trip to Chicago with the girls to visit a quack doctor Carmen had met at Sugar Shack who injected them with hog tranquilizers, swearing the treatment would help the women lose weight. It was really speed, that's all it was. The girls ran around like they were being chased by bolts of lightning.

One afternoon, Sherri finished her shift and saw that Ola had left her another note:

ARTHUR CALL HE MISS YOU

She felt a tug in her gut when she again saw Arthur's name in Ola's block handwriting. He called and left messages all the time, and when he did, he briefly came alive to her with a startling vividness. She could practically hear the low timbre of his voice as he spoke to Ola. Sweet, sweet Arthur. She hungered for his touch, so intuitive she swore he knew what it felt like to live inside her skin. But what good did it do her to miss him? It was the end of July, the very height of summer, and he wasn't due back for almost a month. He couldn't go away for so long and expect her to stand frozen in place, waiting for him. She needed to prove to herself that she could be OK on her own. He was perfect in so many ways. He was a little older than she was. He was worldly and smart. Yet he was also a burden—a delicious, intoxicating burden. Thoughts of him set off an emotional tug-of-war, a push/pull where one minute she would marvel at her independence, and the next an image of him walking naked in his bedroom would flash in her mind and she'd think about his smile.

Restless and throbbing, she headed back to the dorm without waiting for a security guard to take her. It was a gorgeous afternoon, and she was cold from the air-conditioning. She needed clarity—clarity that was interrupted when a man in a black shirt called after her. She picked up her pace and tried to ignore him. She was used to getting hit on, especially lately. She'd seen other Bunnies exude a strange magnetic energy, and now that she felt desired and adored, it was happening to her.

"Hey," he said. "I want to spend some time with you."

She didn't have time for this guy. In two hours, she was supposed to work a Bob Hope charity fundraiser that she'd been looking forward to for weeks. She'd planned to return to her dorm room, take a quick nap, and shower. If she had time, she'd sneak off to the VIP lounge before it opened so that she could play piano, though what she truly craved were the pedals of the organ. She couldn't explain it, but some days music built up inside her. On that day, she'd been hearing the complex melodic lines of the andante of Handel's organ concertos op. 7 and she wanted to work it out on the keys.

The man heeled her like a dog. "Don't you know who I am?"

"No. Why should I?" She tried to walk faster. She'd heard enough stories of guys who hung around the resort to make her wary. There were men who wanted to lure Bunnies into their cars. She'd heard that the previous summer a troubled Vietnam vet had accosted a Bunny in the parking lot and cut up her face with a razor. But that day, Sherri wasn't too worried. It was a perfect, sunny afternoon. She had Arthur's note in her pocket, she had her job, and she had music. What could go wrong?

He followed her, and she quickened her step. "I sat in your section last night," he said.

Sherri slowed to look at him. He wasn't familiar to her, and she had a good memory for faces. Then again, it was dark in the Cabaret. Frankie Avalon had performed, and the place was packed.

"I'm Mr. Saito," he said. "Hinata Saito. Doesn't that name ring any bells?"

"Sorry, no bells."

"People call me Johnnie." He opened the big black bag he was carrying, and Sherri worried for a moment that he was about to pull a gun. Instead, he lifted out a fancy camera. "I'm from the magazine."

"Yeah?" That got Sherri's attention. She'd heard about girls getting discovered by visiting photographers. That winter, Gloria had invited Tina, Carmen, and Bunny Autumn to participate in a photo shoot by the ski lodge, and the photographer took photos of them learning how to cross-country ski. Bunny Tina was friends with a Bunny in the St. Louis club who'd become a centerfold; now she was married to Jimmy Connors. It wasn't unusual to have a photographer at the resort. What was unusual was that he was talking to Sherri.

"They don't like to announce that I'm coming. I'm like a famous food critic who dines undercover. I try to see you girls when you're acting natural." He began to clean the lens with a soft chamois cloth. "I have a feeling about you. You've got great bone structure, and your smile is absolutely radiant."

"Radiant?"

"Brighter than the sun. So, tell me, you want to test?" he asked.

"Me?"

"Who do you think?"

The word "test" sounded official and reminded her of school. It was something to be administered. "I guess," she said. "As long as I don't have to get naked or anything. I'm not like that."

"You didn't strike me as a square. Why would you be embarrassed of your perfect body?"

"I'm not," Sherri said. "It's just—"

"Don't worry, don't worry. I get it. You don't have to do anything you don't want to do. Look, all I'm interested in right now is how your face comes across on film. Please, can I just take a few photos? You never know what might come of it. If they turn out, I'll send them to corporate."

Corporate? That sounded official. "I guess."

"Good, let's go tell my assistant. We were just about to leave when we saw you. Perfect timing." He walked her to a tan van and rapped on the window with his knuckle. A young man with hair the color of the burnt-red peanuts her mom used to eat stepped out. "Ron, I found that girl we saw last night, the one you said would be perfect."

Ron smiled. "Oh, that's great. The hair, the attitude. I told Johnnie you're the whole package."

"He's learning," Mr. Saito said. "It was Ron who noticed you first. He's developing a good eye, gotta say. Ron, you got that bottle of Jim Beam? Let's pour her a shot."

"No thanks," Sherri said. "I've got to work after this." Gloria was part bloodhound—she could smell alcohol from a mile away. Once, Ginger had gotten busted for drinking before work, even though she'd gone to great lengths to cover it up. She'd brushed her teeth, gargled with mouthwash, smoked a menthol cigarette, and swallowed a spoonful of mustard. Still Gloria sniffed it and gave her a demerit.

Mr. Saito said, "I'll let you in on something: this *is* your work. You don't want to come off as stiff, do you? This is your big chance. Just one shot to loosen you up. The people in charge won't mind. Every club wants one of their own Bunnies to make it into the glossy pages. What we're doing? This is what your job is really about. Management knows we're here." He handed her a plastic shot glass. "Bottoms up."

What was one shot? Sherri loved the idea of being discovered, and Johnnie was right, she didn't want to blow her chances by coming off as stiff. The alcohol burned the back of her throat and made its way to her always empty stomach.

"OK, guys, follow me. Let's go where we can take photos without distraction."

He led her away from the parking lot and down a steep embankment to the woods at the edge of the golf course. Ron stabbed an umbrella-like contraption into the grass and adjusted it while staring at the sun. "Let me test the light. Stand there, don't move."

"Should I smile?" She was nervous. Her legs shook and sweat dripped down her sides, but the shot was already beginning to relax her.

"Yeah, smile," Ron said. "There's nothing men love more than a smile on a pretty lady's face."

A cloud obscured the sun. There were more on the horizon. Johnnie looked at the sky with satisfaction. "I was hoping we'd get some clouds to filter the light. Everything is working out perfectly."

She wanted to do a good job for Mr. Saito; her whole life at the resort was centered on pleasing the guests. They took her photo on their cheap cameras all the time, but Mr. Saito's big camera had a lens that was practically as long as a telescope. He seemed incredibly serious and professional. He began by focusing on her face. That was OK, safe. "Oh honey, I wish you could see what I see."

"What?"

"The camera just loves you," he said.

"Yeah," said the assistant. "You're really beautiful."

Her customers always said she was beautiful. Arthur said she was beautiful. But these men? They really knew beauty. Beauty was their job.

"Move around a bit, loosen up. Like you're dancing," Mr. Saito said. Sherri swayed awkwardly, grateful that she had some alcohol in her to put her at ease. "You've modeled before, right?"

"No! Never."

"Get out of here! Look how natural you are. And that hair!" He took more shots, the lens fluttering in a staccato rhythm she found mesmerizing. Her eyes began to feel heavy. Why was the shot affecting her so quickly? Johnnie walked behind her and off to her side, checking every angle. The trees felt like they were closing her in, and mosquitoes were beginning to bite. Her father had met a poet from Fort Atkinson, Lorine Niedecker. He'd read some lines of one of her poems to Sherri and they floated into her consciousness. "What horror to awake at night / and in the dimness see the light. / Time is white / mosquitoes bite."

"OK, let's drop our top," he said.

"Excuse me?"

"Your top," he said, "take it off." He flicked his finger in the air as if he were flipping on a light switch. His tone was cold, almost scolding, as if she were slowing him down, and made her feel like a little girl. She wondered what would happen if she said no. She wished she had the nerve to deny him. Her thinking had grown foggy. She looked around. There were men out there on the golf course, but they couldn't see her. Nobody could. Wasn't it illegal to take off your clothes in public? But she wasn't in public, not really. The resort was private property, and they were pretty well hidden.

"Go on, darlin'," he said. "These shots are just for evaluation. A test, like I said. We can send them in to corporate and see what they think." There was that word again. "Corporate" sounded very serious, very buttoned-up. "You never know, they might want to fly you out to LA, make you a centerfold."

She knew plenty of Bunnies who would jump at the opportunity to find stardom, no matter the cost. But she had complicated feelings about the word "centerfold." To men, it sounded glamorous. Well, not all men. She knew Arthur wouldn't approve, but Arthur was across the Atlantic. To women—to her mother, if she were alive—it would sound horribly cheap and tacky, not to mention permanent.

"You can make some big money. Travel. Get into television and movies. You never know." He adjusted his lens. "You'd be amazed at the careers our girls have found, the money they've made."

"I don't—" she stammered. It was hard for her to find words. She was oppressively tired, and her brain felt like it was turning into soup. *Time is white.* "I don't think so." The last person to see her breasts was Arthur. He didn't make her feel funny the way Mr. Saito suddenly did; he didn't look at her to see if she met his expectations. Then again, Mr. Saito was an ambassador to "corporate" and readers of the magazine. In that moment Mr. Saito wasn't just one man, he was all men, and she wasn't a woman but a product. Shouldn't Sherri let him take a look? Did she measure up? Was her body magazine-worthy?

"These aren't the kinds of photos your boyfriend would take of you in his basement," Ron said.

"This is high concept," said Mr. Saito. "Real art. You could hang these photos in a gallery in SoHo. Your top," he said, raising his finger. He seemed so focused and important, so busy. She didn't have the confidence to say no, even though something was off.

Ron came over and pinched the hem of her shirt with his fingers. "Here, let me help you." She could push him away. She could run for it. And if she didn't feel like she had molasses running through her veins, she might have. "I can get it myself," she said, slurring her words.

"There we go. There's my girl." That was what Sam had said to her, and again it made her feel dirty.

It was one thing to expose her shoulders at work, another to bare her breasts. Sherri wondered if she was pretty enough, if her big breasts were the right shape and size.

"You are a work of art, Shelly."

"Sherri," she said. She heard the plodding bass line of Handel's chaconne. Her mother had said the bass line was often the walking part of music, moving the piece along, step by step. Each step grew longer, heavier.

Mr. Saito took more photos, then he set his camera down and frowned. He asked Ron for the plastic cup he was holding, walked closer to her, and pulled out an ice cube and set one on her nipple. She jumped. The cold shocked her, but not as much as the feeling of his hands on her breasts and the thought that she ought to do that herself. She felt angry and powerless. Her body was no longer her own, but had it ever been? He stepped away before she could push him. "Now we've got some raspberries. Yum, yum." He stepped back. "Arch your back, kitten," Ron said. "Push out those titties."

That was a record scratch. She hated the words that only men used to describe women. A mosquito landed on her forearm. Slapping it felt like it would be against the rules, rules that weren't made by her. "Arch more," Mr. Saito said. "Come on, smile, arch, really arch, *more*. More arch." Sherri didn't want to, but she did. She tried her best to smile and she arched until she thought her back would crack in half. It was as if she were under some kind of spell. She wasn't in her body. She was hovering somewhere in the distance, watching.

"These shots are good. So good I know what'll come next: the folks at the magazine will want me to come back out and take a full body. Why don't you save me that trip. Just for spec—they won't get published or anything. What do you think, Ron?"

Why was he asking Ronnie what he thought instead of her? Ronnie's grin was that of a hungry dog just before sinking its muzzle into a steak. "Yeah, yeah. More would be good."

Sherri shook her head. She tried to say no but her lips felt numb, her tongue fat. That wasn't just alcohol in that shot. Her eyes were starting to feel heavy. She worried she might fall down, and then who knew what would happen?

"Ron, help her with her shorts."

He walked to where she stood. The acne pits in his face seemed deeper and darker than they had at first, a face like tree bark. He began to work the snap. Sherri tried to push him away, but her arms were like rubber. She felt like she was locked in one of those dreams she would have first thing in the morning, where she was awake enough to know she was dreaming, but unable to wake fully. Ron pushed her down onto the grass and began to yank her shorts down to her knees, along with her underwear. She looked up and saw the branches of the oak trees scratching the sky. She was so tired, but no, *no*, she couldn't sleep. She mustered up some energy and rolled away and began to run, stumbling and shirtless, toward the golf course. Danny! She saw him in the distance, caddying for James, the golf pro. She gathered all the strength she could muster and screamed at the top of her lungs. "Danny! Help!"

Everything that happened next was a blur. She heard Danny on his walkie-talkie calling security, she saw a golf club fly through the air. Johnnie and Ron gathered their things and began to make a run for it up the hill, toward the parking lot. They were met midway down by Paul, the security guard. Small Paul, everyone called him, even though he was a former linebacker for the Bears and was built like a dumpster.

"Get your ass out of here or I'll call the cops," Paul said. Sherri was too grateful to argue that he shouldn't give those jerks this ultimatum; he should call the cops anyway, and take the film. "I told you to stop tricking the girls."

Sherri burst into tears. "This was a trick?"

Danny helped her get her shirt on, and he led her, limp and tired, to the cart. "Let's get you back."

"What were you doing walking, Sher? You know you're supposed to let us drive you to the dorms," Paul said. He sounded angry, as though the whole experience had been her fault, and it had. She was an idiot, an idiot!

"They said they were with the magazine," Sherri said.

"And you believed them? Those guys have your pictures now."

They had more than that, she thought. Even in her stupor, she understood that those men had taken a piece of her.

Danny took her to her dorm room and told her to lie down. Val rushed to her side, shouting expletives as Danny relayed the situation. The couple seemed like older siblings to Sherri. Danny's hand was on Val's shoulder, and the three of them felt like they were linked together in a chain. "Oh, Sher," Val said, her voice softer and kinder than anyone would ever have believed possible. She was moody and difficult, but in that moment, Sherri loved Val with her whole being.

"You aren't the first girl those guys have tricked," Danny said. "Believe me."

"What am I going to do about work? I have the Bob Hope event tonight. I can't even think!"

Val said, "I'll cover. As far as Gloria is concerned, you came down with food poisoning."

"I'm sorry." Sherri began to cry. "I should have known better."

"Don't be sorry," Danny said. "Those guys are scum. I'm just glad I was with bad golfers who shot their ball into the rough or I wouldn't have found you."

"Why can't I be more like you?" Sherri asked Val.

"You don't want to be like me." Val smoothed Sherri's hair. "You get like me from having bad stuff like this happen all the time."

"Your problem," Danny said, "is that you're so surprised by everything."

Sherri couldn't stay focused. Whatever the guys had given her made her sleepier than she'd ever felt. "I'm so stupid. They used me. I was *used*."

Val and Danny were gone, and night descended. Sherri had strange dreams that she was in Arthur's cottage with Johnnie and Ron. Arthur was outside, but she wouldn't let him in. He knocked on the doors and banged on the windows. "Let me help you," he said. He even tried climbing down through the chimney and up through the crawl space. She awoke to the sound of Val banging on their door because in her rush to leave she'd forgotten her keys.

"Look," she said, excited. She turned in to the hall and pushed something big and heavy into their room. "It's too bad you missed the event. Bob Hope gave us *mopeds*! We each got one. Ryan O'Neal was there! Oh, and these came for you. I told Ola I'd deliver them."

Val set a bouquet of flowers on Sherri's bed like a consolation prize.

The overpowering scent of white lilies cut through Sherri's fogginess. Arthur had inadvertently bookended her whole experience with the "photographers." She pulled the note card off the stem:

All being like the moonflower is dissatisfied
For the dark kiss that the night only gives,
And night gives only to the soul that waits in longing
And in that only lives.

—F. T. Prince.

My soul (and the rest of me) waits in longing. Remember me.
Remember us. Soon.

—Arthur

The sentiment of the poem combined with the sweet odor of the lilies brought Sherri back to herself, rescued her from a bitterness so tangible she knew it might otherwise stick with her forever. She hated knowing that she was an easy mark and that she meant nothing to those men. She meant something to Arthur. She couldn't shake the spooky feeling that he was tuned in to her on a cosmic wavelength. Even from a distant continent he'd somehow sensed that, more than ever, she needed to know that she mattered.

CHAPTER THIRTEEN

It was the last week of August, and Arthur was due back after a summer that had surely been more refined than her own. Sherri imagined that he'd spent his months away in museums and cathedrals, while she'd shot like a metal ball rolling through the playfield in the pinball machine, wildly careening off the bumpers. While Arthur sipped expensive wine in vineyards, Sherri worked as many shifts as Gloria would give her. When she wasn't working, she partied, throwing back shots of Rumple Minze and Jägermeister. After her incident with that awful Mr. Saito she did her best to lose herself, and to never, ever be alone.

When Biata handed her a message telling her that Arthur was due to pick her up at noon that Friday, she felt a nervous, confused thrill. She wanted to see Arthur. She did. But she'd lost track of her emotions. She'd close her eyes and try to remember him, but he came to her in parts: arms, eyes, shoulders, hips, toes. She decided it was time to come off the booze and the speed to prepare, the way she'd floss the night before having her teeth cleaned. Besides, what good was speed out on Jesuit Island? She'd go crazy there, lazing around with Arthur and Goldie while the world sped by elsewhere.

Withdrawal was brutal. Her insides felt like they were being scraped dry. She wanted to snap at customers when they complained that their steak wasn't prepared the way they liked it, and she had little patience for Carmen, who constantly barged into Sherri's room and yapped incessantly while trying on her makeup without asking. Ginger came across as bossy, taping notes to the bathroom mirrors reminding the girls to rinse the sink after they brushed their teeth. Boo sat back and took it all in, and Sherri wished she'd say something, do something. The only person who didn't bother her was Val, because she was hardly ever around. Curtis placed more demands on her time, showing up in his yellow truck at the end of her shifts to drag her back to Beloit with him.

Even though it was still technically summer, Sherri could feel a slight shift in the atmosphere at the resort. The kids who were usually underfoot, threatening to knock her down while she carried her tray or begging her to play backgammon with them when she worked her shift in the game room, were instead back-to-school shopping. The college girls dribbled back to their campuses with their stashes of saved tips, and the guests returned to their old lives. Gloria said it was the start of the shoulder season—not peak, not off-peak. The upcoming weekend would be one of the last big blasts of the summer before Labor Day.

The changes ushered in with the transition between seasons snuck up on Sherri. She found the rusty smell of burning leaf piles and the slightest hint of cool, dry air from the north unsettling, because they evoked sharp memories of her mother's decline. One of Sherri's last good memories was of wheeling her mother to the square. Muriel had been so frail, her muscles atrophied from disuse. Still, she'd managed a smile when a monarch butterfly alit on her arm. That time of year had felt like an end then, and it was a new kind of end now.

Everything felt off, and Sherri's nose was out of joint as she began her Thursday-night shift. A week earlier she'd suffered a bruised rib at a charity basketball tournament for the Boys Club in Waupaca, when the Bunnies played against the volunteer police department. An officer who must have weighed three hundred pounds fell on her. Everyone thought it was hilarious. She winced when she zipped her costume, and she had to suck in her breath every time she had to lift her tray or dip to deliver a drink.

Beyond the big windows in the Cabaret a big thunderstorm inched closer on the horizon. The trees swayed in unison, and the golf carts zoomed back to the clubhouse fairway, small as Matchbox toys. Sherri spied Danny with a big bag over one shoulder, his blond hair almost as white as his golf shirt and standing straight up off his head. Off to the side the surface of the pool was rough. Only a few brave souls swam laps. The light was slant and hazy. It was just after six o'clock and already it was getting dark, a darkness that seemed to press against the windows and make Sherri's life feel small in a place where she'd expected it to be large.

Carmen and Sherri were rolling silverware into napkins. "Gloria only gave me seven lousy shifts this whole week. How many are you working?"

"Five," Sherri said. "And she took me off the schedule for tomorrow."

"What'd you do to piss her off this time?"

"I breathed."

Carmen spoke in a quiet voice. "Have you noticed she seems different, like she doesn't care as much lately? She didn't even weigh me in today."

"Probably because it's all old people coming to the Don Ho show tonight. Who wants to listen to a guy in a Hawaiian shirt playing the ukulele? We could look like pack mules and they wouldn't care."

"The cane-and-crutch crowd can't even see us. Do you see how they have to hold the candles to their menus? And they always complain it's too loud. I have to repeat the specials over and over and over."

Carmen pretended to stab herself in the chest with a butter knife and dumped another tray of silverware on the table, where it landed with a clattering thunk. "Tina was here looking for you."

"Tina?"

"Yeah, before you got here. She wanted to say goodbye. She called off her engagement, can you believe it?"

"She did? What about her grandfather?"

"I don't know. I guess she told him to go to hell. She and Bunny Starr are headed to LA to work at the club there. Tina is next-level pretty. I'll bet she'll make mountains of money. Sounds way better than getting married and joining the Junior League."

Sherri swelled with pride for her friend, but she was also jealous. California had always been *her* dream—well, hers and Roberta's. They planned to have picnics at the base of the letters on the big Hollywood sign and look for handprints on the Walk of Fame. She saw celebrities at the resort, but in Los Angeles they'd be in their natural habitat.

"Guess what?" Sherri said. "I put a deposit down on a car."

"Yeah?" Carmen seemed impressed. "I want one, but once I pay my brother's medical bills, I'm going to start saving for nursing school."

"You want to be a nurse?" That was the last job Sherri would ever want after so many years of taking care of her mother, but she could picture Carmen holding someone's hand at their bedside, distracting them from their pain and suffering, or maybe just driving them nuts.

"I watched them work with my brother and I thought to myself, you know what? I could do that, I could! And let's be honest, I'm a terrible stripper, and I'm not much better as a Bunny. After watching Mark's skin blister and melt, nothing could gross me out. The burn ward is the third ring of hell."

"I can just see you in comfortable white nurse shoes," Sherri said.

"Doesn't that sound like heaven?"

"I've thought about going to college myself," Sherri said. She'd never spoken these words aloud before, and to do so felt like a commitment.

"What do you want to study?"

"Oh geez, I have no idea! Remember Linda? The tall girl who goes to Madison? She told me there's such a thing as an undecided major." Linda had taught Sherri drinking games she'd learned at fraternity parties. She said she had classes in big lecture halls and went to football games and hung out in the bars on State Street. Another Bunny, Pamela, went to Wash U. in St. Louis. She majored in statistics. One day when it was slow, she taught Sherri how to figure out standard deviation by quizzing all the Bunnies about their cup sizes and creating a graph. "This is easy," Sherri said. "Anything bigger or smaller than average becomes increasingly rarer." When Sherri told her that she had an almost perfect score on the ACT, Pamela encouraged Sherri to apply. Going to school in-state was one thing, but college in another state at a school she'd never heard of before sounded impossible. Besides, Jerry still hadn't found anyone to buy, rent, or lease her building on the square. She couldn't make any major plans until that was taken care of. And now that she'd put a deposit on the car, any ideas about college had to be put on hold. She'd opted for wheels, her most immediate form of freedom.

"You must be excited. Did you get the Monte Carlo?"

"Sure did. Burgundy. They had to order it from Detroit. They said it'll be at the dealership in East Troy tomorrow. I can't wait."

"That's a big purchase. Did you get a good deal?"

"I think so." Sherri didn't want to tell Carmen that she'd been so nervous and excited that she hardly knew what to say when she found herself in the salesman's office. Sherri frowned. "The guy said he gave me his best price. Bunny Boo was with me."

Bunny Boo? "Hon, don't ever shop for a car without a man. If I'd known, I would have sent Mark to go with you. He's six foot four, and as wide as he is tall. Nobody messes with a guy that big, or with his messed-up face."

"I wish I'd thought of that," Sherri said. "I practically had to wave a wad of cash in front of the salesman before he believed I was really serious. He kept calling me 'lady' and tried to get me to pay list. He said he'd shave three hundred dollars off the price and he even threw in a cassette player."

"You could have done better."

Bill, the manager, walked past. "Oh hey, Billy," Sherri said, tilting her head and offering her most winning smile, but he was grim-faced and anxious, like all the other managers who had lately been called into meeting after meeting. Sherri and Carmen exchanged glances when he didn't acknowledge her at all. A few days earlier she'd heard that Toyo, who managed the golf club, had quit abruptly and left to work at a resort in the Bahamas, and the couple that ran the ski chalet decided to move to Vail.

The guests would arrive soon and the Cabaret would magically transform from this massive, empty space to a darkened den of chatter and clinking silverware. She couldn't have known this would be her last shift, yet, without speed or alcohol, her senses came alive. She found herself paying attention to the way the atmosphere thickened with smoke, the smell of prime rib, the sound of the glassware clinking at the bar, and the tech tapping the microphone to make sure it worked. *Hello, hello. One two three. Can you hear me? Testing, testing.*

The evening took a surprising turn when Sherri struck up a conversation with a big, bearded man who said he was the band manager for the Allman Brothers.

"I'm a fan," she said. "A huge fan."

He smiled and nodded. "That's great, sweetheart." It was clear everyone told him that.

"You don't understand. I grew up listening to every album they made with my friend Roberta. 'Whipping Post' is my favorite song ever!"

"That's the saddest damn song he's ever written."

Sherri said, "*Good Lord, I feel like I'm dyin'!*" loudly enough for the room captain to look in her direction with alarm. "Roberta made me learn that song so I could play it for her on the organ."

"You play?"

"Not like Gregg Allman, but yeah, I guess. I play mostly hymns."

"We'll have a Hammond onstage tomorrow night. Cost us a pretty penny to get one."

"Tomorrow? They're playing Alpine?"

Frank overheard their conversation. "You didn't hear? Where've you been?"

Where *had* she been?

The manager pulled a little notebook out of his breast pocket. "Give me your name. I'll put you on the list for backstage passes."

"Can I bring Roberta?"

"Only if she's as cute as you are."

"She's cuter." Sherri meant it. She'd always thought Roberta was the prettiest girl in the world.

"I doubt that. What's your name, honey?"

"Bunny Sherri," she said. "I mean, I'm Sherri. Sherri Taylor."

"I'll put you down for a plus-one. Just go to the backstage door after the concert, tell them you're on the list."

She couldn't believe it. Her name was on a list! And she'd discovered a novel way back into Roberta's good graces after the tension between them at the party earlier that summer. They hadn't spoken since, and while Sherri was too busy to actively think about Roberta, her friend's displeasure hovered over her thoughts.

Roberta's first love, before Ian, and before the Sex Pistols, was Gregg Allman. She had a poster of the Allman Brothers Band in her bedroom that her mother, a devout Catholic, absolutely hated because the band members sat naked in a creek. The other poster over her bed was of Allman alone in his golden glory, his straight, silver-blond hair long enough to brush his fingers while he was bent over his guitar. The glossy surface of the poster was smeared from lipstick stains and spots where Roberta touched it, closing her eyes and making a wish—for good luck on a test, or for a thunderstorm to save her from running laps outside in gym class. "Greggy loves me," Roberta said to Sherri. "He just doesn't know it yet."

Allman was like the family dog for Roberta, a constant source of watchfulness and comfort. She'd study the poster and say to Sherri with a dreamy look in her eyes, "He looks like a little boy trapped inside a man's body, doesn't he? Just look at him. He's lost so much. He's hurting. When I meet Greggy—and someday I will—I'm going to make him a pot roast. I can make him happy, Sher. I just know I can. I understand him, and I know he understands me, too, even though we've never met."

Once, when Roberta's family drove to Florida for a vacation (Sherri was so jealous; it was a big deal to go anywhere farther than Des Moines), Roberta told Sherri that she'd convinced her parents to stop in Macon, Georgia, on their return drive because she wanted to lay flowers on the spot where Gregg's brother Duane Allman had been killed by a truck carrying peaches, the tragedy that inspired their album *Eat a Peach*. Just a few blocks away was where bassist Berry Oakley had been killed in a separate motorcycle accident. Roberta said she'd stood in front of the old house the band lived in and waited in vain for Allman or guitarist Dickey Betts to emerge.

On the day Allman married Cher, Roberta wore all black to school, and then, when Cher filed for divorce just nine days later, she danced through the halls. "Now *I* can marry him." She remained devoted to the Allman Brothers even after Ian came along and introduced her to punk rock.

Sherri loved the Allman Brothers because she loved Roberta. She admired Gregg Allman, too, but not for his looks—he was pretty with his soft lips and blue eyes, but too pretty for Sherri's taste. What she admired about him was his musicianship. She and Roberta would lie on the shag rug in Roberta's basement and listen to her *Brothers and Sisters* and *At Fillmore East* albums over and over again, the sound big, jazzy, and Southern. They had two drum sets, and Allman was the only rock and roller she knew of who played the organ. She'd read that he'd said playing the organ "is like kissing a lady." She thought of that often when he rocked the pedals and the three-note chords. She wondered when Allman decided he could play whatever music he wanted, find his own sound, join a band, become an actual artist, do his own thing. Could he do that because he was a man, or because he was really that talented?

She took a fifteen-minute break and ran to the dressing room phone to call Roberta at her parents' house, a number Sherri had known by heart most of her life. "Berta, are you sitting down? You're going to die when you hear what I'm about to say."

Roberta screamed at the top of her lungs.

The next day was her first day off in ages. Arthur was due to pick her up around noon, and she felt nervous about seeing him again. She wasn't sure what it would be like—easy and passionate, or awkward and strange? She knew he'd be disappointed that she'd made other plans for later that night, but they'd have the afternoon together.

That morning she wanted to enjoy the pool and the sunshine and get a nice tan for the concert, but she still felt awful without speed. Every noise irritated her, from the sound of the music pumping through the speakers to the crickets chirping in the tall grass at the edge of the golf course. The click of her fellow Bunnies' heels on cement reminded her of the alarming sound of the shutter clicking in Mr. Saito's camera. She tried to push the memory into the back corner of her mind, along with all the other bad memories and her nagging bouts of insecurity and grief that haunted her when she wasn't on pills. The sun was offensively bright, and the humidity from the previous evening's storm made her hair look like a mess of broken springs. Instead of mingling, she sank into a lounge chair, exhausted and cranky.

She knew she had to come down, although she hadn't anticipated that she'd land with such a heavy thud. She could sleep for days. Her desire for sleep was almost as great as the sudden unwelcome desire for food. She closed her eyes and imagined herself biting into a big burger. Maybe she'd ask Arthur to take her to the A&W. Maybe they'd skip the boat ride and spend the afternoon in bed and he could cook for her the way he had during the week she spent with him, when he made pasta. It was delicious, even if she only had a few bites. She closed her eyes and tried to remember the feel of Arthur's hand gliding over her hip.

She woke to the feeling of someone blocking her sun.

"Hey." A familiar, laconic voice.

She opened her eyes, convinced she was still dreaming, and saw a man wearing a pair of big reflective sunglasses and a navy shirt tucked into his tight jeans. His ash-blond hair was longer now, almost to his shoulders, and fell in a lazy Andy Gibb wave. He looked like one of the rock musicians she saw in the hallways of the resort. He was impossibly beautiful and cool.

"Mitch?" Her stomach lurched. She sat up and wiped the drool from her mouth with the back of her hand. Off in the distance she saw the pool captain watching her; even on her day off she could get written up. "What are you doing here?" She wiped the sweat off of her brow with her towel and adjusted the bra top on her bikini.

"You said I should come visit, so here I am." He pointed at himself as if he were a gift.

She'd almost forgotten how desperate she'd been to see Mitch again; she used to check with Ola and Biata every single day to see if he'd called, but lately she hadn't even had a fleeting thought about him. He made her feel nervous, as though she needed to meet his standards.

"You came all this way just to see me?"

"Yeah, sure I did. All the way from California." His glasses refracted the sun into explosions of russet light. "It was a convenient excuse to buy a car."

"A new one? What kind?"

"An Excalibur. Just picked her up. She's a beauty."

Sherri tried to sound impressed. She remembered the Excalibur from the car show she'd worked with Val her second month on the job. Janesville was the sister town to Beloit and home of the massive GM plant. Val, like everyone from that corner of the state, knew all about cars. Val thumbed her nose at the showy, low-slung antique-looking roadsters that were manufactured in Milwaukee. "They design them to look like the pre–World War Two Mercedes," Val said between forced smiles. Excaliburs belonged in a black-and-white mobster movie from the thirties, outfitted with features she was paid to point at as the MC narrated the car's benefits: luggage racks, chrome wire tires, and exhaust pipes like rib cages. It was the kind of car a mayor would drive in a parade. Occasionally, Sherri would see one parked in front of the resort. The valets didn't bother moving them to the lot—showy cars like that they kept near the entrance, like the stretch Rolls-Royce the musicians used.

"Those cars are classy," Sherri had said.

Val had rolled her eyes. "They're stupid fiberglass kit cars built on a Pinto chassis. Piss elegance. Phyllis Diller drives them."

"Piss elegance" was the term that jumped into her mind that morning while she spoke to Mitch. "What about the Ferrari?" Sherri asked. "Isn't that a new car?"

"Who says I can't have more than one?"

"Nobody, silly. Drive a whole fleet if it makes you happy." Sherri tried to sound bright, but she could hardly open her eyes. Why did he have to show up on the day she was trying to come clean? "I bought a car, too." She thought she sounded very established. "A Monte Carlo."

"Why not a sports car?" Mitch looked around, unimpressed. "Hey, want to get out of here?" He pulled a crushed pack of Camels from his pocket, lit one with a shiny gold lighter, and exhaled slowly through his nose, dragon-style. "Let's go."

Sherri hesitated. She didn't know what to do. Arthur was probably driving to Lake Geneva in his cool red car at that very moment.

He feigned sadness. "Sherri, you don't seem very happy to see me and I came all this way."

"Oh, yes, I sure am!" Sherri jumped out of her chair, feeling dizzy from standing up so fast.

"You haven't even said hello."

"Hello, hello!" She hugged him but looked beyond where he stood, paranoid that Arthur would arrive at just that moment.

"That's more like it."

She pulled away. "I'm just surprised is all. A happy surprise. I was convinced I'd never see you again. I thought maybe you'd gotten yourself killed on some movie set." She laughed at herself. "That sounds terrible. What I mean is that I thought you were in LA thinking *Sherri who?*"

He smiled, revealing perfectly straight, pearl-white teeth. "I didn't die, and I didn't forget you. How could I? You're a blast. Let's go have some fun."

She looked at her watch. "Can you hang on a sec?" She stood and gestured for him to sit in her chair. "I'll be right back."

She ran into the resort, panicked, and looked around. She knew the right thing to do, but the right thing with Arthur meant a missed opportunity with Mitch. What if Mitch was the perfect guy for her? Besides, Arthur had been gone for ages, and she could see him any old time now that he was back. What was one more day?

Honey sat at a table at the Sidewalk Café reading a book, her beautiful dark hair cascading down either side of her face like black syrup. Honey was Korean. Her real name was Ha-yoon, and she was married to Bill, the Cabaret manager, who was British. The Bunnies were mostly local, but all the managers, it seemed, and even their wives and girlfriends, were from faraway places Sherri knew little about. They never lasted long, because management moved them from the clubs to the resorts in order to get experience.

She spied Arthur stepping into the lobby, looking out of his element, as if he knew he was wrong for the club and couldn't wait to leave. He walked with his hands stuffed deep in his jeans pockets. Sherri's heart lurched. She both longed to rush toward him, and run away.

"Can I hide in Bill's office?" Sherri asked. It felt like it was Honey's office. Bill was always rushing off to some meeting or other, but Honey was in there all the time.

Honey stood. "I hate it when these creeps won't leave you girls alone. Hurry!"

Sherri followed Honey into the office with the tinted interior window that overlooked the café. The clock said noon. Arthur's timeliness and obliviousness made Sherri feel a painful tenderness for him. He hadn't seen a thing, she could tell by the expectant look on his sweet, awkward, familiar face. He stopped and stared at the ceiling, no doubt considering how the place had been constructed—he liked to talk about joists, fluting, and eaves. "See that guy?" Sherri pointed him out to Honey. "The skinny one? Will you go out and ask how you can help him, and when he says he's looking for me, can you tell him that I had to work an off-site at the last minute?"

"I tell him go to hell!"

"No, he's not bad. Just . . . can you make him disappear?"

"Sure, baby." Honey called everyone "baby." "You got too many men?"

Sherri smiled, remembering what she'd been told shortly after she'd started—that she would need to arrange shifts for all the boyfriends she had. "Tell him it was a last-minute sort of thing."

"He don't need a story!"

Sherri peered through the window and watched Honey approach Arthur. She felt terrible. Arthur was there for one reason: to see her. But so was Mitch.

Honey returned. She clapped her hands together twice. "Bye-bye!" She flipped the blinds shut, and just like that, Arthur was gone.

Sherri sank into the desk chair. "Thank you."

"You're tired, baby. Here." Honey opened one of Bill's drawers and pulled out a mirror and a ziplock bag and set them on the desk. "You need a bump."

Honey sprinkled some white powder on the mirror, grabbed a razor blade, and began to *tack tack tack tack* it against the surface. Sherri was nervous. There were rules against drug use, including the rule Sherri had set for herself. Coke scared her. It seemed so frightening and unnatural to sniff powder up your nose. Technically she could get fired for this, but everyone did it, and besides, Honey was her manager's wife! What was one time, just to see what it was like? Honey pulled her gorgeous hair back, pinched one nostril with her finger, leaned over, and efficiently vacuumed one of the lines up her nose. It looked easy enough. Sherri's legs shook. "Now you go." She stepped aside, handed Sherri her rolled-up dollar bill, and put her hand on Sherri's back. When she leaned over, she saw her reflection in the mirror. *What am I doing?* she wondered—about the coke, about Arthur and Roberta, about her life. She sniffed hard. The texture was like cakey powdered sugar. It didn't burn, but ran into the back of her throat, where it felt like liquid metal.

Just before Sherri left Bill's office, Honey gestured for her to wipe the powder off her nose. "You can do it here next time," she said, pointing at her rear end. "Keep your nose good."

"You can put that in your butt?" Sherri was disgusted.

"Sure you can!" Honey began to laugh so hard she couldn't stop. "In your butt!"

When Sherri returned to the pool, she wiped her nose again and grew taller with every step, proud of what she'd done. She found Mitch surrounded by bikini-clad Ginger and Carmen and a few middle-aged golfers, chatting and drinking, already the life of the party.

"You're right," Carmen said admiringly. "Mitch really is cute!"

"You have any brothers?" Ginger asked. She was as tall as Mitch. "All the guys around here are two inches shorter than I am."

"He's mine!" Sherri said, playfully inserting herself into the group, coming back to life. The water, the sky, the trees: everything was in technicolor. Her rib no longer hurt. She felt like helium had been pumped into her veins. She looked at the lifeguards and the guests in their lounge chairs, Mitch, her friends: Did they feel what she felt? She was queen shit, that's what she was, illuminated from the inside. All this time she'd been told she was beautiful: by those creeps with the camera, Arthur, the guests, the little kids who stared at her in the hallway. She'd been flattered, but she hadn't really believed them. Now she knew what beauty really felt like.

"Guess what?" She reached into her purse and pulled out the tickets, scraping them playfully under Mitch's chin. "Allman Brothers are playing tonight at Alpine Valley, and I'm on the list for backstage passes. Want to go?"

CHAPTER FOURTEEN

They drove to Lake Geneva in Mitch's shiny beige Excalibur with the hood down. She loved the warmth of Mitch's arm resting behind her on the leather seat, and the feeling of her hair whipping into a crazy froth.

The fields were lush and green, punctuated with rolls and rolls of hay. "Hey Mitch, see those cows? I feel sorry for them. You know why?"

"No, why?"

"They can't get a square meal. Get it, square?" That was Roberta's joke. It always made Sherri laugh and laugh.

Judging by the slow traffic heading into downtown, it seemed everyone in the world wanted to be on the lake that day. On Broad Street, the tacky souvenir shops and ice cream parlors were jammed with people, and the sidewalks bustled with pedestrians who openly admired Mitch's car. He smiled, smug and confident. With all the news of the recent wedding of Lady Di and Prince Charles, Sherri felt she understood what it meant to be royalty. When they parked, he wiped the bullet mirrors with his handkerchief and fixed the collar on his shirt before opening her door.

At Popeye's, they sat at a table near the water even though the simple act of sitting seemed impossible now that the coke was in full effect—she could practically hear the orchestra of synapses firing in her brain. The host smiled at Mitch when she handed him his menu. "Welcome back." She left.

Sherri leaned forward. "Did she say welcome back?"

He flipped the menu open and pretended to inspect it. "I've been here a few days," he said.

Sherri wanted to clean out her ears. She'd blown off Arthur and nearly cheated Roberta out of Gregg Allman for him, and he hadn't told her he was in town? Wasn't *she* the reason he was there? "Why didn't you come find me sooner?"

"I did, all right? I asked around. You were busy working and I had stuff to do. What's the big deal? I didn't think you were one of those clingy girls. I thought you were cool. Really cool."

"I am, I just, you know. I could have seen you."

"I'm with you now, aren't I?" He reached across the table and grabbed Sherri's hand. "I flew halfway across the country to see your pretty face." He leaned forward and kissed her on the nose, then the mouth. "Can't you just appreciate that I'm here? We're together now." He tickled her under her arm the way he might tickle a little kid, and Sherri laughed loudly enough for all the people at the tables around them to turn and look. "Let's have a good time."

A good time? Those were magic words for Sherri, who'd already forgotten why she'd been upset. Coke was an independent drug, making her fall more in love with herself than with Mitch, free of the complicated and deep feelings she had for Arthur. She ordered a Cuba Libre. And another. After they ate, they wandered over to the bar. Soon Mitch was striking up conversations with people who seemed as impressed by him as Sherri was. He stood with his arm draped around Sherri's shoulders and told people that his father had been nominated for an Oscar, and said that his family's cook used to work as the cook for Elvis, and that he'd had to work in a zero-gravity chamber once when he worked on *Battlestar Galactica*. He was good at reading the crowd. He knew that his stories of Hollywood glamour would appeal to them.

"It must be so exciting in LA," Sherri said. "The only thing that's ever happened in East Troy was a visit from Grover Cleveland a hundred years ago."

Mitch laughed—it made Sherri feel good to make him laugh. "You'd love Venice Beach. It's like this"—he gestured at the pavilion on the waterfront just beyond the window and the crowds of people walking past—"only you can surf, and it's sunny all year long."

"California sounds perfect!"

"It is. Hate to say it, but everything is just better there."

This sentiment, so definitive and absolute, appealed to Sherri, who believed there was an established collective conscious she was only beginning to tap into, one that ranked people and places and behaviors from worst to best.

A freckly guy named Rye with brassy hair and madras shorts invited Mitch and Sherri to see the lake on his wooden Chris-Craft. They jumped at the opportunity, especially Sherri. She hadn't been on a lake since the night of her party at Arthur's, and summer and lakes were interwoven in her mind.

Rye tooled around the shore in his fancy wooden boat, skirting the ends of the long piers that stuck out into the lake. Just beyond them, walkers strolled along the community footpath that circled the shoreline. He pointed out all the big estates perched on grassy bluffs, each one different in style—some old-timey and Victorian and others glassy and modern, but all grand and impressive. When she was a girl and her family had taken a tour of the lake, she had been awed by the homes. "These houses are for just one family?" Sherri had asked her father. "I'll bet they're mortgaged to the hilt," he said. Her mother was not impressed. "Too many bathrooms to clean."

"They call this the Newport of the Midwest," Rye said to Mitch. "You've got movie stars out West, and here we've got captains of industry. Sears, Wrigley, Maytag, Schwinn. All those families have houses on the lake." Rye waved to the sailors in their fancy boats. "Oh hey, Mr. Levy," he said. "Hey Mrs. Pierce. Great day, huh?" It was clear from the easy, familiar interactions that Rye had known his lake neighbors his whole life. The culture of the lake was easy. It was a place where the playing field between kids and adults was more level. You could buy your way into this world, sure, but it was better to be born into that net of connections.

Mitch sat with his hands behind his head and nodded as if he knew everything already. Sherri sympathized with Rye. There was something about Mitch that made them both want to impress him.

"See that?" Rye pointed at a massive boathouse built to resemble a lake steamer that sat in front of a Spanish-style mansion. "That's called the SS *No-Go*. The people who own the place, the Bells, created the soap opera *The Young and the Restless*."

Sherri's mother had loved that soap. It wasn't like the other soaps; it was modern. It had mood lighting, a gorgeous soundtrack, lesbians, sex, women having breakdowns. "My friend Roberta calls it *The Young and the Rest of Us*," Sherri said. Roberta, Roberta. She was probably in her bedroom getting ready for the show at that exact moment. There was still time for Sherri to ditch Mitch, although she knew she wouldn't. That afternoon, she gave herself credit for merely having the intention to do the right thing.

Sherri snuggled into Mitch's side as if they'd been together for years. He was the kind of boyfriend she'd always dreamed of: handsome, popular, fun. Sherri giggled and bit his earlobe. "We had a good time in Galveston, didn't we? Remember how soft those sheets were?" She ran her finger down the side of his golden face and down his chest. "How about next time I come visit you in California? A bunch of girls have been to the Playboy Mansion in LA. Hef says any Bunny is invited." She said "Hef" the way the girls at the club did, as if they were old friends, even though she'd never laid eyes on the man. Still, his name had currency. "Bunny Lisa and Bunny Karen went there and stayed a whole week." She didn't tell him that they seemed changed from the experience. Damaged. Lisa took money from the gift shop to buy drugs and was fired; Karen just stopped coming to work—who knew what had happened to her. "Maybe I could take you there for a party."

"Yeah," Mitch said. "You should come out. That would be great."

Sherri nuzzled her face in his neck. His jaw was smooth and soft, nothing like the scratchiness of Arthur's face. She pictured herself in the passenger seat of Mitch's car in LA with big sunglasses on, cruising down some road with palm trees lining both sides, the sun high in the sky.

Motorboats zipped around them, and the air smelled of gasoline. Mitch asked Rye to teach him how to water-ski. Sherri was surprised that a stuntman didn't already know how, and surprised that it took him so many tries before he got up. She clapped and cheered for him like a real girlfriend over the sound of the motor. After his last effort, they stopped in the middle of the lake, a lake so big that she could hardly see the shore. This, she thought, must be what it was like to be out on the ocean. She could feel her face and shoulders burn from the sun.

Mitch took off his skis and threw his life preserver on the back of the boat and swam around, leaving Sherri alone with Rye. His leather Sperry Top-Siders were so worn that they looked like they'd been passed down from generation to generation. Sherri didn't know what to make of this trust-fund guy who acted like he was used to getting whatever he wanted. He was about her own age, but their lives couldn't have been more different. He abandoned the captain's chair and moved to the bow of the boat to sit with her. "Mitch is a great guy and all that, don't get me wrong, but he doesn't seem like he's your type," he said.

"What does that mean?"

"I don't know. After he leaves, you and your friends should come to a party at my place." He looked at her the way Mr. Saito and Ron had. That was an experience she still hadn't made sense of. She wanted to just forget it and move on, and the drugs made that easier, but even through the haze of drinks and coke she felt his leer igniting a combination of fear and anger, both at him (and guys like him) and at herself because she'd been such an idiot—so stupid she'd even missed out on earning a free moped, and who knew where those photos might surface?

"Do you have some blow?" she asked. She craved that feeling again, craved the way the coke sealed her up inside, made her impervious.

"Sure," Rye said. He licked his finger, reached into a bag, and covered it with powder. "Open up," he said, and he rubbed his finger over her gums. Sherri's mouth turned instantly numb, a strange and wonderful feeling, followed by that explosion of confidence and energy she'd felt earlier that day.

"I want to swim!" Without even taking off her T-shirt or jean shorts, she jumped into the lake. The water was freezing, much colder than Beulah had been a month ago. It sucked the air out of her lungs. Mitch was about thirty yards away, and she swam toward him. It was one thing to swim in the deep part of Lake Beulah, but she'd heard that Lake Geneva was almost a hundred and fifty feet deep, almost as deep as the Water Tower in Chicago was tall.

Mitch began to swim to the metal ladder that hung off the back of Rye's boat and Sherri followed him, giggling and splashing. But then she stopped, and the bubble of her enthusiasm was momentarily ruptured when she remembered her watch, the one her father had given her. She felt for it, but her wrist was bare. For just a moment she wondered if she'd put it on, but she was sure she had. She wasn't allowed to wear jewelry with her costume, so she made a special point of wearing it when she wasn't on the job. It must have slipped under the water, and she went back under in hopes of finding it. When she surfaced,

Rye gunned the engine and drove away, with Mitch waving goodbye, laughing. Some of the water from the choppy wake went up her nose and she began to cough. "Hey!" she called out. "Hey, that's not funny." She slapped the water in frustration. What if a ski boat headed in her direction? How would the driver ever see her? "Come back!"

They looped back around to get her, but those few minutes when she wasn't sure if they would return felt like a lifetime. She pulled herself back on the boat and wrapped herself in a towel. "That was a horrible thing to do. You guys are assholes, you know that?"

Mitch handed Sherri a beer, and Rye looked at her wet T-shirt clinging to her chest. "Hey, come here," Mitch said, and he wrapped her into a hug. "I'm sorry, we were just fooling around. Don't go getting all sad."

She gazed at the choppy surface of the water and thought about her watch sinking to the bottom of the massive glacial lake. It had been her last connection to who she was; part of her drowned along with it, and there was no going back.

The concert would soon start, but just as they got ready to head to shore, Rye backed the boat up over the ski rope and it fouled the propeller. "What'll we do?" Sherri asked.

"Well," Rye said. "You guys can swim to shore, or we sit here and wait for another boat to come by and tow us."

The water was too cold and the shore too far away for the first option. They sat on the boat for an hour as the sun began to slip behind the horizon. Finally, they waved down a ski boat whose skipper offered to pull them back, a slow process, moving inch by inch. Sherri thought she'd die of impatience as they puttered back to shore in the waning light. By the time they ditched Rye, got back to Mitch's car and drove up the long gravel drive that led to the parking lot at Alpine Valley, everyone was already there. The guys from her high school whose job was to direct cars stood around in their money aprons.

"You want VIP parking?" Trent Eagan, her old lifeguard crush, spoke to Mitch without registering that it was Sherri sitting in the passenger seat.

"Yeah, VIP," Mitch said, but Sherri stopped him.

"Don't fall for it. It's a scam. There is no VIP parking. He just wants to pocket the extra five bucks."

"That you, Sherri Taylor?"

"Yes, and I'll tell Dave D what you're up to if you don't let us park for free." Dave Dodge was the manager. Everyone knew him. He was referred to as Dave D, Double D, D Squared.

Trent laughed. "You got me." He waved Mitch in and smiled sheepishly at Sherri. "I hear you're one of those Bunnies now."

Sherri smiled and waved as Mitch drove away. They parked, and she pulled down the visor to inspect her appearance. Her hair had dried into ringlets like Nellie Oleson's on *Little House on the Prairie*, and her jean shorts were still damp. She put on a fresh coat of lipstick and some mascara while Mitch pulled out an eight ball. Within moments she was lit again, full of energy, no longer nervous about running into. She led Mitch by the hand past the campgrounds and the woods, and when they crested a hill Mitch looked admiringly at the sea of fans. They could have been explorers discovering a lost civilization. They walked through clouds of marijuana and cigarette smoke and stepped on beach blankets, towels, and crushed red Solo cups.

The band started to play "Blue Sky." Everyone stood and cheered, singing along: "You're my blue sky, you're my sunny day." Roberta loved that song. On their way to the stage they passed Tony McKenna, who had nine brothers and sisters whose first names all started with the letter *T*. It had been a game to memorize them: Tony, Tracy, Tia, Travis . . . The whole concert venue seemed to be run by her high school. If her former classmates didn't work parking cars or selling tickets, they printed tickets and volunteered as ushers, just as Roberta had for the Jackson Browne concert the previous summer. She told Sherri that the fans played volleyball naked, and that the flatlanders from Illinois drank Michelob while the locals drank Bud. She was taught to hold the flashlights to check tickets, but that also the flashlights were weapons to push drunk and unruly concertgoers out of her way. It was important, she said, to keep fans out of the fire lanes.

There, standing at the stage with a clipboard, was Paula Kipp, who used to call her "Sherri Taylor Trash."

"Hey Paula," Sherri said. "I'm on the list."

"Right. Everyone says they're on the list."

Sherri was once again queen shit. She had no patience for Paula. "I am! Just look." Sherri aggressively flicked the back of the clipboard with her painted fingernails. "You'll see."

Paula offered an indulgent sigh, shined her flashlight on the page, and scanned it. There it was, Sherri's name, with a "+1" next to it.

"I told you."

"But you can't go back there until after the show." Paula looked at Mitch, who stood with his hands on his slim hips, gazing off in the distance. "Is this your boyfriend?"

"He sure is." The word "boyfriend" conjured Arthur, although Sherri had a feeling that Paula wouldn't be as impressed if it were Arthur by her side, because he wasn't cool the way Mitch was.

"Wow."

Fortunately, Gary, the band manager, recognized Sherri. He smiled and gestured for her to join him. "The Bunny is here!"

"See ya, Paula," Sherri said. She threw her cigarette butt on the grass and ground it down with the toe of her wooden Dr. Scholl's.

Gary opened a cooler, tossed Mitch and Sherri cans of Michelob, and led them to the back side of the stage. And there he was, Gregg Allman in the flesh. He was sitting at a Hammond B-3 organ, mimicking the rhythm guitar with the percussion tab set to the third harmonic. He looked older than the image that was burned into Sherri's mind. His hair was less lustrous, his beard scraggly, but he was still handsome and cool in his T-shirt and a black leather vest. He glanced to the side and Sherri swore he saw her, really saw her. His eyes were the same sad, soulful eyes from Roberta's poster. She was close enough that she could study his hands while he played and watch his sweat fly into the lights like dust in front of a window on a sunny day.

The wooden floor hummed with the bass. She understood now how musicians felt like gods when she saw the red, yellow, and blue lights pan over the screaming sea of audience members. Beach balls bounced in the air. Sherri's whole body, and even the aluminum of her beer can, pulsed with the vibrations of the drums and the sizzle of electricity running up and around the heavy stage curtains and the pipes, tubes, and wires that held everything in place.

She reached for Mitch's arm and began pressing her fingertips into his flesh the way her mother had once pressed invisible piano keys while Sherri played. She wished she could sit down and play a duet with Allman. She could almost imagine all the hours he'd sat on a piano bench with his teacher, all the recitals and practice books, and now he had effortless mastery of his craft. She loved the way he bounced the single nondominant seventh and repeated the hooks. She wanted Mitch to be impressed that she understood this language, that she knew how to play, that she felt the music, that she was special, but he wasn't paying attention to the band at all, didn't care that she'd tried to turn his arm into a keyboard. He'd started talking to the guy standing next to him, who said he airbrushed nature scenes onto the sides of vans. How could Mitch talk through that song? If only Roberta were there with her. They would have been having the best time.

The band started playing "Ramblin' Man" and the crowd went wild. So did Sherri. She raised her arms in the air and shook her hips. She mouthed along with the words. *When it's time for leavin' I hope you'll understand.* The guitarist leaned forward and dug his guitar into his thighs, holding the instrument like a wild animal he'd just caught with his own hands. Sherri closed her eyes and wished the moment would never end. But it did, and after the hysterical clapping, Sherri wondered why the band refused an encore. Then she realized that *that* was the encore. She couldn't believe it. They'd missed the entire show!

The drawbar setting Allman chose for the finish was dark but honest. The somber notes echoed ominously off the hillside and into her future.

After the show, Sherri and Mitch were walking along the heavily wooded path that led up the hill to the parking lot when, just ahead of them, Roberta caught sight of her. "Sherri?"

Sherri felt terrible. "Oh hey."

"'Oh hey'? I waited for you for over an hour. I was stuck by myself on the lawn."

"Yeah, well I was busy."

Roberta pointed at Mitch. "With him?"

"I couldn't reach you."

"You didn't fucking try."

Mitch walked ahead of them, clearly uninterested in getting caught up in a drama between two women.

Tough as Roberta was, Sherri hadn't ever seen her angry, not like this. "I don't even know you anymore."

"I'm still me." Sherri pointed at herself, her words slurred. Her blood was slushed with alcohol and her head was buzzing from a pill someone gave her backstage. She did nothing but stand there with a dumb grin on her face. She grinned!

"You *aren't* still you. The Sherri I know would have never ditched me."

Sherri tossed back her hair.

"You're a slut," Roberta said. "Everyone in town thinks so."

"I'm not a slu—" She couldn't even say the word, but she still felt the sting of it. Before she could say more, Roberta ran off and Sherri started to run after her, but Mitch grabbed her arm.

"Don't worry about her. She'll get over it," he said. In her state of mind, it was easy to take his advice.

The party moved from Alpine Valley to the Hogs & Kisses bar in Lake Geneva. Sherri loved being part of the rock-star entourage, and so did Mitch—this was what it must have felt like to be on homecoming court, only better. After her encounter with Roberta, Sherri was determined to have fun. She snorted some more lines of coke in the bathroom, only this time the drug made her nerves feel frayed. Her jaw seemed to come unmoored, rocking back and forth, and she couldn't control her body language. She climbed onto the bar and danced with the other patrons, although she couldn't seem to move with the music.

Next thing she knew, she was partying in Hugh Hefner's suite at the resort after Small Paul snuck her in. Even if she was caught, she had a feeling Gloria wouldn't mind, because the rules were bent for celebrities or high-ranking keyholders with gold-tipped keys.

She would remember the rest of the night in fragments. The suite had carpeting on the walls and a giant, round bed. Gregg Allman flopped down onto it and fell fast asleep, a shot glass resting on his stomach. At some point, Paul snuck down to the kitchen refrigerator and entered the room holding lobsters in each hand. He took the rubber bands off their claws and the pathetic creatures flailed around on the carpet for what seemed like forever. After a while, people just stepped out of their way. Finally, a stagehand threw them out the window onto the golf course, shouting, "You're free, motherfuckers!"

The next morning, the room was gassy from all the bodies flopped on every surface. Mitch and Sherri had fallen asleep on the couch. She was on top of him, and woke to see his face—just a mortal, puffy face. She stood up, and saw the outline of Allman's figure on its side in Hefner's bed. He snored loudly. If only Roberta were there to see Gregg Allman right there, snoring. Sherri felt sick with guilt. How could she have betrayed her best friend?

She walked into the bathroom and made herself throw up. It was easy, because her stomach turned as much from all the crud in her system as from the memory of Arthur walking back out of the building without her, and the scene with Roberta. The word "slut" hit the sides of her head like a moth against a light bulb that awful, hungover morning. What was a slut, anyway? Why was it so terrible for a woman to want to have unadulterated, boundless fun? All anyone seemed to think about anyway was pleasure, so what was it with all the puritanism? She was free to do what she wanted. She was independent! Liberated! It wasn't lost on her that she wrestled with these thoughts while showering in Hugh Hefner's bathroom, in the very place where he'd stood naked. But did he ever feel such poisonous shame?

Before she left, she kissed Mitch on his lips. Who knew someone so handsome could have such sour breath? "See you later?" she whispered.

"No. I've got to head back today."

"Today?" She couldn't believe it. "To California?"

"Yeah, where else?"

"But I'll come visit you?"

"Sure, sure. That'd be great. We'll have a grand time." He gave her half a hug. "Thanks for the show." He pointed at Gregg Allman, asleep on the round bed. "I mean, look at that. Just look! It's great here, Sher. *You're* great. A ton of fun."

She stumbled, still drunk and a little coked-up, out the door, creeping down the carpeted back stairs all the way to the basement locker room. It was surprisingly empty. She took forever to get dressed. Just turning her black tights right side out felt like a Herculean task. She'd lost so much weight that she could get her uniform zipped without much effort, although her hands were so shaky that she wished someone were in the locker room to help her. She sank onto the bench and closed her eyes. What she wouldn't give for some sleep.

Gloria emerged from her office, took one look at her, and frowned. "Well. Look what the cat coughed up."

"Thanks a lot," Sherri said. She couldn't argue. She did look like shit. She opened her locker and pulled out her makeup bag.

Gloria shook two aspirin out of the bottle and handed the tablets to her. "You can't go out on the floor like that."

"I just need some coffee."

"No. What you need is to slow down."

Sherri tried to line her lips. A three-year-old could have done a better job. She needed another bump, that was what she needed. Every cell in her body cried out for cocaine. "I just had a long night, OK? I couldn't sleep with Val snoring."

Gloria put her hands on her hips. "Look in the mirror, sweetheart." Did Gloria just call her "sweetheart"? "Look at yourself!"

Sherri was gaunt and ghostly, with dark circles under her eyes, and her face was puffy and red from sunburn. She was so thin that someone could crack her in half like a twig.

"I know all about you, Sherri," Gloria said. "I've known all along. I know about your mom. Your dad. Your 'brothers.'"

"How?" All this time, Sherri had been so careful to keep her old life separate from her new one.

"Your friend you came here to interview with, she told me. I knew before you even showed up in my office. That was why I let you interview."

"Because you felt sorry for me?"

"Listen, I don't feel sorry for anyone. Life is tough. Just ask any of the girls. You aren't the only person here with a master's degree from the school of hard knocks."

"And?" Here it was. Sherri waited for Gloria to lower the boom.

"And nothing."

Gloria picked some dirty cotton balls off the floor and threw them in the garbage with a look of disgust. "You want to know why I hired you? It's not because you were the prettiest girl to walk through that door. It's because you wanted to work here so badly that you were willing to lie for the job. You were hungry."

"Don't fire me, Gloria. Please." Sherri didn't want to cry in front of Gloria. Not Gloria!

"I could have fired you a long time ago. Believe me, I've thought about it. For someone who's a quick study at everything else, you're slow to learn about yourself. You're slipping. I see it. Everyone sees it. But you?"

"I'll do better. I will. Please, I've got nothing else."

Gloria put her hands on her hips. "You really believe that, don't you?"

Sherri couldn't answer, because Gloria was right, as usual.

"I don't think it's the *job* you want," she continued, after a pause.

"It is. I love it."

"Get out of here, Sherri." She pointed at the door.

"Please. Don't." She was so desperate she wanted to hurl herself at Gloria, grab on to her, beg. "I'll go out there and bust my ass. You'll see. I'll be fine."

"Clean up. Grow up. Get all that shit out of your system. Get your act together."

"You mean I can come back?"

Gloria turned and began walking toward to her office.

"Please?"

"Take care of yourself. Dry out, Sher. No more pills. No more sleigh rides." She clicked the door shut behind her.

Sherri, angry, looked at herself in the full-length mirror and began to pull off her eyelashes, tugging the ends so hard that her eyelids were distorted and her vision blurred. But if it was from pain or the tears that had gathered against her will, she wasn't sure.

CHAPTER FIFTEEN

Sherri emerged from the locker room and considered her options. She had no idea that every move she was about to make on that fateful day would, in effect, be like sprinkling bread crumbs of guilt in her memory, creating a path of mistakes that she'd travel again and again long into her future.

She felt trapped, with nowhere to go but East Troy, the great boomerang. If she went to her house, Roberta would see her, because Giles was just across the square, and her stomach turned with shame at the thought of what she'd done. Worse, she couldn't stand to see all the people in town who apparently thought she was a slut. She could go to Arthur's, and she would, eventually, but she sure couldn't ask Mitch to drive her there.

Mitch! She could still catch him. She kicked her stiletto heels off her feet and ran barefoot up the carpeted stairs one, two flights up, and raced down the hallway to Hugh Hefner's suite. She'd go with him to California in his Excalibur, that's what she'd do. Screw this place. Screw Gloria. Screw East Troy. Nobody would even miss her—nobody but Arthur.

Arthur, Arthur. What was she supposed to do with him? She

compartmentalized her thinking, pushing the image of him and his sweet smile and low voice and soft, broad back into a separate closed space in her mind, like one of the many hotel rooms she passed with DO NOT DISTURB tags hanging on the door handles. He was too good for her. She didn't deserve him. He'd believed she was smart enough for college and she couldn't even keep it together as a Bunny.

She reached Hefner's suite, perched at the edge of the lobby. She took a deep breath and knocked on the door, a light, polite tap that belied her desperation. Nobody answered. She hadn't been gone that long—maybe an hour. Was everyone still sleeping?

She knocked again, this time louder, louder. "Mi-*itch*," she said, her voice carrying downstairs and echoing off the glass walls surrounding the indoor swimming pool. "Open up."

Finally, the door swung open and a groggy Gregg Allman himself stood there in a pair of saggy white briefs, the gold mushroom charm with the band's name resting on top of his chest hair. Even after a night's sleep his hair was still perfectly parted down the middle; his part was so neat and straight that it was the only thing in her life that made sense that morning. He rubbed his eye with the back of his fist. He didn't seem to recognize her from the night before. "Yeah?"

"I'm looking for my boyfriend. He was, I was—we were both here last night."

Allman scratched his head. "Sorry, honey, everyone's gone now." He had a gentle Southern accent and a sweet, shy way of speaking. "I told 'em to scram. I've got a gig tonight in Chicago and need some rest. So if you'll—"

She peered beyond him to see if she could see Mitch on the couch she'd slept on. "Everyone?" Her voice was small and sad.

"Yup, it's just me here."

She was worried she'd start to cry. "Gregg?" Sherri reached into her purse and rifled around for something, anything to write on. "Is there any way I could get your autograph? For my friend Roberta? She loves you. She really does. She always has."

His sigh was impatient and laced with irritation. "Sure, but then you've got to go, OK?"

"One sec." Lipstick, nail polish, powder, a comb. There was a felt-tip pen, but no paper. Nothing. He yawned. She bit her lip. She had to find something, she just had to. She wanted to make things right with Roberta, with Gloria, with Arthur. With everyone.

"You take care," he said, and he began to shut the door.

"Wait, here." Sherri pulled out the only thing he could possibly write on: a maxi pad. She unfolded it and handed it to him.

He seemed amused. "What'd you say her name was?"

"Roberta. And could you do me a favor? Could you sign it Greggy? That's what she calls you."

"Now, which one of us is going to tell her I hate that name?" He winked and handed her the maxi pad and pen. "Now get lost." He paused and looked right into her eyes. It was as if he saw something in her that he recognized. "And honey, watch yourself." The door shut with a soft clicking of the bolt.

Sherri held the maxi pad in her fist. Now what? Just like that, with Mitch and her ticket to California already gone, an impulsive plan she'd made for the rest of her life burst as quickly as it had come into her head. She needed to replace it with a new impulsive plan.

One thing became clear: she needed her car in the same way that Raylee had needed her old Sundance bike. Wheels meant freedom.

She went to her dorm room to grab a few of her things. Val and Danny were asleep in her little twin bed, wrapped around each other like pretzels. She used to think they were a cute couple, but she was too fried and hurt for anything to strike her as cute. She resented their closeness. Her gaze rested on the moped, a horrible reminder of that awful day, leaning against the far wall of her dorm room.

She threw as much into her bag as would fit, trying to be quiet so that she wouldn't have to explain her latest failure. Just before leaving, she grabbed her wad of tip money. She stuffed it into her purse, as big as the signed maxi pad, and took one last look at the careless comfort of the messy room they'd shared—the Miss Breck hair spray, a tube of lipstick on the window ledge, the bikini top hanging out of the drawer, the fermenting pile of laundry at the foot of the rumpled bed.

She ran to the locker room and asked Ola if she could use the phone. Ola and Biata were like mothers to the girls, always fussing over them, always concerned. They loved the activity and drama of the dressing room, and they loved the girls, every one of them. They kept extra tampons, hair spray, bobby pins, and deodorant in their office, and were always available with a dab of nail polish to stop a run in their nylons from getting worse, or a needle and thread when a seam split, and club soda to treat a stain. "They're like the world's best bridesmaids," Bunny Tina had once said to Sherri, and it was true. Ola could see that Sherri was in a bad state. "Sit, sit," she said when she saw her. She offered her a pierogi, a small, kind gesture that almost made Sherri fall apart. She knew this was likely the last time she'd see the women who'd so steadily buttressed her days.

Ola handed her the phone and left the room carrying a basket of dirty uniforms. Sherri called Jerry Derzon to ask him to come get her. She knew his number by heart, because she called him twice a week to see about the building. "You're going to have to wait while I get going," he said. "I'm not a taxi."

"It's not like I've got anything better to do."

Ola saw her as she was leaving. "Oh, *biedne dziecko*," she said. Sherri didn't need to speak Polish to know that she was saying "poor baby." How she wished she could collapse in Ola's talcum-scented embrace. She longed for someone to fret over her well-being and ached for her mother. She kissed Ola on the cheek and squeezed her muscular hands, unable to bring herself to say goodbye.

Back in the lobby, the sound of Muzak piping through the speakers was oddly comforting. She plopped into a big chair by the entrance and waited for Jerry to arrive and whisk her away to the dealership. At least she had her new car to look forward to.

Bored, she pulled out her money and began to count, trying to be discreet the way that Arthur had taught her. Twenty, thirty, sixty, one hundred and forty, three hundred, five hundred and fifty, seven hundred and ten, eleven, twelve . . . She stopped and counted again. She was sure she'd saved over a thousand dollars, absolutely sure. She'd put five hundred down when she'd ordered the car. She'd planned to pay another eleven hundred for 20 percent down.

"Oh hey, Sherri."

Sherri looked up from her money and saw Rhonda. She looked like Tinker Bell with her pixie haircut. Now that she worked the coat check, she wore a brown polyester vest and pair of slacks like the ones the switchboard operator wore. Still, she looked cute in them. Adorable even. She glowed. "Rhonda! Wow, you're so big now."

Rhonda turned so that Sherri could see her profile. A neat little mound stuck out, a bump of caution. Suddenly tiny Rhonda appeared so grown-up, so brave. She was managing. She thrust her hand in Sherri's face. A tiny chip of a diamond sparkled in the platinum band on her ring finger. "Look, I'm married, Sher! Can you believe it? I'm a 'Mrs.' now. Mrs. Frank Mitten."

It was one thing to lose her last name, but her first name, too? Sherri swore she'd never, ever get married, never change her name (especially to Mitten), never have a baby, never get dragged into the world of responsibility and obligation, never become a Rhonda.

"We're really happy," Rhonda said. "We snuck off to the Walworth County Courthouse last week. Our parents still aren't talking to us. They wouldn't even throw us a reception. But you know what? We're going to be fine, just the two—no, three—of us!"

"That's great," Sherri said, trying to sound sincere. Then she had an idea. If she couldn't be at the resort, the resort could come to her. "Let me throw you guys a party. How about Sunday?"

"Sunday as in *tomorrow?*"

"Yeah, tomorrow. Tell everyone. We'll have way more fun than some stuffy reception in a church basement."

Rhonda beamed. "Seriously?"

"Come to my friend's house on Lake Beulah." Sherri saw Jerry's car in the entranceway. "Two o'clock. It's on the tip of Jesuit Island. Invite anyone you want, OK? Danny knows where it is."

"Sounds great," Rhonda said. "Speaking of Danny, have you seen him? Some guy says he left his nine iron in the cart but housekeeping can't find it."

"He's in my room with Val, as always. Those two can't keep their hands off each other. I wish they'd get a hotel room for once." There it was, Val's secret. Sherri didn't care that she'd spilled the beans. After all, Val had stolen from her.

Rhonda's expression darkened. She pointed discreetly at something behind Sherri. Oh, no. Sherri turned and there was Curtis, standing behind her, fuming as usual. He wore a stiff jean jacket with a giant comb sticking out of the chest pocket. She felt heat rise to her cheeks. Was it possible that he'd heard her? As upset as Sherri was with Val, she took no satisfaction from the predicament her friend was about to find herself in, not after seeing Curtis's face flush with rage. Sherri prided herself on being good at keeping secrets, but she'd blown it this time. She wished like crazy that she could rewind the last five minutes—the last five days.

Jerry stepped into the lobby and waved, gesturing at his car. Who could have imagined that of all the people in Sherri's world, he'd be her knight in shining armor, that his car was the carriage that would take her away from this very bad day? "I'll see you tomorrow." She threw her bag over her shoulder and brushed past Curtis without even looking at him. She dashed out the front door and sank into the passenger seat of Jerry's car, replaying her conversation with Rhonda in her head, trying to figure out if Curtis could have heard her over the music and the din of conversation in the lobby. "Drive fast."

"What's up, buttercup?"

Sherri didn't know where to begin. "I don't think I'm cut out to be a Bunny, Jer."

"I could have told you that a long time ago, saved you some trouble. That job is too easy for you."

"Too easy? No, it's too hard. I screw up all the time."

"Cut yourself a forest of slack. Screwing up is what you do when you're young. Only some of us, including yours truly, never stop making mistakes." He patted her on the leg in a fatherly way and offered her a piece of Hubba Bubba. She'd never before looked straight into his eyes. Something had broken down between them. She was no longer a Bunny, and he was no longer Monopoly Jerry or the Barnacle. They were just a couple of locals heading home.

"Can you take me to Frascona's? I bought a car."

"Listen to you. That's really something, your own car."

"Jerry, can't you do something about the building? It's just been sitting there for months now. I can't stand it. I need to move on."

Jerry seemed to agree. "Well, I do have an idea, as a matter of fact. I don't know if you'll like it, but hear me out. It could help us both."

"Yeah?"

"How about we take out a mortgage on the building. Thirty grand, something like that. You take the money from the bank, and I pay the mortgage and the taxes and pocket anything extra. And if I can't rent the space, I lose. If I can, and I make more than the bills, I win. Either way, you're free and clear. Once the mortgage is all paid down, say thirty years from now, the building is still yours."

Sherri turned that idea around in her mind. They were on Highway 120, passing over Sugar Creek. Thirty years was an eternity, an amount of time she couldn't wrap her head around. "Thirty grand?"

"That sounds about right to me. That's enough to get you a fresh start somewhere else."

"What do I do about Arthur?"

"So about him—" Jerry was going to say more but he slammed on the brakes abruptly, throwing his arm in front of Sherri so she wouldn't fly through the windshield. She became acutely aware of her bruised rib again.

"Hang on." Jerry pulled over to the side of the road and threw the car into park. He stepped out and clomped along the asphalt in his wing tips. She watched him bend down to pick up a giant turtle from the middle of the road. He carried it to the other side, walked down a berm and into the wetland to set it free. He returned to the car wiping his hands with the stained linen handkerchief he kept in his pocket. Mud was caked onto the sides of his shoes.

"The turtles don't stand a chance with all the trucks. You know those buggers can live to be almost two hundred years old? That big guy I just moved, he was probably older than I was. Older than my grandpa. You should have seen him kicking. Mad as a hornet."

"I didn't have you pegged as the kind of guy who saves turtles."

"I think I know what kind of guy you had me pegged as."

He was right. "Jerry, I'm sorry—"

"Don't be. You weren't entirely wrong." He stared straight ahead.

"That's nice you saved it."

"Nice? It's what you do. I'll tell you something about turtles, Sher. They have a slow metabolism. They move slow, but they also die slow. Say a truck ran him over. It could take him weeks to pass. We don't want that."

"No," she said. "We don't."

"Once you get that car of yours, you watch out for the turtles, OK? And you drive in the center of the road when there's no traffic so you won't hit a deer if it darts out of the woods." He pressed the accelerator. "And when you're waiting to turn left in an intersection, always, always straighten out your wheel. Otherwise someone hits you from behind and bam! You're history. So where were we?"

Sherri was so hungover she couldn't remember what they'd been talking about. Arthur? All she cared about was the mortgage. She didn't fully understand Jerry's plan, and she didn't need to. "The building?"

"Right. This business arrangement we discussed, it could really help me out, kiddo. Maybe you heard Doris left me."

"She did?" Sherri wasn't all that surprised.

"She says I'm a hopeless drunk, and I'm trying to prove her wrong. I haven't had a drop of alcohol in over a month. I'm trying to be a better man."

"Doris will come back."

"Nah. It's over. It's been over for a long time. I've worn out my second chances. And now she's squeezing me for everything I've got, and I can't say I really blame her. This arrangement would allow me to live in your apartment and rent out the store space. Plus, I think it would help you out, too. I like you, Sherri. You're doing what you need to do to keep going. I get it. I promise I'm not trying to cheat you."

He drove around the square. Giles was packed. Roberta was probably somewhere inside, making sure none of the customers gave her any shit. Just off the square he pulled up in front of Frascona's. The shiny new cars with their bright yellow price stickers were lined up in neat rows in the parking lot, the windshields glinting in the sun. She itched to pass over her wad of cash to the salesperson and hold the steering wheel in her hands. Getting the car would be the easy part, or at least that's what she thought.

The hard part? Arthur. She'd go see him next. She'd have her party, only it would be as much a going-away party as a celebration of Rhonda and Frank's wedding. She knew this, but Arthur did not. He might be the perfect person for her, but that was the problem. She was torn between missing him, and missing out on life. Moments of clarity were rare, but that late morning it hit her: she couldn't stay in East Troy any longer, and she couldn't go back to the resort. She also couldn't let Arthur hold her back. She'd have to hurt him, have to find a way to tell him goodbye. Maybe not for forever, but for now. Now was all she could think about.

She was going to drive her new car to California, that's what she was going to do.

Before she stepped out of the car, she said, "I like your plan, Jerry. Let's do it."

Raylee, walking home along Highway 15, carried a bag full of corn on the cob she'd bought at the produce stand. She spied Sherri the minute she stepped out of Jerry's car. "Sher!" The girl ran over to where Sherri stood, an inch or two taller than she'd been at the beginning of summer. "Why you been gone so long?"

"Hey twerp." Sherri had always thought of Raylee as a pest, but that morning she was happy to see her, grateful for the company. She wanted someone to share the excitement of her first major purchase. "I'm picking up my new car. Want to be the very first passenger?"

"Your own car? Yeah, sure!"

Even on a few hours' sleep, the thought of the car made Sherri giddy. It had seemed so far off for so long, but Rick, her salesperson, was someone she didn't know from town. He clearly didn't share her thrill. He gave her a Styrofoam cup filled with burned coffee to drink while she filled out paperwork. She wasn't his priority now that he'd made the sale. "This your kid?" he asked, looking at Raylee, who sat next to her with all that corn in her lap, the delicate hair at the top of the stalks looking unruly and earthen in the lobby that smelled like oil and vinyl.

"God no!" Sherri said. It never occurred to Sherri that someone would think she could be Raylee's, or anyone's, mother.

"We're sisters," Raylee said. She smiled smugly.

Rick took plenty of other sales calls, talked to someone on the phone about his golf game, and slipped into a back office to do God-knows-what. Meanwhile, Raylee walked around the used cars in the showroom, intrigued by the designs of the cars, noting the boring Citation, the boxy Malibu, and the shoe-like profile of the Chevelle like Roberta's, and the yellow C/K pickup truck like the one Curtis drove. "There's a car for every kind of person," Raylee said.

"I think you're right," Sherri said, trying to figure out what kind of person Mitch was if he liked both an Excalibur and a Ferrari.

"Can we go?" Raylee groaned. "There's nothing to do here."

"You can go if you want."

"No." She grabbed Sherri's hand. "I want to stay with you."

Half an hour later, Raylee had eaten the contents of an entire fish bowl filled with Tootsie Rolls and talked Sherri's ear off. She told her about the new swim instructor at Booth Lake, the girl she'd met at camp that summer who said you could read satanic messages on the top of a Ritz Cracker, and the Princess Diana doll with her pouffy wedding dress that she wanted to buy at the The Trading Post, but it cost almost twenty dollars.

Finally, Sherri passed the wad of cash across Rick's desk—more money than she thought she'd ever be able to spend at once. She wanted to put as much down as possible to keep the interest low. The rest she would pay monthly. Even car payments sounded grown-up and exciting. She strummed her hands on the faux-wood finish of his desk.

Rick passed some paperwork across his desk and asked her to sign. She did so without even reading what it said. She was too tired and hungover to process all those tiny words. All she cared about was the key that he tantalizingly twirled around on his desk.

"All right, missy. You ready?"

"I've been ready forever!" It wasn't just a car Sherri felt she was buying, it was a lifestyle. It was her independence. A new, different future. He walked her out onto the lot, and Raylee trailed behind. "Here you go. She's a beauty, and she's all yours. Well, yours and the bank's." He pointed at a brown car.

"That's not mine," she said. "My car is red."

He tapped the rolled-up paperwork against the hood. "Says here you wanted brown."

"I said red. Burgundy, actually."

"Red, burgundy. You ladies sure can be fickle. See now, brown is what you asked for, Miss Taylor, and brown is what we ordered. They hauled this here on a flatbed all the way from Detroit just for you."

Sherri was so mad she could cry. "I said burgundy, I did! That's the only color I've ever wanted. I'd never ask for brown. It's ugly. Dirty." Carmen was right. She should have never bought a car without a man, any man. "I didn't change my mind. You didn't listen to me."

"Sure I did. Besides, you don't want burgundy. Stands out too much."

"I want to stand out!"

"I'll bet you do. But trust me, brown is nice. It's a *dignified* color."

"I don't want to look dignified."

"Well, maybe you should. This color is more becoming of a lady." Suddenly it clicked: he knew she was a Bunny. When she filled out the credit application, she'd listed Playboy Corporation as her employer. She saw the light glint off the gold cross on his necklace. He was doing this on purpose! This lazy son of a bitch with his big desk and big chair. She'd like to see him make a living with stays cutting into his back and corns on his toes from pointy shoes. He could try to dip and smile for tips. He could work a double or a triple and know what that felt like. He could end up with a shit-colored car.

"This here's what you bought. You can trade it for burgundy, I suppose, but there's a five-hundred-dollar up-charge, not to mention the shipping and wheel tax, and who knows when it'll get here. Could be a few weeks, could be a few months."

"I want my money back. I don't want this car."

"It doesn't work like that, sweetheart. See here?" He pointed at her signature. "It says plain as day that this is the car you bought. This is your signature, right? Sherri with an *i*?"

"I want to talk to Mr. Frascona."

"He's on vacation, and I'm in charge. I suggest you calm down. If you have a tizzy fit, I'll have to ask security to escort you out."

"You're going to call security? On *me*?" It was all she could do not to hit him with her purse, lunge at him, put her hands around his neck and squeeze with all her might.

He handed her the key and opened the driver's-side door.

"Get in," Sherri said to Raylee, who scrambled into the passenger side. Her dirty shoes left marks on the soft velour seat.

"Let me show you how this works." Rick leaned in through the open window and pointed at one of the gauges.

Sherri would have none of it. "I'll sue you."

"You go ahead." He handed her the receipt and title, and she tossed it into the back seat like trash.

"You're a fucking asshole, you know that? A goddamn liar." She pumped the gas and backed away so fast she could have plowed into someone if they'd had the bad fortune to stand in her path.

She tore down Highway 15 clutching the wheel so hard she could have ripped it off the base. Tears stung her eyes. Usually when she was upset like this, she would head to St. Peter's and release her wrath on the organ—just sitting at the console calmed her. She could practically hear the toccata from Boëllmann's *Suite Gothique* raging in her head—it sounded like Dracula music. Her mother loved that piece. "Imagine what it was like for some poor sinner in the nineteenth century to walk into a cathedral and hear this! Who wouldn't believe in God's wrath?"

Raylee sat quietly with her chubby hands on her lap. She had dirt under her nails. Sherri appreciated her silence. She wasn't a bad kid, she was just painfully lonely, and here Sherri had gone and abandoned her—she hadn't even given her more than a passing thought all summer long, and soon she would be gone for good.

"Sher, I forgot my corn."

Sherri reached into her bag and handed the girl a twenty-dollar bill from her separate stash of spending money. "There's no way I'm going back there. Here, go get some more. And use the rest of the money to buy that doll you were talking about, OK?"

"For real?"

"Yeah. At least one of us should get exactly what we want."

CHAPTER SIXTEEN

Sherri dropped off Raylee, picked up a quarter barrel of beer, and drove to Arthur's house in her new boat of a car. Mitch had asked her why she didn't get a sports car, and she wondered the same thing as she steered. It seemed to hug both sides of the road. She absolutely hated it.

Arthur's sleek red car sat in his driveway. When she knocked on his front door, nobody answered. It was funny, she thought, how she could feel the soullessness of an empty home—it was the same bad feeling she'd had on the few occasions she'd returned to her apartment on the square.

She stood on the landing long enough to recognize that the cottage felt different to her in ways she couldn't explain. The window boxes had been repaired and filled with geraniums. The intricate spiderwebs that once cluttered the overhangs were gone. There was a raw stump where the elm tree had once stood, another victim of the Dutch elm disease that had ravaged the trees on the square. The once-lush lady ferns that had been sheltered by the leaves shrank pitifully in the harsh glare of the sun. She knocked again. The only movement was a hornet with a drooping stinger that hovered in front of her. She was scared to death of bees and turned, running for the lake. She should have known better than to wear yellow this time of year—the bees loved that color.

At the resort, she'd been sheltered from what she knew of late August. It was the time of year when Wisconsin summer overstayed its welcome. Fruit flies congregated around the drain of the kitchen sink and carpenter ants skittered across countertops. Winter, as harsh as it was, seemed a necessary antiseptic, a chance to wipe away the overabundance of life and start fresh.

"Is that you, Sher?"

Arthur's head floated above the still surface of the turquoise lake, followed by a dripping, waving arm. He climbed the wooden ladder on his pier and made his way up the small bluff behind Goldie, who ran ahead and pressed her damp head against Sherri's legs, her fat tail thumping madly. Sherri wondered who'd watched the dog while he'd been in Europe. Arthur wore a pair of teal-colored swim trunks. He looked a little bit like the runner Sebastian Coe with his lean frame and muscular legs and his hair that was black as oil when it was wet. "I thought I was going to see you yesterday. What happened?"

"Oh, everything," Sherri said. The tenderness in his gaze when he looked at her made her feel as awful as she deserved to feel. "I'm so sorry."

"You're here now." He reached his hand out and twirled a strand of her hair in his fingers, tentative in a way he wasn't before. He pressed his damp forehead against hers. She could feel his breath. His voice was low, guttural. Adult. "Damn I've missed you."

Sherri touched his chest the way she might test an iron to see if it was hot. When she'd allowed herself to think about Arthur, he was a fuzzy abstraction, more an insistent idea than an actual person. Now he was real, and his presence overwhelmed her—intimidated her even, and jostled loose her decision to leave for California. There was the squareness of his jaw, the dip of his sternum, the arc of his clavicles, the patch of dark hair that spread across his chest. She stood on her toes to kiss the tiny scar on his collarbone that nobody else could see or know about unless they got close enough. His skin was soft and slick, and her hand lingered on the nape of his neck. What was it about him that scissored her heart?

"Whose car?" he asked.

"Can we not talk about it?"

"Uh, sure."

"There's a lot I don't want to talk about. Arthur, I need you to take me to bed."

He led her back inside. The musky scent she associated with his place hit her in the back of the brain. What a fool she was to think she could make a decision to leave Arthur.

The old wooden stairs creaked less now that it was humid and the grain had expanded—everything felt full. Arthur pulled back the quilt and she crawled into his bed. How she'd missed rolling around with him in those soft sheets that smelled like they'd dried on the line outside, reminding her of her childhood. They made love quickly. After, she drifted to sleep to the sound of the curtains rustling in the gentle wind and the distant hum of a ski boat followed by the slap of waves on the shore in its wake.

She slept like a fairy-tale princess. When she finally woke the next day, she had a vague memory of making love to Arthur again in her sleep. He was next to her, propped on one elbow, his other arm resting on the rise of her hip. He smelled like her, she smelled like him.

"What are you doing?" she asked.

"I'm memorizing you. Every inch."

She ran her fingertip down the side of his stubbly face. "I'm memorizing you, too," she said. She vowed to never forget his skin mellow and golden against the white sheets. How could she have left him in the lobby looking for her, oblivious? It was easy to rationalize her behavior when he wasn't around—they weren't married, they hardly even knew each other, or at least that's what she told herself. But in person, it was another story. He seemed so true. So honest and pure. And she'd let him down.

"So," she said. "It feels like you were gone forever. How was your summer?"

"Remember when you said there's a lot you don't want to talk about?"

"Yeah."

"Same. Nobody wants to hear about someone else's vacation. Just know that the whole time I was gone, this was where I really wanted to be. Here." He kissed her. "With you."

"You wanted to be in East Troy more than Europe?"

"Just because you know a place well doesn't mean there's anything wrong with it."

"I guess." She instinctively raised her wrist to check the time, and it all came back to her: the lost watch, Lake Geneva, Mitch, Gloria, Curtis, the bargain she'd struck with Jerry, the turd of a car. The party! She sat up abruptly. "Arthur, what time is it?"

"It's around one."

"One on *Sunday*?"

"I know. I thought you'd never wake up."

"Please don't be mad." She paused and bit her lip. "I invited some friends over. Rhonda, she's a Bunny from my training group. Well, she got pregnant, and they got married at the courthouse, and their families aren't speaking to them now. It made me so sad to hear about it. So I told them we could have a little party here."

Arthur rolled onto his back. "Sher, you can't just offer up my place to your friends. I'm still finding empties in the bushes from the last party."

"I'll clean up. I promise I will."

"That's not the point. This isn't your party palace. You're with your friends all the time. This is my rare chance to spend time with you after a long summer apart, and you invited your friends over without asking me?"

Why couldn't Arthur be the kind of guy who loved parties? Mitch would have jumped at the chance to invite a bunch of people over. "Gosh, I'm sorry. I wasn't thinking. I mean, I was. I was thinking I was being nice. Poor Rhonda, she's like a little girl having a baby. I feel so bad for her, and—"

"Cancel. Please."

"It's too late." She bit her lip. "Arthur, they'll be here any minute."

"We don't even have beer."

Sherri sprang out of bed. "Actually, I do. I bought a quarter barrel. It's in the trunk of my car."

"It's been in your car overnight? Sher, it's ninety-two degrees out."

Sherri laughed. "Arthur, is this our first fight?"

He raked his fingers through his hair, frustrated. "I resent that you didn't ask first."

"I couldn't really. It was all very spontaneous." She wrapped her arms around him. "Parties are fun, don't you think?"

"You don't understand. This is my house. I just can't—you can't—we need to talk"

"Please? Summer is almost over. It's not like I'll ever do this again. Just this one time. We can go out on the pontoon, we won't even be here." She pushed him back onto the mattress and straddled him. At first he didn't respond, but Sherri kept at it.

He sighed, resigned. "Why can't I be mad at you?"

They were in the middle of Mill Pond on Arthur's double-decker pontoon. The boat had a name now: *Omniboat*. Sherri didn't like it at all, mostly because Arthur had left her out of the decision process, and because she'd hoped for a more romantic name. Arthur had once told her that Lake Beulah used to be called Crooked Lake, and a farmer renamed it Beulah after his wife. If a whole lake could be named after a woman, why couldn't he name his boat after her? Arthur said he thought *Omniboat* was funny because the double-decker buses in London were called omnibuses.

Funny to you, Sherri thought. She knew she was in no position to complain. They were, after all, having a party, even if it wasn't nearly as fun as the last one. Not even a dozen friends from the resort showed up. The first party had had a frenetic energy because the whole season stretched out in front of them. This party felt like it needed a snap of electricity—something, anything. It was hard for her to believe that just a few days earlier she'd been backstage with Gregg Allman, every cell in her body exploding. Now she didn't have the energy to explode, and either did anyone else, not in the thick, muggy air the storm had ushered in. Nothing moved, there wasn't a breeze. Before they stopped to swim, Arthur had toured around, and the Jewish camp on the other side was already closed up for the season. The paddleboats and canoes were stacked up on the shore, and tarps were pulled tight over the cabins.

"My grandparents have a place in Wheatland," Frank said. "There's a boat there called the *Filthy Whore.*" Frank wore a black bow tie around his neck, and Rhonda wore a veil. They looked like a real couple, not just some scared kids. They sat next to each other on the hot vinyl seat holding hands, having more fun than everyone else.

Everyone had a buzz on, although the beer was warm and soupy. The tap had leaked, and when she and Arthur pulled the keg out, her new car stank of hops. Sherri had almost forgotten what it was like to be drunk without speed. Alcohol sloshed around in her system, slowed her down. She jumped into the lake and swam with Boo and Paul. She held her breath and dove so deep that her ears popped. Boo was showing them how to perform some water ballet moves. "This the clam," she said, throwing her arms and legs up in the air so that they touched, sinking down and rising again. When Paul tried it, he looked like a thrashing whale.

Sherri climbed back onto the boat and discovered Carmen and Ginger leaning over the rail on the bottom deck. Carmen wore a turquoise bikini with sequins all over the cups, and they glinted in the dim light. The women were dangling their fingers in the water, gossiping about the resort's financial trouble. Sherri overheard them talking about auditors in gray suits who had started showing up, asking questions, disappearing into the managers' offices for hours on end. The head of catering had been let go. Sherri couldn't stand to hear it. "You guys are buzzkills."

She climbed the metal stairs to the top deck. Val was asleep on her *Jaws* towel snoring gently, a sound Sherri was familiar with. Sherri had avoided her the entire afternoon. She felt guilty about what she'd said in earshot of Curtis. She couldn't confront her about the missing money in front of everyone, nor did she think she could do it straight to Val's face. Earlier she'd noticed Val and Danny holding hands like any old couple. They didn't seem too concerned that Carmen would see. Once Carmen got word of something, the whole world heard.

Danny and Arthur were talking about boat stuff. Horsepower, inboard, outboard, tow capacity. Arthur was more outgoing than he'd been at first, clearly more comfortable with a smaller group. Sherri's idea of a bad party was his idea of a good one. "Danny," Sherri said, trying to get a party started. "Show me your corkscrew. Remember?"

Danny smiled and took off his shirt. "Think I can splash all the way up to the second level?"

"Sure you can."

Danny took a running jump off the top deck and flew through the air with one knee bent up to his chest. Water shot up when he landed, but not a lot.

"I think it's time for me to show you people a cannonball," Paul said. He lumbered up to the top deck, jumped with both knees up to his chest, and landed with such force that Sherri swore the entire lake could have emptied out. The splash startled and soaked Val. She sat up and looked around, confused after being woken up so abruptly from her nap. "What the actual fuck?" Everyone laughed. Sherri was happy—her party was beginning to feel more lively. The boat rocked from the ripples in Paul's wake, followed by the sound of metal on metal. Sherri thought nothing of it, nor of the commotion on the first deck of the pontoon.

"Arthur, will you jump?"

"How about I go backwards? I have a special move I've perfected over time. I'm not as good as one of the Acapulco cliff divers from *Wide World of Sports*, but I'm trying. This is why I got a double-decker pontoon."

Sherri clapped. "Do it!"

He gave her a kiss and winked before walking to the edge of the boat. "Anything for you, Sherri." He made a big show of it, which surprised Sherri, because he didn't seem like the kind of person who sought attention. He bent his legs, lowered his arms, and with great force drew them up over his head before he vaulted up and back, high into the air. The sun was setting just behind him, and a crack in the clouds revealed a dazzling blast of orange and yellow light. His jump seemed to happen in slow motion. It was a thing of beauty to see Arthur in the sky, his dark hair hanging down, arms outstretched. She was certain in that moment that she loved him.

But then she heard the most awful sound. It was quick and definitive, like the sound of a baseball hitting a metal bat. *Glunk.*

All the people below deck saw what Sherri didn't. A collective chorus of screams and groans burst out. Sherri couldn't make sense of the sound, but she knew it was bad. She ran to the side and saw Arthur's rowboat tied to the pontoon. "What's the rowboat doing here?"

As if in a dream, she ran down the stairs to investigate, feeling like she couldn't move fast enough. She was followed closely by Val and Danny, who pulled up short when they saw Curtis standing hunched on the deck, looking dumbfounded.

Distantly, Sherri heard someone ask what he was doing there, but her only concern was looking past him, eyes scanning the water. Where was Arthur?

It was so simple. All that needed to happen was for Arthur to surface. But he didn't. She told herself that he'd gone down deep, and would take time to come up for air. The horrible sequence of events was taking shape in her mind.

"Curtis, what did you do?" Val asked. She was bent over onto herself, biting her fist. "Oh, honey, goddamn it, why'd you come here? What did you do, what did you do?"

"I didn't do anything. I wanted to talk to you is all." Whatever jealousy and rage Curtis had felt had been replaced with astonishment.

"Since when do you ever just 'talk' to Val?" Danny asked. "You came here to beat the shit out of her, didn't you?"

"I came to beat the shit out of *you* if you want to know. Look, I didn't do anything to your friend. I saw you out here on the pontoon, and I helped myself to the rowboat. That's all I did."

"But why are you here?" Val asked. "Why?"

"Because I heard there was a party."

"A party you weren't invited to!"

Rhonda shot a look at Sherri. Curtis *had* overheard their conversation. He'd heard about the party, heard about Val and Danny. Everything was Sherri's fault, that much was clear. She'd spilled secrets, forced Arthur to have a party, asked him to dive. Her guilt, anxiety, and fear felt bigger than she was. "Arthur, come on, Arthur." She banged the metal railing with her hands. "Don't do this!" She paced back and forth along the edge of the boat. "Don't mess with us."

"It was a freak accident," Curtis said, sounding more like a scared little boy than a tough guy.

"I'm going in," Danny said. "Maybe he's under the boat."

"It's so deep," Sherri said, remembering the first time they'd gone out, when Danny tried to drop anchor. "Arthur, come back. Come back! Damn it, Arthur, you can't—"

She couldn't say the word "drown."

Paul yanked Curtis's arm. "Come on, don't just stand there. Let's go get help." He untied the fateful rowboat Arthur had hit his head on, and he and Curtis rowed toward the eastern shore.

Rhonda was in a state of panic. She had a high voice and began to scream at the top of her lungs. "Mayday! SOS! Help! Please help!" The sound was so loud, piercing and pure, that it split time into before and after: the Sherri she'd been, and the Sherri she was about to become.

The lake was hungry, just as Jerry had said, and the water was dark, growing darker by the second, glowing dark green. Sherri couldn't stop looking into it while wondering how many seconds someone could live without oxygen. Finally, Officer Henley, whose son Charlie had been in her grade, showed up at the scene in a police boat. He might have arrived within minutes or hours, Sherri couldn't say. She'd become an island of worry, her brain overrun with panic. He and the other offi-cers turned on a floodlight so white and so powerful they might have pulled the moon down from the sky to shine it closer to the lake. "You've got to let the divers do their work, Sherri. You've got to go."

"But Arthur—"

"He's been down there a long time. Too long."

Danny drove the boat back to Arthur's pier. Sherri's friends hud-dled around her in the dark in their bikinis and swim trunks. Val said, "You're going to get through this. It'll be hard, but you will."

The wind had changed direction and was coming from the north. Suddenly she was freezing, and she didn't care. She couldn't think, couldn't focus. Her head was filled with static while she waited for news. Finally, she saw the police boat slowly approach the pier, the lights, once purposeful and dramatic flashing red and blue, were off now, replaced by only the small white boat light. Officer Henley stepped up onto the pier with his heavy black shoes.

"Is he—" Sherri began to ask. She wanted to ask if he was alive, but deep down she knew the minute she heard his head hit the boat that he couldn't have survived.

The officer put his hand on her bare shoulder. She was struck by its warmth. "If it makes you feel any better, your friend went fast."

The word "friend" was all wrong, everything was. "Probably never knew what hit him. He died instantly. Didn't even fight to breathe. His lungs were still filled with air."

Sherri couldn't process the news. "No, he can't—he was just—here. He was right here!"

"We're all going to meet our maker someday. That's the way you do it. Die young, before life gets hold of you. Think of it. The last thing he saw was the sunset over the lake. Still a tragedy, don't get me wrong, but now he'll never suffer the indignity of growing old. That's a good death. Maybe the best I've ever heard of."

This was no comfort for Sherri, who was dumbfounded and numb. She approached Arthur's house one last time. Goldie waited expectantly by the door, her brown eyes sad and hopeful.

"Danny?"

"Yeah?"

"Will you do me a favor?" She petted Goldie's broad head.

"Sure," he said. "Anything."

"Will you take the dog? Her name is Goldie."

Sherri would have taken her, but she felt so responsible for Arthur's accident that she knew she couldn't be trusted with any creature with a heartbeat. She ran inside and grabbed her things. She took Arthur's pillowcase and inhaled the scent of him. She took his newspaper, scribbled with notes. She went outside and opened the door to her car. It stank like a barroom floor.

The car had come with an atlas. She opened it up and found the arteries that led to California. She inserted the key, backed out of Arthur's driveway one last time, and sped past the attendant in the booth without so much as slowing down. She'd hardly remember that stunned, silent drive to the West Coast. All the music that once filled her head was replaced by the very last words Arthur had spoken in an endless loop:

Anything for you, Sherri.

CHAPTER SEVENTEEN

The atlas got Sherri to California without problems, but the blurry inset map did little to help her navigate the endless sprawl of Los Angeles. Her first mistake was to arrive during rush hour. The most traffic she'd ever experienced before that early California evening was at Alpine Valley. She'd never before seen, or even imagined, such serpentine freeways. They were as big and as jammed as the parking lot at the resort on a Saturday night, as if a giant octopus had descended on the city, wrapped its arms around it, and the arms became roads. In her abrupt departure, she hadn't thought to bring her sunglasses with her, and the bright California sun left spots in her eyes from the light bouncing off the gleaming metal and glass of the cars.

Her face was wet from tears and she smelled faintly of the musty towel from the roadside motel she'd stopped at, where she had tried without success to get some sleep. Every time she closed her eyes she saw Arthur hanging in the sky. She was certain she'd never sleep again.

Impatient to get there, wherever "there" was, she rode the bumpers of the cars in front of her. She lit cigarette after cigarette, her hands jittery from nicotine and speed. She didn't even bother with the ashtray, so the ashes were sprinkled like dirty snow across the brown velour seat.

Every lane change felt like a death-defying act. All the other drivers, especially the ones who drove in convertibles, seemed so impossibly blasé. How she wished she could trade places with people who had a place to go; for them, this was just another day, and they were in the middle of their lives. Her only reassurance was that, aside from Mitch and Tina, nobody knew her there, not a soul. She could start fresh, but then she dismissed the thought. She'd never be fresh, never again.

Sherri saw some shiny tall buildings that rose in the distance. She figured she'd discovered downtown, she'd arrived. Until that moment her heart had felt dead, but at the initial sight of the LA skyline, she managed to feel the smallest surge of excitement. Except then there were more clusters of buildings, and still more, and the roads didn't lead to any one place. As someone who had grown up on a square and had spent the previous year in a town with a main street, Sherri assumed that all places had a center. Not LA. It went on and on and on and on. She felt like an imposter, surrounded by strange brown hills, palm trees, and cars, cars, cars.

She wanted to find Venice Beach because Mitch had said it was like Lake Geneva, only *better*. From the map it looked like the interstate 10 should take her straight there, but it turned into the Pacific Coast Highway and she missed Venice Beach completely, heading north instead. She saw signs for Santa Monica and, finally, for Ocean Avenue. She had to get out, had to pee and stretch her legs. She found a parking spot near the little shops and vendors selling drinks and ice cream. She wandered down the crowded pier. Her first feeling of greeting came from the tinkly sound of a Wurlitzer rising above the din of the crowd in the Hippodrome. She followed the noise even though it sounded out of tune, all wrong. She walked into the vast, barnlike building that housed the carousel, her eye drawn to the instrument belting out music that seemed as maniacal as she felt. There was no player, no keyboard, just a drum rolling around the belly of the unit.

She ran back outside and burst onto the wooden pier with its giant moorings. Couples walked hand in hand, children heeled their mothers. A homeless man jingled his cup. A barefoot Hare Krishna in an orange robe ran up to her and tried to give her a book. She'd only heard about them on television and worried they'd try to get her to join a cult. "No!" she said, picking up her pace, terrified. "Stay away from me!"

She returned to her car and stopped at a 7-Eleven. Mitch Spaulding: there was his name, right there in the phone book that hung off a metal chain in the phone booth. He lived on Pico Boulevard. How cute that word sounded: Pico. She imagined a mansion sitting on a bluff overlooking the ocean, a circular driveway with the Excalibur parked in front of a grand entrance. Sherri wrote down his address, went inside, and asked the attendant for directions. "Is this far away?"

"Just a few blocks east of here," he said, pointing toward the parking lot.

"Seriously?" Sherri began to laugh—a shrill, manic sound. She couldn't believe that in the huge city, she'd ended up so close. She chose to take it as a sign. As far as she could tell, the downtrodden neighborhood didn't seem to change much within a few blocks of that grungy convenience store.

She cleaned up in the bathroom and put on a dress and heels. When she applied makeup, she thought of how Val had called it "putting on my face."

The last stop before Mitch's was a seedy liquor store that specialized in forty-five-ounce cans of malt beer. She splurged on the nicest bottle of champagne she could find and paid for it from the shrinking wad of remaining bills that she kept in the inside pocket of her purse. She didn't like how she was back to worrying about money. That was what she'd loved best about the resort. She'd experienced many freedoms there, but the one she valued most was financial. She'd have to call Jerry as soon as she was settled and get the ball rolling on the mortgage, a deal she'd made that she still didn't totally understand.

She pulled up in front of a run-down apartment building with a one-eared cat sitting on the stoop. This couldn't be where Mitch lived. It was dark now. A streetlight flickered. Surely this must be a mistake. He was the only Mitch Spaulding in Los Angeles, but maybe there'd been an M. Spaulding?

Sherri plumped her hair and reached into her collar to lift and reset her breasts to show more cleavage. She grabbed the champagne by the neck and passed a woman standing by the road in a terry cloth tube-top dress, big hoop earrings, and stilettos. The past year she'd heard the words "prostitute" and "bimbo" bandied about, always with incredible derision, but until that moment she'd never seen a real hooker. Sherri tried to walk quickly past the woman and everything she thought she represented, but when they caught each other's glance, she saw only another woman who might have been a Bunny or a teacher or a wife.

"I saw your Wisconsin license plate. You're new in town?"

"Yeah," Sherri said.

"You be careful."

"I'll be fine."

"Famous last words, honey."

Sherri walked up to the apartment building. It was long and narrow, with exterior steps that led to the upstairs apartments. Blue light from televisions lit up the windows. Children screamed. She could still hear the traffic from the next street over, a siren. Apartment 2C.

She walked upstairs, her heels clicking on the concrete. When she reached the landing, she approached his door and tried to get a glimpse inside the pulled shades. Was Mitch in there? The *wrong* Mitch?

One knock. Her bracelets jangled. Another knock. No answer. He wasn't home. That was OK, this wasn't the right Mitch, anyway.

Tomorrow she'd find him. And she'd find Tina. She'd get something to eat, find a place to sleep, start fresh. Forget about Arthur and the accident. Tomorrow, tomorrow.

Suddenly the door flew open and there was Mitch, shirtless, his hair a mess, a cigarette dangling loosely from his fingers.

"Surprise!" The word sounded like a question.

"Sherri?"

"I told you I'd come visit. We talked about it." She smiled her brightest, fakest smile and held the bottle of champagne in front of her. "You actually live here?" Sherri asked.

"What does it look like?"

"But the cars. I thought—"

Mitch paused, and suddenly his entire demeanor changed. She felt like he was leveling with her for the first time. "Look," he said. "Those cars aren't mine. I drive them for other people. Rich guys hire me to pick them up and drive them back here."

"You lied?"

Mitch began to inch the door shut. "I never said they were mine, did I?"

"Mitch!"

He ran his hand through his messy ash-blond hair. "Sorry. Yeah, I lied. I did. You're a Bunny. I wanted to impress you."

Sherri couldn't believe her ears. "You were worried about impressing *me*? You're not a stuntman either, are you?"

Mitch took a drag of his cigarette. "I'm just me." His expression softened. "I feel bad. You seriously drove all the way to California?"

Sherri nodded. It wasn't so much that she came for him, it was that she needed to leave home. But it was too big and too complicated to explain.

"I'm just a fuckup, honestly." He gestured at his messy apartment.

"I don't even care. I'm a fuckup, too."

She wasn't looking for love. She didn't care about being in a relationship. She didn't think she deserved anyone especially someone as good as Arthur. All she knew was that she couldn't stand to be alone. "Look, it took me two days to get here. Please. Can I come in and crash on your couch for a while?"

He shrugged and opened the door further. Sherri walked into his disgusting apartment, and stumbled into what would become a lost year in her life.

CHAPTER EIGHTEEN

The money Sherri had borrowed against the building in East Troy went right up their noses. Sherri and Mitch lived large in Los Angeles, and they spent a fair amount of time partying in Palm Springs, a town that felt refreshingly small, like East Troy. Mitch had a friend who managed the Riviera. The low-slung hotel, like the Playboy resort, had a history, but their history ran deeper. The hotel now also billed itself as a family resort, and the hallways were filled with framed photos of celebrities like Frank Sinatra, Dean Martin, Elvis Presley, and Sonny and Cher. The pool was designed like a spoke wheel, and had been the site of psychedelic bashes in the sixties. She felt at home there, like she could pick up where she'd left off, only now she didn't have to work. She could walk into a guest room, wake up late, and lounge by the pool while someone else served her. The freedom and lack of rules went to her head. Because she could do anything, she did.

Palm Springs was where Sherri went hiking in the mountains in her bikini and flip-flops, and it was where she discovered the joys of the desert, even in the middle of summer. She liked the flat, dry landscape because it bore so little resemblance to what she'd known in East Troy that she might as well have been on another planet.

She and Mitch made a striking couple, and they were always up for a party or a late-night hike in the nude. They hopped the fence of Elvis and Priscilla Presley's former house and took a dip in the pool, and after all the bars closed, they'd hang out at the airport because it stayed open all night long.

Mitch, a mere mortal now, was on a level playing field with Sherri. When she told him about what had happened with Arthur, he gave her space to indulge her frequent bouts of melancholy, and he'd hold her when she woke from nightmares screaming Arthur's name. He'd had his own trouble. His mother ran off with another man when he was a kid, and his father had been a car wrangler for the movie studios, finding automobiles for various films, or for the movie stars to drive around in, looking like swells. But he'd wanted to live the same high-profile lifestyle as the people who drove the cars, and began staging crashes in order to collect insurance. Mitch's world had crumbled when his father ended up serving a prison sentence for manslaughter and insurance fraud.

Mitch and Sherri could be down together, but they could also escape their troubles by having fun—too much fun. Sherri had always thought of men as a different species, mysterious, impenetrable. Mitch rid Sherri of that notion. Once he descended from the pedestal she'd put him on, she realized he wasn't much different from her. He could be craven, insecure, desperate, sweet, greedy, moody, kind. This knowledge endeared him to her. It was better to be messed up together.

When the money began to run out, Sherri tried to get serious and send her résumé around. The economy was bad, and the words "Playboy Bunny" in her "Work Experience" section only seemed to attract lecherous managers and business owners who called her in for interviews just to ogle her, more interested in her measurements than her abilities.

"I can't get a job in this town," she said. "Temping pays dirt."

"Baby," Mitch said, "why don't you just go back to being a Bunny?"

He was right. It was a job she knew how to do, a job she'd been good at, even if she felt she'd left the resort a failure. Yet she was haunted by what Arthur had told her: that she needed to focus on becoming rather than being. But Arthur had been all wrong about her.

There were two Playboy venues in town. She decided against the Mansion, because it loomed too large in her imagination after what she'd heard about it from the Bunnies who'd visited back in the day. She still had small-town sensibilities, and the promise of a bacchanalian scene exceeded her comfort level. There was a grotto, they'd said, and there were peacocks strutting across the yard, and orgies. Sometimes they said Hef would show up in his silk smoking robe, quiet and observant, a Bunny always at his side. Sherri had never once laid eyes on the man and put him in the same category as Oz and Willy Wonka. It seemed everyone was so quick to judge her, but look what Hefner got away with. A Bunny was always just a Bunny, but people insisted he was a misunderstood genius. That's what Sherri used to think, but not anymore. She figured he was a pervert, and just plain weird.

She and Jerry spoke occasionally. He called to check up on her and tell her stories about AA and the twelve steps. Forgiveness was one of them, but the idea seemed remote and strange to Sherri, who blamed herself for everything. Jerry knew this, but he was careful to never bring up Arthur. It was through Jerry that Sherri heard that the resort had closed. "Some brothers from Houston bought it," he said. "They set up a giant bonfire out back and torched anything with the logo: golf score cards, boxes of swizzle sticks, pens, mugs, matchbooks. Anything with the bunny. They even tore up and burned the carpeting. I'm glad I kept all the keepsake mugs you girls sold me. And I'll take my key to my grave." Even with her complicated memories of the resort, it seemed wrong and dishonest to dismantle its history. Her time there ended so abruptly that she had frequent dreams of wandering around a gutted version of the place. She'd show up for her shift but nobody was there, only Gloria.

She set out to get a job at the club in Century City, because that was where she might find Tina. Her friend had helped her become a Bunny before; maybe she would help her again. Sherri had no desire to go through the motions of properly applying—why should she audition for a job she'd already had? But her confidence crumbled the closer she got to the Shubert Theatre, which housed the club. The first time she'd seen the Playboy logo writ large, back when she was with Roberta, it had been carved onto a wooden sign and tucked into a thicket of trees in Lake Geneva, innocent and unthreatening, like the sign for the YMCA camp. Here in LA, the logo was less subdued. It screamed at her, and it was massive, as tall as the first floor of the building, ablaze in white neon. A line of customers stretched around the block. That was when it hit her like a blow to the gut: she was just a customer now, a civilian, wasn't she? She'd have to stand in line like everyone else. She couldn't bear that thought, so she decided to get a drink first, thinking it would get her out of her own head. She drove right past the club and found herself gliding aimlessly through the city in her big brown car. She loved to explore Los Angeles, and still gawked at the Columbia Records building and the Hollywood sign. She was even amazed by lesser-known landmarks like Gelson's Market, the biggest grocery store she'd ever been in. It was nothing like Ray's Save-a-Lot back home, where Ray, the owner, would dress up in a trench coat, hat, and sunglasses and lurk in the aisles trying to catch shoplifters. Who knew you could feel homesick for a grocery store? The fact that Gelson's impressed her made her feel like she'd always be a hick. She'd feel like a perpetual tourist in Los Angeles no matter how long she lived there.

She didn't know where to go or what to do. The massive Century Plaza Hotel caught her eye. It was a place to get lost in. She was greeted by doormen in red beefeater costumes. The lobby, with its marble columns and massive chandeliers, housed travel agencies and fancy boutiques. She imagined the shopkeepers looking down at her wearing the nicest outfit she owned, a cheap May Company dress.

The swanky restaurants, the Vineyard and Yamato, with menus displayed near the entrance like fine art, made her acutely aware of her dwindling cash reserves. Now, after her year of excess with Mitch, she hardly had enough money to buy a dozen eggs. She stopped to look at the framed, signed black-and-white photos of people who'd been there who were far more important than she was or would ever be: Prince Andrew, Richard Nixon, Bob Hope, and the Apollo 11 astronauts. If Sam had thought that the Rice Hotel was impressive, imagine what he would have thought of the sparkling Century Plaza. She fingered the Texas pendant Sam had given her. She'd started to wear it every day to remind herself not to be an idiot. Little good it did.

She walked into the bar and took her place on a stool. She ordered a rum and Coke, knowing that she wouldn't have to pay for it. Sooner or later, dressed the way she was, her face caked in makeup, some guy would show up like an ant at a picnic. The bartender set her drink in front of her. She peeled the wrapper off the straw from the bottom up, the way she always had with Roberta at the Dairy Bar, back in the days of sticky candy bracelets and cigarette gum. It had been a long time since she'd had a friend.

A man in a plaid sport coat and gabardine slacks tapped her on the shoulder. "Ask me what time it is," he said.

If she didn't need him to pay for her drink, she'd have swatted him away like a fly. "OK, what time is it?"

He lifted his arm to check his bare wrist. "Half past a freckle. Pretty bad, huh? I'm Gabe."

Sherri shook his hand. His fingers were soft and sweaty. Everything about him, even his name, was soft. She didn't want to tell him her real name. "I'm Roberta." She lit a cigarette and tried to act as tough and as cool as her old friend, speaking with him just enough so that he'd keep her from dying of loneliness and cover her tab. But she stubbed out the cigarette after only a few puffs. It didn't taste good. Neither did the drink. Gabe said he ran a company that made the rolling mechanism for credit card machines. He lived in Orlando, had

she ever been there? "Yeah, sure," she said, because Roberta actually
had. "Disney. Oranges."

She pretended not to notice the outline of his wedding ring in his
shirt pocket, visible when he took off his suit coat. "Listen," he said,
tapping his nose. "Want to go up to my room? I've got blow." He put
his sweaty hand on her back.

"Yeah, sure. One minute," she said, excusing herself, saying she had
to go to the bathroom. A month earlier she might have taken him up
on his offer, but something was changing in her. She slipped away, returned to her car, and drove back to the Playboy Club. All the lights of
the city twinkled. She found a parking spot a few blocks away, reached
into the glove compartment, and grabbed the bunny tail that she'd
taken with her the last time she worked. She walked down the dirty
sidewalk and passed everyone in line. When the bouncer tried to stop
her, she held up the tail, smiled sweetly, and said, "Oh honey, I work
here. I'm Bunny Sherri." She dipped and smiled, and he raised the
velvet cord, waving her through.

The lobby was crowded and elegant, with a swirling staircase that
reminded her of her old Barbie Dreamhouse. She stopped when she
saw a Bunny in a green outfit.

"Can you help me find Bunny Tina?"

"Tina?" She looked confused. There were so many Bunnies at that
club. It was nothing like the resort where everyone knew each other
and most of them lived together in a dorm. Sherri had always had a
sixth sense about who was working which shifts and where. Here, this
was just a job. The Bunnies were employees.

"She's tall, blond," Sherri said.

"You just described all of us."

"Tina *Schnitz*," Sherri said, knowing how ludicrous it was for her to
say her last name. "She's from Wisconsin. Maybe she goes by Mary?"

"Wisconsin? Oh wait, I think I know who you mean. But I don't
know if she's here tonight."

"If you see her, could you tell her that Bunny Sherri is looking for her?" That name didn't feel like it belonged to her anymore. "Can you take me to the Bunny Mother?"

The Bunny seemed irritated, rushed. "Follow me," she said. She was a million times more glamorous than any of the girls in Lake Geneva. She had the sort of confidence you only got when you had to exercise it a million times. She pushed open a service door and pointed up a flight of stairs. "Evelyn's office is the second door on the right."

Evelyn: such a pretty name. Elegant. "Is she nice?"

"Nice?" The Bunny shook her head and walked away.

Evelyn's amber hair was pulled back into a tight updo. She wore a fitted boiled-wool suit. "Can I help you, dear?"

Sherri hadn't worn heels in a while, and her ankles felt like they might crack. "I'm Bunny Sherri," she said. "I'd love to work here."

Evelyn looked her up and down, unimpressed. "Lots of girls would," said Evelyn. "It's a dream to be a Bunny. You can fill out an application, just like everyone else."

"But I already am a Bunny. Or I was, in Lake Geneva." She thought "Lake Geneva" sounded more sophisticated than "Wisconsin." Sherri smiled brightly, remembering what Tina had said—smile until your mouth breaks—only this time her smile was different, because she could tell that Evelyn had no intention of hiring her. There would be no conversation about the East Troy Lioness cookbook or lop-eared rabbits, no conversation at all. "Listen, I need the money. I work hard. I'm fast. I know all the drinks."

"I thank you for your interest. Now, if you'll excuse me—"

"You know what? I don't want to work here anyway." Sherri felt more clearheaded than she'd felt in a long while. She'd wrestled with just about every emotion possible in the past year, but anger? This was something new. It welled up inside of her. "Let me tell you something: I don't want to stand on a scale for you. I don't want to call you 'Bunny Mother.'" It had never occurred to her until that moment that even Gloria knew how ridiculous her title was. "I don't want to walk around with ears on my head. Good Lord, I walked around with *ears* on my *head*!"

Evelyn pointed at the door. "Go."

"I'm already gone." Sherri pulled her tail from her pocket and set it on her palm, letting it linger for a few moments, white and light, before doing something practically sacrilegious: she threw it in the garbage. And then she left.

On her way out, she passed Tina on the stairs. Her hair was brassier than Sherri remembered, and her legs were longer. She was such a welcome sight.

"Sherri? Is that really you? I heard someone was looking for me and I—what on earth are you doing here?"

What on earth *was* she doing there? "I guess I thought I wanted to work here."

"You don't. Trust me. Back in Lake Geneva it was different. It's like going from *The Love Boat* to *Fantasy Island.* As soon as I get my real estate license I'm out of here. So what happened? You met Evelyn?"

"She doesn't want me. I guess I'm only 'Wisconsin cute.'"

Tina paused and really looked at Sherri. "Not to be mean, but honey, you don't look great at all. Are you, like, pregnant or something?"

As Tina's question lingered in the air, time seemed to crystallize while Sherri did the math in her head. She blanched. "Oh, Tina, I kind of think I might be."

CHAPTER NINETEEN

August 2019

Sherri is too busy to travel to Wisconsin to see poor, sick Jerry, really, she is. The annual gala is coming up in eight months, and nobody can agree on the theme. Her diva event planner at the museum, Marco, is pushing for Arabian Nights Under the Stars. He imagines tents, magic carpets everywhere, go-go dancers on plinths above the guests, little monkeys on leashes, a genie in a bottle. "Hummus!" he says. "Grape leaves! Fig everything! Lamb on a spit. We'll drink wine out of old-school chalices, sit on pillows, and smoke hookahs. We could have two-humped camels trucked in."

Margie Kent taps her pen on the table. "It all sounds a bit too *Aladdin* to me."

"Or *Raiders of the Lost Ark*," says Yvonne Blaisedell.

Sherri's student intern, Chase, is just learning how to speak up in meetings, at her insistence. She loves interns and makes a point of giving them meaningful work to do. "Um, excuse me, but do we need to worry about cultural appropriation?" *Oh, Chase. Not now*, Sherri thinks. *Not this meeting. Not on this day.* Chase has unwittingly just become Marco's enemy.

"Good point," says Terrence, the head of membership. "This reeks of Orientalism."

"OK, find me a theme that won't offend someone," Marco says. "Just try."

"Cats?" Chase says.

Sherri wishes she could laugh. Oh dear. Marco shoots a look at Sherri and mouths *Help me.*

Terrence leans forward. "Excuse me, but what does Arabian Nights even have to do with our collection, and, well, art in general?"

Marco rolls his chair back to the wall. "What did Great Gatsby have to do with art? That was last year's theme, and we raised almost a million dollars."

The last thing Sherri needs is the staff disagreeing with each other at a board meeting. Terrence and Marco recently broke up, and they both came into her office on separate occasions to cry on her shoulder. She advised them to keep it professional, and here they are, arguing in front of board members. They are both her friends—they are like family, really. Everyone at the museum is. Nobody has done the other wrong. Sometimes, Sherri explained to them, playing the role of the sage older woman, that's just how relationships end. She is beginning to think that's the way her relationship with Bayard might end, maybe soon. No hard feelings. She always broke up with men when they cared too much for her, and Bayard has already proposed a few times. Each time she says no he kisses her and says he hopes she'll change her mind someday. He put the ring in her nightstand drawer. She's dated plenty of men over the years, but ever since Arthur, she's been superstitious that loving her comes with a high cosmic price.

Margie looks at Sherri and says, "I'm just worried that the theme might seem a little . . . tacky."

Marco puts his hand on his chest, offended. "Did you just say *tacky?*"

They have no idea how to work with a visionary like Marco. Sherri does. She always starts by telling him he's the smartest, most creative person in the world and he can do whatever he wants, and once he has some time to think about it, and a budget to work against, he reins himself in. Like Sherri, he pays attention to every single detail. He's the best event planner she's ever hired.

Margie is one of their major funders; Marco knows better than to spar with her. The museum needs people like Margie. She's a pain in the ass, but she's money. Oil money, but still, it might as well go to the arts instead of some nutty right-wing cause Margie could easily get behind. Sherri smiles her most winning smile. "I think what Margie means is that we want to have fun, but show some restraint, and Marco knows exactly how to do this. He's always so good at hitting just the right note."

Terrence circles the rim of his tea mug with his fingertip, which is what he does when he's upset. "I'd like us all to think for a moment about drunk people with swords." He pauses. "Next, I'd like us to think about camel droppings."

Everyone laughs—except Marco.

Chase says, "Should we go back to the Casino Night idea?"

"She's on to something," says Margie.

"*They* are on to something," Terrence corrects her. "Honor the pronoun." Chase gives him a thumbs-up. Sherri thinks about transferring Chase to work for Terrence in membership. They'd work well together.

"Casino Night just isn't a fresh idea," Sherri says. "Nobody even knows who Bonnie and Clyde are anymore, and there are all kinds of legal hoops to jump through, gambling licenses. It's tricky, and we don't want to compete with the casino." Sherri stands and gathers the pile of papers on the conference table. "Thanks to all of you for your input. Lots of good ideas. We'll meet again next week. I've got my next appointment." Just before she walks out the door she says, "And for the record, I think the Arabian Nights theme is an absolute riot." She winks at Marco, who beams.

She doesn't really have an appointment, she's just been to enough meetings to know when productive conversation has ended. She'll follow up with a lovely email that will make everyone feel smart, and Marco will get his way and the event will be a smashing success.

She steps into her office, shuts the door, sinks into her chair, and kicks off her heels. Maybe Bayard is right. Maybe it's time to think about retiring. Why is it that everything feels like it's coming to an end? She's been working special events in one capacity or another for almost forty years, ever since Tina got her a job staffing the information desk at the Los Angeles County Museum of Art. The young people who work for Sherri now expect raises and promotions before their butts have worn grooves in their office chairs. Sherri had to claw her way up to special events after paying her dues in HR, the budget office, *and* marketing, all while raising a kid and attending night classes. They have no idea.

She checks her phone. She missed a call from Tina, who calls her all the time. Her friend is constantly on the road and feels naked without her Bluetooth headset in her ear. Sherri dials her back. They speak so often that they don't even bother to say hello.

"I can't name names," Tina says, "but let's just say my potential new client is an actor in a Marvel movie. He thinks he can get over six million bucks for his house. The guy is interviewing every Realtor in LA until he can find someone to agree with him. He's like a patient with a terminal disease in the seeking phase, going from doctor to doctor, hoping to find someone who'll tell him he's fine. At first I thought, well, maybe the young stud *can* get that much. He's got a great location in Malibu, halfway up Clifftop. I'm walking around taking inventory. Pool is nice, a little old-timey, you know, not an infinity but OK, big bedrooms, lots of closet space, mostly decent view, some good landscaping. So what's the problem? I don't see mold, mudslides, termites, the usual. But then he takes me downstairs to the lower level and Sher, the guy has built a secret apocalypse vault. You have to tap the floor and drop into it through a trapdoor with a rope ladder. No windows. He's got four walk-in freezers stuffed with wild game, machetes hanging on hooks, a gun cabinet. A whole camo wardrobe. This guy has a hard-on for the apocalypse, like it would be the best thing that could ever happen to him. I either need to find a buyer who's an end-timer or have him gut the whole thing. And get this: he thinks it's a selling point."

"So what'd you do?"

"I tell him sure, I can get you more than six. And maybe I can. Just takes one crazy buyer. But anyway, when do you leave for Wisconsin? Is it this weekend already?"

"Tomorrow," Sherri says. She picks up a foam stress ball, a leftover giveaway from last year's gala, and squeezes it, hard. "I don't think I can do it. I can handle everything remotely."

"Honey, Jerry has been like an uncle to you for almost forty years. You have to go see him. Take Violet. She needs to connect with her Midwestern heritage. She doesn't even like cheese."

"Or beer. What can I say, I raised her wrong. Anyway, she can't come. She's helping her dad with a big shoot. It's set in the fifties, so of course she and Mitch are in heaven sourcing Studebakers and Hornets. She picked up a Bel Air convertible from one of our board members. She was in heaven." With Sherri's help, Mitch started his own business like his dad's, only without the racketeering. Violet grew up around cars. She knows how to buff a fender, source parts on the aftermarket, and sweet-talk nervous collectors into letting her borrow their precious keepsakes for movie shoots. She can even change the oil by herself. Now she and Mitch, both good-natured, are partners in the business, and they are inseparable. Mitch hadn't been the greatest husband—their marriage had only lasted a few years—but he's always been a good friend and devoted father. When Sherri had told him she was pregnant, she'd expected him to leave her. Instead, he began to cry tears of happiness. "I guess I'm going to have to straighten my shit up," he said, and he did.

And Sherri got her life together, too. But she needed order and consistency, while Mitch liked to shoot from the hip. His was a life of empty pizza boxes stacked on the coffee table, hours at the arcade, and weekends playing volleyball on the beach. He's remarried and had five more kids with Beth, his funky second wife, who runs a vintage-clothing store in Silver Lake and dresses in hoop skirts paired with argyle sweaters and Doc Martens. Now Violet is part of the big family Sherri never had. She has Sherri for structure, and Mitch for ease.

Tina says, "It'll be nice for you to go back home, Sher. You need to come full circle."

"I'm fine."

"No, you're not. I can hear it in your voice. What happened, you know that was a long time ago. It wasn't your fault. It was an accident."

They've gone over this a thousand times. There was no way Tina could convince Sherri that Arthur's death wasn't her fault. She's blamed herself every single minute of every single day for almost forty years. She dedicates each yoga practice to Arthur, donates money to nonprofits in Arthur's name. Forty years was a long time ago, but to Sherri, the memory is as fresh as the morning. "Are you sure you can't come with me?"

"I promised Julia I'd babysit." Tina is one of the highest-grossing Realtors in Los Angeles, yet she's also a doting grandmother. "She and Connor are going on one of those ridiculous babymoons. Nori and I never did anything like that when I was expecting."

"None of us did." The only indulgence Sherri had experienced when she was expecting Violet was a small shower arranged by Mitch's stepmother and Tina.

"Just bring your CBD, practice your loving-kindness meditation, and text me every five minutes."

Sherri actually wishes Tina could come for another reason. "Guess what?" she says. "I'm seeing Val." Sherri found her on Facebook and sent a message. Val responded instantly, her reply typically curt. *Yeah sure. Come by. We'll rendezvous.*

"Get out!"

"I'm flying into O'Hare, and Beloit is right on the way home. She'll be my first stop."

"Ooh, take pictures! God, just hearing her name still scares me to death. Sorry, gotta go, I've got another call coming through. A beauty on Tigertail in Brentwood. She wants to sell before another fire races up the ravine. Who wants to watch their life get destroyed at three o'clock in the morning?"

"Tell her to buy the apocalypse house."

"Love you. Keep me updated."

Sherri has to admit that Tina generally knows what's good for her; it was Tina who'd sensed that the museum world would be a good fit and made sure she'd gotten hired before anyone in HR could see she was pregnant. The pay was terrible, and working the information desk was incredibly boring compared to the resort, but boredom was what she'd needed. It was a time for her to clean up and get her head back together. On her breaks she'd wander the galleries and visit paintings and sculptures the way she might visit friends. Never in her life had she seen art like that, from ancient pottery to Japanese woodprints to her favorite contemporary painting, Alex Katz's *Round Hill*, featuring a bunch of friends lounging on a beach, some spacing out, one reading, others in conversation. It reminded her of the feeling of togetherness she'd shared with the other Bunnies at the resort.

When the market crash wiped out much of the museum's endowment, Sherri was worried she'd lose her job after some of the top brass were let go. Then again, she worked in development, and they needed people who were good at raising money—and good at accounting for it. Sherri could do both. She was almost done with her finance degree after taking night classes at UCLA in tax, audit, financial accounting, managerial accounting, and business. Brian, her boss, told her that she was valuable because she could work a spreadsheet as well as a fundraising event.

Tina was like an older sister even as Sherri became more independent and accomplished. She helped Sherri find a good divorce attorney when it became clear that her marriage was going south, no matter how much she and Mitch cared about each other, or how much they doted on little Violet, with her curly blond hair, rosy cheeks, constant smiles, and chubby ankles. Tina babysat when Sherri had night class, and when she got her degree, Tina arrived at the graduation-ceremony venue two hours early to stake out front-row seats for her, Violet, and Mitch.

Tina was the first person Sherri called after she'd gotten off the phone with Jerry one afternoon when Violet was five years old. The little girl was engrossed with the Matchbook cars Mitch had given her. "I've got a pile of mail from Lehman Brothers to forward to you," Jerry had said. "And it doesn't look like junk."

"My pension is with Northern Trust," Sherri said. "I already get those statements." There wasn't much in her account after such a short stint at the club, and that was money for later, much later. "Can you open one, see what it says?"

"I feel funny opening other people's mail, but here goes." She could hear Jerry's fat hands tearing open the envelope, heard him exhale sharply. "Wowie, Sher," he said. He paused for a long time. Then he whistled. "You never told me you were loaded."

Sherri laughed. "That's because I'm not! I'm broke."

"Well, I'd say three hundred thousand eighty-four dollars and seventy-nine cents is pretty loaded."

Sherri had no idea what Jerry was talking about. "Three hundred what?"

"This is your name right here on the paperwork, Sherri Taylor. Account opened May twenty-first, 1981." That felt like another life to her. Sherri hadn't forgotten about the money she'd given Arthur to invest that morning at Giles, just as she was falling under his spell. But she hadn't followed up on it, because anything that had to do with Arthur and every step that had been set in motion leading to his demise made her feel pained and guilty. May 1981? This had to be the account, but there was a mistake. "Looks like you started out with a hundred forty thousand," Jerry said. "Sherri, where'd you get that kind of money? Did you get involved with the Mafia out in Lake Geneva?"

"There must be a computer glitch. This is off by several zeros. Arthur opened the account, but I only gave him a few hundred dollars. It couldn't have grown that much." She was dumbfounded. "Arthur sold some gold and added the rest."

"You and Arthur opened an account together?"

"He said he'd heard a stock tip and wanted to invest, but not under his name."

"Well, Digital Switch was one hell of a damn good investment. You've made a small fortune."

A small fortune? She looked at the pile of bills on her kitchen counter. She had tuition payments, gas, electricity, food, day care. More money meant she could get a master's degree in business. It meant she could hire babysitters, go out, date, have a life. Still, she couldn't spend it. "Jerry, that money was Arthur's. All but a very little bit of it."

"You know he was a St. John, right? He paid cash for that place on Beulah. His dad was a big commodities trader. They've got a place on Lake Geneva with a garage for ten boats."

She knew that Arthur's father had been on the Chicago Board of Trade, but she had no idea Arthur was one of the "trustafarians" she'd met on Lake Geneva. He hadn't seemed like those guys.

"Maybe Arthur had a premonition that he was going to pass on," Jerry said. "Maybe this was his way of looking out for you."

The conversation with Arthur at Giles haunted her in a new and fresh way. She remembered the line she'd uttered: "Money is external." The rest of Berryman's poem came back to her, and gave her the chills. "'Soon part of me will explore the deep and dark / Floor of the harbour . . . I am everywhere . . .'"

Arthur was gone, and yet he was everywhere, lurking in the corners of her conscience. Sherri still couldn't believe this was real. "Jerry, can you send those papers to me? I should give it back to his family."

"They don't need it, honey. Listen to me: don't say a single word about it. All the documents are in your name, and your name only. Nobody else even knows about it. You didn't do anything under-handed, he did. But he's gone now, and that's tough, but you've got a kid. And frankly, you owe me some of the money I loaned you last year for the deposit on your apartment when you broke up with what's his name. Congratulations, Sher. You're rich. Don't blow it this time."

She didn't. She would always feel funny about spending Arthur's money—that's what it was to her, Arthur's. The quarterly earnings statements felt like hauntings. She mostly reinvested the dividends, and only spent her earnings on things she believed Arthur would approve of: her education, Mitch's business, Violet's private school. The initial stock had split like an atom in a nuclear reactor, and she'd used some of the money to diversify her portfolio. Now she sits on a mountain of money. She doesn't need to work at the museum, but she's stayed on. She likes to work, likes people, and she likes to be on a schedule. Plus, she's always found that staying busy helps her to forget. She's only ever wanted to forget, which was why she's stayed away from Wisconsin. She's forgotten for so long that she's almost forgotten how to remember.

Back at home, Sherri's reflection bounces off just about every surface of the Palm Springs home she shares with Bayard, from the surface of the pool to the sliding patio doors to the gleaming quartz countertops in the kitchen. One full wall of her bedroom is mirrored. She sees her-self from every possible angle in her bathroom, where she even has a mirror that she can pull away from the wall and flip this way and that to reveal each pore and wrinkle in horrifying detail.

Ever since Sherri bought her plane ticket to Wisconsin, she's begun to tear through all of her outfits and consider an assortment of possible versions of herself she might project during her visit to East Troy. Nothing seems right, and she's suddenly exhausted from a lifetime of constantly turning the volume of her personality up and down and never quite landing on the right setting. She's on day four of a strict five-day mail-order cleansing kit that she discovered on Instagram, featuring all kinds of horrible powders she blends into neon-colored smoothies that turn her gut into a cement mixer. Bayard says her skin has started to smell like burning plastic.

She's standing in front of a full-sized mirror in Bayard's late wife's closet, which is now her closet, although some of Nell's better clothes—her rabbit-fur coat and Chloé dresses—still hang there in a small, cordoned-off section. Two years ago, Bayard's rock-climbing, Patagonia-clad daughter in Seattle, Meg, said she wanted to claim her mother's clothes for herself, although they'd never fit her. She's stocky like her father. Violet, on the other hand, is tall and slim like Mitch. The dresses would fit Violet perfectly but would look laughable on her, with her shock of purple hair and pierced nose. She has a tattoo with a Buick Riviera tail fin on the back of her neck. She's used to dealing mostly with men, and it shows. She's tough and jaded in a way that Sherri never was. Meg disapproves of Violet and Sherri, these ragtag women her father has pulled into his life, although she's never explicitly said so. Sherri doesn't take it personally, because Meg wouldn't want her father to date *anyone* new, especially someone who, at nearly sixty, still wears stilettos and bodycon dresses.

Nell had been a society wife. She sat on the board at the art museum where Sherri works, which was how Sherri had met Bayard. Nell never missed a fundraiser. She was the kind of woman who didn't flinch when she spent two thousand dollars on a dress or thirty bucks on a bar of French milled soap. Sherri was a long way from East Troy, but her Midwestern upbringing stays with her. She has a lot more money to her name than Nell ever did, but she suspects Meg thinks she's a gold digger. Still, she prefers to shop the sale racks. She often thinks about taking all those old dresses to an upscale resale store on Palm Canyon Drive (the drag queens would love them), but that is Bayard's job. Three years after he'd buried his wife, he still isn't up to the task. Sherri understands. She hadn't spent the bulk of her adult life with Arthur—really, she'd only spent just over a week with him. Still, to this day she feels his presence alongside her. She even sleeps on Arthur's threadbare pillowcase.

Bayard walks into the dressing room, so distracted that her nakedness does nothing for him. The recessed lights bounce off his bald head. Shirtless and tan, he reminds Sherri of Yul Brynner from *The King and I*. Sherri adores him. "Have you seen my yoga shorts?"

"I don't keep track of your shit, my dear." She bet that Nell had never spoken to Bayard like that.

"But they aren't in my blue bag where I left them."

"Then you misplaced them."

He's incredibly fit for a man his age, although he's barrel-chested and thick-necked, and has the breathless look of someone who could suffer a heart attack at any moment, especially in the heated vinyasa classes he attends. Hot yoga in the desert? Sherri is perpetually amazed that that's really a thing.

"Still fretting about what to wear in Siberia?"

"Stop calling it that." She yanks out a satiny pink dress with a bow at the neck and holds it against her torso.

"No," Bayard says. "Too Melania."

"It's awful, I know. Nothing's right."

He pauses, stands behind her, sets his hands on her shoulders and smells her hair. "You're scared to go back there, aren't you? You're scared of all those people."

"I'm not scared." She says this quickly—too quickly. She's terrified, and he knows it. "I just want to look my best."

"You always do." He moans with pain—he's wearing his Slendertone belt, which zaps his abs with an occasional electric jolt—kisses her on the forehead, and disappears. A few seconds later she hears him shout "Found 'em!" with delight in his voice, followed by the chime of the security system indicating that the front door has opened and closed. Finally, she hears the hum of his Audi sliding into the quiet desert streets. She is grateful for Bayard, and as she gets older and experiences the loss of friends, she grows increasingly grateful for days when the worst thing that happens is misplaced gym shorts.

Sherri's gaze drifts over to Nell's dresses. She eyes a tasteful white Alexander McQueen A-line with cap sleeves and tiny ruffles near the hem. She slips it off the hanger and discovers that the tags from Berg-dorf Goodman are still attached. Nell paid fifteen hundred dollars for this thing? It was like pulling teeth to get her to donate half as much to the museum's annual campaign. Bayard said she wouldn't even put dill in her famous potato salad because she thought it cost too much.

She slips it on. It fits, although it feels stiff. She stands in front of the mirror and smooths the fabric over her hips. This is the kind of dress a woman her age would wear to a courthouse wedding—maybe she can even wear it to her own if she ever decides to take Bayard up on his proposals. Imagine marrying someone in his dead wife's dress! She's always felt she was married to one man: Arthur.

CHAPTER TWENTY

Val's Beloit house is an old Victorian with chipped purple paint and turquoise blue shutters. It sits perched on a small hill with a view of the Rock River and, beyond it, the main street downtown, with a hippie co-op. There are antique stores, and even a sushi restaurant.

Plastic children's play toys are scattered all over her lawn, as are piles of leaves from the previous fall, sitting in rotting lumps under the late summer sun. A hummingbird drinks nectar from a plastic bird feeder that hangs from a metal hook. Sherri, already nervous for this encounter, nearly trips on the long dog chain with one end wrapped around the porch column. She feels ridiculous in her heels. Is it really time for her to switch to more comfortable footwear?

Val sits in a rotting rattan chair on the porch smoking a cigarette. "You've still got that crazy fucking hair."

"You used to say it looked like pubic hair." Val had a way of saying things that stayed with Sherri.

"Did I? Sounds like me." Val laughs and coughs—she is clearly used to both activities. "Of all the things to remember."

"I remember you were nice to me, too."

"Don't tell anyone." Val eyes Sherri from head to toe. "Do you have weigh-ins out in California? Because you still look like *this*." She holds up her pinkie finger, and Sherri remembers how Val once told her that she was big-boned. Is she saying she actually thought Sherri was thin? Has Sherri's conception of her own body for the last forty years been defined by the old woman sitting in front of her?

Everyone tells Sherri that she looks great *for her age*—and she imagines it's their way of saying she looks good enough to model for an ad for Metamucil. What, she wonders, does great "for your age" even mean? Is there some agreed-upon aesthetic template for an almost-sixty-year-old woman? She looks OK, she supposes, but she has to work at it—and pay for it. She's grateful she can afford Coolsculpting, BBL, and Pilates. She has time to play tennis and swim and go for hikes in Joshua Tree. So far, thank God, her joints and back haven't failed her. She's tried hard not to make Violet crazy about her weight and her looks, but it's always been difficult for Sherri to bite her tongue when she notices that her daughter has gained a few pounds, or her outfit isn't flattering, or she could use a bit of lipstick, just as she finds it hard to be kind to herself when she notices the way time has changed her body. She knows she's not young anymore, not like those girls who drive out from Los Angeles in their boho sundresses and booties. They have gleaming skin and lustrous hair and little dogs in their purses.

She stopped turning heads the way those girls do a long time ago, and she likes to think she's OK with it, but she can't shake the feeling that she'll be weighed-in and judged. She's not old, but she finds it disconcerting to be at the end of the middle part of life. Her crow's-feet grow deeper and longer by the minute, she's got elevens between her eyes, and tiny vertical lines like a bar code have appeared on the skin above her lip. She happily forks over hundreds of dollars for the occasional fillers, but they can only do so much.

Sherri smiles. "I guess Gloria has taken up permanent space in my brain."

"Mine is filled up with too much other shit to make room for that old hag. But you look good, Sher. You really do."

"So do you."

"Shut the fuck up. Five kids and a busted knee have done a number on me. At least my grandkids keep me moving around. Jason, my oldest, he's got four now, and my girl Jenny, she's on her third. I'm on granny duty most days—who would have thought we'd be grandmas?"

"I'm not."

Val seems confused by this. "So that's why you look so good. Never married?"

"Once. We didn't last long." She still speaks with Mitch often— she even called him on the drive to Beloit. His laconic voice always calms her. He makes for good company, but they're better off as friends. After Arthur, she knew there was more, and she's happy that that's what Mitch found with Beth. They visit Sherri and Bayard in Palm Springs all the time. Mitch loves to park whatever car he's driving in front of their house. Cars, he says, look best in the desert. Last time, it had been a green Triumph that he and Violet had rebuilt together. Beth and Bayard never mind when Sherri and Mitch wax nostalgic about their wild days in Palm Springs. They aren't jealous when Mitch winks at Sherri as they drive past the O'Donnell Golf Club and says, "That's where I knocked you up."

"Kids?" Val asks.

"One. Violet."

"Why just one? Problems with the plumbing?"

Who would have thought that between the two women, Val would turn out to be the maternal one? "No," Sherri says, not expecting such a direct, personal question, but then again, this is Val. "I wasn't cut out for kids." That's what she always says when people ask, which they do. The truth is that Violet saved her. Once, when Sherri was a girl, she watched a story on the news about a woman who'd jumped off the observation deck of the Empire State Building, but she was saved when a gust of wind pushed her onto the ledge on the eighty-fifth floor. Violet had altered Sherri's path the same way that wind did, blowing up out of nowhere at just the right moment, even though it felt like the wrong moment back then.

"Well, it's too late for me to change your mind about not being cut out for it. None of us are, but we make do. Come on, let's go inside. I won't keep you long. You probably have people to see, things to do. Everyone's so busy these days."

The television is on in the living room. On top of the coffee table Sherri eyes back issues of *Better Homes and Gardens* and *Highlights for Children* and a plastic bottle of spray butter. "Take a seat." Val gestures at a massive Barcalounger where a curled-up dog raises its furry eyebrows to register Sherri's appearance. "Tommy, get down!" Val barks, shooing the dog away. "He's Tommy Two. Tommy One ran into the street and met his maker in the grille of the recycling truck, so we recycled the name."

"Oh God, I'm sorry."

"Honestly, Tommy Two is better. He's a good boy, aren't you? Let me get you a soda." The dog leans into Val's legs the way Goldie used to. Sherri envies Val. Her house is a mess, and her body is blown out, but she seems so comfortable with who she is. Not since she was a girl has Sherri known comfort like that.

Val returns from the kitchen and sets a can of soda on the end table. Sherri's eyes have adjusted enough that she can just barely make out the seam running down her pair of lightly pressed slacks. She's ironed for her. Val pulls a framed family photograph off of the wall and hands it to Sherri. Her entire family is dressed in jeans and white shirts. "That's from a few years ago."

"Five kids, huh?"

"Four pregnancies. First came the boys: Jason, Peter and Jimmy. Scott was happy. He had his fishing buddies, someone to sit next to him on game day. But damn it if I didn't want a girl, even though you and I both know how much trouble they are. Careful what you wish for, right? The good Lord gave me two. Jenny, she's a saint. She looks after all of us. But Molly? She's a piece of glass in my eye."

"You have a beautiful family," Sherri says.

Val laughs. "Damn, I wish Scotty could be here, but it's Friday fish fry. We own Murphy's, the supper club down the street." She points out the side window. "Scott can cook anything, but we keep it old-school because the young people think it's campy. We've got relish trays and pickled herring, cinnamon rolls, the whole bit. I used to help him out until someone rammed a cart into my knee."

"I'd love to check it out next time," Sherri says, although she knows she'll probably never see Val again. "What ever happened to Danny?"

"Oh, he lives in his grandmother's place now. He's still at the resort. It has a new corporate owner now. You'd almost never know it had anything to do with Playboy back in the day."

"Did he ever get married?"

Val raises her hand and spreads her fingers wide. "Last time I checked, about five times. God love him, he'll always be Danny. Falling in love never gets old for some people. He kept your friend's weird dog, you know. I swear Goldie was scared of her own tail." She pauses. "You sure left on a low note. That was tough, what happened. It sure was."

People change on the outside, but not so much inside. After all these years, Sherri can see that Val, in her gruff way, is trying to address Arthur's death as gently as possible. Sherri's pain has been so private for so long that it feels good to talk about it with one of the few people in her life who'd actually known him.

Val continues, "When you left, I honestly thought you'd come back. I kept everything on your side of our room just the way it was. But you shot out of here like a bat out of hell."

"I guess I did," Sherri says.

"I can see why." Val grows quiet, reflective. "Forty years almost. How did that happen? Days are long and all that."

"I can't believe it myself. The days really do run away like wild horses over the hills."

"Well, you're back now. Took you long enough to return. Everyone does. These kids, they try to live in big cities and then they discover the traffic and the sky-high rents. Suddenly Wisconsin doesn't look so bad—"

Sherri interrupts her. "Val—"

She leans forward, curious. "What's on your mind? You didn't just come here to say hello, did you?"

"No, I have something I want to say to you. I—" Sherri pauses. "Val, I'm so sorry. I've been sorry for such a long time."

"What on earth for?"

"I told Curtis about you and Danny. You told me to keep it to myself, and I did, right up until I let it slip. Curtis overheard, and, well." Sherri looks at her hands. "We both know what happened next."

Val sinks back in her chair, amused. "Oh, for fuck's sake, Sher. You can let that go. Curtis knew about Danny and I long before that day. He came to Lake Beulah because he thought he could change my mind. And if you want to know the truth, if your boyfriend hadn't hit his head on the rowboat, you might have ended up attending my funeral instead of his, and none of these people would exist." She waves at her family photograph. "I think about that more times than you'll know."

Sherri has replayed what happened that day so often and for so long that her memory of the events leading up to Arthur's death is like a well-traveled road in her mind. What Val tells her is a strange detour. "You're kidding."

"I told him to stay away from us, but, well, that's all she wrote." Val reaches for Sherri's hand. Her nails are long and perfectly painted. "I never had a chance to tell you how sorry I was about Arthur. Talk about being in the wrong place at the wrong time. I don't think Curtis ever got over it. He changed after that. Not a lot. He's still an asshole, only now he doesn't seem like he wants to kill someone, just give them a hard time."

"I keep thinking of everything that went wrong that day," Sherri says. "What if we'd taken the boat out five minutes later? What if—"

"Don't do that to yourself, Sher. Awful as it was, it happened the way it was meant to happen. You can't beat yourself up."

"But I do." Sherri hasn't ever admitted this out loud to anyone before. As far as the people closest to her know, it's old news. But Arthur's death never feels old to Sherri.

"Curtis owns Wilson's Carpet—did you see it by the exit off 39? He makes a fortune. Burns me to think that he bought that place with the tip money I gave him."

"You're kidding me." Sherri thinks maybe even some of her own tip money had helped Curtis build his carpet empire after so much of it had gone missing. "You couldn't get your money back?"

"Nope, no paper trail. I couldn't even prove I gave him the time of day."

Sherri checks her phone. "I should get going," she says. Truthfully, she wants to leave; she needs some time to reorganize her memories around this new truth. "I'm happy it worked out to come see you."

"Are you going to see the other Bunnies?"

"Not this trip," Sherri says. "But we're still in touch. Well, just a few of us. Ginger visits me in Palm Springs each winter. She and Lizzy. Her wife."

"Oh boy, I sure saw that one coming. You know Ola and Biata are gone." Val points at the sky with her index finger. "They owned a tailor shop in Lake Geneva up until a few years ago. And Boo isn't with us anymore," Val says. "We've lost more than a few rabbits."

Is that what they are now that they're older? Rabbits?

"It's a shame the cancer came back," Val says. "She gave it a good fight, I'll tell you that. We stayed in touch until the end."

"And Gwen?"

"Oh, she's a bigwig at Northwestern Mutual. She serves on all kinds of boards. I see her name in the paper all the time and I think, there's our Gwen." Val mentions some Bunnies Sherri has forgotten or remembers only vaguely, which she finds disconcerting. Karen, Jessica, Kris, Peggy, Ann, Jin, Susy, Denise. It amazes her that people can pass through her life and fade out of her memory, like last season's reality television contestants.

"What about Carmen?" Sherri asks. She's tried to find her, but with no luck. It's hard to find old friends when so many of them have married and changed their names. Not Sherri. She went right back to Taylor as soon as her divorce was finalized.

Val winces with displeasure at the sound of Carmen's name. "I ran into her at the State Fair a few years back. She looked like she'd seen a ghost. She had to break away from her family to talk to me. She's in Mequon now, married to an anesthesiologist. A real North Shore Nancy in her white jean jacket. She doesn't want anyone to know about her past."

"Carmen? How'd she keep her mouth shut about that?"

"I guess it's one thing to talk about other people's business, and another to talk about your own. Even her kids don't know. It was all I could do not to chase after them and say something about Sugar Shack."

It makes Sherri sad to think about shunting such a major part of your life's story, although part of her understands. People look at Sherri differently as soon as they find out that she's a former Playboy Bunny, as though they've just discovered that her brain is stuffed with cotton tails. If she were to make a pie chart of her life, the eight months she spent at the resort would hardly account for a sliver of time, yet her experience as a Bunny overpowers her identity, like too much bitters in an old-fashioned. The way she sees it, she can either turn her past into a secret, the way Carmen did, or capitalize on it and endure the consequences.

"I caught her in our room once, going through our drawers," Val says. "She stole from me. I'll bet she stole from you, too. I was going to tell you about her sticky fingers but just like that"—Val clapped her hands together—"you were gone. Anyway, those girls never liked me, and I gave them no reason to. They have their little reunions sometimes, and they had a big one after Hef died a few years ago. I don't go anymore. They turn those get-togethers into competitive aging events. They spend the whole time counting each other's wrinkles."

Sherri reaches for her bag and remembers how long goodbyes take in the Midwest—it's a long, slow march to the door, and a real accomplishment to finally put your hand on the handle. But Sherri senses Val's hesitation isn't rooted in politeness. She doesn't seem to want Sherri to leave.

"Gloria's in Phoenix now. She runs a dog-grooming business."

"Poor dogs!" Sherri says.

"She wasn't so bad. That was a hard job for her to do. And Rhonda and Frank bought Zuhde's Resort in Kenosha. They're on the God squad now. Frank is a preacher at one of those big churches that looks like a hotel. Guess his stripping days are behind him. Maybe Carmen's a parishioner."

A truck rumbles over the bridge that runs across the Rock River. Off in the distance she can see Beloit College perched on the hill, pretty and old. "Let me get a photo," Sherri says, remembering that Tina wanted a snapshot. She flips her phone around.

Val puts her arm around Sherri and smiles broadly. "Just look at us," Val says. "A couple of old roomies. I didn't like you at first, you know that? But you turned out OK I guess."

Sherri puts her phone away and begins to walk back to her car. "You ever regret it?" Sherri asks.

"Regret what?"

"Being a Bunny."

"A Bunny? Oh hell no. That was the best time of my whole goddamn life."

CHAPTER TWENTY-ONE

Home is a place best arrived at on your own terms. This is what Sherri finds herself thinking as she looks out at the square from the driver's seat of her rental car. It seems smaller now, and achingly familiar. It's funny what you don't realize you remember. She used to rub her hands on the rough bark of the ash trees, read books in their shade, and feed peanuts to the squirrel with the crooked tail. Her father loved those trees because, in the fall, the leaves turned a shade of purple he said he'd never encountered anywhere else. He said the ash tree was considered the Venus of the woods. When they had picnic lunches on the square, he'd lie on the blanket, look up at the leaves, and say, "'The song of the Ash Grove soft as love uncrossed.'" Those trees were the first to explode into leaf in the spring, but also the first to drop. The leaves were in full bloom. She could make out the knots of squirrel nests in the branches.

When Violet took scuba diving lessons, she told Sherri about the process of reentry, of slowly rising back to the surface in order to avoid the bends if oxygen entered her system too quickly. Sherri can feel herself going through her own kind of reentry in those first few moments back home, as though she were under water, rising slowly, allowing East Troy to seep back into her system one molecule at a time.

She braces herself for this return to the site of her lost childhood, and her former self. She's never before appreciated how lucky she was to grow up on a square, a place that made her believe there was a center to everything, like the "home" square in the middle of a Parcheesi game board. It was a destination, a goal, a safe zone, the emotional vortex of her life. She realizes now that this was exactly what Arthur recognized when he arrived in East Troy.

She's long since stopped paying attention to the meditation and mindfulness podcast she was listening to and only in that moment becomes aware of the host yammering on. "The first step of mindfulness is to inhabit a beginner's mind," he says in his mellow voice. He sounds like he's prone on the floor with a cat on his belly. Sherri doesn't buy it. After all, wasn't it a beginner's mind that got her into trouble? She flicks off the radio and steps out of the car. Her phone rings. Marco. He only calls with bad news.

"No camels," he says. "Apparently we need a livestock license."

Sherri pretends to sound disappointed. "And we can't get one?"

"It's not as easy as all that. What sort of Nights of Arabia party doesn't have camels?"

A livestock license shouldn't be a big deal, but then again, it seems livestock is everywhere in southeastern Wisconsin. On the drive to East Troy from Beloit she watched as countless livestock trucks rumbled past her car on the freeway. She was relieved the cages were empty, sparing her a glimpse of the watery orbs of the animals' eyes when they were headed for slaughter.

"It's a public-health issue," Marco says. "I've tried everything."

"How much?"

"You know what? It doesn't matter how much," Marco says. "We don't have enough time to get it approved. We just can't have camels.

It was a bad idea anyway. Terrence was right. The smell alone would be a problem."

Sherri thought camels were a bad idea when he'd first made the suggestion, although she hadn't said so out loud because she knew that Marco would discover this on his own. She's having a hard time caring about the gala. Her entire life in Palm Springs feels unreal, because she is overcome by the sight of the bandstand and the giant spruce the town decorates for Christmas.

The lovely lilting sound of Marco's voice is drowned out by the rumble of a passing motorcycle. There are still little flags stuck in the grass, left over from the Fourth of July more than a month ago. She's forgotten what a big deal Independence Day has always been here, and she's sad she missed it, sad that Violet never experienced a small-town Fourth of July when she was a kid: the floats, carnival, ETBT, and fireworks she'd watch on the lawn by the library. As much as Sherri used to love the activity, she also remembers how happy she was when it was all over and the people who'd come from everywhere else, the lake people and the campers, even the carnies, would leave and she'd have her town back. Her town.

Marco says something about an ordinance against tiki torches and Sherri gasps. "Giles is gone?"

"What's gone? What's Giles?"

"I'll call you later. Don't worry about the camels or the torches. We'll figure something out."

"Well OK, bye then."

The entire building that once housed Giles has disappeared. It seems impossible. Not just impossible, but a betrayal of memory and history. At first, she thinks she's entered the square from the wrong corner, got turned around. Is she dreaming? A plot of grass stands in its place, just grass like any old mowed lawn. Businesses didn't get tombstones, yet she wishes they did.

Her eye is drawn to a massive vinyl overhang that reads PUFFY's VAPE on what used to be Bev's Flowers. There are signs on the big glass windows that say ASK ME HOW FLAVORS SAVED MY LIFE and URBAN SMOKE. Marshall's Department Store is now an upscale café, and the town has a bookstore, quaint and classy. Just seeing it makes her want to weep. Her father would have loved that—he'd always bemoaned the lack of a bookstore in East Troy.

Finally, she turns and musters the nerve to look at the building—*her* building, the former home of Taylor's Timeshop. All those hours of her childhood in that store! She could smell the chicory scent of her father's polyester shirts, hear the cuckoo flying through the little door, all the clocks ticking and chimes ringing in her head.

The stenciling on the big windows reads LAKE COUNTRY YOGA. Jerry had turned the building she'd grown up in into a yoga studio? She walks to the door and gives it a push. The wall between the office and the showroom has been knocked down, and the lowered ceiling had been removed, revealing ornate, painted tin tiles. Sherri can't believe they've been there all along. The space is beautiful, bright and spare, painted a pleasant off-white with gray undertones. The once scratched and scuffed wood floors gleam. A middle-aged woman with a long braid stands behind the reception desk. "Can I help you?"

"No," Sherri says, overcome. "I'm in the—"

"*Sherri?*" She steps away from the desk to approach her. "Sherri Taylor? Oh. My. God. Is that really you?"

"Raylee?"

"I go by Lee now." She's taller than Sherri, and her hair is marked by dramatic stripes of gray, but the gentle brown eyes and friendly, curious nature are unmistakable. "What on earth are you doing here after so long?"

"Well, Jerry, you know, he's sick, and the building is technically mine. He's been managing it for me for years. I'm here to sell it . . . or something."

"Oh, don't sell. Please. Jerry gives me a break on rent. I shop for him, take care of stuff. I don't make much on this place, but you'd be surprised how busy we get on weekends, especially in the summer. We have an intro class, and a power flow, and the first Sunday we practice asanas and—"

"You still don't stop talking, do you?"

Raylee laughs. "I missed you so much when you left, Sher. You were always so nice to me. Hey, do you still have that brown car? I thought you were going to back up and drive right over that dealer, I really did."

"I sold that car long ago," Sherri says. "I couldn't wait to get rid of it."

"I still have my Princess Di doll I bought with the money you gave me. She's probably worth a fortune now. So, what are you going to do with this place?"

Sherri shrugs. "I don't know. I'm about to talk to Jerry, see what he thinks. Speaking of—" Sherri points at the ceiling. "Is he in?"

"He just left for a doctor's appointment. He should be back in a few hours. He looks terrible. Breaks my heart." She pauses. "It feels so good to see you, Sher. I always thought of you as the sister I never had. I looked up to you so much. I tried to walk like you, do my makeup the way you did. You gave me your bike."

Sherri is touched. "Honey, I was just a goof."

"I never thought so. You were my North Star. Nobody else paid any attention to me but you and your mom. You taught me math, made me cookies, let me bang on the organ. Without you, I probably would have never left my house or made friends."

"You're hard to resist," Sherri says, and she means it. She'd always had a feeling Raylee would come into her own. "Do you have a family?" She feels like Val asking that question.

"I guess so, if you count goats and chickens. My husband Dave and I, we've got a little farm on Carver School Road. Can you believe it? Now *I'm* the one in the country."

Sherri *could* believe it. Raylee's hands are muscular and weathered, and her face is ruddy from time spent outdoors. Every muscle in her body looks like it is regularly put to productive use. "I love the farm. It keeps us busy. We're growing hemp now. It's good business. And I shear my sheep and sell the wool on the internet. I hardly have time for yoga, but I need it. It's my touchstone. Speaking of—" Raylee reaches for one of many stone pendants hanging from leather cords on a display stand on the information desk. "I want you to have this. It's black obsidian, a spiritual protector."

Before Sherri can refuse, Raylee slips it over her neck. "It looks great on you." She beams. "Just great."

A young woman with colorful tattoos up and down her arms walks into the studio, her mat tucked under her arm. She's followed by a man with a long beard. Hipsters! In East Troy!

"Darn, I've got a class starting in a few minutes. I could talk to you all day. You haven't even told me what you've been up to. Come back, OK? There's a class tomorrow morning at eight. We could have coffee after at the café. I can have you to dinner at the farm. You can meet Dave. God, it's just so great to see you!" Raylee squeezes Sherri hard. "You're still so beautiful."

"*You're* beautiful. You really are. Inside and out." Sherri gives Raylee a long hug—long because she doesn't want her to see the tears welling up in her eyes. Even after all these years she feels she needs to stay composed in front of her young charge.

CHAPTER TWENTY-TWO

She might as well get it over with. She's avoided the lake long enough, ever since her abrupt departure.

Sherri feels so discombobulated from her encounters with Raylee and Val that she doesn't trust herself to remember the back roads to Arthur's cottage. She takes Highway 15, now called Highway ES, to J, wishing the letters would spell something that made sense. The wetlands between ES and the freeway have been destroyed to accommodate self-storage sheds that go on and on and on. Who are all these people with so much junk they can't part with when she'd spent most of her adult life trying to let go? At the edge of East Troy and Mukwonago she is disheartened by the discovery of characterless exurban cul-de-sac homes where there'd once been an apple orchard. They looked temporary somehow, as if they were parts of a movie set. The beautiful old oak trees she remembers lining the road had been cut down to make way for sewers, electric and gas lines, and there was a sea of manicured grass where there'd once been prairie. There is so much people neglect in their lives; why, she wonders, are some homeowners inclined to tend so devotedly to something as mundane as a yard—space made only more boring and nondescript by their effort?

Up ahead she is happy to see that the old barn that housed the Elegant Farmer is still there, only now it is decorated with big black eyes and a grinning smile. She and her mother used to go there to buy produce and milk, or to pick strawberries in the adjacent fields. Now the fields, aside from a small orchard, are gone. A sign says they are famous for their home-baked pie in a bag. She pulls into the parking lot and wanders through the aisles of the farm store, stalling, her stomach in knots. Why was she going back to Arthur's? Why return now? She worries she might run into Roberta at the store. Would she even recognize her old friend? They'd made plans to meet later that day, another miracle of Facebook. They exchange messages occasionally, and like each other's posts, but they are both uncomfortable with social media, too uptight to share anything of real substance. It makes Sherri nervous to think about seeing her in the flesh. She has no idea what her old friend thinks of her after all these years.

The store caters not to the locals but to parents dropping their kids off at one of the area camps, or visitors from Milwaukee who want to experience some idealized version of "the country." They sell popcorn, heavily scented candles, ice cream, every kind of cheese she can imagine (she really is back in Wisconsin), refrigerator magnets shaped like cows, and massive lollipops. She loads up her cart with hundreds of dollars' worth of cheese, summer sausage, and knickknacks and asks the girl at the register to ship it all to her office at the museum so that her colleagues can get a dose of exactly what they think Wisconsin is. Sherri is always extravagant with gifts.

Back in her car, she rolls down her windows to get some air. The August heat is oppressive. High temps are nothing new to her after living in the desert for so long; but she had forgotten about the Wisconsin humidity she'd once loved, and still does, even if it took some getting used to.

She turns onto Highway J and enters the eastern edge of East Troy. Everything she sees—the hills, railroad tracks, shrubbery, slouching barns, cornfields, farmhouses, churches, the sign for the Phantom

Lake YMCA, even the rusty weather vanes—register inside her like pulled stops and depressed keys on the organ.

It is beautiful here—she hasn't forgotten that, but she had forgotten how incredibly verdant and lush it is, the fields peppered with daisies, coneflowers, allium, and purple loosestrife, sandhill cranes standing in pairs in the fields, the hills gentle and rolling. A summer day in Wisconsin feels golden, buzzing with life and activity.

After the Lake Beulah Country Club golf course, she spies the open water of Mill Pond where the road is so close to the lake that there are no houses to block the view. The water is choppy from a motorboat whizzing past hauling a banana-shaped tube with a bunch of kids screaming with delight on the back. Don't they know what could happen to them? Of course they don't. Sherri looks out on the part of Mill Pond where Arthur died. Even after that awful tragedy, the lake still strikes Sherri as strangely benign, a thing to be enjoyed.

The bar across the street is packed. Sherri had walked over there once with Arthur to play bar dice. Motorcycles are lined up in the parking lot, and the tables on the deck are filled with people lounging in the sun and drinking beer out of giant plastic cups. A pair of cyclists in Lycra zoom past her. This was what summer should really feel like, treasured and fleeting, and approached with gusto. Here, because of the weather, everyone feels the need to pack an entire year into three months. It is nothing like Palm Springs, where the seasons all run together without the intense cycles of nostalgia, loss, or anticipation that come with the changes in the weather.

She turns off the main road and passes the sign for Jesuit Island. Massive, droopy weeping willow trees glaze the surface of the water, and the boathouses sit sentinel, as if waiting patiently for the boat traffic to die down so that they can see their reflections again. Tall, old trees and brush front the channel by Beber Camp. She remembers the joyful sound of camp songs skipping off the water and the flotillas of counselors in training who'd pass by the point in their

canoes when she'd spent that week with Arthur. They sang about Old
Mother O'Leary's cow tipping over the lantern in the shed to start the
Chicago fire, and Father Abraham who had seven sons, seven sons
had Father Abraham. It is refreshing to see that the camp is still there,
but where is Javell's, the old lodge with the public beach where she
and Roberta had bought Popsicles and candy when they were girls?
It's gone, replaced with matching, suburban-style McMansions squat-
ting hip-to-hip across their lots. They seem wrong for the lake with
their boring, pristine yards, greedily hogging the newly private sandy
frontage, their Jet Skis and cigarette boats propped on the shore sta-
tions next to their fancy fiberglass piers. This isn't the Lake Beulah she
remembers. It was better when lake property wasn't thought of as such
a luxury, back when the divide between rich and poor wasn't as stark as
it is now, back when Jet Skis didn't buzz around like angry hornets. It's
strange. When she was young, Sherri thought East Troy was slow and
small. Now that she's older and it isn't as slow or as small as it used to
be, she wants it back the way it was.

She steels herself for her return to Jesuit Island, half expecting to
pass the ghost of her frenzied, grief-stricken former self driving in
the opposite direction the last time she'd left. The gatehouse where
the gatekeeper had turned Gwen away has been long since abandoned, judging from the moss-covered roof tiles and empty cans
of Miller Lite on the ledge. She drives past it, feeling rich because
she *is* rich now, but what difference does that make? Money doesn't
calm her nerves. Money doesn't make her feel she's gotten her shit
together.

The fancy new homes that had seemed so raw when Sherri first
visited Arthur are still nice, but they aren't so new anymore. Now they
are swallowed by overgrowth, at least on the sides of the homes that
face the road. The old oak and ash trees have a thick, shadowy canopy
for her to drive under. After so many years in the desert, she's forgotten how wise and reassuring trees feel—tall trees, not like the Joshua
trees that grow only a few inches a year. She doesn't realize until that

moment that she's missed them, just like she's missed the smell of damp soil and leaf dust, which is the pervasive scent on that shadowed stretch of land. Nothing is damp back home.

She follows the road for a quarter mile or so before the woods thin and the marsh becomes visible. If she goes to the right at the fork, she knows she will end up at the white Mediterranean-style house that looks out onto the main lake. A left should take her to Arthur's old cottage, but when she takes it and drives to the end of the other point, his house isn't there. Sure, she's a nervous wreck, but it would be impossible to have forgotten where it was on this spit of land, wouldn't it?

Once, when Bayard had meetings in D.C., he'd taken Sherri to see the starter home he'd shared with Nell in Leesburg, where they'd lived back when he'd worked for Xerox. That place had been his home for a dozen or so years, but even after all that time he drove from street to street, unable to remember which block they'd lived on, which threshold he'd carried Nell over for the first homecoming as a married couple, which front door he'd walked through holding newborn Meg, which yard he'd mowed and driveway he'd shoveled. Sherri thought about breaking up with him right then and there. What kind of person forgets where they'd lived? Was this a kind of domestic absent-mindedness only men could enjoy?

But there she is on that simple little island, home to only ten or fifteen houses, feeling confused herself, wondering if dementia is setting in. Now that she is almost in her sixties, she feels worrisome anguish every time she forgets a name or misplaces her reading glasses or walks into a room completely forgetting what it was she'd meant to get there. Watching her friends' parents—and, lately, some of her friends—battle with Alzheimer's makes her worry about her memory the way she'd once worried about her weight. She completes cross-word and sudoku puzzles every day and takes Spanish lessons. But this afternoon, she wonders why she worries so much about staying sharp. She almost wishes her memory could be erased like the ink on a dry-erase board, or at least the bad parts. She wishes she could only remember the exquisite pleasure of new love without feeling the horrible pain of loss.

She pulls to the side of the road, throws her car into park, grips the wheel, and lets out a scream. It feels good, necessary, cleansing. The sound scares a heron wading in the lily pads. It abruptly takes flight, seeking a quieter refuge.

There are only two points on the island, like the barbed end of a snake's tongue, so what's her problem? She's crazy, as absentminded as Bayard! She backs up and returns, and again she can't find the sweet little cabin with the fieldstone fireplace and the sunporch with the rusty screens. Where were all those sugar maples with squirrels and raccoons rustling in the branches? Gone—gone! But then she spies the shed she and Arthur had so urgently made love against. She realizes his sweet little cottage has been torn down and replaced with a modern, glassy structure so flashy and contemporary that it seems to have been designed with the sole intent of obscuring the past.

She turns off her car and pulls the mirror down to inspect her face, haunted as always by the lines from Auden: "O look, look in the mirror, / O look in your distress." She applies a fresh coat of lipstick, kisses a napkin, and steps out of the car. She adjusts her outfit, now wrinkled and damp. She'd chosen it carefully: a simple black pantsuit with a colorful silk scarf to conceal the infirmity of the skin around her neck. She wanted to return to East Troy looking more confident and classy than she felt.

Although she disapproves of the coldness of the new home, she is grateful to be spared the house she once knew. The replacement is tall and narrow, almost prisonlike, reminding her of one of Louise Bourgeois's "personnages" sculptures she saw at the Tate Modern when Bayard took her to London to celebrate their six-month anniversary. He surprised her with tickets for a sightseeing tour on one of those awful double-decker omnibuses. Sherri lied and said she had a migraine in order to avoid it.

Giant windows face every which way. It makes sense, she supposes, to want to optimize those views, but the openness changes everything. Sherri is so overcome with memories that she swears she can almost see her old self there, so young, sitting by the bonfire with her friends. She pictures Goldie tapping the front door with her paw, asking to come inside. And she's overcome with the image of Arthur, shirtless and wet and alive, walking toward her from the pier.

OK, Sherri thinks, *enough. Enough!* She wants to leave. She's been there, she's seen it, yet she is transfixed. The door opens, and a woman walks out. She's younger than Sherri by a decade or two. Her blond hair is pulled back into a tight ponytail. She's about to go for a run. How strange to think of other people living here in this other house on this sacred ground, yet she looks at Sherri as though *she's* the imposter.

"Can I help you?"

Sherri wants to dislike this woman who had something to do with the bulldozing of her past, but she seems harmless. For her, this is just another beautiful summer day. She'll get some exercise, invite some friends over, cook out on the grill, cruise around the lake in a pontoon—

"I'm sorry," Sherri says. "I thought I was lost. Everything's changed. I—I used to know someone who lived here. In the old house. A long time ago."

"Do you mean Arthur?" There it was, the name Sherri hardly ever spoke out loud. It startles her to hear it.

"Yeah. He's—I'm—"

"Hang on a moment, will you? Let me get my husband," she says, running back to the door. She opens it and yells, "Arthur? Arthur! Come outside for a second."

There was no way Arthur could be alive. Sherri breaks out into a sweat. This was like an episode of *The Twilight Zone.* She holds the key to the rental car tight in her hand, ready to make her escape. She needs to leave this weirdness behind. And then—

Arthur.

She gasps.

The man who approaches her is older than she'd ever seen Arthur, but younger than Arthur would have been if he'd lived. He possesses Arthur's same wiry build, his lustrous hair. Only the symmetry is off. The lips are fuller, his eyes more heavily lidded. It takes Sherri's breath away to look at him.

He reaches for her hand to shake it—such a simple gesture but she hardly knows what to do. Words come out of his mouth as if he's trying to speak to her underwater, the way Sherri and Roberta had tried to speak when they were young. *I'm going to tell you a secret,* they'd say, and they'd sink down to the bottom of Booth Lake, trying to sit cross-legged on the sandy floor of the lake, the words always muffled and confusing. It takes her a while to process what he's saying, but as soon as she does, the words bang against the back of her brain with such force she thinks she might faint.

"So," he's saying, "you were friends with my dad?"

CHAPTER TWENTY-THREE

Sherri stands in front of now-closed Lake Country Yoga, takes a deep breath, shoves her hand into her pocket, and reaches for her keys. Her body still knows this building as if she's an extension of it. She's kept her worn brass key on her chain all these years. She knows its weight and shape, and can blindly distinguish it from all the others.

She slips the key into the lock and listens for the pattern of clicks, knowing the sticky parts, waiting for the moment she'll need to push it at the farthest point in the turn and lift the doorknob to nudge the stubborn lock loose. The tall old door creaks on its decorative brass Victorian hinges. She feels as though she's moving a giant boulder away from a mouth of a cave.

She reaches to her right and flips the switch, still exactly where she remembers it, and braces herself for the fluorescent fixture's antiseptic illumination and insidious hissing sound (her father had replaced the dingy bare yellow bulb during the energy crisis). She counts out the eleven creaky stairs that take her up to the landing with the coat tree where she'd had her own hook, only now Jerry's giant overcoat slumps from it.

The hallway now smells like an old wool blanket. She continues from the landing up a shorter flight of stairs to the door. *Tap tap tap*— how strange to have to knock to enter her own home.

"Come in," Jerry barks. He sits at the kitchen table with a napkin tucked into his shirt like a bib. "Well, well, there she is. How's the return to your old stomping grounds?"

Jerry's voice was so big on the phone. She isn't prepared for how small he's become, like a freeze-dried version of the Jerry she used to know. He is sick, but he has the same twinkle in his eyes. He's clearly glad to see her.

Sherri tosses her purse on the old couch. Jerry hadn't replaced anything in all these years. It was as if he'd been living in a museum of Sherri's life. Everything is the same, just more worn down, like the faded upholstery on the his-and-hers wing chairs her parents used to occupy. Sherri is surprised the old sheet music she'd last played wasn't still sitting on the rail of the piano, yellowed with age.

"You look like you've seen a ghost," Jerry says. He's eating a slippery-looking hard-boiled egg. The room smells of sulfur.

"I feel like I have." She plunks down in the chair across from him. "You knew."

"Is this how you say hello after all this time?"

"Jerry." Her hands shake. "Why—why didn't you tell me?"

"Tell you what? Slow down. Are you mad about the yoga studio? I know some people around here think that yoga is the devil's doorway, but you ask me, Raylee's the perfect tenant. Those kooks are real quiet until they start with their 'ohm's."

"I'm talking about Arthur," Sherri says. "And, well, his son."

Jerry reaches for the napkin and wipes the sides of his mouth with it. "Oh."

"All these years you knew. I feel like such a fool." She wants to be angry, but how could she be when Jerry is so sick?

"Yes, I knew, I knew."

"Jerry, why didn't you tell me?"

"Because, well, what difference would it have made if you'd known, huh? Would his death have been any less tragic?"

Sherri has to give this some thought: Would it have been better or worse if she'd found out that Arthur had been married, that he'd had a family?

"When did you find out?"

He sips his water out of Sherri's old juice cup. This is a conversation he's been expecting, Sherri can tell. "'Son of Prominent St. John Family Drowns While Partying with Playboy Bunnies.' Salacious stuff. It was all over the news back then, but of course you weren't here to see it."

"But *you* were. We spoke. You could have said something." Sherri stands up and walks to the kitchen window, too agitated to sit still. She fingers the edge of the yellowed lace curtain and looks out at the tar rooftop of the building next to her. It's so hot outside that the tar looks like it's melting. It is getting dark. The sky is dusty pink, a hue she doesn't see in Palm Springs. Sherri will meet Roberta at the tavern for a drink soon. "Did you know about his son even before—?" All these years later she still can't talk about his death openly, still can't bring herself to say "before he died."

"Do we really need to go through all this? Nothing I tell you will bring him back. This is old news."

"But Jerry, when did you know?" Sherri is insistent. Questions swirl in her brain. "You were the one who made such a big deal of him being single."

"I thought he was. That house, he bought it in his own name. With money from a trust."

"And?"

"And then somewhere along the way I found out he had a wife. I wish I'd warned you. I was going to. I was. When I brought you home that last time, before you bought your car, I lost my nerve. I think I'd started to say something, and then—"

"The turtle."

"That's right. If it makes you feel any better, I'll bet that turtle is still alive. That little fucker is going to outlive both of us."

Sherri almost has to laugh. Here she is learning a truth that will forever scramble her thinking, and they are talking about a turtle.

"I've never felt I was one to get involved in other people's, erm, *affairs*. Doris had just left me. I was a mess. Who was I to tell you what to do with your life?"

It was one thing for Jerry to have found out about Arthur after he'd died, but to have known beforehand? What an idiot she'd been!

"Besides," Jerry says, "I thought you might have figured it out on your own and been OK with it."

"I was such an idiot! I didn't figure things out back then. And I definitely would not have been OK with it." Sherri remembers Jerry as blustery and brash, but the poor guy sitting in front of her is so uncomfortable that she feels sorry for him, and she recognizes with embarrassment that her drama is insignificant compared to the situation he's facing. She sits back down across from him and exhales all her frustration. "I really can't blame you. It was my life."

"I don't know, Sher. Maybe everything would have been different if I'd put my neck out. You wouldn't have gone to his cabin, or if you did you would have given him a piece of your mind. Instead, you had your party, and that's all she wrote."

Parties were all she'd cared about back then. No wonder Arthur had been hesitant to let her invite her friends to his new place.

"How'd you find out about him, anyway?"

"I went to see the house."

Jerry whistles. "Ooh boy."

"I thought I needed closure, but instead of closure I got something else entirely, that's for sure. His son. He looks just like him. I thought Arthur had come back from the dead. When I said I'd been friends with his dad—"

"Friends, huh?" Jerry smiles and winks.

"Yeah, well, I think he was thinking the same thing judging by the way he looked at me. Like he knew I was a Bunny and that's it, just a Bunny. Like what had happened was all my fault. And you know what? It was. I've never forgiven myself."

Jerry leans forward and places his hand on her shoulder, a fatherly gesture. "You should have never been there in the first place. He's the one that lured you there. But look, we all make mistakes. What happened, it was nobody's fault. Let that sink in. Life is random, Sher. Why did Arthur die that day? Why do I have cancer?"

How, after a lifetime of blaming herself for what had happened to Arthur, could she let go of her guilt? She wasn't ready. Sherri's mind is still racing. "Was Arthur just using me, you think? Maybe he planned to keep me on the hook long enough for his stock to take off. Then he could sell, have me sign some paperwork, he'd get his money, his dad would never get in trouble for insider trading. What was I to him, just a name on an account that would have made him rich?"

Jerry stood up on his spindly legs and took his plate to the kitchen. Sherri followed him. "I don't know, Sher." He pushed the eggshells into the dish disposal—didn't he know not to do that? "I wish I did."

"What do you know about his wife?" That word felt so loaded on her tongue. All these years there'd been another woman who'd known, loved, and mourned Arthur.

"Her name was Margaret. She wasn't bad. Stiff. Very businesslike. She contacted me about selling the place shortly after Arthur's accident. She didn't want to deal with the bad memories and the gossip, and who could blame her? She said she never liked it there anyway. It had all been Arthur's idea, his project. She was perfectly happy to spend summers with their families on Lake Geneva, but Arthur and his dad didn't see eye to eye. He wanted their kids—"

"Wait. Kids *plural*? There was more than one?"

"Twins. Arthur, Jr., and Charlotte. I think that was her name."

Now that Sherri had a child herself, she couldn't imagine being involved with someone and keeping Violet a secret.

"They were little, must have been about two years old at that time. Anyway, the market wasn't good. I told Margaret to wait to sell. And she did. Anyone with that much money can keep an extra house the way some people keep a pearl necklace in their drawer. The place fell apart. The trees grew around it so you couldn't even see it was there."

It pained Sherri to think of the house dying, too, after all the work she and Arthur had done to bring it back. He'd really loved that place.

"Last I heard, Margaret passed on, and the kids tore the old cottage down and built their dream house."

"Oh, it's new all right. I hate it. It looks like a prison."

"That's what they like, I guess. If we all liked the same kinds of houses, the world wouldn't be what it is." Jerry's smile is kind. "Speaking of real estate, about this place—" He pulls out a legal-sized envelope filled with documents and hands it to Sherri. "These are all the receipts for work that's been done here. We got a new boiler just last year, and the roof is only six or seven years old. Here's Lee's lease, and the assessment if you decide to sell. This is all the stuff you're going to need. I sure hope you don't do what Arthur's kids did and tear this place down. It needs work but it has good bones and an important history."

"The thought never would have occurred to me." She couldn't imagine the square without her building, couldn't imagine East Troy without the square, couldn't imagine a world without East Troy.

"Isn't it funny? I dealt in real estate all these years but I'm like the cobbler's son with the torn-up shoes living here in a rented apartment. Turns out I don't much like owning my own place."

Sherri holds the envelope with trembling hands. She'd been so preoccupied with Arthur that the gravity of Jerry's prognosis starts to hit her. She worries she might start to cry.

"There's so much we'll never know in life, kid. I don't know why Arthur didn't tell you the truth. My two cents? I saw the way he looked at you. You two were electric. Maybe he was up to something, and sure, he wasn't entirely honest, but I think he really was in love with you. Maybe he would have told you about Margaret and the kids if he'd had a chance. Maybe he would have even wanted to leave her. Who knows? People have complicated lives. I'll tell you what *I* hold against him: They weren't in Europe that summer. They were right here in East Troy."

"They were here that whole time?" Sherri feels her face go numb. How stupid was she? How many different ways can she be wrong about the past?

"Arthur didn't think it would get back to you. Guess he figured we'd all stay in our lanes, the lake people and the townies, never the twain shall meet. But that's yesterday's newspaper nobody wants to read again." He reaches for Sherri's hand. His skin is translucent, and his skinny white arm is scarred from IV needles. "My doctor, I just saw him today. He says I don't have long."

This wasn't news. Anyone could look at Jerry and see that he was near the end. Still, Jerry has been a constant in her life for so long, she can't imagine him gone.

"I'm going into hospice, kid," Jerry says. "All the beautiful nurses are waiting for me to arrive. That's my last stop before I meet the angels." Sherri wonders what it must be like for him to hover on the edge of death, to wake up each morning wondering if that day would be his last. Maybe Officer Henley had been right. Perhaps Arthur really had died the best kind of death. To never have to say goodbye, to slip out the back door of life without suffering or awareness.

Jerry continues, "My son is going to help me move my things out of here tomorrow, and then the place reverts back to you. This is a great apartment. Aside from all the stairs, I've liked living here. I really have. It's worked out great, financially and everything."

For the thousandth time, Sherri wonders what she's supposed to do with the building without Jerry to take care of it. The square has really come around. It is much more upscale now, and surely the real estate is worth a fair amount. Monopoly Jerry had gotten the bad end of the deal in the end. If he'd bought the building outright for what it was worth back in 1981, instead of allowing her to take a mortgage for half its value and paying it down, he would have come out ahead. He wasn't even making money on the rent, not with Raylee down there. It occurs to Sherri that the deal had never been a strategic arrangement; it was a favor. "I'll help you move, Jer. I can come over tomorrow."

"That's OK, I don't have much. We've been getting rid of things since my diagnosis. I live like a monk, anyway."

Sherri's voice cracks when she says, "Oh, Jerry, I couldn't have made it through these last years without you. Our conversations kept me tethered. You helped me out when I needed it. I feel like you're family."

Jerry waves her sentiment away. "Don't thank me. I've spent my whole damn life here. I got to live somewhere else vicariously through you." Jerry gazes out the living room window that looks out on the square. The upper branches of the giant spruce tree are visible. He grows serious. "I'm sorry you felt you had to leave this place. East Troy was never your problem." He pauses to gather his strength. What he wants to tell Sherri takes great effort. "I've been thinking about this a lot lately: I couldn't have lived anywhere better than here, Sher. I really believe that. This town has its drawbacks, like any place. But I love it. I love the square. The lakes. The trolleys. The people. The history. Everyone knows me. They don't all like me, but they know me. And I know everyone I want to know and avoid the ones I don't. I'm very sorry it's now my turn to leave. I sure am. I don't think I'll ever be ready, but what choice do I have?"

Sherri hugs him for the first and last time. His body is fragile, and feels as if it is filled with air. He takes a raspy breath before he speaks again. "My two cents? If you want to be upset with Arthur, be mad at him for any role he might have played in making you feel you had to leave your home. This is your house and this is your town. And it always will be."

CHAPTER TWENTY-FOUR

Sherri weaves through the crowd at the bar, feeling like an imposter in a space that is filled with people who are known to each other. They are in book clubs and cookie exchanges. They play "sheeps" (or Sheepshead) and bridge. They see concerts, share recipes, go for walks, sit in the stands to cheer on their friends' kids in volleyball, deliver meals when someone falls ill. They know each other's brothers and sisters and cousins and parents. They are part of a giant, tightly woven net, a net she thought she'd slipped out of forever.

Still, Jerry said that East Troy is Sherri's town, and though she's spent nearly forty years trying to prove otherwise, she can't help but wonder if he's been right all along. Everything is so familiar to her, in a way no place has ever felt since. Until that moment, she's never truly appreciated the weight of her decision to leave, never realized how much she'd given up, or how she'd let guilt rule her life. She has friends in Palm Springs, good friends. But the friendships in this small town are born of constant, repetitive exposure.

Sherri sits on a stool at the bar and considers what to do with the building. She finds it easier to think about real estate than this new information about Arthur. She'd always assumed she'd sell, and is surprised to find herself thinking instead about keeping a stake in her past. Maybe she and Bayard can "summer" in East Troy the way that people "winter" in Palm Springs. She could ask Jerry's son to manage the property, or maybe Raylee would want to take it on, in exchange for reduced rent? Sherri thinks about updating the kitchen, sanding the floors, covering the drab walls with a fresh coat of paint, buying some new furniture. She could even get a boat and rent a slip on Booth Lake—Beulah was out of the question. She'd never be able to swim in that lake again.

Beulah, Beulah. She finds it difficult to peel her version of the events leading up to Arthur's death away from this new narrative. The conversations and moments she'd shared with Arthur were perfectly preserved in her mind, like specimens suspended in resin. But that evening, she thinks not of what she and Arthur had said to each other, but of what they *hadn't* said. She'd always assumed Arthur had wanted her to be part of his life. What a fool she was! The only future he'd spoken about was Sherri's alone. Her "becoming." That last day with him—she'd slept. Any conversation they might have had didn't happen, and then she had that horrible party. He'd tried to tell her something, hadn't he? Something had been on his mind. Had she noticed the slightest hesitation in his manner, a twinge of guilt?

"Why can't I be mad at you?" he'd once asked her. Anger might have been the appropriate response for Sherri now, but what good was it? Arthur was dead, and what a shocking but wonderfully affirming miracle it had been to see part of him alive in his son. Any stirrings of anger she felt weren't directed at Arthur, but at life itself—how fast it goes, how strange it is. She knows she'll never get answers to the questions that swirl around in her head.

She orders a brandy old-fashioned, press. It is the perfect Wisconsin drink. While she waits for Roberta, she listens to Tom Petty—she has a feeling the jukebox selection hasn't changed much over the years—and overhears people talk about the heat, who is winning the fastball league, and how the local sports teams are going to look for the fall season. They discuss the parties coming up, the ones they just went to and who they saw—who was wasted and who screwed who. The guys on the other side of her are strangely passionate about the ethanol-free gas at the Kwik Trip.

East Troy has always been a progressive farming community, but it is now a more conservative part of the state. She has a hard time putting her finger on the political climate. It strikes her as a place of contradictions. She weighs the We Back the Badge yard signs and organic co-ops, faded Scott Walker bumper stickers and Raylee's yoga studio. A bookstore and a Lions Club. Lattes and custard. Titanium racing bikes and bratwurst.

The bars in Palm Springs are sleek and fancy. She doesn't realize how much she's missed the basement-like atmosphere of Wisconsin bars until she sinks back into the ambience of faux-wood paneled walls, baskets of free popcorn, electronic dartboards, and vintage beer signs.

"Sherri Taylor? My God, girl. Is that you?"

Roberta takes her place at the stool next to her. Sherri is so relieved to see her old friend on this strange day that she wishes she could fall into her arms in a deep hug. She would never guess Roberta was approaching sixty if she didn't know that they were born on the same day. Her hair is dyed a striking jet black. Sherri doesn't know many women their age who still wear tank tops, but Roberta does—as she should. She is incredibly fit and toned. She has an actual waist, and the arms of a twenty-year-old. Even her face is muscular. Roberta waves to the bartender, revealing a tattoo of a barbell across the inside of her wrist.

He sets a gin and tonic in front of her without her having to order it. "Bombay with lime, just like you like it. Made it as soon as I saw you walk in."

"Thanks, Jimmy." Roberta takes the drink.

"I figure if I take good care of you tonight, you'll be nicer to me when I see you at five tomorrow morning."

"Never." She winks.

How the tables have turned, Sherri thinks, remembering how

Mike at the resort had so much power that all the Bunnies had to kowtow to him. Now this twentysomething Jimmy was at Roberta's beck and call.

Sherri had been anxious about seeing Roberta, but she's surprised she doesn't feel more awkward with her. Some people are perpetually familiar. They make time collapse.

"Jesus, you look good, Berta. What's your secret?"

"My son and I own the CrossFit studio on Main Street, where Neighbor's Laundromat used to be. Remember when we used to spin each other around in the dryers, and Mr. Neighbor would chase us away?"

"He had that beautiful Ford convertible hardtop."

"A Ford Fairlane," Roberta says. "We did our homework there in the winter because the dryers were so warm."

"Your house was always freezing."

Sherri hadn't thought about the laundromat in almost forty years, and suddenly she could remember it with startling precision, right down to the powdery scent of laundry detergent and the mesmerizing hum of the massive dryers. No wonder Sherri still loved the sound of a running appliance to this day.

Roberta says, "You know, I thought of you when we bought the building and they hauled the machines away. I found so many dimes and nickels. We used to search every corner for loose change for candy."

"How do we even have teeth still? Remember how we wrote secret messages in the steam on the windows?" Sherri said. "The hearts with our initials. Yours and Trent Eagan's."

"Little did I know I'd one day marry the guy," Roberta says.

Sherri is genuinely shocked. "Get out!"

"We had a good run until he left me for Kelly Eberjay a decade ago. Cut me in half. I was a mess. I blamed myself, thought I wasn't pretty enough, supportive enough. That's when I got into fitness. I needed a release. Jeanne, you remember her?"

"I do! She told me not to be a Bunny and after that I pretty much avoided her."

"Sounds like her. She lives in the Cable house now, and she works for the DNR. She told me after the divorce that it's such a relief to be middle-aged because people stop looking at you, and I was like, fuck that. That's our consolation prize after busting our asses with work and raising kids? To not be seen? I hit the gym extra hard after that. I wanted to show Trent what he was missing out on. The irony is that now I could give a shit what he thinks. He and Kelly had a nasty divorce. And you know what she told me?"

Sherri had forgotten how much fun it was to gossip with Roberta, how she shares information with you in a way that makes you feel chosen.

Roberta leans close and whispers, "He's *impotent*. Good thing I got him while the plumbing still worked. We've got three strong boys."

"You always wanted boys."

"Sometimes things work out," Roberta says. "Even our marriage falling apart, hard as it was, was a good thing in the end. The way I see it, Trent was just my starter husband."

"I had one of those, too. Mitch."

"You mean the guy from California?"

Sherri nods. "We're good friends now."

"That's great." Roberta clicks her drink against Sherri's. "Trent and I aren't exactly friends. But I've got to hand it to him: He was good with the boys. He liked to mow the lawn and cut wood and fix shit. Now I'm single, and that's just fine."

Roberta tells Sherri about all her boyfriends, most of whom are in the fitness world. Some are Violet's age. They cook for her, give her back rubs, bring her gifts, take her to Chicago for romantic weekends. "One guy, Dylan," she says, "I met him at a conference in San Antonio. He flew up here and spent a week with me. The longest week of my life. He's into tantric sex. I told him I'm too old for that. I just want it to be over. I have things to do."

Sherri laughs, but in the back of her mind she remembers how she'd been called slut and bimbo, and how those words had reduced her to nothing. It's nice at their age to be more free of those labels.

Roberta says, "The business is great. This time of year, we take groups out into the park next door for outdoor circuits. Honestly, it feels amazing to tell these three-hundred-pound muscle-heads to do something, and they do it. My son, Brett, he teaches, too. He's big in the CrossFit world. We go to all the conferences, compete. The industry is like a family, I swear. I love it. Doesn't even feel like work."

"I just can't believe my ears," Sherri says. "You would have done anything to get out of gym class, and now look at you. You could lift a refrigerator."

Roberta takes a sip of her drink. "Not to brag, but I can still bench my weight. You work out?"

"Not like you. I take Pilates."

Roberta laughs. "Listen to us. We're still on brand. I'm CrossFit, you're Pilates. Cheers, Sher."

It's hard for Sherri to believe she'd been nervous to see Roberta. They can't talk quickly enough—there is so much to say. They keep interrupting each other in a conversation that is frequently punctuated by the word "remember."

Roberta says she lives in a new house just off Stringers Bridge Road with her youngest son and a couple of dogs. She knows everyone in town, it seems. As they sit perched on the sticky wooden stools, people swing over to the bar to talk with Roberta, mostly about exercise. "You remember Sherri Taylor?" she says, and a few of them do: Barb, Sue, Linda, Dave, Randy, Kayleen. It's strange how warmly they greet her. Nobody even remembers that Sherri had been a Playboy Bunny, and if they do, they don't say so—well, except for Pete Becker, who is fat and balding, his fingernails still dirty from oil. "You look *good*," he says, and winks. "California agrees with you." Roberta rolls her eyes and sips her drink out of her straw. She waves him away like a fly.

Sherri tells Roberta about Mitch and Violet, her job at the art museum, about Bayard and his many proposals. "He sounds perfect," Roberta says.

"Please don't say that," Sherri says, troubled.

"Why not?"

"Well, speaking of men who sound perfect, I was in for a big surprise earlier today." Sherri waves down Jimmy and asks for another round to fortify her before launching into the story.

When the drinks arrive, Sherri tells Roberta about the spooky encounter with Arthur's son, and the conversation with Jerry afterward. "I mean, I know this sounds crazy, but I got it in my head that in some parallel universe Arthur had kept on living the life he was meant to lead—that we were supposed to lead, together. I don't know how to explain it, Berta. He never even told me he loved me, but all these years I've been obedient to that story." She was more than obedient. She'd mythologized Arthur, choosing to forget that she'd ever had ambivalent feelings about him when he was alive. Perhaps she should have given her younger self more credit for her intuition. "I convinced myself that Arthur was the yardstick I needed to use to measure other men against."

"Some yardstick." Roberta puts her rock-hard arm around Sherri's shoulders and gives her a surprisingly soft hug. It is exactly what Sherri needs in that moment. "I have a lot of thoughts," she says. "The first is that it isn't the worst thing in the world to suffer under a beautiful illusion for most of your life. There are lots of stinkers out there, and he raised the bar for you. Why not have high expectations?"

Over the years, Sherri had met plenty of men who'd let her down, both emotionally and in the bedroom, but the idea that an Arthur existed, someone who could cherish her body and soul, had bolstered her, given her confidence that she deserved more. Sherri *is* grateful for that. "What's your other thought?"

"Well, that it took you long enough to realize that we're all just a bunch of dented cereal boxes."

Sherri gives this some consideration. She is beginning to see how much stock she'd put in a certain idea of perfection—that Arthur had been perfect and blameless, and that she alone was responsible for his death. It isn't so black-and-white; it never had been. Is this why she keeps saying no to Bayard's proposals? He is perfect in his own way. He's loyal. He adores her. They have fun together and make each other laugh before they fall asleep each night. Who would have thought that this trip to Wisconsin would free her to say yes? She's almost giddy.

Roberta continues, "I'm sorry Arthur died and all that, but I never liked that guy. I had a feeling about him when I was at your party. You left me alone with him when you went on your boat ride, and you know what he did? He went right inside and read a book. He just left me out there by the campfire. And then that summer, he came to Giles with his wife and kids. He didn't even recognize me. So you know what I did? Oops! I spilled coffee all over his lap."

"Berta!"

"It was real hot, too." She smiles. "I was going to warn you about him, but then you blew me off for Mitch at the Allman Brothers. I was so angry with you, Sher."

"I could tell. I deserved it. That was an awful thing for me to do. I was so caught up in it all. Actually," Sherri says, brightening. "That reminds me. I have something for you." She reaches into her bag—she's a regular Mary Poppins with her enormous shoulder bags—and fishes around until she feels it: the maxi pad. She pulls it out and sets it on the bar.

"Um, I haven't needed those for about a decade, Sher, but thanks."

"Open it!" Sherri said. "I've kept it all these years."

"Open the pad? What are you smoking in California?"

Impatient, Sherri grabs it and unfolds the wad of cottony tissue. "Look," she says, excited.

Roberta seems confused. "What exactly am I supposed to be looking at?"

Sherri flips it around and can't believe her eyes. Gregg Allman's signature is so faded she can't even see it. All she sees is a dark blue stain on the middle of the pad. She begins to laugh. "That was—" She can't talk she's laughing so hard.

"What?"

Soon Roberta is laughing, too. Sherri hasn't laughed like this with anyone in ages. It feels good, cleansing. "That was Gre—" Sherri knocks her drink over and Roberta begins to wipe it with the maxi pad. "No! Don't!" Sherri gasps, trying to catch her breath. "Gregg Allman signed that for you!"

"This is Greggy's signature? You had him sign a *maxi pad*?" They're laughing so hard they teeter on their barstools. Everyone looks at them. Tears roll out of the corners of their eyes.

Roberta lifts the pad, kisses what's left of the signature, and puts it in her purse. The Rolling Stones play "Let It Bleed," which seems appropriate for that moment. "I'll always treasure this. And you," Roberta says. "It's good to have you back."

As they talk and drink, Sherri finds herself clutching the pendant Raylee had given her, a stone that makes her think of all the years she's moved through her life weighted by guilt, dutifully attending to Arthur's memory. She thought she'd ruined what would have been *their* future—only to discover that the future she'd imagined wouldn't have even been an option.

She can feel herself finally releasing Arthur and reentering her own life, her own story. The sensation makes her delirious with lightness instead of the grief she'd always associated with acceptance. Some kind of compass arrow inside her heart, rusty and stuck all these years, is suddenly free to spin in a new direction.

Acknowledgments

This novel wouldn't have come into existence without my incredible editor, Sarah Cantin, who was willing to take a chance on me with a second book. She was open to the concept right from the start and provided me with a deadline, patience, and the support and encouragement I needed to complete a novel that I can be proud of. I wish every writer could have the experience of working with someone as passionate, thorough, insightful, and responsive as Sarah.

I wouldn't have found Sarah without my beloved agent, Marcy Posner at Folio Literary Management. Marcy is more than an agent to me—she's also a friend. I always know that she's in my corner, even after I shared some pretty embarrassing early drafts with her. Thanks also to my film agent, Don Laventhall, and my foreign rights agent, Melissa Sarver White, also at Folio.

Boy did I ever luck out when I landed at St. Martin's Press. Everyone I've worked with has made me and my work feel valued. Thanks to Jennifer Enderlin, Sally Richardson, Andrew Martin, Lisa Senz, publicists extraordinaire Katie Bassel and Dori Weintraub, marketing dream team Erica Martirano, Brant Janeway, Erik Platt, Alexis Neuville, the experts at Booksparks, and incredible editorial assistant

Sallie Lotz. For their creative talents, I'm thankful to Kim Ludlam, Tom Thompson, and Olga Grlic (love my covers!). And I appreciate the talent of the audio experts, Mary Beth Roche, Robert Allen, and Dakota Cohen. I'm thrilled that Annaleigh Ashford is narrating my audiobook.

I loved writing this book because so much of it takes place in East Troy. My husband's family has deep roots in this unique and lively small town. His great-grandfather was a former mayor, and his family ran the Lacy and Clancy Hardware Store on the square for generations. I loved seeing the sparkle in my late father-in-law Lawrence Clancy's eyes when he told stories about growing up here. A few years ago, Kayleen Rohrer opened a bookstore, InkLink Books, in the very space that was once occupied by the hardware store. That's when I started to form connections of my own in the community, especially with an inseparable trio of book-loving "Chick Peas": Sue Enright, Linda Dodge, and Barb Jones. They brought me into their fold and shared their incredible stories of growing up near so many lakes, a legendary music amphitheater, and the former Playboy resort in Lake Geneva. This book could not have been written without their big hearts and boundless generosity. I tell them this all the time: I'm so jealous of their childhoods.

I also can't express enough thanks to Pam Ellis, or "Bunny Jojo." She worked at the Playboy resort for four years and was my primary source. She met with me on multiple occasions, both in Wisconsin and in Palm Springs. She was always available for a phone call or text if I needed details or information, and she read early drafts to check for accuracy. Thanks to Pam, I can see how work as a Bunny is such a defining experience, and I can also see how it shaped her into the fun-loving, open, and adventuresome woman she is today.

While this is a work of fiction, I had to learn so much in order to write this book that I would physically ache from my desire to step back into another time. Thanks to all my sources for all kinds of information, I feel like I did. Much appreciation and gratitude to Becky

Gross, Dave Hollenbeck, Paula Dornfeld, Francine Inbinder, James Marzo, Susy Cranley, Cynthia Hirsch, Michael Heimlich, John Gilman, Rachel Fashing, Ingrid Pierson, Thomas Alaan, Betsy Dickson, Barb Paulini, Lisa Blue, Don Parfet, Jennifer Snowden, Blake Moret, Kate Twohig, Kim and Jim Engel, Lisa Blue, and Richard Ladwig for sharing what they know.

Fellow writers help keep me sane. Thanks to the world's best writing group: Lauren Fox, Liam Callanan, Anuradha Rajurkar, Jon Olson, and Aims McGinnis. Thanks also to Julia Claiborne Johnson, J. Ryan Stradal, Amy Meyerson, Jean Thompson, Steven Rowley, Kerry Kletter, Karen Dukess, Christine Sneed, Phong Nguyen, Alison Hammer, and all my fellow 2020 debuts. Friends like Ann Conroy, Diane Goldberg, Josh Lieber, Jennifer Thompson, my gang from Shorewood Hills, my Milwaukee crowd, East Troy "Read and Feed" attendees, my former colleagues and students at Beloit College, and all my spinners encourage me to keep writing.

I am so appreciative of librarians and independent booksellers everywhere and wish I could include each one here. They've been so supportive. Special shout-out to Kayleen Rohrer of InkLink, Daniel Golden at Boswell Books, Nancy Baenen, James Bohnen, and everyone at Arcadia Books, Joanne Berg at Mystery to Me, my literary fairy godmothers Pamela Klinger-Horn of Excelsior Bay Books and Mary O'Malley of Skylark Bookshop, Maxwell Gregory, Jeff Peters at East End Books, Stephen Russell at the Wellfleet Marketplace, The Brewster Bookstore, Fitgers, Titcombs, Where the Sidewalk Ends, Warwicks, Chevalier's, Buttonwood Books and . . . and . . . I am in physical pain at having to limit this list. Fortunately, you can find an awesome bookseller near you at IndieBound. They are all amazing and work so hard to find the right book for the right reader.

I appreciate the time and space to write, and thank Shakerag Alley, the Ragdale Foundation, LitCamp, and the Dorland Arts Colony for providing me with opportunities to focus and get work done.

Finally, thanks to my family. My mom, Pat Geiger (AKA Kick

Ass Pat), is always there for me, and knits gorgeous sweaters to match my covers. Thanks to the extended Clancy clan and the Seyferts: my aunt Mel and uncle Bo Van Peenan, Val Piper, my cousins Bob Piper, Wendy (Cutie) Van Peenan, Laura Van Peenan, Kristen (Scuz) Wild, my sisters Sheila Cardenas and Karen Geiger-Niedfeldt, and all my nephews and nieces. Great big love for John Clancy for being such a supportive and patient partner, and to Olivia and Tim, the greatest kids a mom could ask for.

Most special thanks to readers for spending time with my novel, and for keeping the literary arts alive.